Dark Chaos

*Book # 4 in The Bregdan
Chronicles*

Sequel to Spring Will Come

Ginny Dye

Dark Chaos

Copyright © 2010 by Ginny Dye
Published by A Voice In The World Publishing
Bellingham, WA 98229

www.BregdanChronicles.net

www.GinnyDye.com

www.AVoiceInTheWorldPublishing.com

ISBN 150788592X

Printed in the United States of America.

For Pat

I love you, brother!

A Note From the Author

There are times in the writing of history when we must use words we personally abhor. The use of the word "nigger" in *Spring Will Come* is one of those times. Though I hate the word, its use is necessary to reveal and to challenge the prejudices of the time in order to bring change and healing. Stay with me until the end – I think you will agree.

My great hope is that *Spring Will Come* will both entertain and challenge you. I hope you will learn as much as I did during the months of research it took to write this book. Though I now live in the Pacific Northwest, I grew up in the South and lived for 11 years in Richmond, VA. I spent countless hours exploring the plantations that still line the banks of the James River and became fascinated by the history.

But you know, it's not the events that fascinate me so much – it's the people. That's all history is, you know. History is the story of people's lives. History reflects the consequences of their choice and actions – both good and bad. History is what has given you the world you live in today – both good and bad.

This truth is why I named this series The Bregdan Chronicles. Bregdan is a Gaelic term for weaving. Braiding. Every life that has been lived until today is a part of the woven braid of life. It takes every person's story to create history. Your life will help determine the course of history. You may think you don't have much of an impact. You do. Every action you take will reflect in someone else's life. Someone else's decisions. Someone else's future. Both good and bad. That is the **Bregdan Principle**...

**Every life that has been lived until today is a part
of the woven braid of life.
It takes every person's story to create history.
Your life will help determine
the course of history.
You may think you don't have
much of an impact.
You do.
Every action you take will reflect
in someone else's life.
Someone else's decisions.
Someone else's future.
Both good and bad.**

My great hope as you read this book, and all that will follow, is that you will acknowledge the power you have, every day, to change the world around you by your decisions and actions. Then I will know the research & writing were all worthwhile.

Oh, and I hope you enjoy every moment of it, and learn to love the characters as much as I do!

I'm already being asked how many books will be in this series. As of January 2015 there are 7, but the answer to how many are coming depends on how long I live! My intention is to release 2 books a year, each covering 1 year of history – continuing to weave the lives of my characters into the times they lived. I hate to end a good book as much as anyone – always feeling so sad that I have to leave the characters. You shouldn't have to be sad for a long time!

If you like what you read, you'll want to make sure you're on our mailing list at:

www.BregdanChronicles.net. I'll let you know each time a new one comes out!

Sincerely,
Ginny Dye

Chapter One

The loud call of a mockingbird jolted Carrie Cromwell from a deep sleep. Frowning, she struggled to push aside the thick gray fog swirling in her head. A long breath helped to dissipate the lingering fear. The dream had held her tightly in its grasp. *Robert...dead and mangled on the battlefield...* She shuddered as the grim image threatened to pull her back in.

Another shrill cry from the mockingbird made her heavy eyelids flutter open. She sighed with relief when she saw the bright sunlight filtering through her tall windows. It was a dream—just a dream. She forced her eyes open wide and threw back the covers. The terror of her nightmare loosened its grip as the glow of morning chased away the darkness. She reached for her thick robe, wrapped it tightly around her slender form, and stepped to the window.

April had glided into the South, setting Richmond, Virginia free from the harsh grasp of 1863's brutal winter. The rivers flowed freely, and the trees were budding and beginning to bloom. Apple and crabapple trees spread their glimmering pink and white blossoms over the hills of the city. The morning air was chill and crisp, but the brilliant sun suspended above the soft green trees promised a warm day.

Carrie smiled softly, her green eyes exploding with excitement, as the last remnant of her dream dissolved with the light, and she remembered what day it was. She had envisioned this day for so long, so often caught between a hope that wouldn't die and a despair that wouldn't diminish. But it was here. It was really here! She and Robert Borden were to be married today.

A surge of wonder and delight coursed through her. She held her arms wide and twirled around the room, laughing at the wonder of it all. Finally, out of breath, she collapsed on the window seat and rested her head against the sill. She pushed back and flung open the window impulsively. The cool air rushing into the room invigorated her. She knew she should close it to conserve all the heat possible in the war-impoverished capital city, but today she wanted nothing between her and the world she loved so much. Carrie pulled her robe tighter and turned her face toward the east, letting the sun wash her with its brilliance.

Married! She was going to be married...

The shriek of the mockingbird was so close this time it startled her. Pulling back from the sill, she watched as its shadowy form hopped on a branch and then flew into a surrounding bush, only to give another sharp call. Carrie frowned suddenly. Was the bird trying to tell her something? Were its persistent cries this morning a mocking of her happiness? A warning it would be short-lived? A reminder there was still a war going on, and the return of spring was merely the signal for renewed fighting between the North and the South?

Carrie leaned against the sill once more and tried to push away the heaviness seeking to invade her heart. She scowled at the idea that a silly bird could rob her of her earlier happiness. Against all odds, after being missing for eight months, Robert had come home to her. He had been seriously wounded in the Battle of Antietam, but had miraculously survived. Someday she would be able to thank the black family who had saved his life and helped to change his heart.

"Good morning, Carrie."

Carrie started as a cheerful voice greeted her. She leaned further out the window to grin at her best friend. "What in the world are you doing back home, Janie? I thought you had to work at the hospital today?"

"Dr. Wild took pity on me. He knew it was driving me mad not to be here helping you get ready for the big event." Janie pushed aside her soft brown hair, her blue eyes sparkling in the sun. "The truth is, I don't want to miss out on one particle of happy doings in this town. Heaven knows there are few enough of them. I like to get near happiness any time I can." She disappeared under the overhang of the porch. "I'll be right up."

Carrie took one last breath of fresh air and reached up to shut the window. Then she stopped. The sun exploded onto the row of daffodils bordering the walk to her father's house, and for just a moment the beauty transported her back to the plantation. Her eyes glistened with tears as she gazed east, suddenly able in her heart to see beyond the treetops and far down the river.

"Cromwell Plantation would be a beautiful place for your wedding." Janie's voice broke into her thoughts as she entered the room.

Carrie smiled, not turning from the window. Her heart overflowed with gratefulness. She could remember with startling clarity the day she saved Janie from an attack by a drunken soldier. They had been inseparable since then. "How did you know what I was thinking?"

Janie put a hand on her shoulder and shrugged. "I've only been to your family's plantation once, but its beauty, even in the winter, took my breath away. I can only imagine how glorious it must be in the spring. I know how much you love and miss it. It would only make sense your heart would long for it now."

"It almost feels like a physical ache," Carrie admitted with a catch in her voice. "I have so much to be thankful for..."

"And yet there is so much to wish for," Janie finished.

"I feel horribly selfish," Carrie cried. "I have Robert home safely. I have you for my best friend. My father is alive and well thanks to his job with the government. I have wonderful, fulfilling work at the hospital. So many people are suffering so many horrible things. I am nothing but an ingrate."

"Nonsense," Janie said. "Yes, you have much to be thankful for. You've also been through a trying eight months. Robert has been home less than a week." She smoothed Carrie's long, wavy black hair away from her face. "You have a zest for life and a capacity for caring that not many people have. This is one of the most special days of your life. You are wishing you could share it with Rose, Moses and Aunt Abby. You must be thinking about your mother, wishing she had lived long enough to see it."

Carrie whirled away from the window and grabbed Janie in a fierce hug. "Only you would understand all the contradictory feelings raging inside of me. Thank you for making them seem all right."

Janie returned her hug and pulled away. "I'm going downstairs to take care of a few things. Take as much time as you need. Life has been a complete whirlwind since Robert returned. You've had hardly any time to even feel the wonder of the last week."

"Sometimes I long for my special place down by the river on the plantation," Carrie mused. "That's where I would go when I needed time to think and process all that was going on. You're right. I've had hardly any time to feel what has been happening. I seem to roll from one thing to the next."

"Well, this is one thing you're not going to roll through," Janie replied. "Everything at the hospital is running smoothly. I don't want you to come downstairs until you've had all the time alone that you need. Do you understand me?" she demanded.

"Yes, ma'am," Carrie replied meekly, lowering her eyes.

Janie laughed loudly. "And that may be the only show of submission any of us ever sees!"

Carrie laughed along with her, then sobered. "Getting married is a little scary," she said hesitantly.

Janie waited for a long moment. "You're scared of losing your dreams," she said finally.

Carrie saw no reason to deny it. As usual, her friend knew what she was thinking. She simply nodded.

"You love Robert. He loves you. By the time this war is over, all of our dreams are going to have been battered and thrown around. All any of us will be able to do is work to put life back into them. We can either do it alone, or with someone else. You will have someone who loves and respects you. You're not giving up your dreams, Carrie. You're adding a husband who can help you make them come true."

"You're right," Carrie said.

"But..." Janie prompted.

"I didn't say '*but*,'" Carrie protested. Janie's only reply was silence. She turned to stare out the window. "I love him so much," she murmured. "I know he supports my dream to be a doctor, and I support his dream to be a horse farmer. I guess I just don't see how both those dreams can come true at the same time."

Janie eased up beside her. "You don't always have to see the whole picture." She paused. "Isn't that what you always tell me? That you wouldn't have any reason to trust God if you could see the whole picture?"

Carrie nodded as the tightness in her heart began to ease. "You're right," she admitted. "It's easy to say something, but it's harder to live it. You'd think waiting eight months wondering if Robert was dead or alive would have taught me something."

"Or made you so tired you're looking for a reprieve," Janie said.

Carrie laughed and spun away from the window, full again of her earlier wonder. "Thank you for giving me so much space to be human."

Janie watched her for a moment until, evidently satisfied with what she saw, she headed for the door. "I'll send May up with your breakfast."

"No," Carrie responded. "I'll be down in a few minutes. Is my father still here? I'd like to have some time with him this morning."

"He was in the parlor when I came up. He told me he was hoping the governor could do without him today. Something about it not being every day his daughter gets married." Janie grinned impishly and closed the door.

It took Carrie only a few minutes to dress. She gazed at the simple white gown hanging on the door of her wardrobe, then reached for one of the few dresses not yet sacrificed to the cause of the Confederacy. She didn't miss her once huge wardrobe—it had always seemed an extravagant burden—but she wished she had more than her hospital garb today. Pushing useless wishing from her mind, she slipped into a dark blue dress, quickly braided her rebellious hair, and pinned it into a bun. For a moment she allowed herself to imagine Robert unpinning it, smiling as he watched it tumble down her back.

"Behave," she scolded her image in the mirror. "That is hardly proper thinking for a respectable Southern lady." She grinned. She had never made any pretense of being a respectable Southern lady. Why should she start now?

Her mind flew back to the day she met Robert. Much to her mother's dismay, she had almost been late for dinner, caught in a violent rainstorm while riding her gray Thoroughbred, Granite. It had been Rose who worked miracles and made sure she was dressed and ready for their guest. The smile faded from her face, and her lips quivered as the ache for her closest friend filled her heart. How long would they be separated by the war? The days when Rose had been her slave seemed like they belonged to another life. Now, Rose and her husband Moses were free. The last Carrie knew, Rose was in Philadelphia, and Moses was looking for his sister while serving as a Union spy. The aching in her heart was accentuated by the agony of so much unknown. There were nothing but unanswerable questions.

And memories.

Carrie managed a smile as the gentle reminder resonated in her heart. There were so many wonderful memories. Memories she would hold and cherish for the rest of her life. Memories of times and experiences that created much of who she was as a person.

"I hear I have a daughter who wants to have breakfast with me," a strong voice boomed from the hallway.

Carrie leaped up, ran to the door, and flung it open. "I'm so glad you're still home," she said.

"I told Governor Letcher he would have to handle any crises without me today," Thomas Cromwell said. "Except when I was sick with smallpox this past winter, I haven't missed a single day at the Capitol since this war started." His voice softened. "I think my daughter getting married is ample reason." He wrapped his arm around her. "In fact, I can't think of a better reason."

Carrie leaned against his strong body. "I love you," she said as she gazed into his handsome face, ringed by shining silver hair that was a result of the last three years of stress. The loss of his wife and the reality of war had aged him, yet it had also deepened him. Their relationship, close from the time Carrie was a child, had become even more cemented as they met life's pressures together.

"And I love you, Carrie Cromwell," Thomas replied. "I won't be able to say that much longer, you know. After today, you will be Carrie Borden."

"Carrie Borden," she murmured. "Has a nice ring to it, don't you think?"

They were laughing when they entered the dining room. Carrie was disappointed to see two of her father's boarders seated with Janie at the table, but immediately chided herself for her selfishness. The boarders' financial contribution was crucial in this difficult time. Besides, the city was simply too crowded—every home had to be willing to expand to bursting. It wasn't fair to expect all the boarders to disappear simply because it was her wedding day.

"Good morning," she said graciously.

"Good morning," Drew Cummings responded, glancing up briefly from the paper he was perusing.

"Good morning," James Botler said shortly, turning immediately to her father. "Mr. Cromwell, I'm so glad you're here this morning." He stopped short, his round face flushed. "But do you really think this is any time to be away from the Capitol?"

Carrie saw her father shoot James a warning glance, but it didn't stem his flow of words.

"You must realize how critical the situation is!" James exclaimed.

"Oh, keep your shirt on," Drew responded. "Every spring it's the same. Some Union army is coming to take Richmond. They even tried it this winter at Fredericksburg. Haven't you learned General Lee is capable of protecting this city?" He turned to Thomas. "Have you seen everyone down by the river? I walked through some of the markets yesterday. The price they are charging for fresh fish is absolutely ludicrous. Half the town seems to have taken fishing poles and nets down to the water. They're not going to take any more price gouging."

"Price gouging," James snorted. "Who cares what fish costs if we lose our capital? I've heard that the new Union general, Hooker, has over one hundred twenty-five thousand men sitting on the other side of the Rappahannock."

Carrie listened with a sinking heart. Of course she knew of the buildup of the troops, and she was aware the Union Army had been sitting only forty miles from Richmond almost all winter. The Union Army, severely demoralized after their stunning loss at Fredericksburg under General Burnside, had been rebuilding and regrouping under the leadership of General Hooker. It wasn't news to her, it just wasn't anything she wanted to hear right now.

Thomas cut into James' hot words. "I think Drew is right. General Lee is quite a capable commander."

Carrie shot a quick look at her father. His voice carried none of the confidence his words did.

"You can't possibly think General Lee can defeat an army twice his size?" James protested. "Why, we're going to have another Antietam on our hands. No one really claimed that to be a Southern loss, but losing twenty thousand men is not my idea of a victory. The South can't stand many more battles like that, and from what I can tell, Lee doesn't have nearly the same strength in his defensive position that he held at Fredericksburg."

Carrie felt the bile rise in her throat at the mention of Antietam. The horror of the last eight months—imagining Robert dead or horribly wounded after he had been declared missing in action at Antietam—was still fresh in her memory. What if she had regained him only to lose him to another Union bullet?

"What I think," Thomas said sharply, "is that this is no time for such talk. In case you have forgotten, Mr. Botler, my daughter is getting married today."

James scowled. "She won't be the first to become a soldier's widow. Pretending the situation isn't critical doesn't change the reality," he said harshly.

Carrie had heard enough. She put her hand on her father's arm to stop his angry barrage of words. Fighting to keep the anger and fear from her voice, she turned to Mr. Botler. "There is not a person in this room who can change the reality of this horrible war, sir. There is also not a person in this room who cannot benefit from closing out the darkness for a while and letting what little good there is in this mess to become a more present reality. It's called grasping for whatever good there is in a bad situation. It's called hope. It's the only thing any of us have to hang on to." She took a deep breath. "I realize my getting married today doesn't change the fact that Hooker may cross the river tomorrow, but for one day I want the good things in my life to overrule the bad. Is that such a horrible thing?"

James flushed and lowered his eyes. "I'm sorry, Miss Cromwell. I guess I'm just worried."

"All of us are worried," Janie chimed in, "but I've heard a lot of the people in Richmond talking. The last year has toughened them. They made it through last summer when McClellan tried to take the city. They have endured one of the hardest winters anyone can imagine. Now it's spring. They have chosen hope. They are going to live their lives as if the city might not fall in the next few days. There is nothing any of us here can do. It's up to General Lee and his men. We will deal with whatever consequences come. In the meantime, we are going to live our lives."

James nodded. "I won't bother you with anymore of my talk," he promised. "I have a job to do. I guess I'll go do it." He shoved his chair back from the table and reached for his hat on the nearby rack. "Congratulations, Miss Cromwell," he said sincerely. "I hope you have a wonderful day." He moved toward the door, then stopped. "I truly do apologize, but I find myself feeling sick inside when I think of the North coming down here and conquering us. I can't help but be angry." Nodding briefly, he crammed his hat on his head and strode out.

There was silence until James had exited the room.

"I'm sorry, Carrie," Thomas said. "I didn't want anything to happen to spoil your day."

"It's all right," Carrie smiled. "Today, I have Robert. Today, we're going to get married. For this one day, I'm not going to worry about tomorrow."

Carrie fidgeted restlessly as Janie arranged her hair.

"I declare, Carrie Cromwell, if you don't sit still it's going to look as if a flock of birds made a nest in your hair!" Janie finally burst out in exasperation.

Carrie sighed and tried to settle down. "Are you almost done? I'm sorry, but I've never been known for my patience," she said. A brilliant smile suddenly erupted on her face "Can you believe it? I'm really marrying Robert."

Janie nodded. "Your captain should be arriving any minute." She pushed down on Carrie's shoulders firmly. "Two minutes and I'll be done with this. Can you possibly sit still for two more minutes?"

"I suppose," Carrie said, then let her thoughts take her mind off her enforced confinement. Robert had been promoted from lieutenant to captain as soon as he reported back to his unit. She couldn't care less about his military status—she simply wanted him alive. His rank of captain would only make him more valuable to the Confederate war cause. She squirmed and peeked up at Janie. "You don't think they'll make him fight in this new battle, do you? He's only been home a week, and they must know he's not strong enough for that." She knew her voice sounded pathetically hopeful.

Janie tried to sound reassuring. "I'm sure they can do without one captain long enough for you to have some time together."

Carrie knew Janie didn't believe what she was saying, but she decided not to press. She may have only illusions to make her happy, but she was going to live in them until reality forced her to do otherwise.

Janie stuck in the last pin, glided over to the wardrobe, and lifted the white dress off the hanger. "Is the bride ready for her gown?"

Carrie rose in one fluid movement and raised her arms obediently. "Have you ever thought about applying for a job as a servant?" she teased. "You seem to have a natural affinity for it."

Janie stuck out her tongue. "Unless emancipation truly takes place, I don't think it would pay well enough. I would have too many slaves to compete with."

Carrie laughed along with her, but her thoughts soon turned serious "Oh, Janie, this war just has to free the slaves. What if things are still the same when this horrible war is over?"

"Not one word about the war," Janie said sternly. "This is your wedding day. The war will still be here tomorrow. For today, you're just a beautiful bride about to be married to a dashing man." She settled the dress over Carrie's head, buttoned it into place, and took a step back. "Even with such a simple gown, you are absolutely lovely," she said with deep admiration.

Carrie spun to gaze into the mirror above her dresser. "Father wanted to buy a much more elaborate gown, but I wouldn't let him. I think it's criminal to spend gobs of money on a wedding dress when so many people are starving." She spun in a slow circle and looked at her reflection critically. The dress was very plain, but she had to admit it was becoming. The lines hugged her slender waistline and fell outward in graceful folds. "I wish Mother was here."

"She would be very proud of you." Janie reached over to tuck in a final errant strand of hair.

Carrie stared into the mirror for a moment more and then moved away to stand by the window. A warm breeze filled the room with the fragrant perfume of spring flowers, swirling the light blue curtains into a graceful dance. Once again, Carrie felt her heart fly over the treetops to Cromwell Plantation. "Mother used to talk about the day I would get married. She had plans to make it the social event of the season. There was nothing she liked more than large parties attended by the right people," she said. "It used to drive me crazy because I didn't care about things like that, but before Mother died, we had learned to accept each other. I miss her," she said.

She scowled and swung around to give Janie a fierce hug. "Absolutely no more sad thoughts. I have Robert, and Father and wonderful friends like you. My life is incredibly rich." Humming a catchy tune, she pulled Janie into a wild dance around the room, determined to chase the goblins of sadness from her mind. Soon, their laughter filled the room and cascaded through the house.

Janie finally pulled away, gasping to catch her breath. "You're going to be a mess," she accused between gulps of air.

"Poo," Carrie scoffed. "You put enough pins in my head to secure it in the midst of a gale."

A knock sounded at the door. "Is anyone else invited to your party?" a deep voice called.

Janie flew to the door and swung it open. "Your daughter is all ready, Mr. Cromwell. I'll see you downstairs."

"Most of the guests are here," Thomas responded, not taking his eyes off Carrie. "Pastor Anthony and Robert should be here any minute."

"I'll make sure everything is taken care of," Janie said, shutting the door.

Thomas turned to Carrie. "You look absolutely beautiful," he said in a strained voice. He walked closer. "Just as pretty as your mother was on our wedding day."

Carrie's eyes welled with tears at the look of tenderness on his face. "I wish she could be here."

"I have a feeling she knows what is happening," Thomas replied. "And I'm sure she would approve."

Carrie moved closer and wrapped her arms around her father. "Can you believe it's actually happening? That I'm going to be married?"

"I wasn't sure you'd ever find a man good enough for you."

"Good enough—or one who could put up with my stubbornness?" Carrie teased.

"That was something I took into consideration," Thomas admitted with a smile. "Robert Borden is getting the most wonderful girl in the world. Strong-willed, tender, loving, intelligent..."

"You make me sound perfect," Carrie laughed. "I'm afraid Robert knows the truth already. It's too late to trick him."

"I know exactly what Robert thinks of you, Carrie. If he didn't love you as much as I do, I wouldn't let him marry you," Thomas said. "He loves you the way I loved your mother. That kind of love can weather a lot of storms and make your life very rich."

"I'm incredibly rich," Carrie said, wrapping her arms around him. "I have you, and I have Robert." Images of Rose, Moses and Aunt Abby flashed in her mind, but she pushed them away. Someday she would be able to share with them the happiness of this moment, but for now she would simply live it as fully as she could.

She stepped back and stared at her father. "Why are you standing with one arm behind your back?" she asked suddenly.

He pulled his arm around and held his hidden treasure out to her.

Carrie reached forward and took the magnolia blossom he was cradling in his strong hand.

"It's the first one of the season," Thomas said. "Your mother used to tell me how she was going to fill the house with magnolia blossoms when you got married."

"I remember," Carrie whispered, caressing the milky white bloom with her fingers. Fighting tears, she lifted the blossom and inhaled deeply. "So fragrant," she murmured, burying her face in the single flower.

"I couldn't fill the house, but I've been watching that bud for the last few days, hoping it would bloom in time. I went out on the porch this morning and found it lifting its head toward the sun."

Carrie smiled. "I think it's a sign. Magnolias have always been my favorite flower. Rose and I used to pretend each bloom stood for one of our dreams. We would wait for them to bloom and then wish on them." She gazed at the flower, remembering.

"And what is your wish today?" Thomas asked.

"That Robert and I will have a long life of happiness together." She cupped the bloom, lifted it to her face, and pressed her lips against it gently. "That is my magnolia dream for today."

Another knock sounded at the door. "Pastor Anthony and Robert are here," Janie called. "I think all the guests are, too."

"I was just getting ready to come down," Thomas called, kissing Carrie warmly on her cheek. "I'll be waiting downstairs for you."

Chapter Two

Carrie stood at the top of the steps, fighting to control the pounding of her heart. From where she was standing at the top of the long staircase, she could see Robert's wavy, dark hair. Abiding by her wish to not mix the war with their marriage, he was dressed in a dark blue suit instead of his Confederate gray uniform. The firm set of his shoulders and his erect carriage made it almost impossible to believe he had spent months paralyzed, recovering from wounds he received at Antietam.

Pastor Anthony, facing the stairway, glanced up and caught Carrie's eyes. A warm smile spread over his kindly features. Carrie smiled back, her heart full of appreciation for this man who had become such a dear friend. They had grown close during the last year as Carrie worked closely with him to bring medical care to the black residents of the city. She had known instantly that he should be the one to marry them. Pastor Anthony had agreed immediately, but she was sure she had seen a brief flicker of uncertainty flare in his eyes before he smiled and nodded. She had pushed it aside, but in quiet moments, she wondered about what seemed like a flash of fear. Now, as before, she brushed it aside. It was probably just her imagination.

Carrie focused her attention back on the room, where huge sprays of apple blossoms filled the space with their feathery beauty. Thomas stood and climbed the stairs to stand beside Carrie, pulling her arm through his. Janie walked to the piano and settled down, her fingers poised over the keys. She gave Carrie a wink and began to play the wedding march.

"I guess this is it," Carrie whispered as she and her father began to descend the stairs. Down below, the two dozen or so guests rose to watch expectantly. Carrie was glad her father had agreed to keep the wedding small.

"This is it," Thomas replied quietly, his arm gently squeezing hers. "Robert Borden is about to be the luckiest man alive."

Carrie glanced up and caught Robert gazing at her. A smile exploded on her face as the full reality of the moment sank in. His responding smile made her breath catch. She was really marrying this incredible man. They had weathered the storms of their relationship and found their way to this day. The stairs disappeared as she floated to meet him, the rest of the room dissolving in a haze. Robert held her gaze, his dark eyes penetrating her heart. She wanted to both laugh and cry with the wonder of the moment. For today, it was just the two of them. Nothing and no one could steal this day from them. Reality blurred as the magic settled in.

She vaguely heard Pastor Anthony speaking to the audience, his voice seeming to come from a great distance. She felt her father release her arm and place her hand in Robert's. Only then did she tear her eyes away from his and turn to Pastor Anthony. The look on the pastor's face said he knew exactly what she was feeling. Reality settled in again, but the magic still lingered as the pastor's voice rang out clearly.

"Carrie Cromwell, do you take this man...?"

"I now pronounce you man and wife," Pastor Anthony said joyfully. "Robert, you may kiss the bride."

Carrie lifted her face, substance once more fading into fantasy, as Robert's lips lowered to meet hers. Every particle of her being lifted to meet his as his mouth settled on hers tenderly. Every portion of her leaped to quivering, exuberant life as their love met, mingled and meshed them into one.

Sometime later, Robert raised his head. "I love you," he whispered.

"And I love you," Carrie responded, trying to slow her pounding heart.

Pastor Anthony turned them to face the room. "It is my pleasure to present Mr. and Mrs. Robert Borden."

It was several hours later before the last guest left. The sun was sinking low on the horizon, a cauldron of clouds boiling in the eastern sky. The soft green of the trees stood in stark contrast to the gray cumulus, outlined boldly by the last rays of bright sunlight. An occasional stiff breeze amidst the calm that portends a storm kicked up puffs of dust from the road.

Once again, Carrie found herself longing for the quiet and privacy of Cromwell Plantation. She and Robert had nowhere to go. Every house and hotel in Richmond was crowded to capacity, the bulging city barely able to contain the throngs war had heaped upon it. The novelty of ladies marrying soldiers bound for the front had long passed. It was nothing but a commonplace occurrence now, not deserving of special favors. The newlyweds would stay where they would be living for the duration of the war, in Thomas Cromwell's house.

Robert lifted his hand once more to wave at the last departing wagon and then turned to Carrie. "I think we're finally alone."

Carrie flushed at the bright gleam in his eyes but held his gaze. "I wasn't sure we ever would be," she replied, grateful her father had made sure the house would be empty for at least that evening.

Robert continued to stare deep into her eyes and quietly extended his hand. Carrie grasped it, and together they entered the house. The calm before the storm retreated as a strong breeze blew through the hallway, causing the chandelier to sway, its tinkling melody following them up the stairs. Carrie barely noticed. She seemed to float as Robert's gaze held and lifted her.

"Should we shut the window?" Robert asked as they entered what was now *their* room.

"It will be a while before the storm arrives," Carrie replied. "I'd like to leave it open. I love the feeling of the wind dancing into the room."

Robert nodded and took her into his arms. "Whatever you wish, my love."

Carrie raised her head in wonder as he lowered his. Their lips met and melted. She was both frightened and exhilarated by the rampage of feelings exploding in her body as she realized this night was just for them. When Robert finally raised his head, she was clinging to him, her breath coming in gasps.

Robert bent down and easily lifted her with his strong arms. Carrie never took her eyes from his face as he carried her across the room and laid her on the bed. "You're beautiful," he said tenderly, his eyes caressing her face as his hand began to stroke her cheek. He reached up and began to slowly pull the pins from her hair.

Carrie's eyes filled with tears as she felt the tightness of her chignon begin to loosen.

Robert stopped immediately and let his hand drop. "Is something wrong? Am I hurting you?"

"No," she whispered, "it's just... I've dreamed of this for so long. I tried to imagine how it would be when you let my hair down, and now it's happening."

Robert leaned down to brush his lips on hers before he resumed his actions. As he pulled the last pin out, the tightly woven braid dropped down her back. His eyes misted as he lifted her to a sitting position and gently released the strands, catching his breath as her hair fell around her in a thick, dark cloud. Groaning slightly, he lifted it and buried his face in it, taking deep breaths.

Carrie was silent, watching him, overwhelmed by the feelings of awe and desire coursing through her body.

Robert lifted his head. "You're even more beautiful than I imagined," he said roughly. He held her face with his hands for a long minute and then reached back to unbutton her dress. "I love you, Carrie Borden."

"And I love you, Robert Borden." Carrie gave herself over to the wondrous feelings exploding in her body.

The storm had come and gone, washing the world and filling it with fresh fragrances before Carrie and Robert settled back against the pillows to talk. Carrie opened her mouth to speak, but Robert put a finger to her lips. She was startled by the look of urgency and longing that sprang into his eyes.

"I have to tell you something," Robert said quietly.

Carrie felt her heart sink, the magic of the evening taking flight and soaring out of her reach. "You're leaving." It wasn't a question.

"I found out this morning. I was determined not to let it spoil our day."

"How can they call you back to the front?" Carrie cried. "You've already almost died in this horrible war. You're not ready to go back to battle! How can they ask you to fight again?" She made no effort to hide the tears, nor the fear that choked her voice. To go so suddenly from enchantment to cruel reality was more than she could handle. Robert gathered her in his arms, but she pulled back. "They can't make you go!" she cried.

"I don't want to fight anymore, Carrie. You know that. But I don't have a choice. General Hooker is ready to advance on Richmond with one hundred twenty-five thousand men. General Lee has less than half that force to meet him with. He has to have every available man he can lay his hands on." Robert's voice was both pained and resolute.

"He doesn't have to have you," Carrie said passionately, even though her mind told her it wasn't true. The war that had ignited the country was pulling every young man into its flaming path, devouring lives, hearts and dreams with indiscriminate fury. Her heart constricted with fear. Robert had barely escaped the inferno before. Would the flames consume him this time? She had said earlier she would be content with today and let tomorrow take care of itself. Was tomorrow going to come so quickly, snatching away the dreams and love she had tasted so briefly?

Robert said nothing. He pulled her into his arms and held her trembling body close. Carrie clung to him, trying to draw enough strength to conquer her fear.

When Carrie spoke, her voice was calm. "When do you have to leave?"

"Tomorrow morning," Robert said gravely. "Very early." He reached up to touch her cheek, his eyes thanking her for her bravery. "Just about every man who can fight is already at the front. I ride out with a very small contingent tomorrow. We should hook up with our unit tomorrow afternoon."

"What are the odds of this battle?" Carrie asked. She knew nothing would change the dread of waiting for battle news, but any information she could get was better than being in complete darkness. She also knew that as soon as Hooker crossed the river, Richmond hospitals would once more be full to overflowing. Vivid memories of past battle results made her shiver.

Robert shrugged. "Lee has won battles no one thought he had any hope of winning. McClellan faced Richmond with the same number of men last summer and Lee held him off—even sent him running." He paused. "But to be honest, I hear Hooker is a different man. He has none of McClellan's overwhelming cautiousness. I'm sure he knows how outnumbered we are." He scowled. "He just doesn't know what he's up against. He is commanding troops who are far from home, trying to take our city. He is facing battle veterans fighting for their homes, for their capital, and"—his voice roughened—"for those they love."

"How can you stand to fight again?" Carrie asked, her heart going out to him. He had told her of the horrors of battle, of the gut-wrenching things he had seen at Antietam before he was shot.

Robert frowned. "It makes me sick to think of going back into battle. Even when I was struggling so hard to get well so that I could come back to you, I was hoping somehow the war would end, and I would never have to fight again. If it hadn't been for you, I would have been happy staying in that little cabin in Maryland until the war was over."

"I almost wish you had," Carrie responded, tears once more filling her eyes. "I can't bear the idea that I may lose you again...maybe permanently this time." Her voice cracked with pain.

"We have to take one day at a time. I've made it through other battles. I'll make it through this one."

"Won't it be harder to fight when you're no longer passionate about the war?"

"There are countless men fighting who are not passionate about the war. They are fighting because they have to. Because if they desert, they can be shot. Because, unless they win the war, they will no longer have a country to call home." He scowled. "I can no longer fight because of a desire to see slavery saved. You know I will never own another slave. The rest of it is still so complicated." He paused. "I still have a home I'm fighting for. I still have people I love in the city Hooker is trying to destroy. He won't be content only to take Richmond. Just as our government will not be content to step aside and let him have it. If the capital falls, there is going to be a tremendous amount of destruction. I can be passionate about not letting that happen."

"Will this horrible war never end?" Carrie asked in despair. "I feel as if you and I are like a tree trying to take root. Just when it thinks it's going to be left alone, something pulls it up to see if it's growing."

"I want it to end as much as you do, but until it does, I have to fight. I wish I had something to do with making the decisions that would bring it to an end, although, I'm not sure I possess any more wisdom than the men leading us now."

"I would gladly replace any of them with you," Carrie replied. "You're not the same man you were a year ago. You see things more clearly."

"Do I?" Robert asked. "I thought I saw things clearly. Now that I'm back in the middle of the fray, it doesn't seem so simple."

"It will never be simple," Carrie responded, "but you have acknowledged your own humanity now. Because of that you can accept others, including the slaves you once held in such contempt. Too few of the men running our country have recognized their humanity. Their decisions are based on pride and passion. They have ignited a war that could destroy our whole country."

Silence fell on the room as the sound of her words floated away. The cold front delivered by the earlier storm gusted into the room. Carrie shivered and pulled the covers up close around her neck, and Robert padded across the room to push the window shut. As he approached the bed, his eyes met hers in the flickering lantern light. Carrie felt herself grow warm again at what she saw in his gaze. When he held out his arms she melted into them, willing the picture of him riding away in the morning to fade from her mind.

They had today. They had tonight. They had this time to fill their hearts and minds with memories that would carry them through the dark days ahead.

Chapter Three

A full moon hovered on the horizon, its milky glow casting a strange beauty over the fury waiting beneath the surface it gazed so benevolently upon. Its glow cast sparkles across the waters of the Rappahannock and Rapidan Rivers. Hundreds of crackling campfires lent an almost romantic ambience to what soon would be a scene of horrible carnage.

"Bring Moses to me," Captain Jones barked.

Moses was up and moving toward his commander's tent even before the messenger sent word. The still night air, pregnant with anticipation, carried sounds well. The earlier rain had settled the dust. He pulled his coat around him, thankful for its warmth against the suddenly cool air.

"The captain wants you, Moses."

Moses nodded easily. "On my way." Moments later, he stood outside the flap of Captain Jones' tent. He tapped lightly on the side of the tent, and when motioned inside, ducked to allow his massive frame entry.

Captain Jones looked up from his papers, shoved his chair back, and propped his feet up on the makeshift table. "We cross the river tomorrow."

"I see," Moses replied, his voice and face calm, even though his heart was racing. The time had finally come. General Hooker was ordering the long-awaited assault on General Lee's Rebel troops.

"Are your men ready?" Captain Jones asked, eying him closely.

"As ready as they are going to be," Moses said. "My men have wanted to fight a long time. They are eager to prove what they can do. All they need is a chance."

"You realize how much is resting on this," Captain Jones said.

"I joined up as one of the first black spies in the Union Army to help pave the way for black soldiers," Moses reminded his commander. He had put up with tremendous harassment and prejudice to help open the way for the tens of thousands of black soldiers who enlisted as soon as the Emancipation Proclamation had taken effect. "I know people will be watching to see how these troops do. The men are ready," he repeated. "Most of them feel like they have nothing to lose. Many of them are free blacks, wanting to help gain freedom for their race. Most are escaped slaves fighting for their freedom. There is a lot of passion in men like that. They will fight, and they will fight hard. They don't intend to let the South win this war."

"Good," Captain Jones replied. Then his voice softened. "I know I can count on you, Moses."

"Yes, sir." Moses said nothing of the sick dread filling his heart. He would have been content to spend all his days in the army as a spy. He had seen what battle did to men, yet when his captain asked him to serve as a noncommissioned commander of one of the first black corps, he couldn't refuse. He had saved Captain Jones' life when he was shot outside of Richmond a year earlier. In return, the captain had given him enough time to locate his sister June and set her free from the plantation where she was a slave. Moses owed him too much to refuse his request.

Captain Jones resumed studying his papers. Moses turned, figuring he was dismissed.

"One more thing, Moses."

"Yes, sir?"

"Good luck," the captain said with a wry smile. "We have the clear advantage here, but the last couple of years have taught me not to take too much stock in that."

"You, too, Captain Jones," Moses replied. As he walked back to his unit, he recalled the words General Hooker had spoken that evening. He had pulled all the ranks together and announced that he had maneuvered so cunningly, the enemy must either flee ingloriously, or come out and submit to destruction. The confident general seemed to feel there would be hardly any battle at all—that Lee would simply cut and run. From what little Moses had seen of the South's General Lee, he didn't think it was going to be quite so simple.

> *We'll fight for liberty*
> *Till de Lord shall call us home;*
> *We'll soon be free*
> *Till de Lord shall call us home.*

Moses stopped and listened as the song rolled across the night toward him. His men's voices were quieter than usual tonight. They knew what was coming. There was none of the high-spirited singing and dancing that often erupted around the fires at night. Some of the men were cleaning their guns, staring thoughtfully into the distance as their cloths worked up a bright polish. The glow of cigarettes filled the air like fireflies as men contemplated what was to come when the sun rose again. Fervent prayers could be heard around some of the smoldering fires as men prepared for what America had been sure would never happen—black men raising arms against white men in defense of their country.

Moses stood quietly, allowing the words of the song to work their way deep into his soul. He had chosen to fight for the liberty of his people who had toiled under cruel bondage for so long. He had chosen to fight for the freedom of those who would come after. He had chosen to fight for his unborn child.

As they did several times a day, Moses' thoughts flew to the contraband camp located at Fort Monroe. He would give anything to be able to lay down his gun, walk away from it all, and be with his beloved wife, Rose, when she gave birth to their first child.

Moses moved over to a fallen log and sank down upon it, his unseeing eyes staring into the distance. If he concentrated hard enough, he could almost see Rose's beautiful face beaming up at him when she had told him they were going to have a baby. They had only had a few days together at Christmas before he was called back to duty. It ate at his heart to leave her alone in the contraband camp. The fact that his sister June was now living with her was some comfort, but every particle of his heart longed to be there.

The distant call of a hoot owl pulled him back to the present. Would he live to see his baby? Would he still be alive when the dust and gun smoke settled from this battle? Moses heaved a sigh and pushed up from the log. He had made his choices. He would live or die with them.

He had gone less than one hundred feet when a voice called out to him.

"That be you, Moses, suh?"

Moses walked over to the glowing campfire. "It's me, Pompey." He almost smiled at the look of righteous indignation on the face of the man old enough to be his father. Pompey had told him many times he had been the first in line when the federal government opened the army to blacks. The older man had escaped with his wife from a plantation in Georgia over twenty years ago, but he never lost the burning desire to see the rest of his people free.

"There's some o' dese boys here a mite nervous," Pompey said scornfully.

Moses smiled sympathetically. "Battle can be a horrible experience. There's nothing wrong with being a little nervous. It doesn't mean everyone won't fight hard."

"But we be fightin' under de flag, suh!" Pompey snorted. "We got right on our side!"

Moses opened his mouth to tell him *right* didn't always keep you from dying, but Pompey kept talking, standing to add intensity to his words. Moses knew from experience that it was best to let the self-proclaimed orator talk. The gray-haired man often had many words of wisdom.

Pompey positioned himself so that the flames of the fire illuminated his lithe form, and then he pulled himself to his full height, his shadow dancing across the bushes behind him. "Our old Southern mas'rs dey had lib under de flag, dey got dere wealth under it, and ebrything beautiful for dere chilun. Under it, dey hab grind us up and put us in dere pocket for money. But de fus' minute dey tink dat ole flag mean freedom for we colored people, dey pull it right down, and run up de rag ob dere own." He paused dramatically, staring hard at the men gazing up at him.

Moses watched the faces of the soldiers. He knew all of them were brave, good men. Part of him yearned to prepare them for the horrors of battle—the sick reality of thousands of men wounded and killed. At the same time, he knew mere words could never prepare them and would do nothing but instill fear. Their baptism into the truth of war would come soon enough. He welcomed whatever words would give them the courage and determination to fight.

"But we'll neber desert de ole flag, boys," Pompey cried, lifting a fist in defiance to the sky, his voice ringing out into the night. "Neber!" He stopped, letting his words sink in. "We done libbed under it for lots of years. We'll die for it now!"

The cheers and applause of the watching soldiers exploded into the night. "We'll die for the flag!" Their voices rose in unison and were soon caught up by troops in the near vicinity.

Moses listened for a few moments and then moved on. How many of them were prophesying their own future?

Robert threw aside his blanket and walked toward the warmth of the campfire. His gut instincts told him the waiting was over. The last three days of maneuvering and posturing were over. Today they would fight.

One of his men handed Robert a cup of coffee. Sipping it thoughtfully, he moved away to stare out over the morning fog. The events of the last few days had mystified him. Hooker had crossed the Rappahannock with his men three days ago, but not before sending about ten thousand cavalry toward Richmond. Instead of sending General Stuart and the Confederate cavalry after them, Lee ordered them to remain on his flank, depending on Stuart to inform him of Hooker's movements. For the last three days, Hooker moved his men around, but there had been no attack. Had Lee's refusal to respond predictably thrown him? What was happening in Richmond? Were there enough troops to protect the city from marauding cavalry?

A shot rang out in the still morning. Men bolted from the ground. Robert stiffened but continued sipping his coffee. It was too early for an engagement. The sun was barely creeping onto the horizon.

"You reckon it's gonna start now, Captain?"

Robert smiled briefly. "I don't think so, Crocker." The intense lad in front of him reminded him of Hobbs, the youth who helped save his life at Antietam. Hobbs' unrelenting search to find Robert after the battle left him behind the battle lines too long, resulting in one leg several inches shorter than the other. Carrie and Dr. Wild had been able to save his life, but the necessary crutches had ended his fighting days. *Lucky kid,* Robert thought grimly.

"You reckon it's coming today, Captain?" Crocker persisted. "How come Hooker ain't blasting us with all those men he's got?"

"That's a good question," Robert replied, taking another long sip of coffee. "All any of us can do is speculate. From all the reports I hear, Hooker almost had his men in the position they could do us the most harm. They met a small line of our defenders, and instead of ordering their destruction, he pulled his units back." He shook his head.

"I reckon he knows our reputation," Crocker boasted. "I guess we'll smash right through their lines this morning." His eyes gleamed with the light of battle.

Robert said nothing, but he seriously hoped that wasn't Lee's plan. Whether Hooker was playing games with them or was genuinely nervous, Lee's army simply wasn't strong enough to smash into a force twice as strong as their own. Robert felt himself tighten at the picture of how many men would die. As usual, he would simply wait for orders. The lives of almost two hundred thousand men, both North and South, hung on the decisions of their commanding generals.

"Get some food," Robert muttered. "It's going to be a long day."

Crocker nodded and strode away.

Robert ambled over to the fire, filled another cup with strong coffee, and walked over to stare into the woods looming in the distance. Why *had* Hooker moved his men back? The Federals had come close to securing the open farmland that would have afforded them the maneuvering they would need. Instead, they pulled back into what was known as the wilderness—almost fifteen miles of dense, gloomy, second-growth forest full of irregular ravines and low hills. No one in their right mind would choose to stage a battle there.

"Captain Borden, sir," a voice snapped behind him.

Robert spun around to face the messenger addressing him. "What is it?" he asked, sensing that whatever was going to happen was about to begin.

"Pull your unit together and prepare to march."

Robert listened in almost wry amusement as the messenger outlined the plan. Lee was sending over half of his available troops with Jackson to swing around to the right of Hooker's army. Reconnaissance had revealed the weakness of the Federal right-end, and Lee was out to exploit and crush it. Robert knew Lee's decision was the riskiest of all the risky decisions he had made thus far. He also knew the general was counting on Hooker's cautiousness. If the Federals refused to act their part—if they got wind of Lee's attempt—there could be seventy thousand men sweeping down on the approximately fourteen thousand men Lee was leaving to face them. It was a brazen move, even for the daring Lee.

Within the hour, a long line of infantry began its march across the country. Speed was what mattered now. Robert, from astride Carrie's massive Thoroughbred, Granite, stared out over the men marching south. Would their evasive movement make Hooker think they were retreating? Granite strode forward, his beautiful head tossing proudly.

Robert allowed his thoughts to turn to Carrie as the sun exploded onto the morning, dissolving the mist and evaporating the dew. Their night together had been all he could have imagined, but the agony of having her for just one night, only to be wrenched apart again, was tearing at his heart. It would have been almost better never to have experienced her sweet closeness. "Don't be a fool," he muttered angrily. If he were going to die in battle today, at least they had had that one night.

It was three o'clock when Jackson and the marching troops reached their destination. Order and relative calm reigned as the men occupied their positions. Robert could only hope that Hooker's right line was still resolutely facing south, completely unaware that an army was poised to strike from the west and northwest. The afternoon was quiet, the absence of gunfire indicating their ruse was working. Robert leaned back against the towering oak stationed behind him. He knew the order to advance would come soon.

Moses paced back and forth between the cook fires, every nerve taut. The last few days had stretched each nerve until it felt they must surely snap. He watched as his men stacked their arms and prepared supper. Everything in him screamed danger was imminent, but there was nothing on the surface to validate his fears.

They had heard the sound of skirmishing in the distance all day, but the long-awaited battle had not happened. There had been no action on the right wing held by Major General Howard with his company of German soldiers, just another day of endless watching and waiting.

Captain Jones strode up to where Moses was standing, staring hard into the distance. "Do you feel as uneasy as I do?" he muttered.

"Yes, sir," Moses replied, glad someone else was feeling not all was right. "My eyes tell me nothing is happening. My gut tells me something is getting ready to."

Captain Jones nodded briefly. "It wouldn't be the first time Lee has pulled something. I would feel a lot better if Stonewall Jackson wasn't out there somewhere. He has the uncanny ability to appear in places you never would expect him to." He turned around to stare at the men settling down to eat, their rifles stacked nearby. "I have half a mind to tell them to be ready for something, but then I tell myself I'm being foolish. There is no way Jackson could swing his way around here without being seen at some point."

"I sure wish I was a bird," Moses stated. "I'd like to take a look at what's going on beyond all these trees. I can't help but feel trapped down here."

Captain Jones scowled. "I still can't believe Hooker pulled the troops back from the open plain. From what I can tell, it would have taken very little to press forward and push the Rebel troops into retreat. Being stuck down here in these woods feels like being in a cage."

"It's hard to figure the last few days after how confident General Hooker seemed the other night," Moses said, trying to remain casual. He didn't want to sound like he was criticizing his commanding office.

"It's lunacy," Captain Jones snorted. "Hooker gave up the fight before it even started. Now we're sitting here waiting for something to happen. We should have been the ones on the offensive. We could have been in Richmond by now," he said angrily. "Your men could have been marching through the city where many of them used to be slaves."

"It can still happen," Moses offered, even though his heart wasn't in it. He knew nothing of battle strategy, but he wasn't feeling very good about things right now. When Captain Jones didn't reply, Moses broke off his scrutiny of the surroundings. The captain had his head tilted back, scanning the trees towering above them.

"If someone could get up into one of those trees, we might have some idea of what's going on," Captain Jones said slowly.

Moses grinned, relieved to have some kind of action. "Jacob! Caesar! Get over here," he called and then swung back to stare up at the trees surrounding them. "I reckon one of these three will give us the view we need, Captain."

Two men appeared by his side. Moses barked out his orders quickly. "Jacob, take that tree right there. Caesar, you take that other oak. The man who gets the highest the quickest gets extra rations tonight." He smiled at the staring men. "Pretend you're birds, men. That's the only way we're going to know what's going on around here." Spinning around, he swung up into the nearest tree and began to climb.

Moses saw Jacob and Caesar swing into action after him, and then he focused on the tree, searching for the quickest, surest way to make the ascent. For a moment he forgot there was a war going on. He was a little boy again, climbing trees with reckless abandon, finding freedom in the heights that took him above reality. His powerful arms pulled him from branch to branch almost effortlessly. Soon though, he was moving more carefully. The branches were smaller, less likely to bear his weight, and still he wasn't high enough to see beyond the woods. Setting his lips, he continued to climb.

When he looked down again, it was impossible to spot anything or anyone through the thick canopy of leaves spread out below him. He could barely see Jacob and Caesar threading their way through the trees nearby. As he climbed, the reality of the risk he was taking filtered through. He would be an easy target for any Rebel sharpshooters in the area, and there was always the possibility of a fall from what was going to be over one hundred feet in the air. Either scenario meant certain death.

He breathed a sigh of relief when his head broke above the surrounding trees. Exhilaration filled him as the afternoon sun bathed his face and a cool breeze flowed over his sweating body. Squinting his eyes, he stared south. Nothing.

"I don't reckon I ever been this high," Jacob called, a smile spreading across his face.

"Kinda feels like we be on top of the world," Caesar yelled in return.

Moses was smiling when he turned to look north. He stiffened, and his blood ran cold. "Oh my God," he said in a strangled voice. Wave upon wave of muskets gleamed in the distant woods.

"Moses," Caesar called. "What are we looking for...?" His voice trailed off as he turned in the direction Moses was facing.

Moses snapped into action. "Let's get out of here," he called. "We're nothing but sitting ducks!" He began to scale down the tree as fast as he could, leaning over to yell down to the captain. "There's Rebels to the—"

His words were swallowed when the boom of musketry exploded from the woods behind them.

Robert was at the front of the long line when Jackson ordered the charge. The air reverberated with the Rebel yell as the solid mass of gray swept from the woods, muskets firing. It was obvious their flanking movement had been a success. Men were lounging in the clearing eating, their rifles set aside. Robert and his men were on them before they could form a defense.

All around him, the yells of triumphant men rang through the air as Federals turned and ran for their lives. "After them!" Robert yelled, dashing into the timber, stumbling through the dense undergrowth.

Jackson's men continued to surge forward, triggering a full scale rout of Hooker's right flank.

Moses had barely touched the ground before the first of Howard's men stumbled into the clearing.

"The Rebels are after us!" one cried.

"Jackson is upon us!" another yelled. "Run for your lives!"

Captain Jones leapt onto his horse and held his bayonet high. "Hold your ground, men!"

Moses stared around him in amazement as men, their uniforms in tatters from the thick undergrowth, lurched into the clearing. Cattle and mules swept along with the men ran blindly, terrified by the shooting. One cow, eyes wide with panic, ran straight through a cook fire, almost trampling the men caught by surprise.

"Gather your unit, Moses!" Captain Jones called. "We have to stop them."

Moses raced into action. It took only minutes for his men to grab their guns and form a line across the woods. Moments later, the forest exploded with gray uniforms and the flash of musket fire. Moses took a deep breath, aimed, and fired. All around him, his men stood their ground. The Rebels continued to surge forward, their guns firing continuously. Men began to scream and fall around him.

"Retreat!" Captain Jones yelled. "Retreat!"

The remainder of Moses' men, spurred by the panicked flight of the other soldiers, squared off for one final round and then turned and sprinted into the woods. Moses was right behind them. Part of him yearned to stay and fight. The other part of him knew it was useless suicide. Jackson had turned the tables on them.

They fled through the woods for over a mile before two mounted officers, defiantly waving bayonets, swept down upon them. General Hooker was right behind them. "Forward!" he cried. "Forward!" Hooker's band of men cleaved the multitude sweeping toward them as they advanced toward the enemy.

Moses jarred to a halt, his hope renewed. A quick glance told him his men had stopped and were staring at him for direction. His determination steeled as he realized they were counting on him. "Forward!" he yelled. "Follow that unit! Forward!"

With a yell, his men reversed the direction of their flight, grabbed their rifles tighter, and ran back toward the melee. Artillery began to explode around them as the rout was slowed and reversed. Moses fought through the same woods he had fled from moments before, and he took his position with the other men. He raised his rifle and began to fire steadily.

Robert fell to the right as the Federals turned and offered fierce resistance.

A colonel appeared, his cry ringing through the afternoon air. "There is artillery to the right. Forward! Now is our chance to take it!"

Robert and his men were advancing on the clearing full of abandoned artillery and littered with fleeing Union soldiers, when other Confederate units reached the woods surrounding it and prepared to surge forward. Robert called his men to a halt and took up position on the far edge of the clearing. At that same moment, a wave of Federal cavalry swept from the opposite grove. There was a slight hesitation until, with a loud cry, they charged furiously at the advancing Rebels.

Robert stared at what was a certain charge to death. Hundreds of Rebel muskets fired in unison, dropping Federal cavalrymen like dead flies. The leader of the charge was one of the first to fall, his arms flying up before he sagged lifeless from his saddle. Robert felt the bile rise in his throat at the sight of so much senseless death. No matter that it was causing the enemy to fall back—it still sickened him to see so much human life wasted.

The men surrounding him cheered as the Federal forces broke and retreated, their numbers severely decimated. Robert swung his attention back to the clearing, waiting for the order to charge again. The Federals had not been idle during the futile cavalry charge. The ground around the artillery had been cleared of stragglers and vehicles, the artillery turned to face the thick woods. Robert opened his mouth to yell his horror of what he knew was coming...

"Forward!"

At their commander's order, the units already filling the woods poured forth in pursuit of final Confederate victory. A volley of musketry fire dimmed their savage yell as they surged forward. The Federal cannoneers stood their ground, until with one mighty roar, the line of artillery detonated, the explosion shaking the ground and obliterating all sound but its own.

Robert was weeping even before the smoke rose on the suddenly silent scene. Without looking, he knew what he would see. The men around him stared in shocked silence, their faces white with agony. Robert finally raised his eyes. There was nothing left standing in the clearing. Every single man who had rushed from the woods lay where they had fallen, their decimated bodies littering the earth.

Moses couldn't take his eyes from the scene of carnage in front of him. Dimly, he became aware that the Confederate advance had been halted by the lightning strike of the artillery attack. "Poor beggars," he muttered thickly, his loathing of battle intensifying.

Pompey appeared by his side, his sweaty face streaked with soot and powder. "I reckon them boys died fer dere flag, Moses."

"I reckon they did, Pompey. I reckon they did," Moses said heavily.

"You think it be over?" Pompey asked.

Moses stared out at the scene. Every particle of his being longed for this battle to be over, but his heart told him it wasn't so. He shook his head slowly. "I'm afraid there's going to be more dying." His eyes scanned the clearing. "It's not over yet."

Chapter Four

Rose stepped out onto her tiny porch, shielded her eyes against the morning sun, and stared east. She had heard the reports of Hooker crossing the Rappahannock. Somewhere beyond the open fields and dense forests, Moses was fighting a battle.

"Don't you wish you could see right over them trees?"

Rose smiled slightly as June, Moses' sister, appeared at her side. "I do indeed. And by the way, it's *those* trees."

June grimaced. "It's hard enough to learn how to speak correctly without having to think about it when I'm worried."

Rose reached out and put her hand on June's arm. "I'm sorry. It's so automatic to me, I wasn't even thinking. I guess the teacher in me can't be pushed down even when I'm sick with worry over my husband."

"Moses is going to be fine," June said stoutly. "God's done kept him safe this far. I reckon he'll keep on."

Rose said nothing, knowing June was trying to make her feel better. Most of the time it worked. She knew she had to trust God with her husband's life. It was easier during the day when she was busy in the contraband camp, teaching and helping the refugee slaves who were still flooding in, filling the place to capacity. There was precious little time to think of herself. "It's the nights that are so hard," she finally murmured. Her sleep had been disturbed by horrible dreams that would jar her awake and send her out onto the porch. Images of Moses sprawled dead on the battlefield would dim only as the morning light chased away the darkness.

"You look awful tired," June said.

Rose didn't bother to deny the pervasive weariness that gripped her body. Unconsciously, she laid her hand on her swollen belly. She knew she had to take care of herself for the sake of the little one waiting to be ushered into the world, but the demands were never ending. How long before their child was born? She longed to have Moses with her, but she knew it was impossible.

"I'll get us some breakfast," June offered. Just then the wail of her little boy, Simon, split the morning air. "After I give him some," she corrected.

Rose stared after her sister-in-law, reproaching herself inwardly. Here she was pining for Moses, but at least she had seen him five months earlier and received letters from him on almost a weekly basis. June's husband, Simon, had been called to work on the fortifications surrounding Richmond more than a year ago. June had not heard from him since, yet she talked to her little son about his father constantly, and prayed for him every night. She held onto the hope that one day they would be a family.

Rose had a full day ahead of her. She took another deep breath of the fresh morning air and turned to enter the cabin just as the baby residing in her womb erupted with a mighty kick. Rose gasped and reached for the railing to steady herself. "I have a feeling you're going to be a boy, little one," she murmured. "You already have the strength of your daddy." As if in agreement, her baby gave another strong kick before settling down.

Rose swung back around to stare east. "I think our child is going to be born soon, Moses," she whispered, her eyes welling with tears that were at once joy and sorrow. "I promise to love it enough for both of us until you come home." Behind her, a wail burst from the cabin. Rose frowned and hurried inside.

June stared up at her from where she was huddled next to baby Simon's tiny bed. "He's got the fever," she said in a choked voice. "My baby boy done got the fever."

Rose stiffened and moved over to put her hand on the ten-month-old boy's forehead. His glistening skin was frightfully hot. Rose managed to contain her groan. There was no reason to add to June's fear—a fear that was justified. Dozens of babies had died during the long winter months when disease swept through the crowded camp. Hope had risen with the warm winds blowing in from the south. The long days of summer still loomed ahead, but a collective sigh of relief had greeted the moderate days of spring.

Rose met June's frightened eyes squarely. "Simon is strong. He'll make it," she said, praying she was right. She longed for the abundant supply of ice they always had at Cromwell Plantation, but she tightened her lips. They may not have ice, but the thousands of blacks who had fled here had their freedom. "I'll be back in a minute with fresh water," she said.

Rose grabbed a bucket and hurried outside. In the few minutes it took her to return, baby Simon was even more feverish. His pitiful wails made her heart ache. June had already pulled all the covers away from him and gathered a pile of rags. She dipped one into the bucket as soon as Rose set it down and placed it on the tiny body. Rose imitated her actions, wringing out a fresh cloth just as June removed the already hot one.

Rose felt a sick dread grip her heart but pushed aside the paralyzing fear. She needed to channel all of her energy into action.

"He's awfully hot," June whispered fearfully. "Did you hear Willa's baby died last week from the fever?"

"I won't hear any talk like that," Rose said. "It won't help to imagine the worst. We just have to deal with what is." She cast in her mind for a way to help June. "Sing to him," she said suddenly.

"What?" June asked in a startled voice.

"Sing to him," Rose repeated. "The music will help calm him."

June swallowed hard and began to sing in a quavering soprano.

> *Swing low, sweet chariot*
> *Coming for to carry me home*
> *Swing low, sweet chariot*
> *Coming for to carry me home.*

Rose joined in, her soft voice crooning the words that had carried her and Moses to safety during their escape. As always, the words gave her renewed strength.

I looked over Jordan, and what did I see
Coming for to carry me home.
A band of angels coming after me
Coming for to carry me home.

The words faded away, but Simon's cries had lessened and the stark fear was gone from June's eyes. "Thank you," June said quietly. She said no more but continued to hum soothingly as she battled to bring Simon's fever down.

Rose watched for a few minutes and then picked up the bucket to go fetch fresh water. As she hurried down the street, now alive with throngs of people, she nodded and smiled at the many who spoke to her, but she didn't slow her pace. Her bucket full, she made her way back toward the cabin. She wished she could bring a doctor back to treat the sick baby. The government had finally provided one doctor for the thousands of people in the camps, but he was woefully overworked and medicine was scarce. Only the most desperate cases warranted his attention, and by then it was usually too late. Rose ground her teeth in frustration. How long would her people have to continue to pay the ultimate price in their quest for freedom and equality?

Rose could hear Simon's wails as she approached the cabin. She thought longingly of Aunt Abby's luxurious home in Philadelphia, and of the sumptuous bedroom she and Moses shared after they had escaped Cromwell Plantation. Aunt Abby had begged her to return to Philadelphia to have her baby, but Rose had refused, believing her place was here in the camps. Had she made a mistake? Was she bringing sickness and death on her unborn child? Her steps faltered for a moment, then strengthened. Her place was here, with her people. She would have to deal with what came.

Rose and June worked over Simon all morning. Finally, just before lunch, his fever abated and his cries diminished to a weak whimper. Rose breathed a sigh of relief, but she knew the battle was far from over. "I wish I'd listened to my mama more," she said wistfully.

"You mean about all them herbs she used?"

Rose nodded. "I used to look down my nose at them, convinced white medicine was more effective. Carrie, however, learned all she could. I'd give anything to know all the secret things my mama used to bring down fevers and take care of illness."

June shrugged. "Ain't no use wishing for what you can't have." She stroked Simon's forehead. "I don't reckon there's any of us that wouldn't change a lot of things about our life if we had the chance. I guess all we can do is go on, trying not to make the same mistakes and soaking up all we can from each day."

"You're a wise woman," Rose smiled. "You sound just like my mama."

"From all you've told me, I got a long ways to go to be like your mama."

Rose didn't contradict her. Her mama, Old Sarah, had been the wisest, most loving woman she had ever known. Not a day passed since discovering she was pregnant that she hadn't wished for her mama to still be alive. She longed for her baby to know her. She longed for her strength and comfort.

"You need to be getting on to the school," June said.

Rose knew it was almost time for the afternoon session of school to begin. "Are you sure you're going to be all right?"

"Bring me in a fresh bucket of water. If Simon's fever starts to grip him again, I'll be ready. I'm going to sit here with him while he sleeps." June gazed into her baby's face. "I think I'll just be here and talk to God about my little baby for a while. I reckon that's about all I can do.

Rose struggled to ignore the heavy fatigue pressing down on her as she walked toward the little white school in the center of the camp. She gazed around to take her mind off it. Newly planted gardens were beginning to sprout green life from their sandy soil. Laundry flapped in the breeze, while women held infants under one arm and washed clothes with the other. The camp was mostly women and children. The majority of the men were serving in the army now that it had been opened to blacks. Those working at the nearby fort put in long days, leaving at sunup and not returning until after sundown. No one complained. There was a war going on to guarantee their freedom. They would do whatever had to be done.

"Miss Rose! Miss Rose!"

Rose smiled and knelt down to wrap her arms around the little girl snuggling up to her side. "Hello, Carla. How are you today?"

"I be doin' fine, Miss Rose." Carla drew herself up proudly, her black eyes burning intensely. "I made me a decision last night, Miss Rose."

"And what would that decision be?" Rose asked seriously. It was easy to love the little girl with long pigtails and light skin. Her mother and father had helped Moses make it to the camps with June and baby Simon, who was born in the woods during the escape. All of them had become fast friends.

Carla took a deep breath, allowing the suspense to build. "I done decided I'm going to be a teacher like you, Miss Rose."

"I thought you wanted to be a doctor?" Rose asked in surprise.

"Well, I reckon I did," Carla replied, pursing her lips in deep thought. "But then something wonderful happened," she said excitedly.

Rose hid her smile. "And what would that be?" She knew Carla was about to burst with whatever she was holding inside.

"I done taught my little brother Andrew to read last night," she cried, breaking into a glad little dance. Rose settled back in astonishment. Carla laughed and nodded her head vigorously. "I did, sure enough!"

"How in the world did you do that?"

"Why, I showed him how you showed us at school. Andrew has been wanting to learn all winter, but he done been too sick to go to school. I decided to bring school to him," Carla explained as if there were nothing spectacular about what she had done.

Rose stared at her. At ten years old, Carla had taught her six-year-old brother how to read. She shook her head in amazement. "I'm so proud of you," she finally murmured. She wished all the people who thought blacks were inferior to whites could meet the little girl skipping around in front of her.

Carla stopped dancing and snuggled up to her again. "You think I'll make a good teacher, Miss Rose? You think I'll be as good as you?"

"I'll think you'll be incredible at whatever you decide to do, Carla." A sudden thought struck her. "I have an idea." She smiled at the expectant look on the girl's face. "How about if you help me with the younger children? Sometimes there aren't enough teachers to go around. You could help them the same way you helped Andrew."

"Really?" Carla breathed in disbelief. She drew her slender frame up importantly and spoke quickly. "I'd be most obliged to help you, Miss Rose."

A call from the school's stoop drew Rose's attention. She stood awkwardly, swaying a little as another wave of fatigue washed over her.

"You okay, Miss Rose?" Carla asked. Her little face grew serious. "My mama said last night that she reckoned you would be having your baby anytime. You reckon your baby is coming?"

Rose took a deep breath, trying to fight off the dizziness sweeping through her. She had over a hundred women and children waiting in the schoolhouse for her to teach them. As close as she could tell, she still had two weeks before her baby was due. "I'm okay, Carla," she replied weakly.

"You want me to get my mama?" Carla persisted. "You're looking real sick, Miss Rose."

Rose shook her head, straightened, and began to walk toward the schoolhouse. A sharp pain exploded in her body. She doubled over, gasping in agony.

"Miss Rose!" Carla cried. "Miss Rose!"

"Get your mama," Rose managed to whisper.

Then she collapsed.

The sun was sinking low on the horizon when Rose regained consciousness, fighting her way through the dark cloud enveloping her.

"Take it easy, Rose."

Rose turned her head toward the soothing voice. "Deidre...what happened...?"

Deidre squeezed her hand reassuringly. "My little Carla came runnin' to get me as soon as you done collapsed on that road. I sent her to the fort to get some men to carry you here. We been waitin' a right long time for you to come to."

Rose studied her face. Deidre's eyes betrayed the calm way she was speaking. "What's wrong with me?"

"I'd say you done wore yourself right out, young lady," Deidre said. "I done been tellin' you for months that you need to be takin' care of yourself better, but you didn't heed nothing I said."

"So much to do," Rose murmured.

"Ain't nothing gonna get done if you kill yourself in the doin'," Deidre rejoined. Then her voice softened. "Everybody in this here camp knows you would give the very last drop of yourself. That don't mean you have to do it."

"My baby?" Rose whispered anxiously. "Is my baby going to be all right?" Deidre hesitated, obviously not knowing how to respond. Rose's heart tightened in agony. "What's wrong with my baby?"

"I don't know that there be anything wrong with your baby," Deidre protested, "but it ain't good for a woman to let herself get in such a state as this. When was the last time you felt your little one kick?"

"This morning," Rose replied. Her voice tightened. "And then maybe once, right before I fell."

Deidre peered at her sharply. "What do you mean, maybe?"

"There was a sharp pain right before I fell. I don't remember anything but that."

Deidre's lips tightened. "You ain't takin' another step, Rose. Not until this baby be born."

"I can't just lie here," Rose protested.

"That's exactly what you gonna be doing!" Deidre snapped, her kindly eyes filled with anxiety. "I ain't gonna let nothin' happen to you or to that fine baby you be carryin'. You done pushed yourself way past what you can do. I got half a mind to put you on a boat to Philadelphia." She snorted. "I would if I thought you'd have any chance of makin' it. You don't," she stated firmly, "so that means I got to take care of you myself." She stood and put her hands on her hips. "For once you're gonna listen to what people be tellin' you. I don't care if you be some fancy teacher. I be the one that's been a midwife longer than you done been alive. I ain't gonna have you arguing with me. You got that?"

Rose opened her mouth to argue, then closed it and nodded meekly. "I have to admit it sounds pretty nice, Deidre. I guess I'm more tired than I thought."

Deidre stared at her for a minute. Then, obviously satisfied Rose was going to follow orders for once, she turned to where June was watching from a corner chair. "I told you I could do it," she grinned.

June laughed, shifting Simon in her arms. "I haven't ever seen anyone handle Rose like that. I'm impressed. She won't listen to a word I say."

Deidre snorted. "Even a hard-headed young thing like her knows when someone is talking sense."

Rose watched the exchange, tenderness filling her heart for these two women who loved her. "Simon?" she asked weakly. "How is he?"

June smiled. "I reckon he knew there could only be one sick person in this house at a time. His fever completely broke a couple hours ago. I'm just trying to satisfy his appetite now." She shifted her weight and glanced down at him lovingly. "He just drifted off to sleep."

Deidre swung back to the bed. "When was the last time you ate somethin', missy?"

Rose shrugged. "Early this morning. There wasn't time before I went to school," she admitted.

Deidre shook her head knowingly, headed for the door, and stuck her head out. "Carla, get yourself in here." Seconds later, Carla appeared in the doorway, anxiety etched on her face. "Go get your teacher some food. I done baked up some sweet potatoes this morning, and there be a passel of cornbread on the table. Bring a pitcher of water, too. Both she and that baby need somethin' in them."

It was night when Rose woke again. She glanced around the darkened room, lit only with a candle, and saw Deidre rocking contentedly. For a moment, she reveled in the luxury of being cared for. It was almost like seeing her mama rocking in the chair, though Deidre's ample bulk bore no resemblance to her mama's silver-haired petiteness.

"I reckon that sleep was the first good one you done had in a while."

"I feel like I could sleep forever," Rose said with a smile, content to continue lying back against her pillow. "You don't have to stay here, you know."

Deidre nodded contentedly. "I don't plan on movin' in, but I intend to make sure you don't go gettin' stupid on me and try to get up. I done promised Moses before you left that I gonna take care of you. Don't figure I want to have to face him if you and that baby of yours ain't doing just fine when he gets here. I reckon I should have done this a while back, but I was hoping someone as smart as you had some common sense in their head, too. I reckon I was wrong."

Rose heaved a sigh of contentment. "You're just like my mama," she said fondly.

Deidre chuckled, and then a deep silence fell on the room. Rose felt her body relaxing again and her eyes drooped down. A sudden thought caused them to fly back open.

"What's on your mind, girl?" Deidre asked instantly.

Rose hesitated, but decided to ask. "Do you mind being mulatto?"

Deidre peered at her closely. "What you be asking a question like that for?"

Rose was wide awake now. "My baby might be. I was just wondering—just wondering what it was like."

Deidre rose and walked over to settle on the bed. "What you be talking about, girl? You and Moses both be black. How you figure you gonna get a mulatto baby out of that?"

Now that Rose had decided to talk about it, she was eager to express what she felt for months. Instinctively, she knew she could talk to Deidre about it. "I found out a couple of years ago who my real father is. He was the master of the plantation."

"Ain't nothing unusual about that," Deidre stated calmly. "It happens all the time. If that's the way it is, you're mulatto, too. Why you asking me what it's like?"

"Have you always known you were?" Rose asked.

"Kinda hard with skin this light not to know there be white in you somewhere."

"That's just it," Rose replied. "I never knew. I always figured I was black. The only daddy I knew was black, so I thought I was."

"According to the law you *be* black," Deidre observed. "Takes a lot less black blood in you than what you got to be considered black around here. The white part of you don't seem to matter none." She paused and inspected Rose. "The white part of you don't show up too much. You got beautiful caramel skin and coal black eyes. Moses be right dark. I don't think that master of your mama's put too much of him into you."

Rose took a deep breath and decided to tell her everything. "I have a twin brother. He was born white. They sold him when he was only a couple days old. He was adopted by a white family later."

"Do tell," Deidre breathed. "You ain't never met him?"

"Not yet," Rose answered, "but I mean to. When this war is over, I'm going to find him."

"You reckon that's a good idea? That boy been living in the white world for a long time. He might not take kindly to finding out he's half black."

"That's what Moses said," Rose admitted, remembering back to the night on the plantation when Carrie found the papers telling them about her twin brother. The reality of her brother had been much more of a shock than realizing she was Carrie's half-aunt. They had felt like family for so long, it hadn't really mattered. What mattered was that she had a brother she had never met.

She pulled her thoughts back and looked up at Deidre. "You're light-skinned, Deidre. Do you ever wish you could pass for being white?" She held her breath, hoping Deidre wouldn't be offended by her question.

Deidre was silent for a long time. "I'd be lying if I said I hadn't wished that. Yet, I'm also proud to be black. I had some family who escaped, headed north, and then passed themselves off as being white. At first it bothered me real bad. It's like they shoved away who they were." She paused thoughtfully. "Then I realized one day that they be as much white as they be black. I reckoned it was up to them which part they wanted to live more. One thing for sure, I know they had it a lot easier being white. This country ain't an easy place to be a colored person. Ain't too many people wouldn't take the easier road if someone put them on it."

Rose couldn't hold the question bursting from her. "What if my baby comes out white? There must be a lot of white blood in me, even though I came out more colored."

Deidre watched her for a long minute. "Would it bother you if it did?"

"I wouldn't love it any less," Rose replied. "I guess I'm afraid it would make life more complicated for my baby."

Deidre laughed shortly. "Life gonna be pretty complicated for that baby if it be born all black. Like I said, this ain't an easy country to be black in." She leaned forward. "What's really bothering you, girl?"

Rose almost smiled at how easily Deidre could read her, but her fear was too real. "I just..." Her voice trailed off. "I just wonder how Moses will feel about it if it's white."

"Moses know about your brother?"

"Of course. I would never have kept that from him."

"Then he's already thought about it," Deidre said firmly. "That man loves you with a mighty fierce love. He ain't gonna let a thing like that bother him. He's gonna love that baby whether it comes out coal black or lily white." She took Rose's hand. "And you gonna love that baby no matter what it looks like. The future will take care of itself. All you can do is take one day at a time. I reckon God knows what color that baby gonna be. He don't make mistakes, you know."

Rose nodded. Somehow talking about it had made her feel better. "I'm tired," she said, sinking down and burrowing into her pillow.

Deidre pulled the blanket up closer to her chin. "I'm gonna head for home now. June be in the next room. If you need anythin', you let her know."

Rose watched Deidre head for the door through almost closed eyelids. Just as she felt sleep reaching down to claim her, a sharp pain exploded in her stomach. "Oh!" she cried.

Deidre was by her side in an instant. "What's wrong, girl?"

Rose opened her mouth to answer, struggling to rise into a sitting position. "It's—"

Another pain stole the words from her mouth. Grabbing her stomach, she doubled over to escape the hurt.

She heard Deidre move away and fling open the door to the other room. "I think it be time. Get the water ready."

Rose struggled to conquer the fear trying to suffocate her. "Deidre," she gasped.

Deidre was by her side in an instant. "Everything gonna be fine, Rose. Babies been comin' into the world since the beginning of time. Ain't nothing to worry about."

In spite of the pain gripping her body, Rose could hear the anxiety in Deidre's voice. "What's wrong?" she said.

"Something is wrong. Tell me what it is," she demanded, reaching out and grabbing the older woman's hand.

Deidre hesitated. "Them sharp pains ain't normal. They ain't the same as contractions." Her voice grew stronger. "Don't necessarily mean anythin' be wrong, though. Every baby decides to come into the world their own way."

Rose drew comfort from her words. There might not be anything wrong. She relaxed slightly and felt Deidre tilt her chin back so that she could look into her eyes.

"You got a long fight ahead of you, Rose. You're already terrible tired. It's gonna make it harder." She smiled slightly. "But it be worth it, honey girl. When you hold that new baby in your arms, whatever you went through to get it, is *worth it.* "

Rose yelled out again as a fresh spasm of pain overtook her body. She drew her breath in sharply, surprise filling her. "My water," she said. "I think my water just broke."

June eased into the room, carrying a large bucket of hot water and holding a pile of rags. "I sent for Carla. She can watch Simon while I help you, Deidre."

The next thirty minutes passed in a blur for Rose. She would be gripped by a spasm of pain unlike any she had ever known, gasping for breath and wondering if it would ever end. Just as suddenly the pain would end, leaving her as limp as a wet washrag, and feeling just as wrung out. She quickly learned to live for those times.

Deidre moved around the room efficiently, making her preparations. "You're doing fine, Rose," she said softly. "You be doing fine, honey girl."

A pain more ferocious than any yet grabbed Rose. "Mama!" she shrieked, tears coursing down her face. "Mama!"

Deidre put a firm hand on her shoulder, moved to the end of the bed, and turned to June. "This baby be turned wrong," she said. "We got us some work to do."

June stepped up and grabbed hold of Rose's hand. "You're gonna be fine, Rose. Hang on. You're gonna be fine."

Rose hung onto the words for dear life, dimly aware something was terribly wrong but not able to do anything beyond trying to endure the agony her body was producing. She cried out as another fresh wave of pain engulfed her, which left her weak and gasping for breath.

The minutes blended into what seemed an eternity of torment as the night wore on. June stayed at her side, gripping her hand with each fresh spasm.

"I've about got it turned," Deidre finally called. "Rose, you got to push hard."

Rose heard the words through a haze of fatigue and pain. She tried to comply, but her body refused to respond.

"Push!" June cried.

"Can't," Rose whispered. "Tired..."

"You push, girl," Deidre snapped, "and you push now! This baby done fightin' too hard for its life for you to give up on it now. Push!" she yelled.

Rose pushed, straining with all her might to give life to her child.

"It's almost here," Deidre cried. "Push! I ain't gonna lose this battle now."

Rose felt tears coursing down her cheeks, mingling with the sweat drenching her bedclothes and sheets. She screamed in agony and marshaled her flagging strength for one more try.

"Push!"

"God, help me!" Rose shrieked, bearing down with all of her that was left, and then descended into a dark haze. She could hear talking, but the words failed to penetrate the fog engulfing her.

Gradually, she became aware of wet cloths bathing her skin. She struggled to remember where she was, why pain was trying to rob her of life.

"You done got a perfect little boy, Rose."

The words came from a great distance. *A little boy... You have a perfect little boy...* Rose slowly attached meaning to the words. An instinct dating back to the beginning of time made her reach out her arms. She fought to open her eyes. *A little boy... A perfect little boy...*

"He's beautiful, Rose." June's voice penetrated the fog. "Sit up a little bit so I can give you some water. Your son is waiting for you."

Rose found the energy somehow to open her eyes. The water trickling down her throat was like sweet nectar. "My son," she whispered. "My son."

Deidre stepped up next to the bed, her face beaming. "Here he be, Rose. He put up a mighty big fight to make sure he could say hello to his mama."

Rose pushed herself up against the wall and held her arms out in wonder. Deidre laid the tiny little bundle of life, already wrapped in clean cloths, in her arms. She stared down at the puckered face in tender amazement. Tears of joy now streaked her cheeks. She examined him carefully. His dark skin was crowned with a halo of soft black curls. Reaching out carefully, she ran her finger down one soft cheek. "My son," she whispered again. "Hello, little John Samuels. You're named for my daddy, you know." Her voice caught in wonder.

Then she looked up at Deidre. "Thank you," she whispered. There was so much more to say, but she knew words would never express what was in her heart.

Movement caused her to look back down. She laughed as her son turned his face toward her breast and began to move his lips. "He's hungry. Definitely his father's boy," she said, shifting him so he could eat. Rose watched contentedly for a few minutes before a heavy weight pressed down on her whole being. "I'm so tired."

Deidre stepped forward. "You go ahead and sleep, girl. June and I will be right here. Once your son finishes his first meal, we'll get him settled. You need rest more than you need anythin' else."

Rose was almost asleep, but she heard Deidre's quiet words to June. "We almost lost both of them. I reckon God's not done with either of them yet."

Chapter Five

Moses sank down on the ground, fatigue and soreness pressing in from everywhere. Leaning his head back against a tree, he gazed up at the full moon, barely visible as it fought a losing battle against the vapors infiltrating the area. No matter where he looked, all he saw was a hazy darkness. The order had gone out that no campfires be built. Moses knew the Federals were not anxious to give away their position. Jackson had won a stunning victory today, but there was always tomorrow. He reached into his haversack, pulled out several biscuits, and ate hungrily.

Moses felt, rather than saw, the form moving toward him in the darkness. Every muscle tensed as he coiled his body in preparation for action. He reached for his rifle silently. Jackson had pulled one big surprise already today. Was he springing another one?

"That be you, Moses?"

Moses heaved a sigh of relief and settled back. "It's me, Pompey. What are you sneaking around for?"

"I ain't sneaking around," Pompey protested. "I can't help it none that it's so dark in these woods you can't hardly see your hand in front of your face. The stink of all this smoke and gunpowder is enough to suffocate a man."

"Sure makes me long for open spaces," Moses agreed, suddenly glad to have company.

Pompey sank down on the ground beside him. "I don't reckon I'll ever forget my first day of battle."

"I'm trying to," Moses responded grimly, still heartsick at all he had witnessed.

"Caesar and Jacob didn't make it," Pompey said sorrowfully. "They's some of the first done falled when we charged back into that Rebel advance." There was a touch of pride in his voice now. "They died fer dere flag sho 'nuff."

Moses remained silent. He knew war meant killing. He knew that every man who moved onto a battlefield was flirting with death. In spite of the horror, he also knew the only way his people were going to be free was if the North won this war, but it didn't make his loathing for all of it diminish. It didn't ease the ache he felt for the families each fallen man left behind. His mind flew to Rose. He hoped she would not receive news of his death on the battlefield. He hoped he would not have a child who would never get to see their father.

"What you figure tomorrow's gonna be like?" Pompey asked quietly.

Moses shrugged before realizing Pompey couldn't see him. "I don't know. Our side took a mighty hard hit today. I guess General Hooker is going to try to hit back." He paused. "I heard Captain Jones talking today. A lot of the officers are furious with the general. They think he's giving this fight away. I don't know, though. It was Hooker who led the charge that stopped Jackson's attack. I sure wouldn't want to be the one making decisions for a hundred thousand men."

"It ain't possible to get de big pi'ture when you be the little man," Pompey said thoughtfully. "We got to do what we be tole to do. Ain't got no idea what be goin' on even a little ways from us. Ain't no way of knowin' if we be winnin' or losin' this thin'. All we get to see is what be right in front of us." He paused. "That be a might scary at times."

Pompey lapsed into silence again. Moses was content to let the murky night reflect his thoughts back to him. His body longed for sleep, yet his mind desperately needed some time to process the horrendous experiences of the day, all the while knowing no amount of processing could make any sense of it. He had watched hundreds of men and families destroyed because those in power deemed the destruction of humanity would accomplish their means and settle their disagreement.

Given the option to quit, you would choose to fight. Moses almost smiled at the contradiction of his own thoughts. It was true. He would choose to fight. He knew the war hadn't begun as a means to free the slaves forever, yet somehow it had evolved into that. If the North won the war, the face of America would be changed forever—*his* life would be changed forever.

"Why you don't talk like de rest of us?" Pompey asked. "Not dat it bother me none," he insisted. "I know you be a good man." He hesitated. "Some of the men be talkin', though."

"Rose taught me how to talk," he mused, half to himself. Saying her name made the ache more present. Shaking off the memories, he strove to answer Pompey's question. Most of the men knew his story, but there were fresh recruits whose loyalty could be diminished if they doubted his ability to understand them. Pompey was one of them. "A couple of years ago, I was a slave. I'd never had any education."

"Dat right?" Pompey said suspiciously.

"My daddy was killed by a mob when he tried to run away," Moses said, knowing his story would quiet the older man's fears. "My whole family was beaten. I was just a boy. I figured I would always be a slave." He paused, remembering. "A couple of years ago, I was sold to a man outside Richmond. One of his slaves had a secret school out in the woods. She taught me how to read and write. She also taught me how to speak correctly."

"What difference it make how ya talk?"

"It doesn't make any difference to me," Moses said, "but it's going to make a difference when we're free and trying to make it in a white world. People are still going to see me as a black man, but having education will make it a little easier."

"What happened to dat girl who done learned you? Slave owners don't like dat stuff none too good."

"I married her," Moses said, grinning. "Then we escaped and headed north to Philadelphia."

"Do tell," Pompey whistled in admiration.

Moses knew Pompey was solidly on his side now. He also knew he would spread the news around the cook fires. "Rose is teaching in the contraband camp outside of Norfolk." He sucked in his breath at the longing surging through him. "She's going to have our baby any day now," he said. "Might have already had it."

"I got me four little ones back home," Pompey said proudly. "We done took off when some Union troops got near us 'bout a year back. They be stayin' with some kinfolk in Ohio. Sho 'nuff be glad when dis be over and I cans get back."

Moses agreed with him wholeheartedly. He tensed as a sudden rustle in the woods startled him. He could feel Pompey tighten beside him, too. Not until one of his men loomed close enough to identify did they relax again.

"The captain be calling us together," the messenger reported. "Said we ain't done for the day yet."

"What we gonna be doin' in pitch dark?"

"I imagine we'll find out in a few minutes." Moses heaved his body up from the ground, ignoring the fatigue.

The dim light of a single lantern was all that identified the clearing in which Captain Jones was assembling his men. Moses stepped up to the back of the group and waited expectantly. He didn't have to wait long.

Captain Jones cleared his throat. "The general has ordered a night attack. You're going to spread out. Our orders are to charge through the woods with our bayonets, striking down the enemy where we find him. We're to march forward until we join up with our other divisions on the turnpike." Sharpness and compassion merged in his voice.

Moses listened grimly, envisioning the chaos that would reign in these woods when there was no light to reveal their path or their targets. His heart pounded but determination steeled his nerves.

Captain Jones turned to him. "Moses, I want you to take your men with the first line. Make sure your guns are loaded." His voice sharpened. "There is to be no reloading after the first firing. Our orders are to take the area by bayonet. Indiscriminate firing in the darkness could end up killing more of our own men than the Rebels."

"Yes, sir." Moses responded.

It took only a few minutes for all his men to assemble. "Form a straight line," Moses ordered quietly. "Make sure your guns are loaded but don't reload." He paused. "Keep moving forward," he finished.

The orders were passed down the line in hushed voices. Secrecy was paramount in this lunatic plan.

Moses shivered as the darkness pressed in around him. The hush was so complete he had to convince himself he was not alone—that there really were thousands of men forming a battle line. Every muscle in his body drew taut as he awaited the signal.

"Forward!" The hushed voice sounded loud.

Moses shouldered his gun and stepped out. Now that the time was here, he was calm, his eyes searching the murky night before him. Within minutes, he left the sheltering protection of the woods behind. Nearly two hundred yards of open space stretched before him.

"God help us," floated to him in a hushed whisper.

Moses mouthed a silent *Amen* and pressed forward. He sensed prayers going up all around him as the shadow of the woods loomed closer. He could barely discern the outline of the entrenchments. His breath quickened as he waited for the first flash of musketry fire from the watching Confederates. They were letting them draw near to be more certain of their aim. At twenty paces, they would fire their volley. Moses tightened his hold on his gun. Many of them would fall under the barrage of fire, but some of them would get through. He could only hope it would be enough of them.

The anticipated volley of fire never came. The entrenchments rose before him and then disappeared.

"Moses?" came a tentative whisper.

"Forward," was Moses' firm response as he surged into the thicket, trying to ignore the thorny bushes grasping for him. The Rebels may have chosen not to occupy the fringe of the woods, but they were ahead somewhere.

"Halt! Who goes there?"

"Forward!" Moses yelled as a Rebel sentry sounded the call. Raising his rifle, he aimed in the direction of the challenge and fired. Musketry exploded all around him as men yelled, shouted hurrah, and surged forward.

Robert sipped a cup of cold coffee as he stared into the distance. The spirits of the men surrounding him were high. The Confederate forces had taken some terrible hits, but the day had been a wild success. Stonewall Jackson had again done the impossible by swinging all the way around Hooker's massive army and achieving a complete rout. Word had reached them that Hooker was completely confused by their southern feint, evidently believing they were retreating. With the exception of a few slight skirmishes, there was no attack on Lee's tiny force facing the Federals.

"Can I join you, Captain?"

Robert glanced up and nodded. "Help yourself, Crocker." He filled his own cup with more cold brew and then poured a cup for the boy sinking down beside him. "How old are you?" he asked suddenly.

"Turned seventeen last month," Crocker said proudly. "My mama wouldn't let me fight until then. I signed up the next day."

"This your first fight?"

"Yes, sir. I guess we really gave it to them," Crocker said fiercely. "I reckon they'll be gone in the morning."

"Don't count on it," Robert said. "We hit them pretty hard today, but I don't think it was enough to turn them back."

"But it was a victory for our side," Crocker protested.

Robert could almost see his green eyes flashing in the dark. A pale moon filtered down through the towering trees, causing the drifting smoke to swirl in a milky dance. "I'll agree that we came out on the better side of this one," he said. "We'll know how many men we lost when it's all done. Whatever the number is, it will be more than we could afford to lose." He fell silent for a long moment. "Sometimes the cost of victory is stunningly high." He shook his head in the darkness. He should be offering encouragement, but the sight of the lifeless clearing after the artillery smoke faded away continued to haunt him.

"You think we're gonna win this war, Captain Borden?" Crocker asked, the fierce defiance in his voice subdued.

Robert rebuked himself and managed to instill confidence in his voice. "The Yankees don't stand a chance, Crocker. They're going to be sorry they ever came down here."

He could feel the boy straighten. "You got that right!"

Robert was glad the dark hid the skepticism in his eyes. Whatever his own doubts, it was criminal for him not to send each man in his command forward with as much confidence as he could. When a man advanced on a battlefield, all he had to propel him was his own inner conviction that he might come out of this one alive. As a captain, it was Robert's job to help instill courage and hope in his men. Never mind that he hated being in this position. Never mind that he struggled daily to find within himself his own courage and hope.

"Captain Borden, sir."

Robert drained the last bit of his coffee and looked up. "Yes?"

"General Jackson would like you to report to his tent, sir."

Minutes later, Robert joined the small group of men surrounding their commander's tent. "What's going on?" he asked, the darkness making it impossible to determine who he was talking to.

"The general has decided he wants to check things out on the front," came the quiet reply. "He's heard rumors the Federals are getting ready to make a charge down the road from Chancellorsville. He doesn't want to lose any of the advantage we gained today."

"He's going to order a night attack?"

"Who knows what he's going to do. Some of his staff have already warned him it's pretty risky to move toward the front right now. It's too dark to really be able to tell much, but..."

Robert smiled in spite of the foreboding filling him.

"...you know the general. If he thinks something will advance the cause and give him an advantage, he's going to do whatever it takes."

Just then a pale light spilled into the clearing as General Jackson, followed by his immediate aides, strode from his tent and mounted his mare, Little Sorrel. Robert, as always, was mystified that such an unimposing man could indeed be so imposing. His careless dress and posture concealed the rock-hard intensity of his drive and passion.

No one spoke as the small contingent eased forward in the darkness. Robert was alert to every sound as Granite stepped confidently, his gray ears pricked in readiness. Thoughts of Carrie on her Thoroughbred, laughing defiantly as she raced across the pastures of Cromwell Plantation, rose to taunt him. He pushed them aside. They belonged to another time, another day. Wondering if the South would ever again know a time so carefree would do him no good now. He must take care of the business at hand.

Just what that business was, he wasn't sure. It was obvious he had been selected to help protect the general as he inspected the state of events. Practicality demanded acknowledgement that the pitch-black darkness combined with unknown, rough territory would make any kind of protection almost impossible. Robert understood why the general's staff attempted to dissuade him from his action.

A sudden spattering of gunfire in the distance caused him to jolt upright in his saddle. Granite tensed and swung his massive head in an attempt to find the location of the trouble.

"What the...?" Robert muttered.

Moses stumbled and nearly fell as the ground sloped away from him. His shoulder slammed into a tree, arresting his forward movement as pain shot through his body. Gripping his gun tighter, his bayonet pointed in readiness, he gritted his teeth and continued to push on. "Forward!" he yelled again defiantly.

The darkness was as much of an enemy as the Rebel forces. The ground they were fighting through was rough and wooded. Hills gave way suddenly to wet ravines, murky and stagnant. Trees mingled with thorny thickets, ripping at flesh as well as clothing. Sweat poured down his face as he struggled to see beyond the next tree.

Finally, a line of entrenchments came into view. "Forward!" he hollered. He could feel his men moving beside him, but there was no way of knowing how many he had lost in the dark chaos. Far to the right, a burst of fire exploded. He could hear the screams of wounded men as they fell. Setting his lips, he scrambled over an entrenchment, his bayonet thrusting forward. A sigh of relief exploded from him as he realized whatever Rebels had lain in wait there had already fled before the attack.

"What now, Moses?" a voice rang from the darkness.

"We continue forward," he yelled. "Our orders were to keep moving. That's what we're going to do!"

A volley of shots rang out in the distance.

"Get down," Moses yelled, sensing danger before he could identify it.

"I'm hit!" one of his men yelled.

"They got me!" another yelled.

Moses spun around in confusion. There had been no flash of guns from in front of them. Where were the shots coming from? A flash from the rear confirmed his worst fears. The second line, just now entering the woods, had begun to fire. They were being shot down by their own men.

"Stop shooting!" he screamed.

Seconds later, his voice was joined by a hundred others. "Stop firing below! You are firing on us!"

The firing continued, joined sporadically by Rebels trying to hold their positions. Moses quickly considered his options. The lack of resistance thus far would indicate pushing onward was safer than merely waiting to be shot down by their own men. "Forward!" he yelled again. "Forward!" He sucked in gulps of air as he stumbled on, lurching up another crest of ground.

Suddenly, the crest erupted into flame. "Down!" Moses slammed himself to the ground as the hail of lead flew overhead. Its ominous whistle was not accompanied by cries from any of his men. Moses sagged in relief. The Rebel bullets, shot too high, had passed over harmlessly.

"Let's get 'em!" a hoarse voice hollered from the right.

Moses smiled grimly, realizing his men were out for blood. Other voices rose to join the defiant cry as his men burst forward over the entrenchment. Fierce screams mingled with desperate cries. Crackling brush joined with heavy thuds.

Moses gritted his teeth as a dark shape loomed before him. He thrust his bayonet forward with all his strength. He heard a stricken moan and felt a heavy weight at the end of his rifle. Hardening himself against the sick feeling of revulsion, he snatched back his bayonet, leapt over the fallen Rebel, and continued to press forward.

The concept of humanity had been swallowed by the reality and necessity of survival.

Robert peered through the darkness as the distant spattering of fire died away. Suddenly, a volley of fire exploded from the woods on the immediate right of their position. He snatched his rifle to his shoulder and fired in the general direction of the sound, taking scant comfort from the knowledge his enemies could see no better than him.

"It's the Yanks!" one of his party cried, cursing under his breath. "We've got to get out of here."

Robert had already spun Granite around, but he paused now to make sure General Jackson was safe. Staring into the darkness, he could just make out the shape of Little Sorrel dancing in fright.

"Back to our lines!" another man cried.

There would be no more reconnaissance work that night. The Federals, humiliated by the earlier rout, were obviously using the cover of night to wreak their vengeance. They had advanced far into the Confederate lines.

Assured that all their party was together, Robert urged Granite into a gallop, heading left for the shelter of the woods. Just then the misty ground cover dissipated, allowing more of the overhead moon to illuminate the road.

"Yankee cavalry!"

Robert stiffened as the warning call was shouted from the shadowy perimeters. He opened his mouth to yell protest, but his words were swallowed in the explosion of gunfire. Chaos erupted as their own troops fired point-blank into their advancing party.

"Stop firing!" Robert screamed, an instinctive reaction to the horror unfolding before his eyes. "Stop firing!"

Major Simpson, riding only feet from his position, gave an unearthly cry and toppled from his saddle. Ten feet over, another figure slumped and slid from his horse. Granite plunged to a halt and reared in protest at the onslaught of fire. Robert grabbed his mane and leaned forward, lying low against his neck. Turning his head, he watched as Little Sorrel, frantic with fright, raced straight toward the woods and broke again to the rear.

Robert watched as Jackson lurched in the saddle and slumped forward. He had been hit! Little Sorrel dashed into a stand of trees. Jackson, unable to control his mount, was smashed in the face by an overhanging limb. Robert watched, helpless to intervene, as another horse dashed through the woods and approached Jackson. The general was toppling from his saddle as the man reached out and caught his lanky body.

Robert cursed and spurred Granite onward, mindless of the danger. "General Jackson is with us. Quit firing! You've hit the general!"

The firing ceased but distant argument and cursing indicated it could start up again any second. Robert sagged in his saddle and turned back to see what he could do. Moments later, Yankee artillery again split the night with fire and destruction. Robert groaned as more of their party fell from their horses, screaming and moaning in pain. Was there going to be no end to this night?

❧❦❧

"Fall back to the left!" Moses hollered. Ducking low, he darted to the left, uncertain as to how many of his unit were still with him. If they could circle around the entrenchment blocking their way, maybe they could surprise them from the rear. A spattering of fire opened directly in front of him, and seconds later, shooting erupted from the right. Moses stopped, totally confused.

"Who's who?" screamed a frightened voice behind him.

Moses shook his head, his mind swarming. Who was the enemy? Who was on their side? He realized with a sinking heart that he wasn't sure of their location, or even which direction they were supposed to be headed. The obscure labyrinth of ravines and hillocks, of dwarfed thickets and giant trees, combined with the deadly crescendo of gunfire, had completely bewildered him. "Stay down!" he yelled, trying desperately to make some sense of the nightmare he was living.

Moses heard some of his men—at least he thought they were his men—scream in agony and then fall silent. The dark forest was becoming its own cemetery. Gunfire sounded from all around. He could see no more than ten feet in either direction. He cringed as a nearby explosion of bullets struck the trees surrounding him.

"Good Lord, man. What we gonna do now?"

Moses heaved a sigh of relief as Pompey crawled up next to him. He had no answer to his question, but it was good to know he wasn't totally alone. "Our men?"

"Ain't no way of knowin' where they be or how many still be livin'," Pompey gasped. "I reckon we be in a mess sho 'nuff."

"We don't move until we have some idea what we're moving into," Moses said sternly. He hugged the ground tighter as another barrage of lead passed overhead. Groans of the wounded, distant orders and curses, the whistling and roaring of guns, the crackling of branches, and the thunder of artillery all joined together in one diabolical crescendo.

There was a break in the fire to the right, and Moses reacted instinctively. If they were running toward Rebels they would at least be giving chase and obeying the order to keep moving forward. If they were Federals, they could find out where they were and what in the world was going on. "Forward!" Moses cried, springing up and dashing toward the darkened area, holding his bayonet in readiness. He could hear men crashing through the brush behind him, but there was no way of knowing how many there were. He could be moving into more danger than he had already been in. Sucking in his breath, Moses charged over the entrenchment, expecting at any moment to have gunfire explode in his face. Only dark emptiness met his searching eyes. "Whoever it was took off," he crowed triumphantly, relief causing him to sag against a tree.

"What now, Moses?"

Moses looked around to see about fifty of his men gathered in the clearing with him. He grinned, relieved to see so many of them still alive. "I guess we keep moving forward, boys."

"I wouldn't do that if I were you," a rough voice snapped. A tall figure strode from the woods.

Moses tensed, holding his bayonet in position. "Who goes there?" he barked.

"Lieutenant Jamison," the shadow snapped back. "I'm on your side. You and your boys are headed right into a Confederate trap. They've already captured hundreds of our men out there on the road. You'd better get the devil out of here."

Moses peered over to the right. Was the man telling him the truth? Captain Jones had ordered him to continue advancing no matter what.

"Who are you soldier?" the lieutenant asked sharply.

"Private Moses Samuel."

"All right, *Private*," Jamison growled. "I'm giving you orders to turn your men around and head back for our lines. We've done all the damage we can do for one night.

None of you are going to do us any good if you end up in a Rebel prison. Not to mention them Rebs aren't too nice to soldiers they figure are still slaves." He paused and then resumed, more compassion in his voice. "Get going. That's an order!"

"Yes, sir," Moses responded. He decided humiliation was better than putting his men into danger. "Which way are our lines, sir?"

Jamison laughed. "I just found someone who could tell me! Go directly to your left. You'll stumble onto them eventually."

"Yes, sir," Moses said gratefully. He turned to his men. "Left, march!"

Robert wiped at the grime on his face, exhaustion dogging every movement. He knew he needed coffee, but he couldn't find the energy to walk to the campfire. He heard movement and looked up wearily. Crocker was heading toward him with a cup. "Thank you," he muttered gratefully, reaching for the hot, steaming liquid. It made little difference what was being passed off as coffee now, as long as it was hot. He raised it to his lips and drank.

Crocker settled down next to him. "What happened out there, sir?"

"Just routine reconnaissance," he said casually. The officers had decided the men didn't need to know their hero, Stonewall Jackson, had been shot and wounded.

Crocker sat quietly for several moments. "That's not what the men are saying, sir," he said tentatively. "They're saying General Jackson is dead." Fear was evident in his voice.

"Nonsense!" Robert said sharply, realizing the rumors would be worse than the truth. He couldn't be responsible for anyone else's men, but his at least would face battle knowing the real situation.

"I heard some of the fellows from North Carolina thought the general's party was Yankee cavalry and fired on them."

"That much is true," Robert admitted. "Look, the general was wounded, but he wasn't killed. He was hit in the arm several times. It's broken pretty badly, but there's no reason to think he won't recover."

"Lots of others were killed, weren't they?"

"Yes," Robert said, once more reliving the horror of the night.

"I reckon we're gonna draw back then, huh?" Crocker asked.

Robert looked up quickly. "Jackson's orders are clear. We're to hold our line and advance."

"But who is going to lead us? We need General Jackson." Crocker's voice was genuinely alarmed as fear sprang to his eyes.

"General Stuart has been called up."

"General J.E.B. Stuart?" Crocker asked hopefully.

"The same," Robert said. "I have every confidence in his ability to lead."

"I've heard lots of good things about him," Crocker admitted, some color returning to his face. "You say the general is going to be all right?"

"Of course. It's nothing but a wound."

Crocker nodded and stood. "I'll go tell the rest of the men. We'll be ready when it's time."

Robert smiled as Crocker walked off. This boy straight off the farm probably had no idea what this war was all about, but he was meeting it with courage and determination. Robert's smile faded. How many fine, courageous men would die before it was all over?

Chapter Six

The sun was creeping over the horizon when Carrie left her father's house on Church Hill and strode toward Chimborazo Hospital. There had been reports the night before that the first trainloads of wounded soldiers would arrive at the station that morning. Every available space in the rambling hospital had been readied during the last three days. The summer of 1863 was evidently going to be a repeat of the previous two. At least this time they were better organized and more capable of meeting the challenge. Experience had sharpened them.

"Wait for me!"

Carrie stopped at the sound of the distant holler. A brisk breeze teased tendrils from her bun. She pushed at them impatiently as she gazed north of the city, waiting for her friend. Somewhere across the copse of trees only fifty-five miles from where she was standing, another battle was taking place. She knew little of the sketchy details being relayed to the capital. Every waking minute had been spent preparing the hospital for its newest onslaught of wounded and maimed.

Janie joined her, breathless from her rapid ascent up the hill.

Carrie frowned. "I thought you were sleeping in this morning? You weren't feeling well last night."

"I can't lie in bed when our soldiers are coming in today. However I might feel, it's nothing in comparison with what they are experiencing."

Carrie sighed heavily, continuing to stare north. "It's happening again," she said stonily. "All winter I hung onto the hope that maybe the fighting wouldn't start again this spring—that somehow, someone would find the way to stop this crazy war." She clenched her fists. "But it's happening again. More young men are going to be slaughtered." She wheeled and stared at Janie. "How long before there are no more boys and men to die? How long? Will the fighting stop then? When they're all dead?"

She didn't care that her last words were shouted at the sky.

Janie didn't reply. She moved closer to Carrie and slipped her arm around her friend's waist. Together they stood quietly while the sun climbed all the way over the horizon, announcing the advent of yet another day.

Carrie shook her head. "I wonder if God sometimes wishes he could stop the sun from rising—stop humanity from figuring out yet another way to destroy itself and each other." She took a deep breath. "I wonder if it's as hard for him to hold onto hope as it is for me."

Janie turned Carrie toward her. "You're worried about Robert."

"Of course I'm worried about Robert. I'm also worried about every single man who is fighting this war, South *and* North," Carrie said. "I worry about the wives who will never see their husbands again. The mothers who will never see their sons. The children who will never see their fathers, and who are going hungry because their daddy isn't around to take care of them."

"You can't carry it all."

"But how do I keep from caring?" Carrie cried.

"You don't," Janie said. "You'll never quit caring. That's why you're going to be such a good doctor someday." She paused. "But you have to give up the responsibility."

"The responsibility?"

"Yes," Janie replied. "You can't be responsible for the people who come into your life. People make choices, good and bad, but ultimately God is responsible for them. We think we want to be responsible for people, until we realize it's difficult enough to be responsible for ourselves." She stopped and waited for her words to sink in. "You're only responsible for doing what you're supposed to do. You're supposed to be a doctor—right now, a nurse. You're supposed to do your best to help those who come under your care."

"And leave the rest to God," Carrie mused. "I think I'm the one who told you that," she commented. "Why can't I ever listen to my own good advice?"

"Maybe because it's easier to give it than to live it," Janie teased. She sobered and reached for Carrie's hand. "It's perfectly natural for you to be worried about Robert."

Tears welled in Carrie's eyes. "I try not to imagine the worst, but sometimes I get so scared. Other times, I'm mad at myself for being so scared."

"Mad at yourself for being human?"

Carrie managed a smile. "Where did you learn to give people so much room to be human?" she demanded. "Don't you know that takes away half the fun of feeling like you're a horrible person?"

Janie laughed, then looked pensive. "I've told you a little about my Grandma Alice. She was the most special person I've ever known. I was heartbroken when she died four years ago. Now I'm glad she didn't live to see what is happening to her beloved country." She shook her head.

"Grandma Alice taught me to let people be human. She used to tell me folks could play all kinds of games to make others think they were always doing the things God wanted them to. She said it made them feel better about themselves. At least they thought it did. She told me there wasn't a person alive who could always do and be whatever they thought God wanted them to.

"She sat me down one afternoon after a friend had hurt my feelings. I can still see her sitting there, her silver hair outlined by the blue cover on her rocker. Anyway, she asked me if I was angry. I told her I wasn't angry—just a little hurt. Grandma Alice smiled and told me of course I was angry, and that it was okay to feel that way. That it was human." Janie chuckled. "I was pretty excited at first. I asked her if that meant it was okay to feel any way I wanted to, any time. That sounded like a pretty great thing to an angry ten-year-old."

"What did she say?" Carrie asked, caught up in the story, envisioning the wise little lady on her porch.

"She laughed and told me there wasn't anything wrong with being honest about your feelings, as long as you got to work and tried to make them right. She told me it was okay to be angry with my friend, as long as I then tried to forgive her so the bitterness wouldn't eat me up." Janie stared off into the distance. "She told me people could get so caught up in trying to impress God and each other that soon the world was going to be full of people playing games. She said God was perfectly capable of handling honesty."

"Your Grandma Alice sounds like Old Sarah," Carrie said. "She was the wisest woman I've ever known. She could see things so clearly." Carrie chuckled. "And she always saw through my games."

Janie nodded. "I guess the longer you live, the wiser you get. At least I hope so. My dream is to someday be like Grandma Alice."

Carrie hugged her friend to her side. "I'd say you're well on your way." She pulled back. "We'd better get to the hospital. God might ultimately be responsible, but I still have a job to do."

Within minutes, they crested the hill and reached the plateau where Chimborazo Hospital sprawled. Carrie gazed over the rows and rows of long white buildings separated by wide lanes. Less than a dozen of the buildings had patients, mostly men who were convalescing from wounds received from the winter fighting at Fredericksburg.

"Sometimes I pretend this is a normal hospital," Carrie said softly. "Then I'm so proud of its well-ventilated buildings, the gardens, the bakery, the brewery and all the animals we keep to provide meat for the men."

"I know what you mean," Janie responded. "All the pretending will end today, though, when the first trainload rolls in."

"Then it becomes an overcrowded, smelly place where thousands of men will die this summer. Where thousands of men will lose an arm or leg. Where thousands of men will lose their dreams of the future." Carrie straightened and spoke to herself sternly. "But I'm not responsible for that am I? I'm going to do everything I can to make life better for one person at a time."

A vivid picture of Robert flashed in her mind. Her last glimpse of him had been as he turned to wave while riding away from the house, his dark hair shining in the sun, his hand raised as a smile split his face. He had looked so tall and strong, so very handsome. Carrie stifled the ache that threatened to overwhelm her and turned toward the nearest building. "See you tonight." She didn't bother to wish Janie a good day. Under the present circumstances, that wasn't really possible.

Dr. Michael Wild was checking on a few of his patients when Carrie strolled into the building. She watched as his cheerful green eyes beamed down from under his thatch of red hair. Carrie owed this man so much. He had given her the chance to use her medical knowledge, and in the last year, they had become a team. There was never enough medical help when the hospitals filled with wounded soldiers. Though Carrie didn't yet have the credentials to be a doctor, in many ways she acted as one. Dr. Wild had taught her so much. In return, she had passed on the knowledge Old Sarah had bequeathed her about wild herbs and plants. The shortage of medicines was daily becoming more critical as the Union blockade of the coast tightened. The renewal of fighting would mean many men would go without the medicine they desperately needed.

Carrie was waiting at the door to her ward when the first wagonloads of men rattled up the hill. The long morning had passed with no sign of the wounded. It was now early afternoon. Reports of Union cavalry raids had been filtering in, but they were too vague to offer any real information.

Carrie steeled herself as the first men were carried in. A sick feeling pulsed in her throat, though, when her first patient was carried to her. The man looked to be about thirty years old. His face was crusted with blood and dirt, a gory bandage plastered to his filthy, stringy hair. A gaping hole in his tattered pants revealed a ragged bullet wound, and the awkward twist of his left arm told her it was broken. His eyes, somewhere between blue and gray, were already bright with fever from the infection that had settled in.

"Hello, soldier," Carrie said cheerfully.

"Hello, ma'am."

"What's your name?" Carrie asked as she cut away the material around the wound.

"Frank Boscomb," he said weakly. "I don't reckon I'm doing so good, am I?"

"Oh, I'd say you're not doing great, but better than a lot I see go through here."

"I sure don't want to lose that leg."

Carrie inspected the wound. "I think you'll be keeping your leg, Frank. It looks like a clean wound. You'll have a fever for a while, but you'll be all right."

Frank sagged back against the pillow in relief. "Really? You hear so many stories, you know. I got a buddy who lost both an arm and a leg."

"I'm sorry," Carrie said sympathetically. "You're going to be lucky this time."

Now that Frank knew he was going to keep his leg, his mind strayed to other matters. "I guess that's the second time today I've been lucky. I thought those Union cavalry men were going to cart up us north before we ever got to a hospital."

Carrie waited, knowing he would tell her the whole story. The soldiers were always eager to tell of their exploits on the field, and she was always thankful for any information. Especially when Robert was involved in the battle.

"We were coming in on the train. I reckon we were only ten or so miles away when a bunch of Yankee cavalry stopped us."

"Ten miles?" Carrie asked in surprise. The rumors of Union cavalry raids must have been true. What did their presence so close to the city mean? Had Lee been defeated? Was Hooker coming into the city? She pressed down the questions and concentrated on cleaning the nasty wound Frank had received. She would know soon enough.

"Yes, ma'am. We figured those boys weren't going to let us go, but they did. Asked us a bunch of questions and let us come through. I guess they knew we weren't going to do them any harm, and I don't think they had it in mind to take prisoners." He paused. "From all I hear, we did pretty well yesterday. General Jackson took his men around and surprised Hooker at his right flank." He chuckled. "Some boys said those Yankees were running so fast they were stumbling all over each other." Then he sobered. "Don't reckon the luck lasted, though. It's too bad about old Stonewall."

"What is?" Carrie asked sharply.

"You don't know?"

"I'm afraid we're short on news up here in the hospital," Carrie said. "What happened to General Jackson?"

"According to what I heard, he got shot by some of his own men last night. They thought Yankee cavalry was coming through. Killed a bunch of his party and wounded the general."

"How badly?" Carrie asked in alarm. She knew how important Jackson was to the Confederacy.

"Hard to tell." Frank shrugged with his good shoulder. "Some rumors said he got killed. Others said he'd lose his arm. Some guys said his arm was hurt, but he would fully recover. Take your pick," he grinned. Then he sagged against the pillow, pain rippling over his strong features.

"Enough talking, soldier," Carrie ordered. "We're going to get that bullet out, and then I'm going to set your arm."

"I didn't know the South had women doctors."

"They don't." Carrie smiled. "Yet," she added. "Would you like someone else to care for you? Once the wounded really start rolling in you won't have a choice, but you do right now."

Frank regarded her evenly for several long moments and then shook his head. "It looks like you know what you're doing." He paused. "I had a lady friend up north who wanted to be a doctor."

"You're not from the North with that accent," Carrie teased as she leaned closer to make sure the wound was clean.

"Went to school in New York," Frank grunted, his face tightening as Carrie probed deeper in the wound. "Came back south a few years ago."

"What happened to your friend who wanted to be a doctor?" As long as Frank had the energy to talk, Carrie had decided to let him. It would help keep his mind off the pain.

"She started going to the Women's Medical College in Philadelphia, but she dropped out. Said she didn't want to be a doctor bad enough to stand people yelling and spitting on her. Seems some people up there don't like the idea of women doctors."

"I see," Carrie said casually, knowing Frank was watching her closely. "I'm sorry she gave up on her dream."

"Why do you want to be a doctor?"

"You mean why would I want to put myself through what your friend went through?"

"I guess that is what I mean."

Carrie shrugged. "I've always dreamed of being a doctor. I guess I believe that's what God means for me to be. If I have to go through hard times to realize that dream, so be it." She looked at Frank squarely. "I *am* going to be a doctor. I'm not going to let anything stop me. Not even this crazy war. One of these days, it will be over, and then I'm going to school." She knew she was talking more to herself than to Frank. "One of these days, this country is going to be full of women doctors."

Frank looked skeptical but didn't argue.

Carrie finished cleaning the wound and stepped back, straightening her shoulders to relieve the tension. "That should take care of you for now. You'll be taken into surgery as soon as there is space. In the meantime, drink all the water anyone brings you. It will help your fever." Carrie smiled warmly and turned to look for her next patient.

The first ambulance wagon was followed by hundreds of others. Time blurred as Carrie moved from one wounded soldier to another.

Carrie wearily climbed the steps to the house, aware it was close to midnight. Janie had come home several hours earlier, but she herself had decided to help Dr. Wild with two cases he had saved for last, believing they were hopeless. Necessity deemed that the soldiers most likely to live were treated first. One of the two had died on the table. The other had a good chance of survival if infection and gangrene did not set in. Carrie tried to push away the question of whether they had really done the man a favor. He had told her earlier that day that he was a farmer and a father of three. He was now a farmer with no legs.

Carrie pushed open the door and headed for her bedroom. All she wanted was a bath to wash off the stench of the hospital, and a good night's sleep.

"Carrie? Is that you?"

Carrie sighed and veered toward the parlor. "Why are you still up, Father?"

Thomas looked up from where he was seated next to the window, his face lined with worry and fatigue. Though it pained her, Carrie was accustomed to that look. It had settled on her father's face after her mother died. The years of war had simply defined and deepened it. She walked over and sank down into the chair opposite him, grateful for an opportunity to at least get off her feet.

"I'm afraid this might be it," Thomas said.

Carrie sat quietly, almost too tired to care what he was going to say next but still needing to know. Robert was out there somewhere. Had Hooker beaten Lee?

"Yankee cavalry is rampaging everywhere," Thomas scowled. "They're slashing in and out right up to the lines of the city, cutting telegraph lines and destroying railroad bridges. They've destroyed trains and torn up miles of track. Horses and mules are disappearing, and warehouses full of supplies are being burned."

"Has Lee been defeated?"

"No one knows," Thomas said, frustration oozing from his voice. "Since all of the telegraph lines are down, it's impossible to know what is really happening. Some messengers have gotten through, but the information is mixed. Some say Jackson and Lee pulled off a stunning victory. Others talk of defeat. We just don't know."

"One of my patients told me General Jackson was wounded," Carrie offered, wishing she had something positive to offer her father.

"That's what the reports say." Thomas sighed. "That one at least seems to be accurate. His arm was broken and caught several bullets, but his men got him to safety, and he is being treated by his doctor. All the reports indicate he will recover."

"Are people leaving the city?" Carrie asked. The last scares had resulted in a mass exodus of Richmond's citizens. People left the city as rapidly as those from the outskirts retreated to its confines when the enemy approached.

"Not this time," Thomas said. "Richmond is rising to the occasion. We won't let the city go without a fight. Citizen companies have been filing into the fortifications prepared by Lee last year. Doctor McCaw up at Chimborazo sent out a couple hundred convalescing soldiers to patrol River Road. Other hospitals are sending out the men who are able."

Carrie grimaced, all the while knowing it was necessary. She shuddered to think of the chaos that would reign if Richmond fell. What would happen to all the soldiers in the hospitals?

Thomas stood slowly. "I'm going to get some sleep, but I wanted you to know what is happening. I leave early in the morning to join a company of government officials."

"Leave to go where?" Carrie asked in alarm.

"Governor Letcher has called us to duty. We're going to the outskirts of the city to stand guard."

"But you're not a soldier," Carrie protested. She wanted to scream that she had already sent her husband to battle. She wasn't going to send her father, too. She remained silent. Many women were making a much greater sacrifice than hers.

"And you're not a doctor," Thomas reminded her calmly, "but you're acting as one. The times, rather than our credentials, seem to be the commander of our actions."

"Be careful," Carrie said, rising and walking over to kiss her father on his cheek.

"Are you coming up?"

"In a few minutes," Carrie replied. She wasn't ready to face her empty bed yet. Janie had moved to the room next to hers, and she had to admit she missed her friend's company. Every night when she walked into her bedroom, the emptiness seemed to mock her, reminding her of the brief ecstasy she had known as Robert's wife.

Carrie watched her father move slowly up the stairs, and then she eased out onto the porch. Her earlier fatigue was forgotten as fear for her father compounded her fear for Robert. A full moon shone down, its milky whiteness outlining the houses surrounding her, casting shadows from the trees. A soft breeze whispered through the leaves as a chorus of frogs sang to the night. Carrie sank down on the step and cupped her chin in her hand. She closed her eyes tightly, hoping her mind would transport her to her special place on the plantation along the bank of the James River. Spring had intensified her longing to be there again to rejoice in the constant discovery of new life.

Carrie sat expectantly for several long minutes, then sighed and opened her eyes. It was no good. Richmond, a city under Union siege, was her constant reality now. She grimaced. Why had she ever thought she wanted to grow up? Right now, she would give anything to go back to the carefree days when her biggest concern was fighting for her right to be her own person. She managed to smile as she remembered her frustration when her mother tried to form her into a proper Southern lady.

In the last few years, the whole world had turned upside down. Her dream of going to medical school had been destroyed when the South became a foreign country at war with its northern neighbors. She had barely escaped Cromwell Plantation when marauding Union soldiers invaded it. Her whole way of thinking and living had been challenged and changed when she determined that slavery was wrong, and she decided to open up ways of escape for all her father's slaves. It almost cost her relationship with Robert, yet God changed his heart. They were married now, but the war continued to cruelly rip them apart. She was living in a city, numb and shell-shocked from the constant barrage of attacks aimed at the Confederate capital.

Carrie groaned and buried her head in her hands. The new summer of fighting had just begun, and already she was heartsick and weary to the bone. It would be almost seven months before winter signaled an end to the fighting—if the war was still raging on. How was she going to stand it?

One day at a time.

The words were whispered to her on the breeze. Carrie raised her head, allowing the wind to sink the words into her heart.

One day at a time.

A sudden gust whipped around the corner of the house. The heavy, waxen leaves of the magnolia tree guarding the porch rustled in protest. Carrie looked up just as moonlight rested fully on a limb of the tree. Standing slowly, she moved toward it and reached out her hand, cupping the creamy blossom illuminated by the moon. She pressed it to her face, breathing deeply of its fragrant perfume.

One day at a time.

Carrie understood. She needed only enough courage for one day. Only enough hope for one day. Only enough strength for one day. It was a lesson she knew she would have to learn over and over, but for this one night it filled her with hope and the ability to keep going.

She turned to face the breeze and lifted her face to the moon, still grasping her magnolia bloom. "I love you, Robert. Wherever you are, I love you. I'm holding on to my wish for us to have a long life together. It may only be a dream..." Carrie's voice turned fierce. "It may only be a dream, but it's *my* dream. I'm going to hold on to it for all I'm worth."

Chapter Seven

Carrie leaned out her window and drew in deep breaths of fresh air. It was a beautiful day, but she could find no joy in it. A week had passed since the first wagonload of wounded soldiers rumbled into the city. The men now occupied every available space.

Funeral processions had once again become commonplace in the beleaguered capital, but the one that would occur today cast a black pall over the entire citizenry. General Stonewall Jackson had not recovered. His left arm had been amputated, and infection had set in. Finally, pneumonia held him in its brutal grasp, until it sucked the life from the legendary soldier. The whole of Richmond was in mourning.

Carrie straightened her hat and went down to join her father. The shock of Jackson's death mingled with her worry over Robert. He had not been listed among the dead, wounded, or missing, but that did nothing to assuage her fears. Was she about to relive the anxiety and unknown of the previous year?

"One day at a time," she whispered, holding on to her flickering hope with all her might.

Thomas was waiting for her when she reached the bottom of the steps. It was hours before the actual procession, but it was necessary for him to be there early since he was participating as a government representative. Carrie's heart tightened even more when she saw her father. His face was a strange mixture of pain, bitterness and anger. He looked old.

"This is a black day for our nation," Thomas muttered when she reached his side.

Carrie knew there was nothing she could say to make him feel better. She reached out and slipped her arm through his. "Our ride is waiting."

Spencer, the burly black man who was always on call for her father, nodded his head grimly when they reached the carriage. "How do, Mr. Cromwell. Mrs. Borden."

"Hello, Spencer," Carrie replied. "It's good to see you."

Thomas merely nodded and stepped into the carriage, settling down stiffly. Spencer exchanged a knowing look with Carrie. She had developed a strong friendship with the genial driver who remained a staunch Confederate supporter, while also struggling to help gain freedom for his people. He did not share the hatred and disdain for the South that many of his people did. Free or slave, he was determined to stay in the South. It was his home. He had no desire to live under a conquering Northern government.

"I be real sorry about the General, Mr. Cromwell," Spencer offered.

Thomas grunted, his stony face inviting no further conversation.

Carrie caught Spencer's eye and shook her head slightly. When her father was like this, it was better to leave him alone. He would have to work through it himself.

Carrie leaned back against the carriage seat. She could already hear the church bells tolling all over the city. She knew all the government offices, as well as every place of business, were closed. As they drew nearer to the Capitol, she saw that the flags in the city were flying at half-mast. The streets were already filling with people determined to see their hero's coffin pass by.

It took longer than normal, even by the crowded city's standards, for Spencer to weave his way through the congested streets. Thomas, his face set in a hard mask, stepped from the carriage as soon as it rolled up to the columned Capitol. "You'll wait here?" he asked.

Carrie nodded and watched her father trudge up the sidewalk.

"He be a hurting man," Spencer remarked.

"I'm not sure how much more he can take," Carrie agreed, gazing after him. "He feels as if his whole world is coming apart."

"It be something terrible about the General, sho 'nuff, but our boys *did* win that battle up there," Spencer protested.

"It's not that simple," Carrie replied. "Technically we won, but the South couldn't afford the price we paid to accomplish it. The figures are starting to come in, and it seems General Hooker had seventeen thousand casualties. General Lee lost thirteen thousand. He succeeded in pushing Hooker back across the river, but he lost a huge percent of his army in achieving it."

"But at least he got rid of him," Spencer reminded her.

Carrie shook her head. "My father and I have talked about that. People claim we won a stunning victory. My father believes it was far from conclusive. Hooker is not running to the North with his tail between his legs. He is sitting on the other side of the river licking his wounds. He still has a huge army, much bigger than our own, that will eventually get stronger."

"And then he'll be back," Spencer finished for her. "I reckon I see what you're saying." He stared north. "We ain't seen the end of this trouble."

"I'm afraid not."

Spencer looked around thoughtfully. "A lot of folks done pinned a bunch of their hopes on ole' Stonewall. There be a heap of hurtin' in this town today." He turned back to Carrie. "What else be goin' on out there, Miss Carrie?"

Now that her father was gone, he lapsed into his usual way of addressing her. Carrie stopped looking around and focused her attention on him. She knew he counted on her to keep him informed about the events in the nation. "I'm afraid things aren't looking too good. People are taking hope from this battle Lee just won, but there is big trouble out in Mississippi. There is a new Union general in control out there named Grant. He is determined to take Vicksburg, and all reports say he is accomplishing things none of his predecessors could."

"Is Vicksburg important?"

"It's our only port town left on the Mississippi River. If it falls like New Orleans, the Confederacy will be split in half, and the Union will control that whole segment."

"You still be wanting the Union to win?"

Carrie frowned and fell silent. She had been asking herself that question every day. The answer became harder and harder to be sure of. Finally, she shook her head. "I don't know anymore," she admitted. "I used to be so sure I wanted the North to win—for our country to be reunited. My desire to see slavery abolished hasn't diminished, but the rest of it is so confusing. My father is so sure his whole life will be destroyed if the North wins this war. So many men, including my husband, are risking their lives to protect their country."

She shook her head in frustration. "It's so hard to have an understanding of the big picture when my whole life consists of taking care of wounded soldiers and watching men die on a daily basis. It's as if whatever is happening at the moment dictates my feelings." She realized she was rambling, talking more to herself than she was to Spencer. "Listen to me," she laughed. "Enough of my talk. What about you?"

Spencer regarded her quietly for a long moment. "One thing about you ain't changed, Miss Carrie. I don't reckon it ever will. You still look at people and see them as people. Not black or white." He paused. "Ain't many white people in the South feel that way."

Carrie was silent, knowing he was right, but hoping with all her heart it would change with time.

"I been lookin' 'around, Miss Carrie," Spencer continued, "and I've decided one thing. Your daddy's way of life is gone even if the North don't win this war." His voice was firm. "I've heard lots of Southerners say Mr. Lincoln's Emancipation Proclamation don't mean nothing. They snorted about it for a while, then decided the North couldn't come down here and enforce it, so it weren't nothin' they needed to be worryin' 'bout."

"It means more than that," Carrie protested.

"Yessum," Spencer agreed. "It be like the parting of the Red Sea for the slaves. Having somebody standin' up for the coloreds made them see different. Like I said," he mused, "I been lookin' around. I figure the ole' evil of slavery done lasted so long 'cause the slaves let it. Oh sure, they be plenty enough force to keep it going, but all in all, it kept on a goin' because we let it."

"Now, don't get me wrong," Spencer asserted quickly. "Us coloreds done found ourselves in a nightmare, and too many of us be like helpless children, but still there be plenty of us to turn things around if we really wanted to."

"That's what so many Southerners are afraid of," Carrie replied. "They're afraid the slaves will revolt and try to win their freedom with violence."

"That might have done happened," Spencer nodded. "There been plenty enough talk of changin' things, no matter what it took, but Mr. Lincoln done changed that. The coloreds around here are thinkin' mostly one of two ways. They either walkin' away and headin' north to freedom, or they bidin' their time."

"Like you."

"Like me," Spencer agreed. "I know I'm gonna be free real soon. Even if the South done win this war, it ain't never gonna be the same. The old demon of slavery done been broke forever," he chuckled.

Carrie looked at him thoughtfully, realizing the truth of what he was saying. "Change is never an easy thing, Spencer."

"Yessum, it's gonna be mighty hard on ever'body, but it ain't gonna be no harder than slavery been. I reckon it's time for the white folks to have hard times for a while, too," Spencer stated matter-of-factly, his voice holding no malice.

Carrie turned away and stared out over the masses of people gathering for General Jackson's funeral. She knew Spencer was speaking the truth. How many of these somber-faced people knew that no matter how the war ended, the way of life they had always known would be changed forever? How many of them knew the war they were fighting for *states' rights* had somehow evolved into a war for *equal rights*?

Spencer seemed to read her mind. "It ain't only that things gonna be different for the blacks, Miss Carrie. I reckon they gonna be different for you, too."

Carrie swung around to gaze at him again. "What do you mean?" she asked, even though she was fairly sure she knew.

"You ain't never gonna be satisfied to be a Southern lady," Spencer observed, chuckling. "From what I can tell, you weren't never satisfied in the first place. I reckon you got dreams too big for the South."

"Maybe," Carrie murmured. She knew she would have to go north to get her education, but maybe she wouldn't have to stay there. Would the war make people change how they viewed women?

"That's what I mean," Spencer replied. "There be women who be workin' like men now. With all the men done gone, women be findin' out they can do things they never figured they could. Knowin' things like that changes folks."

Carrie smiled. "You're a wise man, Spencer. I think both of us are going to have to fight for our freedom to be the people we want to be."

A sudden loud noise caught her attention. She turned to stare down the street. Far in the distance, she could see a dark mass moving toward her. "What in the world is that?" she asked. "It's too early for the funeral procession."

Spencer stood on the carriage seat and shaded his eyes against the sun. "It sho be a lot of somethin' headed this way." He stepped back down. "I guess we'll know soon enough."

Carrie watched as the black mass drew closer, and gradually she heard the cries and yells of the crowd. At first it sounded like cheering, but as the sound grew clearer, she recognized angry tones. Soon she could pick out the taunts and calls.

"You got what's coming to you, Yankee!" an angry voice broke above the rest.

"That's what you get for coming down here where you don't belong and killing our men!" another burst out.

Carrie leaned forward, glad the carriage was sitting on a high rise of ground. From here she had a clear view of the street. "They're Union soldiers!" she cried.

"I reckon they be prisoners from the battle."

"There are thousands of them," Carrie whispered in a shocked voice. The street was full of marching men as far as she could see. Units of mounted Confederates rode alongside. "Where in the world are they going to go?" She knew from conversation with her father that the prisons down by the river were almost full to capacity.

"I reckon they'll be putting them men out on Belle Island," Spencer said in a grim voice.

Carrie didn't know very much about the makeshift prison camp out on the island surrounded by the James River rapids. Her heart pounded as she wondered if Robert was right then marching through a city somewhere in the North. Had he been taken prisoner? Was he being ridiculed and taunted by people lining the streets?

The angry calls of the crowd grew louder.

"I hope you die in that prison out there!" one well-dressed lady screeched.

"Y'all killed Stonewall Jackson!" an elderly man hollered, waving his cane wildly.

Carrie watched as the people surrounding the old man ducked to protect themselves from his wicked cane.

"Those men didn't kill Jackson," she protested. "It was our own men. It was an accident!"

The old man heard her over the tumult and turned toward her threateningly. "That doesn't matter. They would have killed him if they had the chance. And if they weren't down here invading our country in the first place, nothing would have ever happened to our general." His eyes flashed as he raised his cane again.

Carrie stared at him in fascinated horror. She tried a different approach. "That could be your son out there, sir. How would you want him to be treated?"

If anything, the old man's eyes grew angrier, almost bulging from his reddened face. "It couldn't be one of my sons!" he screamed hoarsely. "They've both been killed by those Yankee marauders! I'd give anything to know they were in a Yankee prison somewhere." His words seemed to sap him of his frantic energy. He lowered his cane, sagging as if the memory of his boys was more than he could take.

"I'm sorry, sir," Carrie said, her heart aching for his loss.

"Oh, what does it matter?" The old man suddenly looked every bit of his age. He turned away, mumbling under his breath.

Carrie watched as the long line of prisoners streamed by. Her heart ached for each one. The tired faces bore expressions of fear, defiance, sorrow and pain. Many of the men had been wounded and were making their way down the street with the aid of crutches or friends. Some of them stared boldly at the angry crowd assaulting them. Most kept their eyes down, staring stoically at the street. She watched as long as she could stand and then turned away with a shudder.

"War ain't a pretty thing," Spencer muttered.

"It's a horrible, wicked thing," Carrie cried. "Every one of those men have someone at home who cares about them. When will this war end?" She battled the despair pressing down on her, trying desperately to find the hope she needed for that day. Visions of Robert parading through a street overwhelmed her. Was he alive? Dead? Wounded?

Carrie sagged against the seat. It was the same barrage of questions she had been battling since the war began. She thought time might make them easier to handle, but time only seemed to wear her down, making the questions more fearsome and terrible.

The long line of prisoners disappeared into the distance, and the dust from their pounding feet settled again. Now that their anger had been released, the throngs of people were once more somber from their grief. All Carrie wanted was to go home to the quiet of her room, but she knew her father was counting on her to be there. He would never understand if she wasn't there for the funeral of one of the South's greatest heroes. Respect for Robert held her there as well. She knew how highly he had esteemed the man he served under.

Carrie had lost track of time when she heard the boom of a gun from the Washington Monument above where she was sitting. She tensed and lifted her head to peer down the street. The funeral procession was beginning. As the crowd grew silent, the too-familiar "Dead March" drifted toward them on the breeze. Men reached for their handkerchiefs and women cried openly as the hearse eased into view.

Four white horses pulled the hearse decorated with black plumes. The pallbearers were all generals. Following close behind was Stonewall Jackson's mare, Little Sorrel, led by a servant. The saddle was empty, save for Jackson's boots strapped to it. Tears misted Carrie's vision as the somber procession filed by. The *thud-thud* of minute guns accompanied the long line of convalescing soldiers from Richmond hospitals who had pulled themselves out of bed to honor their fallen hero. Many of them wore bandages and moved with the aid of crutches, but their expressions were resolute.

President Davis, looking drawn and haggard, and Vice President Stephens rode behind in an open carriage. Members of the cabinet walked two by two. Then came the long line of city and state officials, followed by a multitude of city employees, friends and common citizens. Carrie searched until she located her father. He was walking erectly, his face resolute. He never glanced in her direction.

The bright sun seemed a cruel mockery as a dark pallor spread across the Confederate capital. People lined the street long after the procession had disappeared, seeming to find comfort in universal mourning.

Carrie knew it would be many hours before her father would be home. She turned to Spencer. "I'd like you to take me down to the black hospital, please."

Spencer hesitated and then looked at her directly. "I don't reckon that be such a good idea, Miss Carrie."

"Why not?" Carrie asked. "We always go down there on Tuesday. There is still plenty of time left. There are people who need me."

"Yessum, I know all about that," Spencer said patiently. "If it weren't for you, them poor coloreds down there wouldn't have nobody to look after them. They think you an angel sho 'nuff." He shook his head. "I just don't figure you should be going down there today."

Carrie could feel her frustration growing. It had been over a week since she had been there. The crush of wounded filling Chimborazo kept her from going to the tiny hospital down on the riverfront in the black part of town. Nothing was going to stop her now. "I want to go," she said firmly.

Spencer shook his head. "You done run into trouble down there before, Miss Carrie. People in this town are pretty riled up about their hero being shot. They ain't got nobody to take it out on, so they's gonna do what they usually do. They gonna take it out on the colored. Lots of them figure this war wouldn't be happening if the North weren't so set on seeing us free." He took a deep breath. "And that ain't the worst of it. There's been talk of coloreds fightin' in the Union Army. If folks weren't riled before, they sho be now."

"What's that got to do with me?" Carrie demanded, even though she knew very well what it had to do with her.

"Folks ain't gonna take kindly to a white woman going down into colored town," Spencer said patiently, his voice imploring her to be reasonable. "You be in right much danger every time you go down there, but this time be different. Some folks gonna be lookin' for trouble. I don't want to see you get hurt."

Carrie patted her waistline. "I'm prepared for trouble," she said grimly. "You know my father makes me carry a gun ever since that trouble last year. I'm a good shot," she added.

Spencer's stubborn expression hadn't softened one bit, though, so she stood up and stepped from the carriage. "I'm going. With or without you," she announced dramatically, knowing he would never let her go alone. "There are people there who need me. I'm not going to let my fear of ignorant people stop me from doing what needs to be done."

Spencer sighed and picked up the reins. "I don't know why I ever try to argue with you. I declare, you be the most stubborn woman I ever done met. Your daddy is gonna have me shot sho 'nuff if something happens to you." He shook his head. "Get in the carriage, Miss Carrie. You know I'm gonna take you."

Carrie grinned and got back in. "Thank you," she said sweetly.

Spencer rolled his eyes and clucked to the horses. "Darn fool crazy thing," he muttered under his breath as the carriage began to move down the street.

Carrie was relieved to see the streets emptying as they headed down the hill from the Capitol toward the river. In spite of the confidence she had displayed to Spencer, she knew she was taking a huge risk coming down here. She still had vivid memories of the band of drunken men who tried to stop her months before, angry because she was doctoring the blacks. One of her father's friends had saved her, but he told her disdainfully that if she wanted to keep doing such a fool thing, he would not step in to aid her again. She now carried a gun tucked into her waistband, but there had been no more threatening encounters. Why, then, was she so nervous tonight? She yearned for Janie's company, all the while glad her friend had not been able to get away from Chimborazo. Together, the two of them made a difference in the lives of their patients. Dr. Wild even came down whenever possible to help with the more difficult cases.

Carrie tensed and reached for her weapon when two scruffy looking men stepped out into the road, glaring at her carriage. Spencer, his back ramrod straight, didn't even look at them. He just continued to drive forward. The two men glared at her for a long moment, scowling, and then turned away. Carrie sank back against the seat in relief but still gripped the pistol. Something about the air today spoke of trouble brewing.

Please God, let it be my imagination.

Pastor Anthony was waiting outside the ramshackle building when the carriage rolled up. He met her as she stepped down, looking around nervously. "Are you sure it's a good idea for you to be here today?"

Carrie managed a casual laugh. "My services are no longer good enough for you?" she teased. "Or have all my patients gotten well and gone home?"

Pastor Anthony grabbed her arm and pulled her into the building. As they reached the door, he turned back to Spencer. "Put the carriage in back and come inside. It's not safe for you to be out here."

Carrie tried to control her growing alarm. "Has something happened?" There was no teasing now.

"Two of my parishioners were attacked this morning. For absolutely no reason." He shook his head, his voice edged with anger. "The group of cowards who jumped them said they were going to do away with them before they could escape and join up with the Union Army."

"Did they kill them?"

"They're two of your new patients," Pastor Anthony replied, his normally kind blue eyes flashing. "It's a miracle they're still alive. They were beaten up pretty badly."

Carrie tightened her lips and reached for her bag of supplies. "Show me where they are."

The usually cheerful little hospital was quietly somber as she walked down the aisle. There were smiles sent her direction, but there was none of the loud calling that usually heralded her arrival. Normally bright eyes were hooded and fearful. Carrie wanted to shout that they were safe here, but she remained silent. She couldn't bring herself to lie.

Carrie approached the beds of the two beaten men. She was sure neither of them would be recognizable to family or friends now. Their faces had been beaten to a pulp, and cuts and lacerations were evident everywhere. One man had both arms broken. They were obviously in shock. She pushed down the anger at whomever had done this and tried to concentrate on saving them.

One of the ladies who acted as a nurse hurried over to her. "I done cleaned them up as best I could," she said breathlessly. "I done found some of that stuff you made up from the persimmon bark and cleaned all their cuts." She paused and then whispered fearfully. "You think they gonna make it, Miss Carrie?"

"They're going to be fine," Carrie stated, hoping she was right. There was no telling how much brain damage might have been done by the savage attack. It would be days before they would know. "I want more blankets on them," she ordered, then turned to Pastor Anthony. "Please bring me a bottle of my stramonium leaves and maypop root. It will help alleviate some of their pain." Carrie turned back to her patients. She needed to set the broken bones first.

It was almost dark when Carrie left the hospital. She had hoped to get away earlier, but two weeks of absence meant there was a lot to be done. Every part of her ached from fatigue.

Pastor Anthony accompanied her to the carriage. "I wish I could take you home," he said anxiously, "but I feel I have to stay here at the hospital." He gazed around at the deepening shadows. "They may need me."

Carrie reached out and touched his arm. "We'll be fine," she assured him. "Spencer and I have done this plenty of times."

Pastor Anthony nodded and stepped back. "Be careful."

Carrie waved as Spencer picked up the reins. "See you soon," she promised, swallowing her fear as she looked down the road into the dark pockets cast by the surrounding buildings. Spencer urged the horse into a fast trot, as anxious as Carrie to reach her father's house. She leaned forward, silently urging the horses to hurry.

They had gone less than one hundred yards when the horse jarred to a halt, rearing up and pawing the air wildly. Carrie gasped and slammed back against the seat as Spencer grabbed the sides of the carriage to keep his balance. She had just straightened herself when a group of about ten men stepped from the shadows of a building. The man in the lead calmly coiled the long whip he had just snapped in front of the horse.

"Miss Cromwell, I presume," he drawled in a nasty voice.

Chapter Eight

Carrie remained seated, fighting to remain calm. "Who is asking?"

"Me and the boys here," he snarled. "The name is Pickett."

"Well, Mr. Pickett, if you'll excuse us, we must be on our way," Carrie snapped.

The skinny, disheveled man stepped closer, hefting his whip in his hand. "It ain't real safe to be out this time of the night." He reached out suddenly and grabbed the horse's bridle. "But I don't reckon you're going to be on your way just yet."

"I beg your pardon?" Carrie could feel her heart pounding in her ears. Spencer was ramrod straight, motionless in his seat. She realized she had put not only herself, but him as well in grave danger. Visions of the two men beaten earlier that day rose to taunt her.

"Now, Miss Cromwell, we ain't aiming to do you no harm. At least not *tonight*," he sneered with an evil grin.

"My name is Mrs. Borden," Carrie said arrogantly, hoping the idea of a husband would cause them to think twice about whatever they intended to do.

"You mean there's a Mr. Borden who lets his wife come down to take care of a bunch of niggers?" Pickett snarled. "He must be one of those cowards who are letting other men fight for his country."

"*Captain* Borden," Carrie said coolly, "has just fought in the battle against Hooker's forces." She took a deep breath and continued angrily. "May I ask where you and your *men* were while that battle was being fought?"

Pickett whitened with anger and quickly uncoiled his whip. "I reckon I've heard all I intend to of your female trash. It's obvious from all the talk that you don't know the proper place of a Southern woman. I know all about you being a nigger lover." He moved closer to Spencer. "I reckon this be one of your niggers, ain't he?" He motioned to the men behind him. "I reckon we'll rough him up like we did them two this morning. That'll be one more that won't be fighting with them Yankees."

"I don't think that would be a very good idea, Mr. Pickett," Carrie said coldly, her voice ringing through the night air.

"And how do you figure on stopping me?" he growled. "You look to be slightly outnumbered." He laughed wildly. "Get the nigger, boys!"

The men ran forward but stumbled to a halt as a shot rang out in the air, immediately followed by another.

"What the...?" Pickett cried.

"The next shot will go right through your heart," Carrie snapped, leveling her pistol at the furious man. "Don't doubt that I can do it. I'm an excellent shot."

"You wouldn't shoot a man in cold blood," Pickett blustered.

"I don't think your behavior qualifies you as a man. I would have no qualms about shooting a wild animal to save a decent human being," Carrie said coldly. She waved her gun at the rest of the group. "The first one who takes another step toward my carriage will be the first to catch one of my bullets."

Pickett tried to regain control. "You can't shoot us all. You're fighting a losing game."

"Maybe," Carrie agreed, letting her eyes sweep over the group of frightened, but still defiant men. "But I've got enough bullets left for four of you. If you think I'm going to sit idly by while you beat my driver, you are sorely mistaken. Four of you will have to die to accomplish what you want." She paused. "Which four of you will it be?"

She swung her gaze back to Pickett. "I promise you'll be one of the four if you don't get out of here."

Pickett stared at her for several long moments, hatred gleaming from his eyes. "You'll be sorry for this."

"And you'll be sorrier if you don't clear out right this minute." Carrie relished the look of fear gleaming from his weak eyes. She pulled back the hammer of the gun. "Make your choice."

Pickett backed up slowly, muttering under his breath. His men backed with him. It was obvious they believed every word Carrie said.

When they were twenty feet from the carriage, Carrie stood up and balanced herself against Spencer's seat. "Drive forward at a slow trot," she ordered in a quiet voice. She raised her pistol higher. "Anyone who makes a move before we're out of sight will be sorry," she called to the sullen men.

Spencer raised his reins and urged the horses forward. Carrie gripped the seat to balance herself and held the pistol steady. None of the men moved. As soon as they were out of sight, she leaned forward. "I'd say a little speed was called for," she managed to say in a casual voice.

Spencer needed no urging. Carrie sank into her seat as the horse galloped forward and up the hill into the heart of the city. They dashed down the darkened, almost empty streets. A couple of stray loiterers jumped out of their way with shouted oaths, but no one stepped forward to try to impede their progress. It wasn't until they were a few blocks from her Church Hill home that Spencer pulled the horse down to a steady trot.

Nothing was said until they were within sight of the house. Spencer pulled the carriage to a stop and turned around. His face dripped with sweat in spite of the cool air, and his breathing was shallow. He stared at her for a full minute. "I reckon you saved my life," he said finally. "Thank you."

Carrie sagged, the full reality of the precarious situation finally sinking in. "I'm sorry," she said. "I would have had no reason to save your life if I had listened to you in the first place. I'm sorry I put you in danger."

"They weren't gonna be content with doin' me in," Spencer said grimly. "Men like that don't have no qualms 'bout hurting lady folks." He took a deep breath and looked at her with admiration. "You were somethin' back there, Miss Carrie. You even had me believin' you would have shot one of them." He paused, his unasked question hanging in the air.

"I meant what I said back there. They weren't acting like men. They were behaving like wild animals. If one of them had tried to touch you, I would have shot them," Carrie said, amazed at the surety she felt. When her father had given her the gun, she hadn't known if she could actually shoot someone. She had her answer now.

"It's late," Spencer said, his voice thick with emotion. "I best be gettin' you home. I figure your daddy be worried sick 'bout you."

Nothing more was said until the carriage rolled up at the house. Spencer jumped down and helped her out. "I won't forget you saved my life, Miss Carrie."

"And I won't forget all you've done for me, Spencer," she said quietly. "You've risked yourself for me time and time again. Thank you."

"Carrie?"

The familiar voice from the porch caused Carrie to spin around with a cry of gladness. "Robert!"

Robert leapt from the porch and grabbed her in his arms. "Where have you been? Are you all right?"

"I think I should be asking those questions," Carrie laughed, her fatigue forgotten. "You're home. You're safe!"

"I just got here. Your father is worried sick about you." He turned to Spencer. "What happened?"

Spencer looked at Carrie. "We ran into a little trouble," he admitted.

Carrie reached out for Robert's arm. "I'm so glad you're home." All she wanted was to have him hold her, to be assured he was really home again.

Robert pulled her into a warm embrace. Carrie clung to him, not caring who was watching. She began to tremble as the emotions of the evening released themselves within the safety of her husband's arms. Silent tears rolled down her cheeks.

Robert finally stepped back. "Are you going to tell me what happened?"

Carrie sighed. "I should know by now I can't hide anything from you." Haltingly, she told him what had happened.

"Your wife be a real brave woman," Spencer interjected.

"We're fine," Carrie finished. "I don't think those men will bother us again." She felt much braver within the safety of Robert's presence.

Robert listened, his face growing white. "Both of you could have been killed. And don't fool yourselves," he snapped. "Those men have had their pride hurt. They'll be looking for a chance to get even."

Carrie was silent, knowing Robert was angry because of his fear for her. After a moment, she turned to Spencer. "You can go home now. I think all of us need a good night's rest." She fought to control the quaver in her voice.

Robert reacted instantly. "I'm sorry," he said. Taking Carrie's hand, he pulled her up onto the porch and stepped into the shadows. "I think it's time I said hello the right way."

Carrie raised her face as Robert lowered his lips. Strength poured back into her as the weeks of fear and uncertainty melted away. She clung to him when he pulled back. "I wish it could always be like this," she whispered. "I wish there was nothing to keep us apart."

"You never know," Robert replied, a mysterious grin flitting over his handsome face. "You might get what you wish for."

Carrie opened her mouth to ask him what he meant, but he held a finger to her lips and shook his head. "Not another word of talk until morning. There will be plenty of time then. I find myself not very content to neck out on the porch. Now that we're married, I discover I would much rather kiss in bed."

Carrie blushed at the bold look gleaming in his eyes but closed her mouth and put her hand in his willingly. "Whatever you say, husband dear," she replied demurely.

Robert laughed and led her inside.

"Carrie! Are you all right?" Thomas rose from his chair.

"She's fine," Robert assured him. "We'll tell you all about it in the morning. Right now your daughter needs some rest. We're going to bed."

Thomas managed a small laugh. "It's so nice to know there is someone else around to take care of this willful child of mine." He leaned over and turned out the lantern. "We'll talk in the morning."

Robert pulled Carrie into his arms as soon as the door was closed.

"I love you."

Carrie sighed and snuggled as close as she could. "I love you, Robert Borden. Everything became right in my world again as soon as I laid eyes on you." She reached up and touched his cheek. "I'm so glad you're home." Leaning back, she searched his face.

Robert's eyes grew moist with unshed tears. "I don't think I'll ever get over the wonder that you're mine," he said softly.

"Forever and always," Carrie promised.

Robert grabbed her close. Once again, Carrie lost herself in his kiss, her heart pounding with love and desire. This time, she pulled away first. She took his hand and led him over to the bed. "Welcome home," she smiled.

Robert stared at her, his dark eyes becoming even darker, his breathing shallow. "I dream of you every night while I'm out there," he murmured.

Carrie's heart ached at the vulnerability flooding his face, the haunted look she was growing accustomed to seeping into his eyes. She held a finger to his lips. "Hush," she said. "We'll talk in the morning. Right now we're going to love each other and celebrate being together." She smiled gently. "That's an order, Captain."

"Yes, ma'am," Robert said obediently. Then he reached up and pulled her down on him.

When Carrie opened her eyes the next morning, Robert was propped on one elbow, watching her.

"Good morning, wife," he grinned.

Carrie grinned back. "Good morning, husband." She looked at him lovingly. "One thing will never cease to amaze me."

"What's that? That you landed such an incredible husband?"

"Well yes, that too, but that's not what I'm referring to," she teased. "I was referring to the fact that one can survive off so little sleep when they're in love. I should be dead to the world, but I feel amazingly alive." She reached up to pull him down.

Robert obliged willingly, and once more she was engulfed in the thrill of his kiss.

She pushed him away playfully. "It's morning now. We can talk. What were you referring to yesterday when you said there may be a way for us not to have to be apart?" Her eyes gleamed with excitement. "I'm dying to know."

Robert leaned back and regarded her. "No one so beautiful could be close to death. I think you will live until breakfast."

Carrie jumped into a kneeling position on the bed. "You cannot possibly make me wait until breakfast! That's cruel."

Robert laughed and climbed out of bed. "I told your father we would eat with him this morning. What I have to say, I want both of you to hear." He leaned down for another kiss. "I promise you'll like it."

"You look like a little boy," Carrie said with delight. She jumped off the bed and headed for the closet. "It must be good news if you can look that excited. I suppose I'll play along with this game and wait until breakfast. As long as you don't make me wait ages for breakfast," she said, waving her fist playfully.

"I believe it's being served any minute," Robert responded. "I thought you were never going to wake up. I've been watching you for almost an hour."

"An hour?" Carrie gasped. "Did I snore?"

"Did you snore?"

"I've always wondered if I snore," Carrie confessed. "I spent the weekend with a friend one time. I could hear her mother snoring all the way at the end of the hallway. I've always been horrified I would sound like that."

"Well," Robert said, considering. "I don't think they can hear you all the way down at the end of the hall." He paused. "Maybe next door, though. You might ask Janie if you kept her awake."

Carrie gasped, searching his face. "You're lying," she accused him. "I don't really snore." She hesitated. "Do I?"

Robert laughed and headed for the door. "I don't know if I'd tell you if you did, but thankfully I can honestly say that you don't."

Carrie ran forward and pummeled his chest. "Don't ever toy with me like that again."

They were still laughing when they entered the dining room. All the boarders had already gone off to work. Thomas looked up from his paper. "I'm glad you two can find something to laugh about."

"We all have to find something to laugh about," Carrie said. She hadn't had time to tell Robert about her father's increasing bitterness and defeated attitude. Now, he would get to see it firsthand.

Thomas scowled and tossed his paper aside. "Well, I'm not going to find it in that paper. I'm afraid there's not much good news for the Confederacy right now."

"Our most recent victory was good news," Robert protested.

"I'm afraid losing thirteen thousand men and one of our finest generals is not much to cheer about. Yes, I'm thankful Hooker is not marching through our capital right now, but I don't think it will take him long to get strong enough to try again." He shook his head dolefully. "This is going to be a long summer." He let out his breath in a heavy sigh. "I wonder if we will still have a capital when it's all said and done."

"Lee has a plan to make sure Richmond is still standing at the end of the summer," Robert said. "I think he shares some of your concerns about Hooker's future plans."

Thomas looked at him curiously but didn't respond.

"Lee is proposing the Army of Northern Virginia head north," Robert said. "There is news that Hooker is going to be reinforced. That is clear indication that Virginia will once more be the theater of action. Lee believes if he moves his troops north, it will ease the pressure on Virginia for a while, as well as keep more reinforcements from heading to Tennessee and Mississippi. Lincoln will be cautious if he believes Rebel troops are advancing in the direction of Washington, DC. He'll have to think more about protecting his own capital than about capturing Richmond."

Thomas looked up, a spark of hope in his eyes. "Lee really thinks he can take on the Army of the Potomac in their territory? Without a ready line of supplies?"

"Lee is considering this as a defensive move," Robert asserted. "He is not going looking for a fight. His aims are more moderate than that. He hopes to disrupt Federal plans for the summer. He also wants to use the tactic to gather supplies from the North. Not to mention that if Union troops leave Virginia, more supplies can reach our state."

"If I'm hearing this right," Thomas observed, "Lee plans on spending the summer maneuvering in the North, hoping to return in the fall in better shape than he is now."

"That's it exactly," Robert agreed. "I think President Davis is going to go for it."

Carrie listened with a sinking heart. She had been so excited minutes earlier. Now, Robert was telling her they were going to be apart for the whole summer. "When do you leave?" she asked woodenly.

"The question is not when *I* leave," Robert replied, smiling. "The question is when do *we* leave?"

Carrie stared at him, confused. "Whatever are you talking about?"

Robert reached over and took one of her hands. "I'm not going with General Lee, my love. *We're* going to London." He sat back, a grin lighting his face.

"London?" she echoed stupidly.

Robert nodded. "Think of it, Carrie. Us...together...in London, England. I've always dreamed of going there."

Thomas cleared his throat. "If I'm feeling confused, I can imagine what my daughter must be experiencing.

Maybe you should start from the beginning," he suggested.

"I'm sorry. I wanted so much to tell you last night, Carrie. I wanted to let you know we wouldn't have to be apart again." He stopped short. "I'm still not explaining myself."

Carrie sat quietly, too surprised by his announcement to say anything or to even know what she was thinking.

"President Davis called me to his office yesterday. I was there early in the morning, before the funeral procession." He paused. "The president looked awful. He took Jackson's death very hard." Sorrow clouded his face. "I was there," he said quietly, forgetting all about London for a moment. "I saw Jackson get shot. I helped carry him behind the lines." His face grew grim. "It was a terrible night."

Carrie watched him closely. His face was saying everything his words weren't. Her heart wrenched as she envisioned what he had experienced. "Tell me about England," she said quickly, reaching forward to grasp his hand.

The jaded look faded from Robert's eyes as he glanced up. "England?" he murmured. His eyes brightened. "Yes, London. I was telling you about President Davis." His voice strengthened as he pushed his memories away.

Carrie regarded him tenderly. She knew he was groping toward the future to help deal with the horrors of the past. She loved him for his strength. She also loved him for his raw vulnerability. He had endured more than she could even imagine in the last two years. A fierce desire to protect him gripped her.

Robert turned to Thomas. "How much do you know about the situation in England?"

Thomas shrugged. "That it seems to change depending on how the wind blows. The English aristocracy seems to be decidedly against the Northern position. I believe if it were left up to them, they would grant recognition of the Confederacy. On the other hand," he continued, "the Queen and many of the English people favor a continuation of Northern control and aggression." He shook his head. "Their official position is one of neutrality."

"President Davis has not given up hope that we might yet gain British recognition," Robert said. "We didn't have long to talk yesterday, but he still believes there is a chance England will swing in our direction."

"And if they do?" Thomas asked. "What good will it do us? It is still the actions of our troops on the field that will determine the outcome of this war."

Carrie found herself agreeing with her father. She wasn't sure what the furor over foreign support was all about.

"England has the capacity to build the boats we need to smash the blockade," Robert interjected. "The Union blockade is strangling us from all directions. Our troops are suffering because we can't get supplies to them."

"And men are dying for lack of medicine," Carrie added. "Not to mention that people are going hungry."

"Exactly," Robert said, turning to her. "Davis realizes this spring is a critical time. If we can convince England to let us take possession of the ships that we need, there is still a chance we can smash the blockade and turn things around."

"How long would it take to build these boats?" Thomas asked.

"They're already being built. Davis had hoped they would be ready this spring, but there have been delays."

"And England is going to release them to us?"

"Well," Robert replied, "they're not clear on exactly what their intended use is. Our man over there has managed to quite cleverly cover any tracks that would indicate Confederate involvement. Davis told me the ships being built are regular battleships, heavily armed and armored. Tremendous advances have been made already in the naval industry, but these boats outshine anything constructed thus far. They are much more seaworthy than the sluggish monitors, and far more powerful than any wooden warships afloat." He stopped, his eyes shining. "With these boats, we can break the blockade all along our coastline."

Thomas leaned forward, genuine interest shining on his face. "That would make a tremendous difference," he said. "If we could equip our armies properly, there is no one who could stop them."

Carrie listened, contradictory feelings raging in her heart. She wanted to scream that she wanted the fighting to stop, but instead, she turned to Robert. "I'm afraid I still don't understand what this all has to do with you."

"I'm getting to that," Robert replied with a quick smile. "Davis wants to keep his pulse on British sentiment as closely as he can. He already has plenty of government officials there. He wants some common citizens who can get a feel for how the general population is reacting. He wants someone with an expertise in farming to determine how hard the lack of cotton is hitting their economy."

"Why would the president be interested in my going along?"

"I convinced him I would have a much better chance of being accepted into British society if my wife went along with me," Robert said, grinning triumphantly. "Think of it, Carrie. We'll be somewhere we can make a real difference. We'll be together."

"How long?" Carrie asked, trying to determine why her heart was so heavy. Wasn't this what she wanted? To be with Robert? To not be constantly wondering if he were dead or alive?

"Six, eight months. Maybe a year. As long as we can send back information that will be helpful, we'll stay. By the time we get back, I'm sure this whole thing will be over."

"When do you two leave?" Thomas asked in a tired voice. He leaned forward and took Carrie's hand. "I'm sorry. I didn't mean to sound like that. It will be the best thing for both of you. God knows, something needs to happen to turn things around here. I think Robert is right. If we can break the blockade, things will be different."

"We leave in three days," Robert said. "We have to take the train to Wilmington, North Carolina and leave from there. It is one of the few places where the blockade can still be run."

"How dangerous will this little expedition be?" Thomas asked. "I can't imagine the Union Navy will simply wave and let you pass through."

"President Davis assures me that there is not a great danger. We are being sent out on one of the newest blockade-running ships. She is fast and sleek. Nothing has stopped her yet."

Thomas nodded and folded his paper. "I have to get to the Capitol for a meeting, but I'll see you two tonight." He turned to Carrie. "You're going to the hospital today?"

Carrie nodded, grateful the morning conversation had allowed no discussion of what had kept her so late the night before. Somehow, in light of Robert's news, it had faded in her own mind. "Dr. Wild is expecting me around lunchtime. I'll be home late."

Robert waited until Thomas left the room and turned to her eagerly. "You can tell Dr. Wild today that you won't be coming back to the hospital. It will take us the three days to get everything ready."

"I'm afraid I can't do that," Carrie said quietly, surprising even herself.

Robert set his cup of coffee down, its contents sloshing onto the table. "What do you mean? Why not?"

Carrie took a deep breath. Somewhere in the last few moments, she had reached her decision. "I can't go to England with you, Robert."

Robert stared at her in astonishment. "Whatever are you talking about?"

Carrie groped to find the words to express what she was feeling. "It's not right. My work is here—the hospital, my patients." She paused, looking at him pleadingly. "They need me."

Robert continued to stare at her, obviously at a loss for words.

Carrie tried again. "I hate this war. The idea of being in London with you... Away from everything... Safe." She paused. "Not to have to worry about you every day..." Her voice caught. "It sounds wonderful."

Carrie shook her head. "It's taken me until recently to begin to make sense of all of it. Not of the war—that will never make sense to me. I mean to make sense out of my purpose in it. As long as this war lasts, there are going to be thousands of wounded and maimed men. I can make a difference to them. I can't go to medical school yet, but I can make a difference to every person who becomes one of my patients."

She stopped. Robert's face told her that he wasn't understanding her at all. "Working in the hospital isn't just a job. It isn't just a way to do my duty for the Confederacy. It's who I am." She gazed into his eyes, willing him to understand. "It's who I am, Robert."

"You're my wife," Robert said, anger tightening his face. "I can't believe what I'm hearing. You're my wife," he repeated.

Carrie stared at him with a sinking heart. "Yes, I'm your wife. And I love you."

"But you won't go to England with me?" he asked bitterly.

Carrie felt sick. Robert had been home only a few hours, and already they were fighting. "It's not only the soldiers. There is also the black hospital to consider. If I leave, they won't have anybody. Janie can continue to nurse, but they won't have anybody to act as their doctor."

"So you want me to go off to London wondering which night you are going to be killed by a band of men waiting to attack you?"

Carrie felt her own anger rising and struggled to keep it under control. A shouting match would do neither one of them any good. "You went off to fight when I didn't want you to," she said. "You weren't ready to go back into battle when you left this last time. You weren't recovered from almost dying last year."

"I had to go," Robert snapped. "It was my duty. They're not the same thing."

"You told me you wished you never had to fight another battle," Carrie reminded him.

"Well, yes, but I still have a home I'm fighting for. I still have people it is my duty to protect—you, your father, my mother out on the plantation. I can't turn my back on them."

"I know," Carrie agreed. "No more than I can turn my back on the people here who need me." She leaned closer. "It would be so easy to go to London and pretend there were not people back here injured and dying. It would be so easy to go and buy fancy dresses and pretend my friends weren't cold and hungry. You have a job to do over there, Robert. In spite of the fact that bringing me might make it easier to be accepted into society, you can still do your job without me." Tears filled her eyes. "My job is here. Please don't make me choose."

Robert stood and stalked over to the window. He pushed the curtains aside and stared out wordlessly.

Carrie sat, waiting for him to speak. Her earlier fears about getting married rose to taunt her. Had she married the man of her dreams, only to find that he was going to rob her of another, equally important dream? Her heart pulsed with a chaotic mix of love and resentment. She knew any of her friends, with the possible exception of Janie, would have smiled sweetly and gone along, burying their own thoughts and desires. She knew her mother would have done that for her father. She wanted to bury her head in her hands, but she remained straight. Was there something wrong with her? Her mother used to tell her she would never find a man who would put up with her willful ways. Was Robert already regretting his decision to marry her?

Robert finally turned away from the window. Carrie searched his face for an indication of what he was feeling. He was silent, looking deep into her eyes. She returned his gaze evenly, not sure what he was looking for, but quite certain she was not going to apologize for what she had honestly said.

"Come here," he said hoarsely, holding out his arms.

Carrie rushed into his embrace.

He held her close for a long minute. "I knew I was marrying a hard-headed woman," he muttered. Pushing her away, he tilted her chin up until their eyes met. "I may not agree with you, but I have to respect how you feel. You've worried and waited for me for the last two years. I guess it's my turn to see how it feels," he said. He took a deep breath and then pulled her back against him roughly. "I'm proud of you, Carrie Borden. I hope every one of your patients realizes how lucky they are."

Carrie made no attempt to stop the tears streaming down her face. "Thank you," she whispered, relief mixing with the ache that was already filling her heart at the idea of saying goodbye again. "I love you."

Chapter Nine

Robert took a deep breath as the train rounded a curve, and Carrie and her father slipped from view. The last three days with his beautiful wife had been wonderful. He smiled, remembering, but his thoughts soon soured. Was their entire marriage going to be one of saying goodbye? He hadn't wanted to let go of her at the train station. He'd wanted to order her to go home, get her bags, and come with him like any good wife would. He hadn't of course. Carrie wasn't *any* wife. She was independent, strong-willed and full of dreams she would do anything to accomplish. It was only one of the many reasons why he loved her.

"Off to the front?" the porter asked cheerfully, taking Robert's ticket as he strode by.

"London," Robert said.

"Yeah? My wife and I have always wanted to go to England. Maybe when this crazy war is over."

Robert bit his lip and turned away. It had only been a few minutes, and already the vision of Carrie's shining green eyes, framed by her glossy black hair, was haunting him—creating a longing in him. He turned to stare out the window. It would be months before he would see her again. What if Richmond fell during that time? What if something happened to her? He groaned inwardly and clenched his fists.

He had no choice but to let her stay. He knew that, but the knowledge failed to offer him any comfort. She would have come if he'd insisted, but part of her heart would have stayed in Richmond. Forced to choose between him and her work, she would have harbored resentment. Robert knew Carrie loved him with all her heart. Why couldn't that be enough for her? Overcome with longing, he pressed his head against the window. Exhaustion blurred his vision. The last few days had not offered much sleep. When he wasn't preparing for his

trip or in meetings, he had soaked up all of his wife he
could.

The clacking of the train numbed his mind after a
long while. The wheels sang to him, their song echoing
the disharmony in his heart.

Carrie... London... Carrie... London.....

Finally he slept.

It was almost dark when the train pulled into the
Wilmington station. Robert stumbled onto the platform,
rubbing his eyes. What was normally a one-day trip had
stretched into two. There were constant stops and delays
as troops were loaded and unloaded, tracks were
switched, and loads of supplies taken on or off. His
growling stomach reminded him he'd had little to eat
that day. The food Carrie had sent with him had long
since run out.

Robert took a deep breath of the salty, port town air
and felt some of his energy return. The cramped confines
of the train had almost driven him mad. He set his bag
down and gazed around. There was no reason to expect
someone to meet him, since trains in the Confederacy
never followed a schedule. You were simply lucky if you
eventually reached your destination.

The streets, even at this time of night, were still
crowded and noisy. Robert gazed around, astonished.
Robert had been to the city many times on business, but
if he hadn't heard the porter call out *'Wilmington!'* he
would never have recognized what had once been a
conservative old port town.

"Ain't been here for a while, boy?" An observant old
man chuckled from where he sat on a bench along the
wall.

"Several years," Robert admitted.

"It's changed a bit," the old man said laconically,
pausing to spit a long wad of tobacco into a nearby
spittoon.

"I'd say." Robert continued to stare around him.

"The war changed things, boy," the old man continued. "We're one of the major blockade-running ports. Got more agents and traders in this city now than we do birds. Why, heck, we got as many Englishmen in this city now as we do Confederates. This town has been taken over by English ship owners and fellows from those huge mercantile houses. They'll spend any kind of money to entertain folks around here," he said proudly. "We got all kinds around here who decided they loved the cause of the South once they realized how much profit could be made." He shot another long string of black juice. "Can't say as how I blame them. I reckon I've made more money in the last two years than I've made in my whole life."

Robert shot him a curious look.

"Built me a few warehouses down along the waterfront. They stay full of stuff being shuttled back and forth. No matter how hard they try, the North isn't going to keep our cotton from going out. Things have slowed down a mite, I agree, but the increase in price has more than made up for it."

Robert wondered how long the man would be talking this way if the Union blockade succeeded in choking off the supplies the Confederacy needed so badly. He also wondered what kind of tune he would be singing if he had to spend a winter in Richmond suffering the privations of the citizens there who didn't have the excesses flowing here.

"You Robert Borden?" he asked.

Robert peered at him more closely. "Who are you?" He was suddenly suspicious of anyone who would talk so freely. President Davis had warned him that all the major Confederate cities were full of Union spies. It didn't seem possible that someone had gotten wind of his mission, but he knew he couldn't be too careful.

"The name is Silas McCormick," the grizzled old man said cheerfully. "You sure fit the description I was given. You're a day late, though."

"The trains were running late," Robert acknowledged carefully.

"So you *are* Robert Borden."

"I might be."

Silas barked a wheezy laugh. "Son, I don't have time for a lot of espionage games. I've been sitting at this railroad station for two days, waiting for someone who matched your description to get off some train. I don't mind telling you I'm tired. Saw another fellow that looks like you get off a couple of hours ago," he offered, "but he didn't have a red handkerchief in his pocket, so I let him go."

"You know about the red handkerchief?" Robert asked in relief, glad the men preparing him for his trip had insisted he carry it.

"You don't think Captain Bueller is going to let just anyone on his fancy new boat do you?" The old man stood, his eyes suddenly shining with purpose. "Are you Robert Borden, or are you not?"

"I'm Robert Borden."

Silas nodded with satisfaction. "I knew I was right. Now, can we stop playing our games?" His voice grew gentler. "I know you have to be careful, boy, but my stomach is saying it wants to eat—not that it wants to play games."

Robert grinned. "Our stomachs are in agreement, Silas."

"Good," Silas said heartily. "Follow me."

Robert was hard-pressed to keep up with the agile old man as he wove his way through throngs of people crowding the streets. Music spilled from lighted saloons. Colorfully dressed women strolled arm in arm with elegantly attired gentleman. It reminded him of Richmond when the war was still young, and before it was a battered, tired city under siege. He watched wistfully as a dark-haired beauty laughed gaily up at her handsome escort. Carrie would love this. An ache shot through him.

"We're almost there," Silas called out loudly, continuing to thread his way through the masses.

Robert took a deep breath and pushed on. Soon he was seated in front of the most sumptuous meal he had seen in months. He felt guilty as he shoveled in the thick slices of ham and turkey, the mounds of hot, steaming vegetables, and the slabs of fragrant bread. Finally, he shook his head. "I don't get it," he mumbled through his last bite. "Fresh food is as scarce as gold in the capital."

"That's what we hear," Silas agreed. "We can get the supplies in here, but getting them to Richmond is another matter altogether. Sometimes the army claims it for their men, sometimes the shipments never get there. Not to mention that we don't get enough. Oh sure, the people of Wilmington are living high on the hog, but you don't have to go far before it changes. Wilmington and Charleston are the two main ports left for the blockade runners. We just can't get enough through here."

Robert looked around, thinking that if the people of Wilmington lowered their standards a little, other people might not be so afflicted. He said nothing, though. He was playing only a small part in Davis' plan, but if the scheme worked, the stranglehold on supplies to the South would be destroyed. Then no one would suffer.

"When do I meet Captain Bueller?" He was anxious to be on his way.

"I'll take you to his ship in the morning. You'll leave as soon as the time is right. The captain is anxious to be on his way. I don't think you'll have too long of a wait." Silas nodded at the bowls of food still in front of them. "You'll want to eat up, boy. Captain Bueller isn't one to take up a lot of space with food. He's more interested in how much cargo he can take. That's how he makes his living."

Carrie smiled wearily at Hobbs as she climbed into the carriage. Janie followed her closely.

"How are the two fellows who got beaten?" Hobbs asked, looking around warily as Spencer gathered the reins and urged the horse forward.

Carrie smiled again, this one genuine. "They're going to be fine. They are still sore, and Henry's broken arms will take a while to heal, but they are going to recover." She leaned back against the seat and waved again to

Pastor Anthony, who was still at the door to the hospital, watching them move down the road.

"Thank you for coming down here with us," Carrie told Hobbs gratefully. "Although, I have a feeling Robert didn't give you much of a choice, did he?"

Hobbs shook his head, one hand resting on the rifle lying across his knee. "I told Robert a long time ago I would look after you. Then you and I became friends. That just gave me more reason to make sure you stay safe. Ain't nothing gonna happen to you and Miss Janie as long as I'm around."

Carrie looked at Hobbs tenderly. At twenty-one, she was only a few years older than he was, but his youthful appearance made him seem much younger. Warren Hobbs had the fierce loyalty common to mountain farmers. She knew he would lay down his life in a second for either her or Robert. Robert had asked him to accompany Carrie when she went down to the black hospital, and he took his duty with solemn seriousness. Hobbs was already invaluable to her at Chimborazo, where he acted as one of her ward assistants.

Still, Carrie was nervous as she peered into the dark shadows. Was Pickett waiting there with his friends? It was no secret which day she came to the hospital.

"Do you see anything?" Janie asked.

Carrie shook her head and forced herself to settle back. Her nervousness wasn't going to help any of them. She struggled to control her shudder. She had been having nightmares ever since Robert left. Without his protective embrace to shield her from her thoughts, the dreams haunted every sleeping moment. They were all the same.

Pickett and his men killing Spencer and then coming after her. Their hideous laughter taunting her just before they grabbed her.

She had almost been too afraid to come down today but had finally scorned herself into facing her fear.

The ride back to the house passed uneventfully. Had Pickett seen Hobbs and his rifle and decided it wasn't worth the risk? Carrie was relieved beyond words when the carriage rolled up to her father's house.

Janie turned to Spencer. "Could you come in the house for a minute? I could use your help with something."

"Sho 'nuff, Miss Janie," Spencer said. "What you need?"

"Micah is waiting inside for you. I would like the two of you to move my things back into Carrie's room," she said.

Spencer nodded easily and swung up the walk.

Janie turned to Carrie before she could say anything. "You are not staying in that room alone another night. I can tell you haven't had a good night's sleep since Robert left. I've heard your cries. You're having nightmares aren't you?" she demanded.

Carrie fought her tears. "I'm such a silly weakling."

"Nonsense," Janie snapped. She reached forward to hug Carrie. "It will be good for me, too. I miss our late-night talks. I promise to move back to my room like a good girl when Robert gets home."

"Oh, Janie," Carrie cried. "Do you think I was silly not to go to London?"

"It doesn't matter what I think. You did what you felt you had to. That's what I love about you, Carrie Cromwell. You're not afraid to live your convictions, even when it hurts." Janie stepped back. "Now, I'm starving. Let's eat."

Carrie was startled awake by another nightmare. Bolting forward in bed, she glanced over at Janie. Her friend continued to sleep soundly. She must not have cried out this time. Shaking her head to cast away the images, Carrie rose quietly and walked to the window.

It was a beautiful night, a crescent moon perched on the horizon, its shimmering sliver hanging as if suspended on an invisible thread. A soft breeze rustled the leaves and fanned her hair away from her hot face. She sank down on the window seat and rested her head against the frame.

As she gazed east, she realized her dreams carried her far beyond Cromwell Plantation. Now they transported her out onto the Atlantic Ocean, searching for the ship that carried the love of her life. Tears spilled down her cheeks as the ache of missing Robert flooded her. Her breath came in shallow gasps.

She felt Janie touch her shoulder gently. "Let it out, Carrie. Let it all out."

Carrie turned and fell into her friend's arms, sobs shaking her body. "I was a fool!" she cried. "I was a fool not to go!" She clenched her fist and slammed it against the window frame. "I could be with Robert right now. I don't care about the hospital! I don't care about sick people! I don't care about being a doctor. I just want to be with Robert," she gasped, gulping to catch her breath.

Janie held her tight. Carrie didn't know how long she cried before she began to gain control of her tears.

Janie stroked her hair back from her flushed face. "It's okay, Carrie. It's okay," she murmured.

"It's *not* okay!" Carrie cried. "Don't you understand? I can't catch a train to go join him. He's probably halfway across the Atlantic now. I have no idea when I'll see him again." The tears threatened to take control again. "He's my husband. I should be with him."

"That's enough," Janie said firmly. "No one but you can say whether your decision was right or wrong. It doesn't matter now anyway. It's been made. Now you have to live with the consequences of it." Her voice softened. "You did what you thought was best, Carrie. Robert respected your decision just as you've respected his decisions in the past."

Carrie choked back her tears and tried to listen.

Janie settled back on the window seat. "My Grandma Alice used to tell me God can use a bad decision as much as a good decision. She figured God didn't turn his back on someone if they made a bad choice. He just got to work to figure out how to make good come from it."

"God makes me so angry sometimes," Carrie cried.

"Angry?"

Carrie nodded. "He knows I'll do whatever he wants me to, but it's figuring it out that's so blamed hard. I felt so right about my decision not to go to London. Now I'm so afraid I made the wrong decision, but it's too late to change it. If God wanted me to go to London, why didn't he make it clearer?"

"If I was God, I would tell you," Janie said calmly. "Since I'm a mere mortal, I'm afraid I have no answer to that." She paused. "What would Old Sarah have told you?"

The mention of Old Sarah's name brought a smile to Carrie's lips. "She would have told me that thin's ain't as black or white as we want them to be," she said softly, slipping into the slave lingo. "She'd have told me God can redeem anythin' if I give it to him." She turned to stare out the window again. "She'd have tole me I was lettin' fear win out. That fear ain't a bad thin' until it takes control of your heart."

The breeze picked up, swirling the curtains around her. Carrie leaned further out the window, relishing the feel of the wind against her face. She closed her eyes, letting it sweep through her soul, blowing away the cobwebs of fear and doubt.

"I may never know if I was supposed to go to London, but you're right—I can't change it. I have to deal with my life the way it is now." She reached out and grabbed her friend's hand. "I'm so glad I have you to share everything with. Thank you."

Robert leaned forward in the small skiff Silas was piloting and examined the ship in front of them. He had learned quite a bit about boats from a college friend whose family was in the shipbuilding business. It took only a moment to realize the war had advanced ship technology faster than anything in years. "What's her name?" he called back to Silas.

"That's the *Phantom*," Silas yelled forward. "Built just this year," he added proudly.

"She's a beauty," Robert responded, leaning forward to inspect her. The *Phantom* was a slender, low side-wheel steamer. From all indications he guessed she weighed about five hundred tons, her length about nine times her beam. Her lead color blended with the ocean perfectly.

"The *Phantom* burns anthracite coal," Silas offered. "The stuff makes no smoke at all. Why, you don't even know she's nearby until you're within a hundred yards or so. You aren't going to have any trouble on board that beauty."

Robert had no trouble believing him. He had never seen such a fine specimen of a ship. He was eager to get on board and look around. Captain Bueller had a boat to be proud of.

Silas had pulled him out of bed before the sun was even up. He had two horses tied up outside the inn where Robert stayed. After several hours of riding, they were met by two men with this boat. The *Phantom* was anchored in a narrow inlet of the Cape Fear River, completely hidden from sight.

"Who goes there?" a strong voice rang out cheerfully. "Silas, is that you, you old goat?"

"Aye, and I got me a spry young buck with me," Silas yelled back. "Pull her alongside, boys!"

Robert was surprised to find himself standing in front of a man he guessed to be no more than a few years older than himself. He had expected the captain of a ship such as the *Phantom* to be much older.

"Robert Borden? Nice to meet you."

Robert recognized the clipped accent at once. "You're British, Captain Bueller?"

"Something wrong with that?" he asked sharply.

"Not at all," Robert said. "I suppose I'm surprised."

Captain Bueller grinned and slapped him on the back. "Welcome aboard, Robert. Hang around the blockade-running squadron long enough, and you'll discover most of us are British. Next, you'll discover that almost all the boats confounding the Union Navy are British-built. My government might not officially recognize yours, but that's no reason to turn down the offer to help a good cause."

"And make a healthy profit in the meantime," Silas added dryly.

"That, too," Captain Bueller agreed.

Robert inspected him more closely. They were about the same height, but there the similarities ended. The captain had a thick shock of blond hair over his blazing blue eyes. A reddish-blond beard stood out against his deeply tanned skin. Powerful shoulders and hands spoke of years at sea. He was not exactly handsome, but Robert suspected he was a man who commanded attention wherever he went.

"Do I pass inspection?" the captain asked.

Robert flushed. "You're not what I expected."

"Good. I hate living up to people's expectations. It's always best to keep them guessing. You'll learn that out here." Captain Bueller turned and snapped orders to his crew. "Mr. Borden is our last passenger. We leave tonight. Prepare the ship." He turned back to Robert. "Come up top with me. I'll fill you in on what to expect. If we're lucky, we'll sneak right through that Union blockade out there. If we're unlucky, we'll have one whale of a good time and have a lot to write home about." He threw back his head and laughed heartily.

Robert joined in, his liking of the captain growing by the minute.

Bueller started talking as soon as they reached the top deck. "You'll only be with me until we get to Nassau. It will probably take three or four days if all goes well. From there, you'll load onto a much bigger vessel to cross the ocean to England." He gazed over his ship. "They started making these babies when it was obvious something much faster was needed to outwit the Yankees. I've been through the blockade with the *Phantom* three times now. They only saw me once. They never came close." He grinned proudly, rubbing his hands together. "I foresee a long, profitable career ahead. At least until the Union Navy catches up with our technology...or as long as your boys can keep the ports open."

Robert listened, fascinated. "How long have you been doing this?"

"Since the war started and Lincoln ordered the blockade. Mother England needed your cotton. You needed our money and goods. It was a match made in heaven. The first year of the blockade was a joke," he snorted. "I could have slipped through it with my eyes closed. The Yanks didn't have a chance patrolling over three thousand miles of shoreline. Especially shoreline like this with all the inlets and shifting sand."

"And now?"

"And now it's becoming more difficult," he admitted. "More of a challenge." It was evident from the gleam in his eyes that he enjoyed it. He frowned slightly. "The Union Navy has undergone a lot of change. They have put hundreds more ships in operation. They are retiring the old, slow wooden vessels and manufacturing a new kind of boat to stop us. They're sending out a fleet of thousand-ton sloops-of-war armed with thirty-two pounders." He shook his head. "So far I've been lucky. They're also developing their own fleet of boats like this to try to stop us. They're armed with twenty-four pound howitzers and patrol the rivers and bays."

Robert stared out over the water. "I see."

Captain Bueller laughed again. "Oh, it's nothing to worry about. There are always ways to get through. He who knows the game best will always win. And I know the game," he boasted.

"Why are you doing it?" He wanted to know more about this man he sensed could become a friend.

"Money." He looked at Robert closely. "I suppose I should say I'm doing it to aid the glorious cause of the South. Don't get me wrong," he added quickly, "I'm on your side. I don't think the North has a right to dictate what you can and can't do. I hate slavery, but I'm enough of a free spirit to think you should be allowed to make your own decisions. On the other hand," he continued, "my thinking you're in the right would hardly be enough to make me risk my life for people who live in a country I'd never visited until two years ago."

He turned to scan the horizon carefully. Satisfied, he turned back. "I do it because I can make more money in one month than I could make my whole life back in

England serving in the Royal Navy. I've also discovered I can spend more in one month than I might have in my entire life," he said. "I've become rather addicted to my lifestyle." He shrugged his powerful shoulders. "So I continue to run the blockade."

Robert wasn't sure what to say. He didn't find it offensive that the captain had mercenary motives. If there weren't men like him, the South would probably have already folded. European supplies were their very lifeblood.

"I'm not a total mercenary," Captain Bueller added. "I do it for the adventure as well. Things were getting rather boring in Old England—haven't had a good war in a while. So, I took leave from the Navy and came to play games with the Union. Whatever I may be, I'm definitely not bored."

Robert laughed. "I like you, Captain Bueller," he announced. "Thank you for having me on board your ship."

"I like you, too, Robert Borden. As I said, you're welcome on the *Phantom*. If you'll excuse me now, I have work to do before we leave tonight." He turned away to examine some charts.

Chapter Ten

Robert was talking with his two traveling companions when Captain Bueller called them together. He was glad for the distraction, as he had found the two older men more than slightly boring. He had no idea why they were headed to London, and he was not about to reveal his own mission. If they could have talked honestly, they may have found more ground for communication, but circumstances demanded discretion. Robert was glad he would only have to share their company for a few days.

"We'll be casting off soon," Captain Bueller announced. "I find my passengers handle things better if they have some understanding of what we might encounter. Since I am not interested in having panicked men on my boat, I'd like you to listen carefully."

Robert was amused at the offended looks on his companions' faces. Captain Bueller exchanged a sardonic look with him, making no effort to hide the smile playing around his lips.

"Once we reach the ocean," the captain began in a commanding voice, "we will likely encounter two rows of blockading warships. The first line will be close to shore, just beyond the reach of the Confederate batteries stationed there. The second squadron will be patrolling some twenty to forty miles out. The first row will be hardest to run. Our low profile and high speed will pretty much guarantee we'll slip by the outer line. They'll probably never even know we're in the area."

His voice grew stern. "Secrecy is what will keep us alive. There will be absolutely no light on the ship to give away our position." He nodded at the oldest man. "Mr. Stanford, I'd like you to extinguish your cigarette. There will be no more smoking until I have given the order."

Mr. Stanford complied silently, his face white, his lips set.

"You may go below. You'll be safest there," Bueller continued and then waved their dismissal.

Robert bit back his disappointment and turned away. He hated to miss the excitement, but he would do nothing to upset the order of the ship.

The captain drew him aside as Robert was going down the stairs. He waited until the other two men were out of hearing and then said in a low voice, "Care to join me up top? Or would you rather hang out with those stuffy men?"

Robert grinned. "Lead on, Captain."

Captain Bueller was silent as they made their way to the bridge. Robert could feel the change come over the man. The confident bearing of the shoulders was still there, but gone was the cocky arrogance. He was all business. Robert understood why his men trusted him, though most of them were years older. He was a commander who inspired confidence.

"Move her out," he ordered.

Robert stared up at the sky as the boat glided smoothly toward the mouth of the inlet. The sky had been startlingly clear earlier. Now, he noted with satisfaction that a thick layer of clouds had blocked out all light. There was not even the dim glow of the new moon to betray their presence to patrolling Union boats.

The silence was soon penetrated by a dull roar. Robert leaned forward expectantly, knowing they were reaching the mouth of the Cape Fear River. Soon they would be making their way through booming surf into the Atlantic. His heart pounded right along with the approaching breakers. The powerful boat eased through the surf effortlessly, any engine noise completely obscured.

The wind picked up, whipping Robert's hair and causing him to squint into the salt-laden air. Excitement coursed through his body as he gripped the railing and peered through the darkness.

He stiffened. A massive, dark outline loomed just to their right.

"Straight ahead," Captain Bueller muttered into the speaking tube to the pilot. "They don't even know we're here."

The *Phantom* glided by noiselessly. The Union blockader remained still and silent. Robert let out his breath as Bueller chuckled quietly. "A piece of cake."

Robert tensed again as another boat came into view.

"Port." Bueller instructed. "Port! Hard a-port," he said urgently.

Robert gripped the railing again as the *Phantom* swung to the port and eased by yet another boat, almost close enough to touch it. His pulse hammered, his breath coming in quick gasps.

A sudden call split the night. "Heave to, or I'll sink you." Lights flashed on the Federal boat as the engines came to life.

Captain Bueller threw back his head and laughed defiantly. "Full speed ahead!" he shouted, all need for silence gone. "Now the game begins!" he called.

Robert looked at the man in fascination. He was actually enjoying this.

Shouts could be heard from the Union boat as the *Phantom* leaped forward, her engines roaring at full speed. Robert grabbed for the railing again and threw his head back in exhilaration. "Yahoo!" he hollered.

"Show 'em what we got, boys!" the captain yelled, his commanding figure casting an impressive outline against the sky.

Boom! Boom!

Robert looked back in alarm and then laughed louder as the shots of the pursuing boat fell far to the rear and the right.

Boom! Boom!

The next shots were even further behind them. Robert relaxed, knowing the Union warship didn't stand a chance of catching them. The *Phantom* advanced at full speed for close to thirty minutes before Captain Bueller spoke into the tube again. "Half-speed, Billy boy. We showed them our heels again," he chuckled. Now that they were safe, his cocky arrogance was back. "Score another one for the *Phantom*." He winked at Robert. "Take us on to Nassau, boys."

Abby Livingston leaned against the railing of the passenger boat carrying her from Philadelphia to New York City. She never got tired of coming through the narrows on her way to the grand city. Dawn was just lighting the sky, casting a rosy hue over the white mansions lining both sides of the waterway. Green trees towered over sweeping emerald lawns. In the distance, the city emerged from the bay, church spires mingling with the masts of anchored ships. The city stood in stark contrast against the water, spotlighted by the morning sun.

"Beautiful," she whispered to herself, pushing back a strand of soft brown hair flecked with silver, her gray eyes flashing with excitement. She was traveling alone this trip and was finding it quite enjoyable. She had only been to New York City a couple of times since she lost her husband several years ago, and always with a friend. Her heart pounded with excitement as she envisioned the freedom of exploring the city on her own.

"I find I never get tired of the sight myself."

Abby started as a voice broke into her thoughts. She turned and smiled at the elegantly dressed man behind her. "I don't know how one could get weary of it. It's so exciting, so"—she searched for the right word—"alive!"

"That it is," the man chuckled. "Please allow me to introduce myself. My name is Marcus Clipper."

"Hello, Mr. Clipper. My name is Abigail Livingston." She turned once more to the view. "Is New York your home?"

"Since I was a boy," he replied. "Has it been long since you've visited our fair city, Mrs. Livingston?"

"At least three years."

"I'm afraid you'll find our city much changed."

Abby stared at him curiously. "That doesn't sound very positive."

Marcus shrugged his stooped shoulders. "I shall always love the grand city, but I'm afraid she's outgrown herself. The population has boomed out of control.

Poverty is rampant, in spite of the grandeur you see from here," he said, waving his hand toward the opulence they were gliding through. "There are still parts of New York that are as luxurious and artistic as Paris. Too much of it, though, seems to have been surrendered to barbarian types."

Abby hid a smile as he sniffed disdainfully. It was obvious which part of New York he hailed from. "Surely it can't be as bad as all that," she said.

Marcus tipped his hat and moved from the railing. "I will allow you to make your own judgments," he said. "You are obviously a lady of fine breeding and taste. If you are traveling alone, I urge you to exercise all possible caution. I'm afraid our city has become quite dangerous, especially for lone women." He smiled. "Welcome to New York City, Mrs. Livingston."

Abby looked around her in astonishment as the carriage that had met her at the wharf wove its way through the packed streets. She had always loved the hustle and bustle of New York, but there seemed to be a strange urgency and tension in the air that both gripped her and made her uncomfortable.

She leaned forward to talk to the driver, Cyrus Paxton. "Please do bring me up to date on the city," she asked. When he nodded pleasantly, she settled back. It would take them quite a little while to meander through the city. Paxton had already told her that Mrs. Stratford, the friend she was visiting, had been called away to a meeting but would return by dinner. They were in no hurry.

"The city is changing faster than most of us can keep up with," Paxton began. "The population is booming. The completion of the Erie Canal, the railroads going west, and cheap transportation from Europe has made it easy for folks to come here. Once they're here, they seem to stay."

Paxton turned the carriage. "The people with money are moving further out. The fancy shops and restaurants are following them."

"It doesn't look that much different," Abby observed. "Just more crowded."

"We're in the better part of the city," Paxton agreed. "You'll be wise to stay out of the lower wards. That's where all the trouble is." He spoke to the horses softly to calm them as children ran shrieking in front of them. "They call that area the *'great workshop of the city.'* There are factories everywhere you look. Most of the city's industry is packed down there. So are most of New York's people." His voice was grim.

"Doesn't that make living conditions rather tight?" Abby asked. Philadelphia had some of the same problems, but instinctively she knew New York's were magnified.

"You could say that," Paxton said angrily. "I'm sorry. I didn't mean to sound like that."

"Do you have family down there?" Abby asked.

Paxton nodded. "Yes, ma'am. Most of my family lives there. I'm lucky, though. I have a place with the Stratfords. I was the first of our family to come over from Ireland about twenty years ago. I was fortunate enough to get a job as a driver for the Stratfords. I saved my money to help the rest of my family get here." He shook his head. "I almost wish I hadn't, even though the potato famine would have killed them. At least they would have died in their own country." His voice was bitter.

Abby realized they had drifted far from a narrative of the city, but she was intrigued by their discussion and filled with compassion because of the pain in Paxton's voice. "Is your family ill?"

Paxton clucked to the horses again and maneuvered around several wagons stopped in the middle of the street. "They're living in squalid poverty down there. At least in Ireland they had space and fresh air. They're no better than rats in a sewer down there in the East End. The Irish and the Germans are coming to New York in swarms, looking for an opportunity to make a life for themselves." His voice became hopeless. "But they don't have any skills and can't make enough money to improve their situation. I've been to London and seen the rookeries there. They don't have anything on New York slums."

Paxton looked back. "If you're a friend of Mrs. Stratford, I guess you're one of those women who care about people."

"I certainly am."

"You want to see how New Yorkers really live, you go down and look at some of the places they have the gall to charge money for. People are crammed in tiny, dark rooms like so many roaches. Some of the buildings are seven or eight stories high. Back behind them, you'll find a whole row of stalls they call lavatories. They aren't ever cleaned. Filth is everywhere. The roofs leak whenever it rains. They're freezing cold in the winter and suffocating in the summer."

His voice grew hoarse. "I have little nieces and nephews growing up in those pig holes," he said angrily. "There aren't any sewers down there. The filth just runs in the street and poisons the water supply." He was forced to stop and wait for an omnibus to rumble past. "Have you ever heard what they give the children to drink down there?"

Abby, already horrified at what she was hearing, was almost afraid to ask. She shook her head mutely.

"They call the stuff *'pure Orange County Milk,'* " he said disdainfully. "It comes from spavined old cows stuck in dirty, dark stalls. Those cows are fed on swill, the residue of grain left from the distillation of whiskey. When they milk them, they get this sick, whitish fluid, so they fix it up a little by adding starch, plaster of Paris, chalk and magnesia. That's what they call pure Orange County Milk."

"That's terrible! Surely the city is trying to do something about it," Abby protested.

"Maybe," Paxton shrugged, "but I think there is going to be trouble before the city does anything to help. I have a feeling it's too late."

"What kind of trouble?"

Paxton lowered his voice before he answered her. "I've heard some of the fellows talking. They're real angry. Have you heard about that Conscription Act, Mrs. Livingston?"

"Of course," Abby responded. Who didn't know about Lincoln's controversial decision to draft eligible men into the army? She understood the bill was needed if the North was going to continue fielding an army, but it was a radical departure from the long American tradition of voluntarism. Distrust of standing armies and centralized power ran so deep in the American mind that conscription inevitably aroused strong opposition. Loud protests were being heard all over the Union. There were strong charges being made that Lincoln was converting the North into a grand military dictatorship.

"Did you also know that a fellow with enough money can get out of the draft? They can either provide a substitute, or they can pay three hundred dollars. Either way, they don't have to serve."

"I remember reading that," Abby acknowledged.

"Well, it isn't fair!" Paxton burst out. "All the rich boys are going to stay home, while the men whose families need them to survive are going to be sent off to fight that war. Three hundred dollars is more than some of them make in a whole year. And you know the worst part of it?" he spat. "We're going down to fight for those colored slaves who are coming up here to take our jobs. Can you beat that?" He was getting wound up. "If it weren't for those coloreds, we wouldn't even be fighting this war. Now they're coming up here to take our jobs and drive wages down."

Abby stared at him, appalled at the hatred she saw flashing from his eyes. She chose her words carefully. "You do know that Mrs. Stratford is actively involved in fighting for the emancipation of the slaves, don't you?" She couldn't imagine her friend's employees would be unaware of her intense involvement.

Paxton sobered quickly. "I've been talking too much," he said, urging the carriage down the road at a faster clip.

Abby looked around, relieved to see they were out of the business district and climbing Gramercy Hill. She knew it was known as the most aristocratic quarter of the city. It still amazed her that her direct, down-to-earth friend lived here. Her husband, Wallace, had done extremely well in real estate. They had bought a mansion on the hill several years earlier.

"Are you going to tell Mrs. Stratford what I've been saying?" Paxton asked anxiously. He shook his head. "I know better than to run off at the mouth like that. Sometimes I just can't seem to help myself. I guess it's my Irish blood," he said ruefully.

Abby knew adding to his fears wouldn't help the situation any. "I don't think it's necessary to tell Mrs. Stratford of our conversation." She wasn't content to leave it there, though. "Do you really carry such intense hatred against the coloreds, Mr. Paxton?"

He had the grace to look uncomfortable. "Sometimes I get so much anger built up inside of me that I feel like I'm going to explode."

"And they're a convenient people to explode on?" Abby didn't wait for him to answer. "Wouldn't it be better to take that energy and figure out a way to improve things, rather than wanting to take your anger out on a people who are struggling as hard as you are?"

"It's not that easy."

"I don't recall saying anything about it being easy," Abby retorted. "Anything worth having is worth fighting for." She paused. "We're not really so different, Mr. Paxton. I realize I have more money, but you have the vote. There are many things you take for granted that, because I'm a woman, I can't have or do. I'm sure if I looked around, I could find someone to take my anger out upon. I find I prefer trying to force change."

The carriage rolled up in front of a huge brick mansion with large white columns and a sweeping drive. Paxton pulled the carriage to a halt and stepped out. He stood silently for a long moment, looking at her steadily. "I see what you're saying, Mrs. Livingston. I'll think about it." He paused. "I appreciate you not saying anything to Mrs. Stratford. I'd sure hate to lose my job."

The front door opened. "Abby! It's so wonderful to see you."

"Nancy!" Abby cried. "I thought you were in a meeting. I wasn't expecting you to be here." She smiled fondly as her petite, blonde friend hurried to give her an embracing hug.

"They canceled it at the last minute. I hurried home so I could meet you." Nancy turned to Paxton. "Please carry Mrs. Livingston's things up to the blue room on the second floor." She turned back to Abby. "You haven't changed a bit."

"With the exception of several more lines in my face," Abby retorted. "You look wonderful. Being wealthy becomes you," she teased.

"Hogwash," Nancy snorted. "Still know how to get me riled, don't you?" She grabbed Abby's arm and pulled her forward. "Do come in. I have tea ready for us. There is so much to talk about."

Abby followed, trying to push away her heavy feelings after her conversation with Paxton. People were predicting trouble over the Conscription Act. Would it be here in New York City?

Abby finished her cup of tea and set the fine Dresden china down carefully. "I want you to tell me all about the meeting of the Loyal Women of the Nation in May. I was sick that I couldn't attend, but my business demanded I be there. I can't believe it's been over a month." She shook her head and leaned forward eagerly. "I hear wonderful things happened."

Nancy reached for a piece of paper on the table beside her. "Let me read you what Elizabeth Stanton and Susan B. Anthony wrote. I'm sure you will agree it bears their unmistakable imprint." She cleared her throat and began to read.

"'*At this hour the best word and work of every man and woman are imperatively demanded. To man, by common consent, is assigned the forum, the camp and field. What is woman's legitimate work, and how she may best accomplish it, is worth our earnest counsel with one another... Woman is equally interested and responsible with man in the settlement of this final problem of self-government; therefore let none stand idle spectators now.'"*

Abby smiled. "They have a way with words," she agreed. "I understand hundreds of women came."

Nancy nodded eagerly. "It was glorious...especially if you have any desire to be on the battlefield." She laughed merrily, then sobered. "You know the meeting took place less than two weeks after the defeat at Chancellorsville. Many of the women present had sent family off to fight. Needless to say, with emotions running so high, it was difficult to find common ground."

"Many of them thought women's rights should have no place in the meeting," Abby guessed. When Nancy nodded, she shook her head. "There must be a way to balance achieving rights for all people without diminishing the fight for emancipation."

"Some of the women didn't even think that fighting for suffrage had a place in the meeting."

"What?" Abby asked, astonished. "Surely they knew it would be on the agenda before they came—what with Mrs. Stanton and Miss Anthony running it."

Nancy shrugged. "That didn't seem to matter. Many of them felt our support of President Lincoln's policies was the sole issue, and all that mattered."

"You're right," Abby chuckled. "I'm sorry I missed the fireworks." She settled back in her chair again. "Since I've been called here to work, I'm assuming it was brought under control at some point."

"The women who spoke did so with an eloquence I've never heard until then. The speeches were direct and impassioned. By the time it was all over, they had actually brought that divergent crowd to some measure of agreement. The resolutions they adopted pledged their support to the government as long as it continued to wage a war for freedom." She paused, smiling. "Here's where you come in, Abby. They also pledged to collect a million signatures for a petition asking Congress to pass the Thirteenth Amendment."

"A *million* signatures!" Abby exclaimed. The very number stunned her. She knew Charles Sumner had introduced a constitutional amendment forever banning slavery. The Emancipation Proclamation had been a first step, but it only banned slavery in the areas still in rebellion. This would be the step the abolitionists had fought for from the beginning.

"In light of the recent string of Confederate victories, it seems uncertain whether the measure can command the needed two-thirds majority in both houses," Nancy explained. "Charles Sumner has asked for our help."

Aunt Abby was well aware of the tremendous effort it would take to collect a million signatures from the North. "What can I do?"

"We need as many women as possible who will lead groups of people to circulate the petitions. We have been making contacts with women as far away as California. We have a couple of women in Philadelphia, but none with the contacts you have." Nancy leaned over and took another long sip of tea. "Will you help us?"

"Of course," Aunt Abby said instantly. "Surely you knew I would."

"Why yes, but one always likes to be asked." Nancy grinned and set her cup back down. "I don't imagine you've heard from your young friend in Richmond? I know you had grown very fond of her."

Abby frowned. "I think of Carrie Cromwell every day. It breaks my heart to know that, but for this war, she would be living with me, going to medical school right now. It drives me crazy not to know if she is all right. I have such mixed feelings when I hear of campaigns against Richmond. I so want this war to be over, and I realize the only sure way to abolish slavery is for us to win, but I ache inside to think she is trapped in that beleaguered city." Her voice caught. "I love her like a daughter."

Nancy laid a sympathetic hand on her arm. "And Rose and Moses?" she asked. "You wrote me about them, too."

Aunt Abby smiled. "I got a letter from Rose last week. She has a beautiful, healthy baby boy. His name is John Samuels." Her brow creased. "She hasn't heard from Moses since he headed north to join back up with the Union Army. He doesn't even know he has a child."

"One more question," Nancy continued. "Have you heard recently from that young journalist friend of yours?"

"Matthew Justin?" Abby responded with a fond smile. "I got a short note from him a few days ago. Of course, it was weeks old. He's down in Mississippi covering the campaign to take Vicksburg." She sighed. "I know we all have to do our part during these crazy times, but I can't help hoping this will all be over soon."

"Don't we all?" Nancy murmured. "Don't we all."

"My turn to ask questions," Abby interjected. "How is your son, Michael?"

"I'm doing wonderfully, Aunt Abby," a strong, young voice boomed into the room. "It's great to see you."

Abby jumped up and wrapped her arms around the strapping six-footer grinning down at her. "Michael! You look marvelous," she cried. "It's such a joy to have someone call me Aunt Abby again. I'm afraid all of the young people I care about have been swallowed up by this dreadful war."

"I've been lucky," Michael said cheerfully, reaching down to pick up some cakes left on the tea tray.

"Being a policeman in this violent town is hardly what I would call lucky," Nancy sighed, rolling her eyes.

"Now, Mother," Michael said casually, "you're the one who taught me to care about people and to fight against wrong. Would you rather I turn my back on my upbringing?"

Abby looked at the young man she had known since he was a toddler. His dark eyes shone with confidence under his thatch of brown curls. "I've heard disturbing things about the New York police department," she said tentatively, hoping she wouldn't offend Michael, but always curious to know the truth beyond headlines.

"They're probably all true," Michael acknowledged willingly. "I'm afraid the department doesn't have a stellar reputation. Until a few years ago, policemen were little more than political pawns, and appointments were bought. Things are different now," he said.

"Their hours are ridiculously long, and the pay is so pathetic that most of the better policemen are leaving the force to seek better wages," Nancy interjected. "*That's* what he calls better."

Michael nodded easily. "It's true. Wartime inflation is doing little to help, but the force has still reached a level of efficiency high above any we've known before." He grinned and patted his mother on the head affectionately. "It's a good thing I don't need the city's money." He grew more serious. "New York City is my home. For all its faults, I still think it's the best place in the world to live. I'm determined to do my part to see it improve."

Michael sat down in one of the chairs, his muscular form dwarfing the dainty furniture. "I don't intend to always be a policeman, Aunt Abby," he said earnestly. "I have a college education. I intend to join Dad in his real estate business, but I couldn't see hiding behind my parents' money during the war. I'm one of the lucky ones—I have enough money to get out of fighting—but that doesn't mean I can't find a way to make a difference." He shrugged, his cheerful grin once again lighting his handsome features. "Until then, my wonderful parents will have to endure my profession. I'll make them proud someday."

"We're proud of you now," Nancy protested. "We're just so worried," she said, a catch in her throat. "The city is becoming so violent." She turned to Abby. "Riots are increasing. People are restless. Inflation is horrible." She shook her head. "I can't get rid of the feeling that our whole city is about to explode. It's probably silly..."

Abby was silent, wondering if she should tell Nancy what her driver, Paxton, had said. Not wanting to add more unnecessary worry, she decided to say nothing.

"Enough about New York City," Michael said, reaching over to take the rest of the cakes. He grinned at his mother, who was looking at him with lifted eyebrows. "I'm hungry," he said, shoving them in. Then he turned back to Abby. "Tell us about Philadelphia. From all the reports I hear, the Rebel troops are uncomfortably close to your fair city. Did you come here to get away?" He threw back his head and laughed heartily. "You don't have to answer that question. The Aunt Abby I know would probably grab a rifle from the nearest soldier and race out to meet them herself. Am I right?" he teased.

"If I thought there was any real reason for concern, I wouldn't have come," Abby admitted with a smile. "Michael, it's so good to be with you. It simply does my heart good to be around young people." *Even if it does make me miss Carrie, Rose, Moses and Matthew more,* she added silently.

Nancy leaned forward. "Do tell us more about the Rebel troops. I can't believe they are invading Pennsylvania."

"Invading Pennsylvania might be stating it a little strongly," Abby replied. "So far there has been no fighting. General Lee seems to be roaming around, getting food and supplies for his troops. General Hooker is following him. It doesn't seem to me that either of them are eager for a fight."

"But so close to your city," Nancy protested.

Abby shrugged. "I've talked to a lot of people. I agree with them that Lee is not foolish enough to attack Philadelphia. He knows he could never hope to win so far from his base of supplies. His army simply isn't strong enough. No, there may be a battle yet, but it won't be in Philadelphia." She pushed down the feeling of discomfort she had since she entered New York City. Why did it continue to persist?

Chapter Eleven

Moses was answering a summons to Captain Jones' tent when an angry voice erupted into the sweltering night.

"Don't you know those blacks are nothing but trouble? I don't know whose idea it was to put uniforms on those woolly-headed creatures, but it's surely not one I support."

Moses frowned as he recognized Lieutenant O'Malley's voice. It was no secret the raucous Irishman had no use for black soldiers. He went out of his way to make life miserable for the men who had to fight for him. Since it was impossible for Moses to be commissioned as an officer because he was black, O'Malley was their commanding officer. Captain Jones had made it clear Moses was the actual leader of the black soldiers, and O'Malley's resentment was growing.

"I'm not interested in your support of the idea," Captain Jones said coldly. "I frankly could care less what your personal opinion of the situation is. All I'm interested in is you obeying my orders."

Moses wondered if he should disappear for a little while. O'Malley would most likely not appreciate knowing one of the men he had the misfortune to lead had heard him being bawled out by his commander. Captain Jones' next words held him where he was.

"General Lee is going to make one final attack tomorrow. He may have won the battle two days ago, but today was a clear defeat for him. Lee isn't used to losing. He will try again, but he only has the strength for one more attempt. General Meade believes he will strike hard at the center since he wasn't successful in taking either flank today." Captain Jones paused and Moses leaned in to listen. "I want Moses and his men in the right of the defense. They are excellent shots, and I know they'll stand their ground."

"You want me to lead that bunch of woolly-heads against Lee's strongest attack?" O'Malley protested. "When are you going to give me leadership of white men again?" His voice was bitter. "It's getting to the point where a black man is considered better than a white man."

"That will be enough!" Captain Jones snapped. "If you want to maintain your command of *anyone*, you will do as I order, and do it right." His voice softened slightly. "I don't know why you have so much hatred in you, Lieutenant. It's not like your own people haven't struggled to fit into American society. I would think you would have sympathy for the black condition."

"I can't seem to drum up any sympathy when it's my own countrymen who are being slaughtered to try to help these woolly-heads be free. It's not our fight!"

"I will not have you call them woolly-heads one more time," Captain Jones snapped. "As far as I'm concerned, all it does is show your ignorance. If I had my way, the black troops would have black commanders, but no one has asked my opinion." He continued, his voice clipped. "And in case you have forgotten, this war is not being fought to free the slaves. It is being fought to save the Union. Lincoln brought blacks into the army to help. I would think you would welcome their presence."

"Why are you so much in favor of them?" O'Malley asked suddenly, his voice deeply suspicious.

"Because they're people," Captain Jones responded. "Just like you and me. I could say I feel sorry for them because they've suffered so much, and even though I do, that's not why I respect them. Every black soldier I have worked with has been a good man. They are committed to winning this war and will do everything I ask them without questioning."

"What's the connection with you and that Moses fellow?" O'Malley pressed.

There was a brief pause. "Moses is a fine man, and he's a good soldier. He also saved my life. I'll never forget that."

Moses frowned. He appreciated Captain Jones' words, but he also knew they would only serve to make O'Malley more antagonistic toward him. Moses had managed to hold his temper in check so far. He hoped he could continue to do so.

The door to the tent flapped back suddenly and O'Malley strode out. He cast a baleful look in Moses' direction but didn't say anything. Moses watched the angry man as he stalked off to his own campsite. He was thoughtful as he entered the captain's tent.

"You hear much of that?" Captain Jones asked.

"Enough."

"Don't worry about it, Moses. It's going to take time for some of the men to accept black soldiers."

"We don't have any illusions about how people see us," Moses responded. "We realize the contempt and hatred our 'liberators' hold for us," he said sardonically. "I guess Frederick Douglass said it best for us." He paused and then recited what he had memorized to share with his men.

"*'Once let the black man get upon his person the brass letter, U.S.; let him get an eagle on his button, and a musket on his shoulder, and bullets in his pocket, and there is no power on earth which can deny that he has earned the right to citizenship in the United States.'*"

Moses smiled. "Me and my men figure that when we put on a United States uniform, we at last had a country. We can put up with a lot for that."

"Good," Captain Jones said briskly. "You've got a big job ahead of you tomorrow." He stared down at his papers. "I don't know that either of our armies actually intended to fight here at Gettysburg, but now that we're here, it's time to turn the table on the Rebels. The few reports filtering through from Vicksburg say things are going well there. It's time for the Army of the Potomac to claim a solid victory. This is our chance."

"General Meade seems willing to press the advantage," Moses observed.

"Exactly," Captain Jones responded with relief. "Hooker was a good man, but he didn't seem able to grab what we needed. The Union doesn't need any more reports like the one they got after Chancellorsville."

"We seem to be in a better position this time."

"We have a fine defensive position," Captain Jones agreed. "General Lee seems willing to take the offensive, which is fine. We have such a strong position, it would be foolhardy to relinquish it. No, I'm afraid General Lee is going to discover how we felt at Fredericksburg."

Moses winced. He had heard the reports of Fredericksburg—the thousands of Union soldiers that had been slaughtered trying to storm an impregnable Rebel defense. "I don't wish that on anyone," he muttered.

"Nor I, but if it's going to happen, I'd much rather be on this side of it."

Moses was already wiping sweat from his face as the morning sun exploded onto the day. Dust and smoke from the previous day's battle lingered in the air, and there was the stench of decaying bodies. He gazed right and saw wave after wave of blue uniforms spread across Cemetery Ridge. The left presented the same picture. Sunlight glinted off the artillery backing them up. The whole line was protected by stone walls, piled fence rails and hastily erected breastworks.

He swung his gaze down the hill they were fighting to hold. He scowled as he took in the half mile of open, slanting fields the Rebels would have to cross to get to them. The Federals had a clear range of fire. There was nothing to offer protection to the men who would soon be surging across it. Did they really think they could take such a formidable position?

Moses turned away and leaned against the stone wall, munching hungrily on the hardtack he had pulled from his haversack. His gut told him the Confederate attack wasn't coming anytime soon. He was content to let his mind roam for a while. As usual, it turned immediately to Rose. And to John. A smile played across his lips as he tried to envision his little son. The letter informing him of his birth had come ten days before. Now more than ever, he wanted this war to be over. The ache of missing Rose was now multiplied by the agony of having a child he had never seen.

"Thinkin' 'bout that boy of yours again?"

Moses turned to Pompey. "How'd you know?"

"You got that silly grin on again. Ain't nothin' but that little boy of yours could make a man smile on a day like today." Pompey squinted over the wall. "How long you figure we got to wait before the devil breaks loose 'round here?"

Moses shrugged. "I don't see any movement down there. It could be a long day."

"I reckon every day done been a long one," Pompey grunted. "We got less than sixty men left out of near ninety. Talkin' 'bout dying and watchin' yer friends die sho do be diff'rent things." He gazed off into the distance, then brightened. "But I figure this here war ain't gonna go on forever. I reckon we gonna turn some things around this summer, sho 'nuff."

The morning passed slowly, the sound of fighting in the distance dying away before lunchtime. And still the awaited attack didn't come. An uneasy silence settled over the blistering landscape. It was as if even the earth was holding its breath in horrified anticipation of what was soon to erupt. The birds fell silent. The wispy breeze died completely away. Moses could feel his breath coming in shallow spurts. Every muscle in his body was coiled tight, screaming for release in some kind of action. His mind raced and then dulled as he strained to catch some hint of what was coming. He looked around at the men lolling on the ground eating, reading, writing letters home. Didn't they feel it? Didn't they know what was about to descend on them?

Boom!

The single shot in the distance caused Moses to roll over and stare off toward the woods. The single shell sailed over the ridge, exploding harmlessly in the distance. Suddenly, the entire wood they faced exploded in a dazzling blaze of light and cacophonous sound. The Confederate attack had begun.

Moses rolled over and flattened himself against the ground as the Rebel artillery blasted their position. He watched in horror as soldiers who had moments before been resting were now obliterated before his eyes. One man, still grasping his book, stumbled to his feet and dashed for cover. Seconds later, a shell exploded directly in front of him. His now limp body sailed through the air, tumbling to a halt feet from Moses' position. Moses felt sick as he stared into the gaping eyes of death.

Horses fell all around, giving shrieking cries before they collapsed. Shards of fence posts, splintered into missiles, filled the air. Chunks of earth darkened the air like a black cloud, blinding men who were hurrying to take their position. Moses gritted his teeth, certain he had descended into the fiery pit itself. Added to the din of the Confederate fire was the answering roar of the Federal artillery. The hissing and shrieking sound of missiles and exploding projectiles seemed to blot out any other reality. The shells fell like hailstones charged with exploding fire. Sulfurous smoke permeated the air, causing him to choke and gasp for air. He rolled over and pressed his face closer to the ground, relieved to find tiny pockets of fresh air. He was quite certain there would be no Confederate advance until the artillery barrage finished. Any orders were lost in the incessant clamor.

Two hours later, the artillery finally ceased. Moses felt as if an eternity of time and death had passed over his head. His lungs screamed for fresh air, his face was thick with grimy soot, his eyes bleary from smoke.

"Here they come, boys!" a loud voice called through the smoke. "Let's show them we're not finished!"

Moses recognized Captain Jones' voice, and his spirits lifted. He wasn't sure if he was the only living person still on the ridge. As he lifted his head, he gazed about in astonishment. The destruction spread out behind him was so horrible as to be unbelievable. Horses and cannon lay piled in hideous heaps. Wagons were splintered and the bodies of mutilated men lay everywhere. But the infantry line! Moses stared in surprise as wave after wave of blue uniforms raised from the ground and took their position along the line. Most of the destructive shell had gone right over their heads.

"The enemy is advancing!" came another loud cry.

Moses turned and lifted his head high enough to peer over the stone wall. He froze in horror. Hundreds of Confederate soldiers, their gray uniforms a dull moving mass of iron, swept toward them across the open fields. Man touched man, rank pressed rank, and line supported line. Red flags waved defiantly, while horsemen galloped up and down. Gun barrels and bayonets flashed in the sun. They seemed to move as one soul, in perfect order.

"Hold your fire, men!" came the sharp order.

Moses gripped his rifle, unable to take his eyes from the drama unfolding before him. Silence extended down the lines beside him. Then, slowly, he could hear the click of the lock as men raised their hammers to feel the cap on the nipple. The rattle of stones penetrated the quiet as men raised their muskets over the stone wall, taking aim. The squeaking of iron axles penetrated the silence as the big guns were rolled up closer to the front.

He tore his eyes away and glanced around, searching. He saw it then—the grand flag waving in gay defiance at the scores of men approaching who would rob it of half its stars and divide the Union it stood for. Moses' heart swelled with pride as he realized he was fighting for his country. *His country!*

"Do not hurry, men. Don't fire too fast. Let them come up close before you fire, and then aim low and steady."

Moses turned back to the approaching storm as a commanding general rode by. His pulse was steady now, his head clear. His hands were firm as he aimed his musket at the nearing wave of Rebels. He knew they were outnumbered, yet they held the stronger position. There was not a man in the Federal line who would give a quarter.

The artillery guns blazed behind them. Moses peered through the smoke, still awaiting the order to fire. Great holes were torn in the Confederate advance but were quickly filled. The gray wave moved inexorably on.

"Fire!"

The infantry line exploded in grim defiance. Mounds of gray uniforms littered the ground in front of them, and still the Rebels pushed on. Moses fired, reloaded, aimed.

and fired again. His hands were steady, though his heart was pounding hard. The Confederates responded with fire of their own, still moving forward. Men fell all around Moses, their shrieks and calls adding to the confusion.

Finally, the Confederate advance stumbled in the face of such destructive firepower. Men fought to clamber over the bodies of their stricken comrades, and then were shot down themselves. Thick clouds of smoke added to the confusion.

"They're turning back!" a soldier to Moses' right yelled in triumph.

"We got them on the run!" another screamed hoarsely.

Moses continued to fire steadily and watched in relief as the giant gray wave, diminished in size, turned and began to flow back toward the woods they had exploded from earlier. They seemed to leave behind as many as were retreating.

"We licked 'em boys!" a man hollered.

"Score one for the Army of the Potomac!" another called.

The Battle of Gettysburg was over.

Matthew Justin ran a tired hand over his thick red beard and hair, and stretched his lanky body. Once again, he vowed to never spend another summer in the South for as long as he lived. Swarms of mosquitoes were his constant companion and thirst dogged every step. His clothes, even close to this midnight hour, were soaked with sweat, and the air hung heavy. He longed for a thunderstorm to break the sullen hold Mother Nature had on the great Mississippi Valley.

"I sure hope General Grant finishes this soon," Peter Wilcher muttered. "I'm not sure I can stand one more day in Mississippi. I didn't know it was possible to breathe water, but that's exactly what this feels like. I want to get my story written for the paper and head north."

Matthew smiled sympathetically at his fellow journalist. "I'm with you. I know how important Vicksburg is to the Union, but I'm about to suggest they give it up and leave it to the Rebels. I feel sorry for the poor suckers left behind to hold it."

Peter nodded emphatically, swatting at another mosquito. "Them, and the pitiful soldiers left to watch over those refugee camps. I don't envy them their job."

Matthew grimaced, thinking about Rose, glad the contraband camp she was staying in was better than the ones he had witnessed in Mississippi.

"I wouldn't want my worst enemy in some of those camps," Peter continued. "I went down to cover one for the paper a few days ago. I almost gagged just walking through it. They're nothing more than slums in the woods." He shook his head. "And they still keep coming."

"They don't know what else to do," Matthew replied. "It's like they've seen the Red Sea part. They can see clear to the other side, so they're just walking on through."

"Yes, but a bunch of them aren't making it to the other side," Peter retorted. "Why, the camp I was at yesterday, they're dying off by the dozens every day. Disease is decimating them." He shook his head. "It's horrible."

Matthew didn't bother to argue. He had seen firsthand the horror of the Mississippi contraband camps. The sad thing was that there was really no one to blame. The government was doing the best they could, but they simply hadn't been prepared for the responsibility thrust on them. Thousands of ex-slaves had left their plantations in search of the freedom they heard was promised them. They came to the army camps because, for the moment, they were totally helpless. Traits such as self-reliance and initiative had gone undeveloped under slavery. They came because they could think of nowhere else to go and knew only that they had to be on their way somewhere. They were lured by the blind hope of a better life than the one they were fleeing.

"It seems to me like they're worse off than they were under slavery," Peter observed. "They should have stayed put."

"They might have been better off physically," Matthew agreed, "but they are running from what slavery did to their minds and their hearts. I've talked to several of them. They agree their conditions are horrible, but at least there is a hope before them. Before they had no hope—only the knowledge they and their children would forever be in bondage. They need help, but they're willing to work to help change things. A lot of them have no idea what they have to do, but they're willing to do it."

Peter shook his head. "Some of our soldiers treat them worse than their owners did."

Matthew scowled. "I know. I think they all ought to be quartered and shot. To take advantage of a people so totally helpless is despicable."

"You really care about these people, don't you?" Peter asked. "They're more than just a story for the *Philadelphia Tribune.*"

"I care about them," Matthew agreed. "They're people. They have the same right to be Americans that we do. They didn't ask to be brought here, but now that they are, they want to be treated as human beings. It's no more than you and I want for ourselves and our children." He knew he was being brusque, but he had been ridiculed too much lately by fellow journalists. "There's a lot of people up north who think the slaves ought to be free, but they don't want them to come up there, and they certainly don't want to be responsible for them."

"What's so wrong with that?" Peter asked, raising his hands in self-defense when Matthew glared at him fiercely. "I'm not saying I agree with them, but I can understand how they feel. It's not really their problem."

"It's everyone's problem," Matthew snapped. "The North might not have had slaves for a while, but until recently they've done nothing to stop the ownership of millions of people in the South. If it wasn't for this war and the Emancipation Proclamation, they still wouldn't be seeing it as a problem, because they wouldn't think it was *their* problem. Anytime people—*any* kind of people—lose their basic human rights, it becomes everyone's problem. We live in a country founded on our desire for freedom. Everyone wants freedom for themselves, but they're not very quick to jump to the defense of someone else who has their freedom stolen."

"But look at all the men fighting this war," Peter protested. "They're fighting for freedom."

"They're fighting because their country is at war," Matthew retorted. "If you sat most of them down, they probably couldn't even tell you what it's all about, except that they have to bring those crazy Rebels under control. Don't get me wrong," he added, "there are a lot of them fighting for the right reasons, but there are way too many who aren't." He paused, staring into the starry sky dimmed by thick humidity hanging in the air. "There weren't very many who went into this war thinking to free the slaves, but the war has changed."

"I think everyone has gotten much more than they bargained for," Peter agreed. "What started out as a fight to save the Union has become nothing more than a remorseless revolution. It's going to change the face of America for everyone. When it's all over, most of us probably won't even recognize our own country."

A sudden shout startled Matthew. "What in the world was that?"

Seconds later, a form materialized out of the darkness. "It's over, boys!"

Matthew sprang to his feet. "What's over?"

"The fight for Vicksburg. The siege finally wore them down." The messenger grinned.

Matthew wasn't surprised. The question in his mind had never been *if* Vicksburg would fall, but *when*. The besieged city had been under relentless bombardment for almost a month and a half. Their people were hungry and demoralized. General Grant's engineers had been bringing the Federal trenches closer and closer to the Confederate works, digging tunnels and planting mines to blow up strong points. The Confederates trying to hold the line to the city had fought long and hard, but finally the walls around Jericho had come tumbling down.

"Was it unconditional surrender?" Peter pulled out his pad and began writing, his eyes shining in the firelight.

"No, but darn close," the messenger answered. "Pemberton is surrendering everything. His only qualification was that his soldiers be released on parole instead of being sent north to our prison camps."

"The Rebels are probably so disheartened they'll go home anyway," Matthew observed.

"That's what Grant figures," the messenger agreed. "Plus the fact that the logistics necessary to ship thirty-one thousand prisoners north was more than he wanted to deal with." He moved off and then turned around. "Get ready for a party, boys. We go in to take the city tomorrow. Independence Day. Fitting, don't you think?" He chuckled before disappearing into the dark to continue spreading his message.

Matthew and Peter sat silently for several minutes, relishing the news they had just heard. Matthew finally broke the quiet. "I guess you get your wish. Will you head north for your next assignment?"

"Yes. I'll cover the surrender of the town, and then I'll get out of here. I won't even give them a chance to wire my next location. I have to get somewhere I can breathe again." Peter stuck a wad of tobacco in his mouth. "What about you? Where to from here?"

"I'm going back to Philadelphia," Matthew said. "I'm feeling the need for civilization like you. I've also got a friend there who is heavily involved in the supplying of contraband camps. Aunt Abby will see that some supplies are sent down for the poor people in these refugee camps. Then," he added, picking up a stick and tossing it into the fire, "I guess I'll move on to wherever the next hot spot is."

"No girl you're going to see while you're there?" Peter questioned.

Matthew shook his head, not willing to respond to the casual teasing. Carrie was still a sore spot for him. He realized the girl he loved cared for another man, but that didn't change his heart. He was hoping time and distance would take care of it. That, and constant hard work. He looked for a way to change the subject. "Lincoln might get what he wants this summer after all."

"You think the war could end this summer?" Peter asked skeptically. "Haven't you noticed this is the first major battle to be won so far this year?"

Matthew shrugged. "Maybe. We haven't heard the most recent reports. Meade is chasing around with Lee up in Pennsylvania. Rosecrans is bound to make his move in Tennessee at some point." He paused. "Losing Vicksburg is a mortal wound to the Confederacy. With the Mississippi open, they simply don't have the power to establish an independent government. It can never be done between the Mississippi and the Atlantic. No," he said shaking his head, "I think the Confederacy is an impossibility."

"Would you mind riding to Richmond and telling Jefferson Davis that? It might save the lives of a lot of our men."

"I've seen all of Richmond I want to see for a while," Matthew grinned. "I find the hospitality of their prisons leaves much to be desired."

Peter nodded. "I heard you spent some time in one of their fair facilities."

"Libby Prison. I hope never to see the place again. At least not as a prisoner. It would be nice to cover its destruction someday. I think I'll let President Davis come to his own conclusions. I'm afraid, though, that he won't see things as clearly as I do."

Peter laughed heartily. "Let's get some sleep. We have a lot of work to do before we leave this swampland."

Early on the morning of July 6, Matthew loaded onto a boat with several other journalists. They had almost pushed off, when Peter appeared carrying his bag and leapt on board. "Heading north?" he grinned.

"You got it." Matthew grinned in return. He was suddenly feeling light at heart. The pity he felt for the citizens of Vicksburg when he saw their demolished city and viewed the impoverished people was fading with the excitement of going home. He had written his stories. He would deliver them himself and then see what the future held for him. *After* a huge dinner at Aunt Abby's, he reminded himself.

They had gone less than two miles up the river when a barrage of fire exploded from the wooded banks of the secluded curve they were rounding.

"What's that?" Peter exclaimed.

"Everybody down!" Matthew hit the floor of the tugboat they were riding in, scanning the woods to catch a glimpse of their attackers.

"It's Rebels!" one of the crew members cried. "Man the gun."

The tugboat they were passengers in had a single gun on board, hardly capable of withstanding a Confederate attack. What in the world were they doing, anyhow? Didn't they know the Mississippi was lost? That Vicksburg had fallen? Obviously, they were intent on doing whatever damage they could.

Another shot exploded near them, sending a spray of water cascading over the deck.

"If we take a direct hit, this barge is gonna sink," Peter said anxiously.

Matthew gritted his teeth but didn't answer. The thick cover of the woods completely hid the Rebel position. Even if he had a rifle, it would do no good. They were at the gunners' mercy.

A high shrieking whistle told him another round was in the air. He ducked just as the boat shuddered and lurched to one side.

"We're hit!" a crew member cried. "There's a hole in the portside. We're taking on water, Captain!"

Another shot exploded seconds later. The boat lurched again violently, and then the engines died.

"I'm afraid the game's up," the captain said grimly.

"Don't give up now," Peter cried. "I have a nice soft bed waiting for me. Can't you get some life into this baby?"

"They'll probably sink the boat and send you on your way," the captain replied, shaking his head. "Me and my crew probably have some beds waiting in a Yankee prison. They don't take journalists much, though. You'll be on your way home soon." He shook his head. "If I thought we could take them, I'd fight till the death, but we're not a fighting ship. I thought we were just shipping some journalists north. I'm not going to get all my men killed." Solemnly, he hoisted the white flag of surrender.

Matthew listened with a sinking heart, trying to take hope from the captain's belief they would be released. He could wait a few more days for Aunt Abby's cooking.

A swarm of Rebel soldiers burst from the woods and tumbled down the bank into their waiting boats. Soon the tilting tugboat was surrounded.

The captain and his crew were loaded into one of the boats and then the commanding officer for the Rebels turned to Matthew. "And who do we have here?" he asked cockily.

"We are Northern journalists," Matthew responded pleasantly, albeit a bit stilted. "We will find another way to return to our newspapers."

"I'm afraid that won't be possible," the lieutenant said genially, his hard eyes belying his pleasant tone.

"Why not?" Peter asked.

"I'm afraid your government is holding some rather important prisoners right now, but they are fairly open to prisoner exchanges. I reckon you boys ought to be worth something to the Yankees."

"But we're not soldiers," Matthew protested. "We're civilians."

"Then you shouldn't be hanging around in war zones," the lieutenant snapped, all pretense of geniality gone. He turned to his men. "Guard these men. We have a long trip ahead of us. I think there are some special places waiting for them in Richmond."

He turned to the group staring at him. "Ever heard of Libby Prison?"

Chapter Twelve

Carrie met the courier at the door to her hospital ward.

"Please deliver this to the doctor in charge," the youthful courier urged.

Carrie wanted to ask questions but silently reached for the sheet of paper he was holding. She had heard bells ringing in the city, their wild clanging reaching up to the heights of Chimborazo. What was happening now?

Dr. Wild appeared beside her. "What is it?"

Carrie handed him the sheet of paper. "This was just delivered. The courier said it was very urgent."

Dr. Wild opened it and began to read. "'*TO ARMS! REMEMBER NEW ORLEANS! Richmond is now in your hands. Let it not fall under the rule of another BUTLER. Rally, then, your officers tomorrow morning at ten o'clock, on BROAD Street, in front of the City Hall.*'"

"There are no military men here," Carrie said sharply.

"There's an addendum from the mayor." Dr. Wild sighed. "I have instructions to send whatever soldiers are able."

Carrie spun around and looked at the rows of wounded soldiers staring at them, straining to hear the latest news. "They're not going anywhere," she cried.

Dr. Wild looked grim. "We'll let that be their choice. They might feel rather strongly about being in a Union-occupied city. The reports coming in are not good. Union cavalry is once more doing their mischief. Evidently they are trying our tactics of threatening the Capitol in an attempt to pull Lee out of Pennsylvania. They are once more cutting the railroads and burning homes. Several plantations along the river have been torched."

Carrie whitened. Was her beloved Cromwell Plantation still standing? What would she and her father find when they were finally able to go home?

Dr. Wild gripped the piece of paper more firmly and turned to the hundred soldiers in his ward. "Listen up, men," he called. He read the missive in a loud, clear voice. "I will not order anyone to report," he said. "It is your decision."

Silence fell on the ward as the wounded men digested the news.

"Do we know what's happening with General Lee yet?" one called.

"What about Vicksburg?" another asked.

"I'd rather be fighting," called one legless man. "At least then I had some idea of what was going on."

Dr. Wild stepped to the center of the ward so he could be more easily heard. "We still have nothing but rumors to go on," he said. "It really depends on what story you want to listen to."

"There is one report," Carrie admitted, "that Lee's army has been practically destroyed and is in full retreat."

"Another report," added Dr. Wild, "says that Meade's army was destroyed, and Lee has taken forty thousand prisoners." He smiled. "Take your pick, men."

"What about Vicksburg?" another called again.

"There have been reports that Grant is being beaten back," Carrie said. "And then there are reports..."

"That we lost the city?" one soldier asked.

Carrie nodded, understanding the frustration her patients were feeling. They had sacrificed the best parts of themselves for a cause they believed in, or were at least willing to fight for, and now they lay helpless, not even able to learn what was happening. She was watching the same explosive frustration build in her father.

One soldier, his arm in a cast, struggled to his feet. "Well, I'm not just gonna lie here. Somebody get me a gun. If those Yankees are coming in to take this city, they're going to have to put me out of commission again," he muttered defiantly.

About a quarter of the men agreed with him. Others knew they were too broken to be of any good. Others simply remained silent, the haunted look in their eyes saying they had seen enough horror for a lifetime. They were not going to voluntarily jump back into the fray.

Carrie turned away. She had her own frustrations to deal with. The Union blockade continued to tighten their stranglehold on the coast. The trickle of medicines had slowed even more. No matter the actual outcome of the battle at Gettysburg, the reality was that soon the hospitals would once more be bulging with wounded soldiers. They were only now recovering from the onslaught of men from Chancellorsville. Lee's move into Pennsylvania had indeed given the capital a reprieve, but the shortage of needed supplies had not improved—it had worsened.

Carrie spun around and walked outside, suddenly in need of fresh air. Any mention or thought of the blockade made her feel sick inside. There had been no word from Robert. Of course she knew mail was almost an impossibility, but still she hoped. Once again, she was gripped with the heart-wrenching uncertainty and unknowing that had held her last year. She had reached an uneasy peace with herself over her decision to stay in Richmond, but it did nothing to ease the aching of missing her husband.

Carrie walked to the edge of the plateau and gazed over the city spread out below, its seven hills shimmering in the heat. Would life ever return to some semblance of normality, or would they all continue to simply survive from one crisis to the next? The city was being worn down. Exhaustion dogged the expressions of everyone she met. General Lee may have lured the enemy away for the summer, but it was their husbands, sons and fathers he had used to lure them away, and now the uncertainty was eating away at their hearts.

"Mrs. Borden?"

Carrie spun around as someone spoke her name, glad for something to do, some question to answer. Activity had been her salvation. Carrie almost welcomed the idea that soon more wounded soldiers would swarm into the city. At least then she wouldn't have the time or energy to focus on her own problems. "Yes, Greta. What can I do for you?"

"Some of the women have come back from a trip into the woods," the plain, stocky woman replied.

"Wonderful!" Carrie exclaimed. She had been training a group of women to identify herbs and other plants. Guarded by some of the home militia, they were making forays into the woods on gathering trips. Carrie was determined to do everything she could to bolster the faltering supply of medicines. "Tell them I will be with them soon."

"Yes, ma'am."

Carrie watched Greta walk away and turned back to her purveyance of the city. A sharp clanging of bells erupted again. It seemed like the city was in a constant state of alarm. Shaking her head, she turned away. She was needed to help the women verify the identity of the plants.

"I hear the women have returned from the woods."

Carrie nodded as Janie walked up to join her. "They are becoming quite efficient. It won't make up for everything the blockade is holding from us, but it will help."

"It's too bad some of it can't be used for the black hospital."

Carrie nodded. "The women down there are learning, too, but it's simply not safe for them to go outside the city. It's ridiculous that the hospital commission won't release some of the medicines to them," she said angrily.

Janie reached out and touched her arm but didn't say anything.

Carrie managed a short laugh. "Don't you get tired of my ranting sometimes?"

"No," Janie replied. "It's another example of how much you care. You've met with the commission twice, asking them to change their mind. There is nothing else you can do." She frowned. "This summer isn't so bad, but this winter is going to be hard. I'm afraid that's when the shortages are going to become even more critical. Everyone I've talked to says this is going to be another hard winter."

"There are still the herbs out at the plantation."

"You know your father would never let you go out there," Janie said. When Carrie didn't reply, Janie took her shoulders and turned Carrie to face her. "Please tell me you're not thinking of going out there. It's too dangerous. There is Union cavalry everywhere."

"They won't be there forever." Carrie had been thinking on a daily basis about all the herbs she had bottled and stored in the basement of Cromwell. She had been able to bring back a few on her trip out that winter. "I could take a wagon out," she said quietly. "There are enough herbs there to take care of the black hospital this winter."

"And what do you think the Union soldiers are going to do?" Janie cried. "Wave you on and tell you to have a nice trip? It's too dangerous, Carrie." Janie looked at her pleadingly. "Please tell me you won't do it."

"Not right away, anyway." Carrie said, determination building in her as she talked.

Carrie glanced up when her father slammed his way into the house. It was obvious from the look on his face there was no good news coming into the capital. She almost wished she could plug her ears, but it would do no good. "Bad news?" she asked tentatively.

Thomas turned to her with the bitter, angry look she was becoming accustomed to. Some days she had to struggle to remember the calm, loving father she had known on the plantation before her mother died, and before the war started.

"Vicksburg has fallen," he announced. "Secretary of War Seddon forwarded the official report today. Pemberton surrendered the city. The Union occupied it on the fourth of July."

"I'm sorry."

Thomas sank down into his chair. He stared out the darkened window unseeingly. "We heard from General Lee, too. He is retreating to Virginia. Gettysburg was a disaster. We suffered terrible losses."

Carrie was suddenly very glad Robert was out on the Atlantic somewhere. Envisioning him out there was much easier than imagining him killed on another battlefield. She searched for words that would make her father feel better, but she knew there were none.

"Union cavalry burned the railroad depot up at Ashland," he continued in a dead voice. "Train service has been severely disrupted."

Carrie watched him closely, her heart aching at the defeat and despair she saw etched on his face. She reached forward and took one of his hands, but he didn't seem to even notice her touch.

"Rosecrans is on the move in Tennessee," he said. "Bragg is being driven out." His voice cracked, and he lowered his head in his hands. "We're losing it all," he choked. "We're losing it all."

Carrie dropped to her knees and wrapped her arms around her father's trembling shoulders. He remained bowed for a few moments and then straightened abruptly. Carrie gazed up at the fire blazing in his eyes.

"We're not beaten yet," he cried defiantly, his fists clenched. "We'll regroup! We'll rebuild!" He stood and stalked to the window. "They will not come down here and destroy everything I've worked for all my life. They will not annihilate our society."

Carrie remained where she was kneeling, a sick heaviness pressing down on her. What was it going to take to end this war? The passions on both sides seemed to be growing, their darkness expanding until surely they would swallow everything in their path. Would it take the entire destruction of one side before the other was willing to capitulate? Would any of them recognize their country—or themselves—when this was all over?

Carrie was once more standing on the Chimborazo plateau when she saw the smoke from the first train approaching Richmond that morning. The muscles in her neck tensed and her head began to throb. She knew it was the first ambulance train from Gettysburg. Her stomach knotted as she imagined what would soon be rolling into the hospitals. Wounded soldiers fresh from the battlefield were gut-wrenching to see. Add to that almost a week of travel with little treatment, and you had all the ingredients for her worst nightmares.

Carrie took deep breaths of the still air and then hurried into her ward. The soldiers would be arriving soon. She wanted to make sure everything was ready for them, even though she had already checked a dozen times. Activity had once again become her salvation.

It was another hour before the first ambulance wagon rolled into the hospital. Close behind was a long line of conveyances stretching out of sight down around the curved hill. Dust rose in a rolling cloud above the road. Shimmering heat was already tightening its grip on the city. Carrie willed the drivers and aides to hurry. The men waiting in those wagons had suffered enough. Heat and choking dust would only add to their misery.

Soon, Carrie was bending over her first patient. "Hello, soldier," she said gently.

"Water," the man whispered. "Water." His wildly searching eyes fastened on her face for a moment. "How's our baby, Sally?" He gave a gasp of pain as Carrie pulled back a bandage to inspect a wound. "The cows need to be let out." A pause. "I reckon the corn is gonna be good this year."

Carrie fought the tears swelling in her eyes. The young soldier was conscious but securely in the grips of delirium. His roving eyes saw nothing, his grasping hands reached for nothing. "It's okay," she said soothingly. She took small comfort in knowing the soldier wasn't aware she was lying.

Carrie turned to look over her shoulder. "Hobbs!"

Hobbs was standing beside her a moment later, using just one crutch to steady himself on his good leg. "What can I do for you, Miss Carrie?"

"Hold him still," she ordered. "He is ravaged with infection." Quickly, she began to unwrap the filthy bandages from his arm and leg. Her stomach churned at the sight of maggots swarming through the angry, red areas. Tightening her lips, she went to work picking out the maggots and cleaning the wounds as best she could.

"This soldier needs morphine," she muttered angrily.

"Would you like me to get some?" Hobbs offered.

"No," Carrie said. "It is being reserved for the soldiers who need amputation. There is simply not enough to go around." She looked up. "Please get me some of the elder salve. It will help with the maggots." She reached down and put her hands on the man's shoulders to keep him from flailing around in his delirium. "And bring me some of the jimsonweed. We have to bring this man's fever down or it's will kill him."

"Don't let me go, Sally!" the man cried suddenly, bolting forward and breaking free of Carrie's grip. The expression on his face changed. "The storm is coming," he whimpered, shading his eyes and peering out. Fear contorted his face. "The fire. The fire is still coming...eating through me...surrounding me."

Carrie stepped back.

Hobbs jumped forward. "You want me to hold him again?"

Carrie shook her head wordlessly. She had seen this look before.

The fear on the man's face changed to one of wonder. His voice grew calm. "They're coming for me. They put the fire out." For a moment, the wildness in his eyes cleared, and he looked at Carrie with a quizzical expression. "I have to go now," he murmured.

"Yes, I know," Carrie replied, a catch in her voice. She stepped forward and smoothed his burning brow, pushing back the stringy hair. "I know."

The man gazed at her for a moment more, gave a long sigh, and closed his eyes. His body slowly sank back against the pillow, his ravaged face filled with peace.

"I won't need that medicine."

"He's dead?" Hobbs asked hoarsely.

Carrie nodded. "He didn't really stand a chance. The fever had already destroyed him." She would never get used to death, but she knew that for some, it brought welcome relief. Shaking her head, she looked up. "Let's find the next patient. There is nothing else we can do for this one."

It was almost dinner before Carrie had a chance to drink the cup of water Hobbs brought to her. She'd finished half of it before there was a disruption at the door of the ward.

"Someone told me he was here," a strident female voice exclaimed loudly. "I'm going to come in and find him."

Dr. Wild looked up from where he was bent over a patient. "Get that woman out of here! She is going to disturb the ones who are resting."

Hobbs began to move toward the door.

Seconds later, a woman brushed by him. "Don't tell me I can't come in here. I *will* find the man I'm looking for. His name is Perry Appleton. Where is he?" she demanded.

Carrie looked up and stiffened. She took a deep breath and stepped in front of the angry woman. "That's far enough, Louisa. You're not allowed in here."

Louisa Blackwell stopped abruptly, her blue eyes flashing below her carefully arranged blond curls. "Carrie Cromwell," she snapped. "I wish I could say it is a pleasure to see you."

Carrie flushed, but her eyes and voice didn't waver. "I'm not interested in your personal feelings, Louisa. I *am* interested in the welfare of my patients. Your intrusion here could put some of them in danger. Please leave."

She almost smiled at the enraged look that erupted on Louisa's face, but the situation was too critical for humor. Her mind flashed back to the carefree days when they were children playing on neighboring plantations. That was long ago. They had both grown and changed.

Louisa managed a haughty laugh. "*Really*, Carrie Cromwell. I don't know who you think you are, but you are certainly misinformed of your importance." She tried to step around her. "Get out of my way."

Carrie remained where she was. The aisle between the beds was too narrow for Louisa to force her way through. She was well aware many of the soldiers were witnessing this undignified exchange. "My name is Carrie Borden now," she said. "I will ask you one more time to leave."

"Oh, Carrie *Borden*, is it?" Louisa sneered. "So you finally managed to trap poor Robert. I guess since he couldn't have me, he decided to settle for you."

Carrie held her growing temper in check with great difficulty. Louisa's anger and jealousy over Robert's lack of interest in her had exploded beyond all reason. Carrie didn't have time to analyze her one-time friend's feelings now, though. Turning to Hobbs, she said, "Please find someone to escort Miss Blackwell from the ward."

Louisa tried once more to step around Carrie.

"That will be quite enough, young lady," Dr. Wild snapped from behind her. "In case you haven't noticed, this hospital is full of sick people."

Louisa whirled on her new attacker, saw he was a young, attractive man, and immediately softened. "Why, *doctor*, I'm so glad you've come over," she said in a simpering tone. "Maybe you can make this troublesome nurse get out of my way. I simply have to find Perry Appleton."

Carrie grinned at Dr. Wild's disgusted look. He didn't seem at all impressed by Louisa's fluttering eyelashes and helpless look.

"That troublesome *nurse*," Dr. Wild said, "happens to be my assistant. If the man you are looking for is in here and alive, it is highly likely she is responsible."

"Your *assistant?*" She spun around and glared at Carrie. "What game are you playing here?"

Carrie remained silent, staring at her steadily.

Dr. Wild stepped up and took Louisa's arm firmly. "I will see you out the door," he said in a no-nonsense voice. "It will be several days before any of the patients can have visitors. If your young man is here, you can come see him then."

Louisa pulled against his hand for a moment, her eyes staring wildly through the ward. Carrie's heart caught as she witnessed the genuine misery and fear shining from the girl's eyes. Anger blended with sympathy as she remembered her own heartache over Robert. Louisa sagged in defeat and wordlessly allowed Dr. Wild to lead her from the ward. After a moment's hesitation, Carrie followed.

She found Louisa standing under a tree just outside the door. Her expression was one of dazed confusion. Carrie walked up to her quietly. "I'm sorry, Louisa."

Louisa looked up slowly, her confusion changing to anger. "Oh, be quiet, Carrie *Borden!*"

Carrie bit her lip, determined to maintain control. Amazingly, she could feel her anger turning to both compassion and pity. "If you tell me what he looks like, I'll go back in and try to find him."

Louisa stared up at her, the anger dissolving once more into confusion. "Why would you do that?" she muttered.

"Robert was missing in action for eight months last year. I worried and wondered about him every minute. I would have given anything to know..." Carrie's voice trailed off as the old pain resurfaced.

Louisa was still staring at her suspiciously. Carrie, looking at her more closely, could see the war years had taken their toll. Louisa retained her beauty, but the strain had added lines and tension to her face. "Who is he?"

"His name is Perry Appleton," Louisa finally answered in a broken voice. "We were to be married when he got back from Pennsylvania. He..." Her voice broke. "He's all I have left, Carrie. He's all I have left."

Carrie was struck by the desperation in Louisa's voice. Memories of Louisa's hateful attacks over the last few years rose up before her, but she pushed them back down. "What do you mean?" she asked gently. "What about your family? Your father? Mother? Nathan?"

Louisa shook her head wordlessly. Her voice was wooden and numb when she answered. "Father insisted on fighting in this crazy war even though he was old enough to be exempt. He died last winter at Fredericksburg. Pneumonia took him." She took a deep breath. "Nathan was killed at Chancellorsville."

Carrie groaned. "Not Nathan," she whispered. She had always liked Louisa's cheerful older brother. He had always been kind to her. "And your mother?"

"Mother is still alive, but she might as well be dead," Louisa said bitterly. "The light left her when father died. When word came of Nathan, she completely fell apart. Two weeks ago, we got the news our plantation had been burned. She hasn't spoken since then. She just sits in the window and stares out like a zombie. She hasn't eaten a single thing. I know she's trying to die." Her voice broke again as tears welled in her eyes.

Carrie stepped forward impulsively and hugged the distraught girl. Now was no time to hold on to past hurts and angers. "I'm so sorry," she murmured. "I'm so sorry."

Louisa finally gained control and looked up. "Why are you being nice to me?" she whispered. "I've been so hateful."

"All of us are just people trying to survive."

"Robert?" Louisa asked. "Did you ever receive word?"

"Yes," Carrie said. "We had a few days together before he had to go back to duty. He fought at Chancellorsville, and then they sent him to London. I've haven't heard anything."

"London," Louisa breathed. "How wonderful that sounds." There was no resentment in her voice. "You couldn't go?"

"I chose not to," Carrie admitted. "I felt my duty was here." She decided to be honest. "There are times I regret it, and I miss him every day, but I believe I did the right thing."

Louisa looked at her curiously. "If someone offered me the chance to get out of this miserable city with the man I love, I would do it in a heartbeat." She paused. "You always were an odd thing."

Carrie stiffened but realized Louisa wasn't being hateful. She smiled slightly. "To each their own."

Louisa continued to gaze at her. "I've been so jealous of you, Carrie. I'm sorry. Can we try again?"

Carrie nodded, tears threatening to choke her. How easy it would have been to turn away completely, to gloat when Louisa had been escorted from the ward. "I'd like that," she said with a smile.

Louisa returned the smile and then asked hopefully, "Do you really think you might be able to find Perry for me?"

"I can try," Carrie promised. "Tell me about him."

"Perry is wonderful," Louisa replied. "He's very tall — about six feet, four inches. He has blond hair and a blond mustache. And the kindest blue eyes you could ever imagine," she said with a wistful smile.

Carrie nodded. "I'll see what I can do."

"I'll wait here."

Carrie hesitated. "It could be a while. There are over a hundred soldiers in there, and I still have work to do."

"I'll wait right here," Louisa repeated. "No matter how long it takes."

Carrie looked at her for a moment. "I'll send Hobbs out with some water." As she walked back into the ward, she knew she would have done the same thing.

It was almost an hour before Carrie could break away from her immediate duties to try to locate Perry Appleton. Walking slowly down the aisle, she smiled cheerfully at each soldier who was awake, searching for tall ones with blond hair. Three times she stopped. Each time they shook their heads regretfully, their wistful expressions saying they wished someone was looking for them.

Finally, she reached the end of the row. The last soldier had been one of the first to come in that morning. She was about to turn around in defeat when she saw a shock of dirty blond hair sticking out from the bandage covering his head.

Please God, not him.

Carrie walked a little closer. The man was unconscious, his breathing shallow and rapid. Sweat beaded on his skin. She winced as she looked at the bloody bandage wrapped where his right knee would have been. He was still out cold from the morphine.

"He gonna make it?" the soldier lying next to him asked.

"I hope so," Carrie responded. "He has a good chance," she lied. Dr. Wild had merely shaken his head sorrowfully after taking the wounded man's leg off and turned to his next patient. She turned back to the awake soldier. "Do you know who he is?"

"Sure," the man responded promptly. "He's from my unit. His name is Perry Appleton. Comes from around here somewhere."

The man kept talking, but Carrie wasn't listening anymore. She turned back and looked at the maimed man with a heavy heart. How could she tell Louisa she had found her man, but that he wasn't expected to live? How could she burden her with one more death, one more heartbreak? Still, if it had been Robert, she would have wanted to know. Taking a deep breath, she turned away.

She found Louisa waiting outside the door, her face pinched with fatigue and pink from the blazing sun. Carrie took her arm and gently led her under the nearby tree.

Louisa peered at her. "You didn't find him," she stated flatly, hope dying in her eyes.

Carrie shook her head. "I found him." She stopped, groping for words.

Louisa's eyes lit with excitement. "You found him? Perry is still alive?" She turned toward the door and then turned back. "Please, Carrie. I have to see him. I'm not going to try to force my way in like I did last time." She hesitated. "Can you help me?"

Carrie fought for the right words. "He's very sick, Louisa."

"Well, of course he's sick. He's in the hospital. But he's alive!" She seemed to be desperately holding on to that one reality.

"He might not make it," Carrie said gently. "He—he—" She couldn't bring herself to say the words.

Louisa straightened and moved over to stand directly in front of her. "He what?" she demanded. When Carrie remained quiet, she took her hand. "He what, Carrie? You have to tell me."

"He lost a leg this morning," Carrie admitted. "Dr. Wild tried to save it, but it was impossible. It had been too long." She saw no reason to give Louisa graphic details of his hideous wounds. "The infection had already set in. He has a very high fever."

Louisa whitened, but her eyes remained steady. "I don't care whether he has two legs, or none. I love him."

Carrie's respect for her spoiled friend multiplied tenfold. She had half-expected Louisa to turn away in disgust when she heard the truth. In spite of her angry outburst this morning, it was clear that the war and suffering she had faced had matured her.

Louisa took her hand again. "Perry needs me. I promise to stay out of the way, but I want to be with him," she said. "Please."

Carrie stared into her determined eyes, then nodded her head. "I'll see what I can do," she offered.

Turning, she went back into the ward. She found Dr. Wild just finishing surgery on another man. She quickly explained the situation to him.

"You say that woman is a friend of yours?" Dr. Wild asked skeptically.

"Louisa was not always the way you saw her this morning. She has been under tremendous strain. I think the war has changed her—some for the good." She took a deep breath. "I will be responsible for her while she's here."

Dr. Wild shook his head. "You are certainly more forgiving than I am," he said, a mixture of admiration and doubt in his voice. "All right. She can come in and be with him. She's probably the only chance he has to make it."

"Thank you." Carrie smiled her gratitude. "I'll go get her."

Louisa was waiting outside in the exact same spot. She turned a hopeful face to Carrie as soon as she walked out the door. Carrie nodded. "You can take care of him."

Louisa began to cry softly, great tears slipping down her cheeks. "Thank you," she whispered. "Thank you."

Carrie watched her ease into the ward door, then walked slowly to the plateau edge. A stiff wind had begun to blow, buffeting her with hot, dry air. Ships bobbed on the water glimmering below. Great flocks of gulls from the ocean flew in lazy spirals over her head, calling to each other excitedly. Carrie stood, letting the breeze whip through her soul and mind. In a world where destruction and hatred seemed to be reigning supreme, she wanted to savor the triumph of forgiveness and hope.

Chapter Thirteen

Wallace Stratford looked up from his paper as Abby entered the dining room. "Good morning, Abby," he said pleasantly. "Sleep well?"

"Wonderfully," Abby responded, slipping into her place at the sumptuously laden table. Nancy, who loved to sleep in, would not be down for several hours. Abby smiled up at the servant who placed a steaming cup of coffee in front of her, then stared out the window. "Dawn has always been my favorite part of the day. It seems as if there is always a brand new beginning."

"Here's hoping for one," Wallace said, laying the paper aside. "This blasted war had better end soon or the entire economy is going to fall apart."

"Real estate not doing well these days?"

"Oh, I'm doing well enough," Wallace admitted. "The rich always seem to have money," he laughed. "It took me quite a while to make mine, but now that it's made, it's safely invested and protected. My friends are the same way." He scowled. "It's impossible not to see what's going on, though. Retail prices have risen forty-three percent since the war began. Unfortunately, wages have only gone up twelve percent. I'm afraid there are too many people who have found their standard of living drastically lowered. There are many living in abject poverty. That, my dear," he said, "is the formula for trouble."

"You're still worried about violence?" Abby probed. "I thought Michael told me everything was under control."

"I'm sure it is," Wallace assured her. "No, it's not violence I'm afraid of, but what is going to happen to our country." He picked up the paper again. "Listen to this.

'Conscription rides roughshod over the rights of the states and has created one of the largest standing armies known in the history of the world. I would not give a rush for the reserved rights of the States or the boasted liberties of the people if this power is granted to the United

States. I fear this is a part and parcel of a grand scheme for the overthrow of the Union and for the purpose of building upon its ruins a new government based on new ideas—the idea of territorial unity and consolidated power. Arm the Chief Magistrate with this power and what becomes of the State Legislatures? What becomes of the local judicial tribunals? What becomes of State constitutions and State ?' "

Wallace laid aside his paper. "I'm afraid I agree with this fine congressman from Ohio."

"You don't really think Lincoln is trying to frame a military dictatorship?" Abby protested.

Wallace sighed heavily and reached for another piece of toast. "Support for the war is fading, Abby. People have had enough. I'm not sure the government has shown enough capacity for effectively using the means it already has at its command to justify this infringement of states' rights. They are walking a very fine line."

"Yet you support abolitionism?"

"Certainly," Wallace said promptly. "I also support the continued union of our country. What happens if we manage to successfully destroy the Confederate rebellion with our superior force? Do we then send that force down to maintain control? It would most likely take over half a million men. What does that do to our freedom?"

Abby sighed. "There are so many questions there seem to be no answers to. I think people are realizing more and more that the tide of passion has pushed them into a whirling cauldron of chaos. There seems to be no way out, yet the only way to survive is to keep fighting. If only we had been able to see clearly into the future before this whole thing started."

"Ah," Wallace said. "Hindsight is always so much clearer than the future. The sad thing is that man never seems to learn from his mistakes. If one would but look at history, there are plenty of examples that would have shouted the perils of unleashed passion. But, like so many generations before us, we chose to follow our hearts and leave the stones of the past unturned."

Wallace picked up the paper once more. "I want to read something else to you. I wish you and Nancy could have attended the governor's speech on the fourth of July."

"I understand he was quite eloquent," Abby replied.

"Yes. Here is an article about his speech." Wallace cleared his throat.

"'Governor Seymour is a strong Union man, as he has just proved by the vigorous measures taken to hurry our militia units down to meet Lee's invasion of Pennsylvania. He is also a firm Jeffersonian Democrat with a passion for civil liberties. His voice is calling out for the North to unite and help the war effort. But, he said, this can never be achieved while the Republicans are trampling on individual rights. The administration is pleading the necessity of strong action to obtain victory.

Seymour's response was direct. "Remember this, that the bloody, and treasonable, and revolutionary doctrine of public necessity can be proclaimed by a mob as well as by a government."' "

Wallace looked up briefly. "I have fervent hope that he is not also a prophet." He continued reading.

"'Pointing to the dangers of military dictatorship, Seymour called on his audience to maintain and defend the principles of the Declaration of Independence and the Constitution. The federal government should be obeyed as long as it does not clearly transgress its constitutional powers. People must do their duty. They must also insist that the government do its duty: uphold states' rights, freedom of the press, and the independence of the judiciary.' "

"I understand he and his cousin, the former governor of Connecticut, are calling for a cease-fire and negotiations for national reconciliation," Abby recalled.

"Yes."

Abby was thoughtful for several moments. "It sounds so wonderful," she said.

"But it's too late for that now."

"Yes, I'm afraid the lot is cast. I'm afraid this crazy war is going to have to burn on until the end."

"I just hope it doesn't destroy everything in its path."

A heavy silence descended on the room, until a slamming door in the distance broke it. Abby looked up, grateful for the reprieve when Michael walked into the room.

"Got enough food there for a hungry policeman?" he asked cheerfully. "I haven't had a decent meal since yesterday."

"If the police force knew how to take care of its men, you wouldn't be starving," Wallace growled. He looked at Abby apologetically. "I'm sorry. It's just that the force works their men such crazy shifts that some of them go almost twenty hours with little to eat. I don't know how they expect men to do their jobs efficiently."

Michael shrugged and grinned. "It's interesting to find out how most of our country lives." He waved his hand over the table spread before him. "I guarantee I'm the only one on the force who comes home to meals like this. Not that I'm complaining," he added, piling his plate high.

He looked up after several large mouthfuls. "The force seems to be keeping everything under control." He looked at his father. "Remember me telling you they were taking the draft down into the lower wards on Saturday?" He shoved another bite in, talking around his food. "Things went smoothly. The captain sent a strong regiment down to protect the draft officers. There was some mumbling and complaining, but no one tried to stop the proceedings. The draft callings went on all day. At the end of the afternoon, they simply closed up shop and went home." He stretched, as a mighty yawn escaped from his mouth. "I guess all those predictions of trouble were a lot of hot air. There is another draft picking today. The captain is certain there will be no trouble."

Abby breathed a sigh of relief. "I'm so glad. This country has quite enough violence without it erupting in the cities as well."

Michael stood and stretched again. "I'm going to bed. I've been dreaming of sleep for the last day. I'm going to indulge my fantasies."

Abby watched him go fondly. "You must be quite proud of your son."

"That I am," Wallace said. "Once he has this policing bug out of his blood, I fully expect he will come to work for me." He smiled slightly. "That boy is the light of our lives."

Paxton was waiting for Abby when she emerged from the Stratford's house and walked to the waiting carriage. "Where to, Mrs. Livingston?"

"I'm going to visit a new friend downtown on Roosevelt Street," Abby replied. "I'm expected there for lunch. I have some shopping I would like to do on the way."

Paxton frowned. "I don't think you'll be wanting to go downtown today, ma'am." His eyes held a hint of fear.

"Why ever not?"

Paxton shook his head. "There's going to be trouble down there," he insisted. "I heard the boys talking. The fire laddies are upset because some of their members got notice of the draft. They think they ought to be exempt just like the city firemen. They're not going to sit back and take it."

"The fire laddies?"

"They fancy themselves to be firemen," Paxton said, "but they are really little more than gangs. They link up with political groups and then they look for exposure and excitement by putting out fires." He shook his head. "You should see it down here when there is a fire. A wild mob rushes through the streets with the engines, bellowing and screaming at the top of their lungs."

"Well, at least they put out the fires," Abby smiled.

"Depends." Paxton snorted. "Those boys care more about winning a race with another company than putting out a fire. I saw a bunch of them one time. They didn't have a pump that would throw a stream high enough to put out a fire in a store, but they refused to make way for another engine that could have done the job." He shook his head. "Those boys have been known to break in and ransack buildings near fires. Some have been known to start the fires themselves, just to have a little excitement." He turned in his seat and fixed Abby with a frightened stare. "They aren't anyone to be messing with, Mrs. Livingston."

"Nonsense," Abby said. "The police are more than competent to take care of any trouble. I intend to go visit my friend. Please take me to the Lord and Taylor store on the corner of Grand and Chrystie. I need to buy a few things to send home. Then we'll proceed on to Roosevelt Street."

"Roosevelt Street?" Paxton muttered reluctantly.

"It's down in one of the black sections of town," Abby said. She held up a sheet of paper. "I have directions."

Paxton whitened. "Please, Mrs. Livingston. Don't go down there today. Especially not into the black section. If there's trouble, it will be worse there." Sweat broke out on his forehead. "It won't be safe for anyone down there."

"Oh, what utter nonsense," Abby said. "I appreciate your concern, Paxton, but I simply must insist you stop this. Michael assures me the situation in the city is quite under control. May we please go now?"

Paxton looked as if he were going to refuse, but he abruptly nodded his head. "Don't say I didn't warn you," he muttered under his breath.

Abby leaned back and breathed in a deep draught of fresh air. Here, above the city's industrial smoke, the air was crystal clear, the sky blue and sparkling. It was a day to be glad one was alive. Abby thought back over the last two weeks. Her time with the Stratfords had been wonderful, and she had made many new friends among the city's abolitionists. One was Dr. Benson, the black doctor she was going to visit. She had talked to him for a few minutes several nights before at a local meeting. Now, she was going to meet his family.

There were dozens of barrels of supplies already on their way to Rose in the contraband camp. The wealthy people of New York had opened their hearts, their purses and their closets when she described the plight of the camps to them. Rose would be thrilled. Tomorrow, Abby would leave to return to Philadelphia. She was eager to get to work on the petition-signing project. Her time in New York had both refreshed and inspired her.

She thought of engaging Paxton in conversation, but his grim face told her he probably wouldn't be interested. It really was a shame he was allowing his fears to get the better of him. Abby had finally triumphed over the uneasy feelings she experienced upon coming to the city. Michael's assurances had done much to help her.

Now that her earlier fear had been dispelled, New York in war didn't really seem much different from New York in peacetime. As the heat intensified, more of the wealthy had fled the city, heading for Newport, Cape May or Saratoga. Along the Bowery, the crowded beer gardens and theaters pulsed with the sounds and sights of the Vaterland. Jewish clothing stores stood like sentinels along Chatham Street, their clothes flapping in the breeze along the walkway. Only the throngs of men wearing Union blue, the army hospitals in City Hall Park, and the placards bearing war news outside the newspaper offices on Nassau Street bore witness to the furious struggle going on far south of them. If one tried hard enough, they could almost convince themselves nothing had changed.

It was almost ten o'clock when Abby emerged from Lord and Taylor, her arms laden with gifts. She smiled brightly at Paxton when she climbed back into the carriage. "I had an idea."

"Yes, ma'am?"

The idea had come to her while she was selecting a crystal bowl for her hosts. "I would like to go down to where they are picking the draft today. I believe Michael told me it was going to be on Third Avenue." She settled her dress around her.

"What?" Paxton asked in a shocked voice.

"I realize it's rather an odd request," Abby acknowledged, "but the draft is a momentous thing for our country. I would like to see firsthand how people are responding to it—how they feel about it."

"I can tell you how they feel," Paxton muttered. He sat silently for a few seconds and then turned to her. "You're crazy to want to go down there," he said, his anger rising. "I realize I'm just a driver and that I could be fired for talking to you this way, but it's the truth. You don't have any business being down there." His expression grew more obstinate. "The Stratfords will have my job for sure if something were to happen to you."

"Oh, come now," Abby countered, battling her irritation at his refusal to do as she requested. "The Stratfords know how independent I am. They are used to my crazy escapades. They will certainly not blame you if something happens to me because of my own willfulness." Her voice became firm. "I quite understand how you feel about this, Paxton. Now, will you please take me down there?"

Paxton stared at her for a moment, gave a deep sigh of resignation, and nodded his head. Without a word, he picked up the reins to the carriage and urged the horse forward.

Abby sat back, satisfied to have won that victory. She felt slightly uneasy, but she wasn't going to let fear stop her from doing what she wanted to do. She learned that lesson long ago. Words a friend spoke years ago popped into her head suddenly. *"Abigail Livingston, there is a difference between courage and obstinacy. Courage is a wonderful mixture of bravery and wisdom—obstinacy is just plain stubborn determination to have something your way."*

Abby stared out of the wagon thoughtfully. Was she being courageous or obstinate? Only time would tell.

The first hint of trouble came when they rounded the corner on Twenty-Eighth Street. A large group of men, shabbily dressed, were milling in front of a building. As they drew closer, Abby identified the building as an iron works. She tensed when she saw the men's angry expressions. Some of them clenched crowbars and heavy sticks. They turned and scowled at the ornate carriage, before turning back to stare at the building.

As the carriage rolled by, they let out a lusty cheer. Abby turned and watched as perhaps a hundred more men poured from the lot behind the building, adding to the mass. Yelling loudly, they surged down the road toward them.

Paxton looked back. His face whitened even more as he urged the horses to a faster trot. "Get on!" he cried.

Abby felt an uncomfortable knot in her stomach but pushed it down. "There are no laws against peaceful demonstrations", she said calmly.

"Peaceful demonstrators don't need crowbars," Paxton growled, looking over his shoulder.

As Abby glanced back, a song drifted to her on the breeze. She strained to catch the words the mob was singing.

We're coming, Father Abraham,
Three hundred thousand more.
We leave our homes and firesides with bleeding hearts and sore,
Since poverty has been our crime, we bow to the decree;
We are the poor who have no wealth to purchase liberty.

Abby stared at the marching mob. Were they right in their assessment that this was a rich man's war, but a poor man's fight? How would she feel if she were in their place, asked to leave home to fight a war she had no desire for? Most of the men in the lower wards of the city were recent immigrants, both Irish and German. Where was their motivation to suffer and die for the Union? They were too busy suffering and dying in their own fight for survival. Abby shook her head. The war's boiling cauldron showed no favoritism in its hunger for destruction.

When Paxton looked back down at her, she nodded for him to continue, ignoring his look of frustrated fear. She was more determined than ever to witness for herself the calling of the draft. These were human beings who were having their lives turned upside down. Just because it didn't touch her personally was no reason for her not to understand what was happening.

There was an atmosphere of eerie expectancy around the draft office when Paxton pulled the carriage to a standstill. The streets were crowded with throngs of people. As Abby craned forward to see if the process of pulling the draft had started yet, a cordon of police rounded the corner, their faces set and unsmiling. The crowd erupted in angry muttering, but they sullenly divided to let the men through. The police took up their positions near the building.

Abby could see the drafting barrel—a large hollow wheel mounted on a stand. Stuffed inside were the names of the men enrolled for conscription. One of the clerks was blindfolded while a handle was attached to the wheel. When the clerk stepped up, the muttering of the crowd dissolved, and they strained forward to listen.

"Patrick Jones at Forty-Ninth and Tenth Streets," the clerk called out loudly.

Someone in the crowd cursed. A nearby lady broke into tears.

"Clancy O'Brien," rang out next.

Abby watched and listened as scores of names were called out. Expressions of anger and dismay, fear and sorrow surrounded her. Her heart ached for the people whose lives had been changed forever by the turn of that wheel.

"They're coming!"

Abby twisted her head as a hoarse shout rang above the clerk's voice.

"They're coming!" the cry was repeated and multiplied as person after person picked it up.

"We've got to get out of here!" Paxton cried to Abby. "The Black Joke fire laddies are on their way. They're going to destroy this place. I thought maybe they had changed their mind, but they haven't. They aren't gonna let anything stand in their way."

Abby was struck by something in Paxton's voice. She hesitated, torn between her desire to stay and the sudden hammering of her heart that told her it was time to leave. She nodded.

Paxton whirled around and picked up the reins. "Get up," he urged to the horses.

Suddenly there was nowhere to go. The crowd had increased and was now pressing closer to the building, completely ignoring Paxton's yells for them to move. All of them were craning to see what would happen when the Black Joke arrived.

With her heart pounding, Abby stood up in the carriage looking for a break in the mob. All she could see in every direction was a mass of bobbing heads. A solid sea of humanity pressed around her. She realized how foolish she had been. Her friend had been right—there was indeed a fine line between courage and obstinacy. She reached forward and touched Paxton's shoulder. "I'm sorry," she yelled above the noise.

Paxton was in no mood to talk. His eyes scanned the crowd, looking for a break. "I'll get us out of here," he muttered.

A Black Joke hose cart pulled up in front of the draft office. Abby could see a large pile of stones inside the cart. She ducked instinctively as a loud pistol shot rang above the tumult of the crowd. A flurry of stones flew through the air, crashing through the windows of the draft office, shattering glass in a million directions.

Abby gasped and ducked down in the carriage as an angry cry rose from the crowd.

"Down with the draft!"

"You ain't gonna send our men off!" a lady screamed.

"How are you now, Old Abe?" a rough-looking man hollered defiantly.

The fire laddies leapt from the cart and stormed the building. Abby watched in horror as the police fought to hold them off. She could just make out the draft officials scurrying to protect their papers. Slowly, the police were beaten back. With a triumphant yell, the angry men rushed into the building, smashing everything in sight. It looked like one man was splashing something around the building.

"They're going to torch the place," Paxton yelled.

Flames of fire began to lick from the door, smoke seeping through the shattered glass, swirling defiantly toward the sky. The angry cries of the crowd increased, fueled by the flames.

"Get out of the way," Paxton yelled again, cracking his whip, trying to get the crowd to move. Several moved toward him threateningly.

"Stop!" Abby cried. She looked around frantically for an escape route. She knew that once this mob was out of control, a well-dressed lady of obvious financial means could easily become one of their targets.

A burly policeman stepped onto the porch of the draft office. "All right, boys!" he yelled. "You've done your work. All the equipment has been destroyed. There won't be any more draft calling today." He spread his hands in appeal. "Won't you put out the fire now? There's innocent women and children in the houses attached to this building. You don't want them to be hurt. They haven't done anything to you."

Abby's heart rose hopefully. Maybe it was still possible to restore order to the chaos. That hope plummeted as a part of the mob rushed forward and clubbed the officer foolish enough to confront them. She gasped as one of his fellow officers rushed to his aid and was also clubbed to the ground.

The sight of the beating sparked the mob's appetite for violence. With a howl, they surged forward. Sounds of smashing doors and tinkling glass sounded above the din as people broke into the burning houses. Furniture and clothing were being tossed out into the streets, swept up by the looting crowds.

"There isn't any way to get around this," Paxton yelled, pulling at Abby's arm. "We've got to get out of here on foot. It's our only hope."

Abby stepped down. Paxton was right. "I'm sorry for getting you into this," she yelled. "I should have listened."

"I should never have brought you here," Paxton yelled back, holding her hand and pushing his way through the crowd.

It was fairly easy to weave their way to the back of the crowd. Everyone's attention seemed to be on the violence and looting in front of them. Several people cursed and shoved back, but no one tried to stop them. Abby looked back as they finally broke free into an open space. From both directions, she could see crowds of people running to join the mob.

"We've got a full scale riot on our hands," Paxton yelled. "I've got to get you somewhere safe."

"What about you?"

"I'll be fine," Paxton insisted. "They aren't after me."

"But surely they're not after me either." Abby battled the fear churning in her stomach.

"Right now they're a bunch of people out of control," Paxton explained. "They're going to go after what's different from them. One look at you, and they'll know you don't belong." He grabbed Abby's arm and began to pull her down the street away from the mob.

"Take me to Dr. Benson's house." Abby stopped abruptly and pulled out her map.

"Not a chance," Paxton snapped, pulling at her again.

Abby forced herself to remain calm. "We have come too far for me to walk back through that crowd. I know no one else down here." She held up the map. "We're just a few streets away. It will only take a few minutes. They're expecting me."

"Are you crazy?" Paxton said through clenched teeth, obviously making an effort to remain professional. "That's right in the middle of a black area. That's the first place that mob will go."

"The police are sure to have it under control by then," Abby protested. "Besides, do you have somewhere else I can go? I can't just roam around the streets." She hated that she had gotten them in this situation, but now that they were, she was obviously going to have to take control.

"You're right," Paxton groaned in frustration. "Why did I ever bring you down here?"

Another wild yell erupted from the mob. A large contingent broke away and began to surge in their direction. Breaking glass and shouts accompanied their movement.

"Let's get out of here," Paxton yelled. "Where's that map?" He glanced at it wildly and began to pull Abby down the street.

Abby's heart pounded with fear, but her head was clear. She looked back over her shoulder as Paxton pulled her down the road. She could see several men cutting down telegraph poles. She understood instantly they were trying to break communication with the outside to keep the police away.

Abby heard the rattle of wheels and the tramping of feet. She hesitated and looked down the side street they were passing. "The police!" she yelled in relief, plowing to a halt. "Look, Paxton. The police are coming."

Paxton scowled. "There aren't enough of them to stop that mob," he insisted. "I've got to get you to your friend's house."

Abby studied the police marching toward them and realized Paxton was right. She hurried on, looking over her shoulder. She had managed to cover a couple of blocks before a cry rent the air. She spun around, stunned by what sounded like a wild animal in horrible pain. It hung on the air for a moment, then swelled through the streets, luring more people to join in the madness.

The police rounded the corner, advancing on the rampaging crowd. With another cry, a flurry of paving stones rained down on the policemen. Abby heard a few shots, but the crowd was upon the men before they could form a defense. She watched in horror as several of the uniformed men crumpled to the ground and then were swallowed by the crowd. Seconds later, she could see the rest of the policemen break and run. The mob, strengthened by its violent victory, surged on.

"Come *on*, Mrs. Livingston," Paxton cried, tugging her hand.

Abby swallowed the bile forcing its way up her throat and blinked back her tears. She could only pray Michael hadn't been in that group. Picking up her skirts, she ran after Paxton.

Minutes later, he was pounding at the door of a simple, well-kept, three-story house. "Let us in!" he cried.

The door flung open. A black man stood staring at Abby in amazement. "Mrs. Livingston! Whatever is the matter?"

"I'm so sorry to bust in on you like this, Dr. Benson," Abby began.

Another roar floated toward them. Paxton pushed Abby in the door. "I'm sorry, Dr. Benson. There isn't time for talk. There's a full scale riot that has erupted. Keep

Mrs. Livingston safe!" He turned to Abby. "I'll be back for you when this is all over." Then he spun and sprinted down the road.

Dr. Benson slammed the door shut and turned to the group of people in the room staring at him in wide-eyed fear. "It's started," he said grimly. "Everyone upstairs." Without a word, they rose to obey him.

Abby watched as a very attractive woman picked up the youngest child who appeared to be under a year old, then ushered the other seven children up the stairs. She paused long enough to give Abby a gentle smile before tightening her lips and hurrying after her family.

Dr. Benson glanced down at Abby. "We've been expecting trouble for some time. We could feel it growing in the air all summer." He paused and walked back to gaze out the window. "Where did it start?"

"Down at the draft office. I was foolish enough to insist the Stratford's driver take me there, even though he was obviously afraid." Abby was angry at herself. "Once again, my impulsiveness has gotten me in trouble."

"More trouble than you might realize," Dr. Benson agreed. "I wish he would have taken you somewhere else, though I realize he would have if there had been other options."

"The mob isn't going to attack the houses of innocent people," Abby protested, watching over Dr. Benson's shoulder for the crowd to appear.

"You're in the black section of town, Mrs. Livingston. That's all it takes to be guilty in their eyes. However wrong they may be, that mob believes their troubles are caused by black people. They aren't intelligent enough to look inside and take responsibility for their problems. They have to find someone to carry it for them. Then they have someone to take their rage out on," Dr. Benson said bitterly. "It's really quite simple. I wish I could say it's something you get accustomed to, but I'm afraid you never do."

Just then a black man raced around the corner and down the street, his head tucked low for speed. Seconds later, a group of white men exploded around the corner behind him, gaining on him slowly.

Abby watched in horrified, helpless silence as the white mob slowly bridged the gap. "Run!" she cried. She realized the black man was limping, obviously already hurt. There was no way he could escape them. Abby grabbed her throat as the mob fell on the fleeing black man. Dr. Benson turned her away roughly, but not before she heard the tortured cry of the captured man.

"Go upstairs," he said gruffly. "I'm sorry you have to be here to see this, but I'm afraid there is no way to get you out until it's over. You will find Elsie and the children in the back room to the right."

Chapter Fourteen

Abby, fighting to see through her tears, climbed the stairs slowly, glancing over her shoulder once to see Dr. Benson staring out the window with a face of stone. She stumbled down the dark hallway to the right. Elsie appeared in front of her and guided her into a room with a single, small window.

"I'm so sorry you are here at such an awful time, Mrs. Livingston," Elsie said, her voice gentle and refined.

Abby grasped her hand and gazed around the room at the frightened children. They stared at her silently, their eyes wide and white in their dark faces.

"These are my children," Elsie said. "The youngest is ten months. My oldest, Stephen, is seventeen." She took a deep breath. "He went out to run some errands for me earlier. He isn't back yet."

Abby stared at her. "I'm so sorry," she finally said. She knew how she would feel if someone she loved were out in that violence.

She noticed a form in the bed tucked against the wall. Elsie followed her gaze and stepped aside to allow Abby to move forward.

"This is Shelby," she said tenderly. "She was very sick with typhoid last winter. I'm afraid it left her very weak."

Abby smiled down at the young girl grinning up at her. "Hello, Shelby."

"Hello. You must be Mrs. Livingston. My mother told me you were coming. It's so very nice of you to come visit us."

Abby stared at her in amazement. "And it's so nice to meet you," she said graciously.

Elsie interpreted her look. "My little Shelby has absolutely no fear. She was quite certain she was going to die last year. When she didn't, she informed us she was never going to be afraid of anything again. She figures that when it's her time to go, she will. Until then, nothing is going to happen that God isn't in control of."

"It's true," Shelby said earnestly. "You don't need to be afraid, Mrs. Livingston. God is taking care of us."

"How old are you?" Abby asked, bemused.

"I'm eleven," Shelby said proudly, "but don't let my age bother you. My daddy says it shouldn't."

Abby felt strangely comforted by the young girl's courage. "Thank you," she said sincerely, turning away to walk to the window.

"Mommy won't let us look out the window," one handsome boy who looked about six called out.

"That's Reuben," Elsie said. "I won't let them look out the window, because there is no need to see what is happening out there." Her gaze swept the room, her voice firm.

Abby totally agreed. Violence was a sad reality of their young lives, but what good would it do to let them watch it explode right before their eyes? However, she also felt the need to know what was going on. Even though it might be horrible, it was better than being stuck away with no clue of what was happening. "I'll be back in a few minutes," she murmured.

Dr. Benson was still standing at the exact spot she had left him. He made no comment about her return, just nodded and moved aside to make room for her. Abby whitened when she looked out. The streets were full of angry people. "There are women and children out there!" she exclaimed.

"I'm afraid passion and the mob mentality is not limited to men," Dr. Benson replied. "Men are not the only ones who throw reason to the wind so that hatred may rule."

Abby turned back to watch. "Where are the police?" she murmured, remembering their aborted attempt to regain control earlier.

"It's going to take more than the police to stop this," Dr. Benson replied. "It will take the militia to break up this mob. I'm quite sure we are seeing only a small part of what is going on in this city. The bomb has been building for quite some time. It was merely waiting for something to light the fuse."

"But the militia was called away to fight at Gettysburg," Abby protested. "They aren't back in the city yet."

"I know."

Abby shuddered as the implications of what he was saying sank in. "What will stop it?" she finally asked, almost afraid to voice the question.

Dr. Benson shrugged. "Oh, they'll bring it under control sooner or later. The government isn't going to allow New York to be destroyed by a riot. The question is, how many people's lives will be destroyed before they do?" He turned back to the window. "My son is out there."

"Your wife told me. I'm so sorry."

"If Stephen realizes there is trouble, he may hide out." He scowled. "There is also the chance he will try to make it home to help protect us here. That's what I'm afraid of."

"It's a good thing I'm sneaky," a strong, young voice announced from behind them.

Abby spun around from the window just in time to see Dr. Benson embrace his oldest son, a good-looking lad already a head taller than his father.

"Stephen!" Dr. Benson made no effort to cover his fear and worry. "How did you get home?"

"Over the rooftops," Stephen said, his eyes wise beyond his years. "You and Mother used to fuss at me for playing up there, but at least I know my way around." He grabbed his father's hand. "We'll have to take the family out that way."

"That mob is not running me from my house," Dr. Benson said angrily. "I have worked too hard for what we have." He paused. "Did you see much of what is going on?"

"Too much," Stephen replied, all the cheer gone from his voice. He sounded old and tired. "They're attacking every black man they see. I barely got away from a group coming after me." His voice choked. "They destroyed the orphan asylum."

Abby gasped. "The Colored Orphan Asylum?" Her voice shook with anger. She had contributed toward the home for black children.

"Yes, ma'am." For the first time Stephen seemed to notice her presence. "You must be Mrs. Livingston. I was sent out to bring home some groceries for your lunch. I'm sorry, but I'm afraid I wasn't able to complete my errand."

Dr. Benson shook his head impatiently. "What did they do to the asylum?"

Stephen's face tightened. "A whole mob gathered around there. I watched from a nearby rooftop. They got all the children out, though."

Abby breathed a sigh of relief. Over two hundred children, all under the age of twelve lived in that building.

"They were yelling things like *'Burn the niggers' nest!'* and *'Down with the niggers!'* " Stephen continued bitterly. "Anyway, I think they took the kids down to one of the police precincts." He shook his head. "They barely had the last kid out the back when the mob broke down the front door. Men were smashing pianos and carrying off everything they could get their hands on. And I mean everything—carpets, chairs, dishes. Why, they even took away all the beds."

Dr. Benson clenched his fists in anger. "It took years to set that place up," he cried.

Stephen wasn't finished. "Once they had everything out, they set fire to the place." He brushed away his tears. "There were some firemen who tried to stop it, but the mob beat them away. I could hear one of the firemen telling the crowd they didn't want to hurt humanity by destroying a benevolent institution."

"And no one listened?" Abby asked.

Stephen shrugged. "Some more firemen tried to put it out. The mob cut their hoses and broke up the hydrants. They finally had to give it up. The whole place was in flames when I finally left."

He walked closer to his father. "I know how you feel about leaving here, but we've got to get out." He hesitated, glancing at Abby. "It's bad out there. They're attacking anyone they can find. It won't be long before they get here. Those crowds out there now are mostly people trying to get in on the excitement, but once the real mob gets here, they're going to follow their example."

Dr. Benson shook his head stubbornly. "If I ran away every time a white person tried to hurt me, I'd never have gotten where I am today." He glanced at Abby. "I also realize I owe much of where I am to white people who have helped me."

Abby stared at him compassionately, understanding the battle in his heart. A clear vision of his family huddled in the upstairs room rose in her mind. "I learned a difficult lesson today," she said. "I thought insisting on coming down here in spite of Paxton's warnings was courage. A friend told me once that courage was a mixture of bravery and wisdom. I'm afraid I threw all wisdom out the window. What I showed today was plain obstinacy, and now I'm paying the price."

Dr. Benson was not persuaded. "I'm afraid I will have to learn my own lessons. I am not leaving my home."

"Learning your lesson may put your family at risk," Abby pleaded. She realized she had no right to try to convince this man of anything, but she couldn't simply sit and watch his family be harmed. Shelby's trusting eyes prodded her to push on.

Stephen stepped forward. "Listen to her, Dad. She's right. You haven't seen it out there." Suddenly, his voice was scared and young again.

Dr. Benson stared at his son and slowly nodded. "We'll scope out your escape route. We'll get your mother and the other children to safety." His voice firmed. "But I'm not leaving this house until I have to. I'm not simply walking away from everything I've worked so hard for."

Abby sagged with relief. Her nervousness was growing as the sounds of the crowd increased.

Stephen nodded. "Come on. I'll show you." He flashed Abby a relieved smile and dashed up the stairway.

Dr. Benson looked around once, gave a heavy sigh, and followed them.

Abby's heart ached for him and his wife. They had done nothing more than be born black. She knew only a little of Dr. Benson's history, but she was aware he was one of a handful of black doctors in the country. Nancy told her he had faced incredible prejudice and persecution, but pressed through until he had his medical degree. He was highly respected in the black community and was gaining grudging respect in the white.

Elsie met them at the top of the stairs, her face pinched and worried. "Stephen! I was so worried about you. Are you all right?"

"I'm fine, Mom. I'll tell you about everything later. Right now, we have to get you and the rest of the kids out of here."

"How do you propose to do that?" Elsie's voice was calm, but Abby could see the tension on her face.

"I've got a plan, Mom," Stephen insisted.

"The roof?" Elsie asked incredulously. "It *was* you I heard a few minutes ago."

"It's the only way," Stephen told her, but Abby thought she saw a flicker of doubt in his eyes.

Abby watched him carefully, aware of the heavy burden he had taken upon himself. "What can I do to help?" she asked, stepping forward.

Stephen smiled at her gratefully. "The adults will need to carry the little ones."

"How are you planning on getting us down from that roof once you get us up there?" Elsie demanded.

"I don't know yet," Stephen admitted, "but I'll figure it out."

"We'll find a way," Dr. Benson added, laying his hand on his wife's shoulder reassuringly. "We won't let anything happen to you or the children," he promised.

A banging at the door downstairs made up Elsie's mind. She spun toward the back bedroom. "I'll take the baby. You three get Mabel, Sandra and Bo. I'm not waiting for that mob to harm my children!"

Minutes later, they were handing the youngest children out onto the roof. Just as Stephen appeared at the window holding Shelby securely in his arms, they heard the tinkling of glass as the windows on the lower level shattered.

Dr. Benson looked back once, tightened his lips, and gathered Shelby gently in his arms. "Come on, baby. We're going to have an adventure."

"Oh, I'm fine, Daddy," Shelby said cheerfully. "Don't look so sad. We still have each other."

Abby was struck again by the child's maturity. In spite of Shelby's youth, she inspired courage in Abby. Taking a deep breath, she stepped out onto the roof, gasping as she looked down. The steep roof sloped away quickly, with nothing to break their fall if any one of them should slip.

Sounds of yelling erupted from the open window behind them. More sounds of breaking glass filtered up to them, followed by a crash as the heavy front door was forced open. Dr. Benson turned around and shut the window with a violent jerk.

"Daddy, why are those people breaking into our house?" Reuben asked fearfully.

Elsie hugged him close. "There are some people in the world who are hungry for power, little one. They'll take it any way they can get it."

"But it's our *things* they're taking," Reuben said in a confused voice. "They aren't taking power."

"They think they are," Dr. Benson said. He forced his voice to become cheerful. "All right. The trick to this adventure is to hang on tight and stay close to each other."

"Where are we going to go?" Elsie asked quietly, gazing down at the maelstrom on the streets.

Abby moved closer and took one of her hands. "We're going to get out of this."

Elsie smiled and turned to Stephen. "What is the rest of your plan?"

For the first time, Stephen looked worried. "I wasn't thinking about the gap between the buildings. I jump over it, but we won't be able to with the children." He clenched his fists. "I'm sorry."

Abby gazed around. Her eyes locked on a large empty lot three houses over. "Is there a rope in the house?" she asked suddenly.

"No, why?" Dr. Benson asked.

Abby shook her head in frustrated disappointment. "If we could get to the next house, we could slide down to that empty lot. Maybe there would be a way around the mob." She sighed. "I thought we could use the rope to lower the children." She shook her head. "I'm sorry. Obviously it won't work."

"Dr. Benson?"

A soft voice arrested their attention. Abby looked over to see a gray-haired, heavy-set woman leaning from the house next door. "Over there," she said, pointing.

"Dr. Benson," the woman repeated. "Maybe I can help your family."

"That's Mrs. Goldberg," Stephen whispered. "We've been next door neighbors for ten years now."

Dr. Benson edged over to the drop-off between the two houses. "You'll endanger yourself if you help us," he said regretfully. "You're a dear friend. I can't let you do that."

"Nonsense," Mrs. Goldberg snapped. "That's what friends are for. Besides, you think I don't know how you feel? The fear and helplessness? The Jews have been feeling it for hundreds of years. It is nothing new to my people. So many of us still live because people were willing to help us. Now, I help you," she said stoutly.

Dr. Benson smiled for the first time. "What do you have in mind?"

Smiling triumphantly, Mrs. Goldberg thrust a long loop of rope through her window. "You can use this to lower your family to the lower porch on my house. There is a window there you can climb into."

"We can't stay in your house," Dr. Benson protested. "It won't be safe for any of us."

"Of course not," Mrs. Goldberg agreed, eyeing the crowd below. "Once you're in the house, I'll take you to my basement. There is a window you can crawl out of. When it's dark, you can make your way to one of the police precincts. You'll be safe there."

Dr. Benson thought for a few minutes and then nodded his head. "It might work."

"Might work?" Mrs. Goldberg chided. "Of course it will work."

Abby sighed with relief, beginning to absorb some of the Jewish woman's confidence.

Stephen walked over to the edge of the roof and lay down flat on his stomach. "Can you throw the rope to me?" he called.

Abby turned back around to peer down into the street. She could see the angry mob hauling things out of the Bensons' front door. Up and down the block, the scene was replaying itself. She could feel the hatred and anger permeating the atmosphere.

"They deserve what they get!" a woman screamed. "If it wasn't for them niggers, my Tommy wouldn't be fighting now."

"Destroy what ain't worth taking!" a man yelled. "I'll be blamed if I'm gonna go down and die for one of these wooly-heads! They've come up here to take what belongs to the white man!"

Abby watched sadly. Maybe one day she would get used to the depths of depravity mankind was willing to sink to. Then again, she hoped not. It would only indicate a hardening of her own heart.

Elsie's soft voice sounded over her shoulder. "Don't they know they are only hurting themselves? That when they try to crush our liberties, they are putting their own at risk?"

Abby nodded. "I hope one day people will realize protecting the feeblest of their fellow beings is the only guarantee they have of the protection of their own liberty—here or anywhere." She smiled suddenly, realizing the incongruity of having a philosophical discussion on a hot roof while a riot waged below. Maybe it was only by maintaining reason in the midst of craziness that the world would survive. She exchanged a long look of understanding with Elsie.

"I got it!" Stephen sang out triumphantly, holding the rope high above his head.

"Good," Dr. Benson exclaimed.

"Daddy, are the bad people going to get us?" Reuben asked.

"I'm awful hot," lisped little Mabel. "Why can't we go in the house?"

Elsie eased over and lifted Mabel in her arms. "No, Reuben, the bad men aren't going to get us," she said. She wiped Mabel's sweating face with her handkerchief. "I'm sorry you're hot, but sometimes when you have adventures you have to go through hard times. We'll be off the roof soon."

Mabel was comforted in her mother's embrace. She hiccupped, then quit crying.

Her husband appeared at her side. "I'm afraid it's going to be a little while," he murmured.

"Why?"

"We can't risk letting that crowd see us. We have to wait until they go away."

"And if they don't?"

"Then, my dear, I'm afraid we'll have to wait until dark," he grimaced. "It's simply too dangerous, and besides, if they see us, we'll compromise Mrs. Goldberg."

Elsie's voice dropped to a whisper so the children couldn't hear her. "And what if they burn the place?"

Abby was wondering the same thing.

"I don't think they'll burn it," Dr. Benson replied. "I've been watching. They seem intent on taking everything they can get their hands on. If they're going to start burning places, I don't think it will be anytime soon."

Elsie nodded wearily, plastered on a smile, and turned to the children. "Let's see if we can think of a quiet game to play."

"I wanna get off the roof," Mabel wailed again in a frightened voice.

Abby took her from Elsie and walked over to join the rest of the children, trying to swallow her own fear. She could imagine the panic the Stratfords would feel once they got news of the riot. A faint spark of hope rose in her. Maybe they would send help. Maybe Michael would come after her. As quickly as the thought rose, she pushed it aside. Michael would be busy saving the city. It was selfish to think he could come after her just because she had made a foolish decision.

Abby set her lips and spoke softly to the little girl. "How about if we sing a song?" More to calm herself than the children, Abby began to sing softly, senseless songs her mother sang to her when she was a little girl. She had not thought of the songs for years, but now they flowed effortlessly, the clock spinning back almost a half century. Little Mabel snuggled close to her. The other children listened, some of the fear fading from their faces.

Elsie gave a grateful, tired smile and sank down against the side of the house.

Somehow the long afternoon passed. The sun began to sink below the long horizon, giving some relief to the exhausted, thirsty family trapped on the roof. Crowds of people still milled in the streets, but the number had lessened.

Abby stood and stretched her stiff muscles, wincing as her scorched skin objected to the movement. Soon it would be safe to try to make good their escape. Curious to see what was going on below, she walked over to the edge and peered around the corner. She found it hard to believe that so far no one had spotted the huddled family. Or had they, but they simply didn't care as long as they got the belongings they were after? Maybe their thirst for blood had been quenched.

A few minutes later, her theory was destroyed. Abby watched as a middle-aged black man, peering around carefully, edged down the alley between two buildings. She opened her mouth to call to him not to come further. A firm hand on her arm stopped her.

"Don't," Dr. Benson said. "Your call will do nothing but broadcast his position, as well as our own. That's Willie Johnson. He's come to check on his family. They live in that house there," he said, pointing.

"But what if they catch him?"

"I know," Dr. Benson said in an agonized voice. He shook his head. "I'm afraid we can do nothing to help him."

Abby watched helplessly as Willie edged closer and closer to the street. Maybe he would make it. Willie paused when he reached the opening of the alley and carefully poked his head out. The attention of the crowd was diverted by something at the far end of the road and they all began to move to the right away from Willie. He watched for a moment more and then darted from the alley, bound for a building three doors down. He had gone no more than ten steps when a man turned around and saw him.

"We got us a nigger!" he howled. "After him!"

Willie ducked his head and ran faster, past the door of his home. He couldn't endanger his family by going there. Several young boys sprinted free from the mob and tackled the fleeing man.

"Oh God," Abby whispered, wanting to turn away, yet held by her horror. Behind her, she could hear Elsie start to sing again in an effort to distract the children.

"Kill him!" one man screamed.

A young child ran up and jumped around in wild glee. "Get him! Get him!" he cried.

Abby could see Willie holding his arms around his head as the savage beating continued. Fists and heavy boots flew as the helpless man was trampled into the dusty road. Tears of frustration and rage poured down her face. She groaned as one final kick snapped Willie's head back into an awkward position. There was no more movement.

"Got another one!" a man yelled triumphantly as the crowd surged away.

Abby looked up at Dr. Benson. "Isn't there something we can do to help?"

"He's dead," Dr. Benson said. "They broke his neck with that last kick." His voice was flat, but his eyes burned with pain.

Abby sagged and turned away. Was this hideous day never going to end? Was it really only that morning that she had been glad to be alive? Now, the thought of living in a world that could do the things she had witnessed made her feel dirty and soiled.

It was dark when Dr. Benson and Stephen came over to indicate it was time to move. The younger children, cradled by the adults and older children, had dropped off to sleep, exhausted by their long ordeal.

Abby gazed down at Mabel's peaceful face. "Wake up, sweetie," she said softly. "It's time to go."

"Home?" Mabel said hopefully.

"Not quite yet, honey," Elsie said, "but we're going to go somewhere safe."

Mabel's face fell and her lower lip quivered, but she didn't cry. "All right, Mama," she said bravely.

Abby squeezed her gently, lifted her in her arms, and walked over to join the family.

"I'll go first," Stephen announced. "That way I can test the rope and be there to catch the ones that come after me."

"You're sure this is safe?" Elsie asked anxiously, eyeing the gap between the buildings.

Abby knew what she was thinking. The older ones might possibly survive a fall from this height, but the younger ones would die upon impact.

Dr. Benson was at her side instantly. "I won't let any harm come to you," he said. "You and the children need to be brave just a little while longer."

Elsie nodded as Stephen wrapped his hands and legs around the rope and slid slowly down. Abby held her breath as she watched him, praying the rope would hold. She heaved a sigh of relief when his feet touched the porch roof.

Dr. Benson moved quickly. He picked up a shorter section of rope and walked over to Shelby. "You first, little one," he said cheerfully.

"It's time for more adventure?" Shelby asked in a weak voice. Her eyes were still bright, but it was obvious the sweltering day on the roof had sapped what little energy she started with.

"Yes, honey," Dr. Benson replied. "I'm going to tie this rope underneath your arms. Then I'm going to attach it to the rope you saw Stephen go down. I promise you'll be okay."

"I'm not afraid," Shelby said, her dark eyes fixed on her father's face.

Abby's heart swelled with tenderness for the courageous little girl. Mrs. Goldberg was going to hide the brave invalid in one of her upstairs bedrooms until control had been restored to the city. There was no way the weakened little girl would be able to make it to the police precinct.

Dr. Benson carefully tied Shelby and pulled out another long section of rope. Once he had Shelby hanging from the rope, he used the longer rope to hold her steady, making sure she didn't slide too fast. Abby held her breath as the little girl was lowered to where Stephen waited with extended arms.

"Got you!" they heard Stephen say in a playful voice.

The rest of the family was passed down quickly, Abby holding Mabel, Elsie clutching the baby close. Mrs. Goldberg was waiting when the entire family was finally assembled in her kitchen.

"Have you seen the police at all?" Dr. Benson asked.

"I've heard reports," Mrs. Goldberg said. "They are simply not strong enough to stop the rioting. Many of them have been hurt—some killed."

Abby stifled a groan, imagining Michael attacked by a marauding gang.

Dr. Benson nodded grimly. "Then we're getting out of here."

Mrs. Goldberg pointed to a door in her kitchen. "The basement is down there. You will find a small window off to the right. It leads out into an empty lot next to the house. There is a high fence that will protect you from anyone still in the streets." She paused. "Most of them have gone home for the night, but there will still be some out there." She stepped forward and laid a tender kiss on Elsie's forehead. "God is looking out for your little family. You will be safe, and I'll take good care of Shelby."

Elsie nodded and gave her a weary smile. "Thank you," she whispered, obviously at a loss for words.

Mrs. Goldberg nodded. "It's what friends are for. You would do the same for me."

"Yes," Elsie replied in a choked voice. She moved over to where Shelby lay on a small cot Mrs. Goldberg had brought down. "We'll be back for you as soon as we can, honey. You'll be fine."

Shelby smiled bravely, but was now too exhausted to speak. Elsie planted a warm kiss on her forehead, then gathered the baby close and walked down the stairs to the basement.

Abby was the last to go before Dr. Benson followed her. She looked back for one final glimpse of the courageous woman who had let others' hatred and bitterness endow her with strong compassion and selflessness.

Stephen already had the family assembled by the window and had pried it open. "We're ready," he called softly.

Elsie turned to Abby as they were waiting for the children to pass through the window. "Thank you," she said. "I'm so sorry you had to be here during this, but I don't know what I would have done without your help with the children." She paused. "You also helped remind me that not all white people hate us. I need to remember that, and I want my children to learn it."

Abby searched for words to express her own horror that people of her race could commit the unpardonable acts they had today. She simply squeezed Elsie's hand. No words could ever express what she was feeling.

The night was beginning to cool when Abby congregated with the rest of the family in the cluttered, trash-strewn clearing. A soft breeze bathed their sunburned faces, while twinkling stars seemed to assure them that not all the world was terror and violence.

"The police station is only a few blocks away," Dr. Benson whispered. "No one says a word until we get there."

"Will we get to eat there?" Reuben asked plaintively.

Elsie put a finger to his lips. "Hush. We'll eat soon."

Stephen led the way through the narrow alleys snaking between the buildings, peering cautiously around all corners before he advanced. Abby snuggled Mabel close and followed, her heart hammering with fear, envisioning what would happen if someone were to spy the fugitive family.

It seemed like an eternity before they finally broke out of the last alley and saw the station standing like a sentinel before them. Abby gathered her skirts around her and dashed across the road with the rest of the family, heaving a sigh of relief when a solidly built policeman stepped forward to confront them.

"Who's there?" he called sharply, peering at them harder. "Is that you, Dr. Benson?"

"With my family." Dr. Benson moved into the light from the gas lamp. "Will we be safe here?"

"As long as you don't mind staying in some jail cells for the night," the policeman replied. "I heard your house was broken into. It could be a little while before we get you back in there. The mayor has called for militia, but it could take them a few days to get here. We simply don't have enough men to bring this thing under control."

Dr. Benson shrugged. "My family is safe," he said. "That's what matters."

"I'm hungry," Reuben wailed.

Abby laughed. The little boy had been brave all day. Now that he was safe, he was going to concentrate on what was important.

"All right, little man," the policeman said. "Let's see what we can do about that."

He turned to Dr. Benson. "It's going to be crowded. We've had folks coming in all day. I'm afraid it's going to be a little uncomfortable."

Abby thought about the misery they had endured all day on the hot roof and smiled.

The policeman turned to her. "Who are you, ma'am?"

"My name is Abigail Livingston. I was visiting the Bensons when the mob started rioting."

"Abigail Livingston?" the policeman repeated, looking thoughtful. "Are you the one Michael has been asking about?"

"Michael Stratford?" Abby asked excitedly. "Is he here?"

"No, but we've had a couple of communications about you. There have been some folks real worried about you. I'll wire over to the main precinct that you're all right." He hesitated. "I'm afraid we can't get you out of here tonight. It wouldn't be safe." His brow creased. "We don't have very luxurious accommodations, but we've got a room off to the back of the building with a small cot."

"I'll stay with my friends," Abby said firmly.

The policeman opened his mouth to argue, then shut it, seeming to realize it wouldn't matter. He nodded. "Whatever you say, Mrs. Livingston."

Chapter Fifteen

Abby woke the next morning stiff and sore from her night in the cramped jail cell. She lay quietly for a few minutes, observing the people around her. All of the jail cells were crammed full of fugitives from the mob. She reflected on the stark injustice of them being the ones contained by bars and forced to hide from those who actually deserved to be in jail.

Abby also had to admit it was rather uncomfortable being the only white face in a sea of ebony. It was rather a new sensation to be the minority. Even though it felt awkward, she was glad for the experience. She had learned long ago that the only way to understand what a person was feeling was to experience it yourself. She knew her limited time in the cell could never truly enlighten her on what it must be like to be black, but for a moment she could feel the loneliness and insecurity that sprang from being different.

Abby heard the jangle of keys and looked up as the officer from the night before swung the door open. His face was lined with fatigue, his eyes swollen. He clearly had not gotten any sleep. What was going on out in the city?

"Mrs. Livingston?" he called.

Abby swung her legs over the narrow cot she had been sharing with Mabel and Reuben and sat up. They stirred but didn't wake. The long day before had left them completely exhausted. She smiled at them tenderly and then looked up. "Yes, officer?"

"Michael Stratford is here for you, ma'am."

Abby smiled in relief. "That's wonderful." The officer unlocked the cell and swung the door open. "What's going on out in the city?" she asked.

Dr. Benson and Elsie sat up to listen.

The officer shrugged his shoulders. "It's still early, ma'am, but it doesn't look good. The crowds are already building up. There's still time for you to make it out of here, though."

"But what about my friends?" Abby protested. "When can they go home?"

The officer shook his head. "I have no idea. I'm sorry."

Abby hesitated, staring at the family stuffed into the cell. "Come with me," she said suddenly. "There is plenty of room at the Stratford's home. I know they won't mind," she said.

"We'll stay right here until it's safe for us to go home," Dr. Benson replied.

Elsie stood and slipped her arm around Abby's waist. "You go. We'll be fine here. One never learns to like it, but we are accustomed to fighting for the right to live our lives." She paused. "Thank you," she finished.

"Thank *you*," Abby said. "I'm quite sure your taking me in saved me from great harm. May I come back to visit when I'm in New York again?"

"We would like that very much," Dr. Benson said. "There is much we were going to discuss. I'm sorry events made that impossible."

Abby forced a smile. "Someday things will be back to normal in our country."

Dr. Benson shook his head. "I most sincerely hope not, Mrs. Livingston. Normal for our people would not be a step forward. No, I rather hope that when this is all over, no one will be able to recognize our country. In fact, I'm counting on it."

Abby stared at him for a moment, realizing the truth of what he was saying.

"Mrs. Livingston," the officer interrupted. "We really must be going."

Abby hugged her new friends and kissed each sleeping child gently on the forehead. "Tell them goodbye for me."

Michael was waiting for her in the main room. "Aunt Abby!" he cried, striding up to embrace her. "Thank God you're all right." He took her arm and began to lead her toward the door. "I'm going to get you out of here before things get too heated again. It took Paxton hours to get home. My mother has been in a panic ever since he told us what happened. I haven't been able to get word to her that you're all right. I've been working straight through."

"You're not in uniform," Abby observed.

"The mayor has called for militia, but it may take another day or so for them to arrive. In the meantime, there are simply not enough police to do the job. Dozens of men on the force have been badly injured or killed. The only way to come into the area to rescue them is to be out of uniform. I didn't want to take any additional chance of having you harmed."

Abby looked at him closely. His eyes held a mixture of both sadness and anger. His face was etched with weariness. "It's bad everywhere?"

"It's bad." Michael's lack of words told her more than if he had gone on at length.

Abby climbed into the carriage with him, then reached over and squeezed his hand. She knew there was nothing she could say to take away the horror. The sun was just climbing over the horizon, but already there were people milling in the streets.

"We had hoped it would rain," Michael said. "Another hot day isn't going to help anything."

Abby gazed around, noting the smashed windows and the household belongings scattered through the dusty roads. "It was worst in the black sections, wasn't it?"

"The workers blame the blacks for the whole draft situation. You can't reason with a mob." Michael urged the horse into a ground-eating trot. People glared but moved out of the way as the carriage swept toward them.

They had almost reached the edge of the crowds when they heard a shout. "Hey, there goes one of those policemen. That there is Michael Stratford. Get him!"

Abby gasped as Michael pulled out a long whip and snapped it over the horses. "Get down in the seat!" he hollered to Abby as the carriage spurted forward.

Abby looked back once and saw a sea of people pressing down on them, anger boiling in their faces. Thinking quickly, she reached behind the seat and found the extra buggy whip drivers usually carried with them. Steadying herself, she uncoiled the whip and grabbed one side of the carriage.

A man lunged out at them from the side of the road, reaching for the horse's bridle in a wild attempt to stop them. Michael cracked the whip over the horses again and they ran even faster. At that exact same moment, Abby leaned out and snapped the whip at the approaching man, feeling a grim satisfaction when the tip of the lash raked across the man's arm. The man screamed a curse and fell back, stumbling until he landed in a pile in the dusty road. Two men following his example crashed on top of him.

"Way to go, Aunt Abby!" Michael cried in admiration.

The last of the crowd melted away before the careening carriage, and they broke out onto an empty street. Michael kept the horses running for several more blocks before he slowed them down and looked back. "We're out," he said in a relieved voice. He turned to Abby. "Where in the world did you learn to handle a whip like that?"

"Just luck." Abby smiled, her hands shaking now that the crisis was past. "I've never touched a whip before in my life."

Michael shook his head and kept going. "Mother and Father will be glad to see you. I'm afraid you won't be able to catch your boat out, though. I know you were planning on leaving today, but no one can get through the streets."

"I'll get home eventually," Abby said. "You know, there's something about almost losing your life that gives you a new perspective on things. Whether I get home in a few days or a few weeks, I'm just glad I'm alive to get home."

Four days later Abby hugged her friends goodbye and stepped onto the boat that would take her to Philadelphia. She stared out over the harbor sadly as they steamed away from the dock. Thousands of New York militia had finally regained control of New York City's streets. Large areas of the town had been burned and destroyed. Looters had wreaked havoc in numerous shopping districts. Bridges had been burned and transportation cars mutilated. Hundreds of people— mostly blacks and police—had been killed or wounded. Order had been restored, but a sullen heaviness pervaded the air and a kind of shame hung over the city.

The loss of life and property made up only a small part of the riot damage. Once again, families were torn apart, and business relationships just beginning to prosper were soured. Hope was blasted, confidence was destroyed and insecurity was fostered. The dark clouds covering America were relentless in their pursuit of innovative ways to darken men's hearts and pull the worst from them.

Robert finished another letter to Carrie, stuffed it in an envelope, sealed and stamped it, then stood to stretch. A large pile of similar letters rested next to him. He added the last one to the accumulation. He had no idea when, or even if, the letters would make their way to her, but he was being faithful. Captain Shoemaker had promised to do all he could to see that they arrived.

Robert strode to the deck of the ship forging through the waters of the Atlantic and scanned the horizon to see if he could catch a glimpse of land. The captain had promised him they would land in London today. He had gotten up early so he could watch England come into view. He had enjoyed his trip for the most part, but he was eager to be on land again. He found the ship to be both confining and boring. The endless expanse of blue possessed a certain beauty, but staring at the same thing day after day wearied him.

"Anxious to be in London, Mr. Borden?" an amused voice asked.

Robert nodded, not taking his eyes off the horizon. "That I am, Mr. Olsen. That I am." He knew Olsen would not be offended by his not turning around to speak to him. The older gentleman was his senior by almost a half-century, but the two had developed a comfortable friendship from the first day of the journey. Neither was open about their reason for traveling to Europe during the middle of a war, but both instinctively knew their reasons were important to the Confederacy. That was enough. Details in such a time as this were simply not important.

"I'll be glad to be back in the old city," Olsen said fondly, tapping his cane against the railing and adjusting his high hat. "I'm afraid I will find it much changed after almost fifty years, however."

Robert glanced at him in surprise. In all their conversations, Olsen had not mentioned being in London before.

"I was here for a year," Olsen said in response to Robert's look. "When I was your age. My father thought it would do me good to expand my horizons, so I came to study." He grimaced. "Can't say I was too fond of it at the time. After twenty years on my family plantation, I found the city both confining and dirty. If it wasn't blanketed in fog, it was blanketed in coal smoke and residue."

"You don't paint an appealing picture," Robert said. "Was there was anything about the city you liked?"

"Certainly. My father was right—it expanded my horizons. I learned to see the world through more than the eyes of a plantation brat. I learned to appreciate politics, art, the theater. Most importantly, I learned to appreciate the freedoms we have in America. Excuse me," he added. "The ones we did have." His words weren't bitter, just matter-of-fact. "I'm afraid our country has changed dramatically since then."

Robert said nothing. They had spent hours discussing the state of affairs in America. He wasn't exactly tired of it, but he was anxious to get on land and get involved in resolving them. The forced inactivity was wearing on him. Discussion was fine, as long as it was accompanied by action.

Olsen was quiet for several minutes and then cleared his throat. "Neither of us has talked about our reasons for going to England and daring to run the blockade."

Robert glanced up. Was Olsen going to confide in him? Part of him was curious to know why the old gentleman was undergoing such an arduous adventure. Another part of him rebelled against knowing—against feeling he should reciprocate the confidence. He had appreciated Olsen's company for the last two weeks. Robert had feared the same boring companions that had accompanied him on the Phantom. The two men were indeed on the ship, but they kept to themselves. Olsen had sought him out at the first meal. In spite of the difference in their ages, they had found much in common.

"I'm afraid that whatever our missions are, they are hopelessly futile," Olsen said heavily. "I've come carrying hope in my heart, but the closer I get to London, the more futile this whole escapade seems. So why did I come?" He chuckled humorlessly, shaking his head. "Maybe to have one last adventure before I die." His voice grew serious. "Our country will never be the same, Robert." He shook his head. "We're putting up a grand fight, but in the end, we are going to lose."

"The Confederacy has won the last big battles," Robert countered.

"As far as we know," Olsen reminded him. "A lot could have happened since we have been gone. But it's no matter. The South doesn't have the industrial strength nor the manpower to conquer the North. It's really only a matter of time."

"If you believe that, why are you here?"

"Like I said, maybe it's just to have one last adventure. I'm old. I'm going to die soon. I wanted to once more see the country where I learned to look at life differently. Oh, I have a mission, the same as you, or I wouldn't be here. I'll try to perform it, but I hold little hope it will make much difference in the end."

Robert stared at the old man, trying to decide what to say.

Olsen laughed lightly. "Don't search your mind for a way to respond, Robert. I'm not looking for one. I simply feel the need to express myself this morning." He turned to stare out at the sea, his silver fringe fluttering in the breeze. "Things change when you get older. I used to insist on seeing the world through idealistic eyes. I scorned those who tried to dissuade me with realism. Then one day, I woke up and realized the world would never be the way I dreamed it would be, because it is peopled with those who are human." Olsen tapped his cane against the railing. "Don't misunderstand me, however. My realization didn't turn me into a cynic. It gave me more compassion and patience. I have spent my life trying to make a difference where I can, but I no longer feel I have failed if the results aren't perfection."

"But if we lose the war, we've lost everything," Robert protested, wondering even as he spoke if he really believed that anymore.

"Have we?" Olsen asked. "We may have lost the way of life we have cherished, but we won't have lost our souls. We won't have lost our ability to love and laugh. We won't have lost our ability to learn and grow."

"Then why are you working for the Confederacy?" Robert asked, confused.

"Because I believe in our right to make our own decisions. I don't believe the federal government should dictate what we do. Even if what we're doing is wrong."

"Excuse me?"

"Slavery, Robert. I believe slavery is wrong. I gave my slaves their freedom long ago." His voice grew firmer. "There are people who feel they are fighting for slavery. Ownership of another human being would never give me the motivation to engage in the struggle we find ourselves in now. No, I'm living the last years of my life in support of the Confederacy because I believe in states' rights."

"I own slaves," Robert confessed. "At least I did. I haven't been near my plantation since the war started. For all I know, they have all run away."

"You don't sound like you would be very distressed."

"I wouldn't. I've changed how I feel about it. I don't believe in slavery anymore. I've discovered blacks are people just like me." He paused. "I was almost killed at Antietam. A black fellow who I will probably never know saved my life. It was a black family that took me into their home for seven months while I healed. Living with them changed my life."

"Yet you are still fighting for the Confederacy?"

"I'm fighting for my home. For my wife. For my right to make my own decisions."

"And if we lose the war?" Olsen asked, watching him closely.

Robert hesitated. It's not that he hadn't thought of it. He feared from the beginning that the Confederacy had taken on a challenge they had no hope of winning. So many thought the North would simply let them walk away—that there would never be a fight. Certainly they never thought hundreds of thousands of their men and boys would die or be maimed for life. Robert finally shook his head. "I don't know."

"Think about it while you're here," Olsen advised. "I find it much easier to deal with a situation if I have come to peace with whatever the results might be."

"But doesn't that make you weak in your fight?"

"On the contrary," Olsen asserted. "I find even more energy to pursue what I'm after because there is no fear of failure to hold me back. I've already decided I can live with whatever happens." He paused and turned to look Robert squarely in the eyes. "What will your life be like if the South loses? Can you live with it?" He turned back to stare at the ocean, obviously not expecting an answer.

Robert stood next to him silently, pondering the old man's words.

"There it is!" Olsen suddenly called out, pointing his cane toward the horizon. "Good old England." He was quiet for a few moments, then asked, "How much do you know about England?"

"Not a lot," Robert admitted. "I've done some studying, but I still feel inadequate. I've always felt you should know as much about a foreign country as possible before you go there. I'm afraid this trip was rather unexpected."

"England is staunchly against slavery. Do you know that?"

"I'd heard they weren't fond of our peculiar institution," Robert said dryly. "Are you afraid I'm going to put my foot in my mouth and embarrass myself?"

"Not at all," Olsen said hastily. "I just find it helpful to understand the mental state of people before I try to develop a relationship with them. *Uncle Tom's Cabin* sold more widely in England than it did in the United States, you know." He laughed. "Of course, English dislike of American arrogance could have much to do with its popularity."

"What are you really trying to tell me?" Robert asked.

Olsen stared at him for a moment. "Don't get your hopes up too high, my boy. The aristocracy is on our side, but the queen and most of the people support the North. Lincoln's Emancipation Proclamation was a stroke of genius. It was exactly what was needed to swing anti-slavery England all the way to their side. Not that it really matters, I suppose. England has rather wisely chosen a position of neutrality. I don't fancy anything we can do will change that."

"It was an English captain who commandeered the boat I ran the blockade on," Robert reminded him.

"Ah yes," Olsen said, a small smile curling his lips. "People motivated by money don't often let a little thing like political persuasion stand in their way. The English aren't fools, Robert. They recognize a way to make tremendous profits when they see it. There are many Englishmen who will become quite wealthy off the misfortune of the South. Not that it's bad," he added. "Were it not for their desire to make money, the South would have been destroyed long ago. If it weren't for the massive amounts of goods being shipped from this country, we would not still be surviving." He swung back around and stared across the water.

Robert wasn't sure what to think of this conversation with Olsen. If all was lost, why not turn around and go home to Carrie? *And more battles,* a voice added. Robert frowned. Was he coming to England because he didn't want to fight? Surely he had never suspected Carrie would choose not to join him. What exactly *was* he doing here?

Robert pushed aside his thoughts for later reflection and leaned against the railing. Soon the other passengers joined them, their laughter and talk reflecting their own relief at finally reaching their destination. The thin line of land grew larger until Robert could finally distinguish church spires and buildings in the distance. Ship masts bobbed in the breeze, looking like a cushion full of needles.

Robert leaned forward excitedly. How many of those ships were loaded with goods destined for Nassau and the blockade runners waiting for them? Which one would take his letters to Carrie? As he watched the city take shape before his eyes, his longing for Carrie gripped him like a physical ache. How he longed to share all this with her. How he longed to explore the city with her, together experiencing all it had to offer.

He swallowed the knot swelling in his throat, and once again reminded himself he had to let her be who she was. He couldn't demand she change. He couldn't make her into something she wasn't. *You knew what she was like before you married her,* he reminded himself. He shook his head heavily. "That doesn't make me miss her any less," he whispered fiercely, glad the sound of the boat and the wind swept away his voice.

Matthew gazed around him wearily as the train carrying him and about a hundred other prisoners pulled into the train station on Broad Street. His mind flew back to before the war when he had arrived to spend Christmas on Cromwell Plantation with Carrie and her family. It seemed a different time and a totally different life. He looked down at his filthy clothes, then contemplated the looks of despair and defiance of the men with him. It was indeed a different time. He pushed the thoughts of earlier times out of his mind. It was now he had to live.

"All right, gentleman," a Confederate soldier called mockingly. "You've almost arrived at your new home. I'm sure you're glad to be here. We'll try to make you as comfortable as possible." His words were accompanied by a harsh laugh.

Matthew gritted his teeth and stood up to exit the train with the other men. He decided he envied the men who had no idea what to expect. They had plied him with questions about the prison facilities of Richmond, thinking that Matthew's confinement here the year before would give them information to make it easier. Matthew had done the best he could to prepare them, but knew his efforts were futile. Only through experience could one understand the humiliation and degradation of prison existence.

He shuddered as he thought of the number of enlisted men who would not even have the dubious *comforts* of Libby Prison to experience. Libby was reserved for officers and civilian prisoners. The enlisted men would find themselves in even more crowded conditions. Matthew had heard rumors of the prison on Belle Island. How many of his companions would end up out there?

During the long ride across the country, Matthew had tried to prepare himself for what was to come. When he had been released in a prisoner exchange from Libby the year before, he hoped to never again experience anything like it. The long nights stuffed into the train had given him plenty of time to relive those horrid months, as well as envision what waited for him. He fought daily to hold on to hope and not let despair completely overwhelm him.

"Well, Mr. Justin, I guess you're home again," a guard sneered. "I'm sure you missed it."

Matthew looked at him steadily but didn't respond. He took a deep breath, stood, and joined the queue of prisoners streaming from the train. It was only now dawn, so the streets were mostly empty as they marched toward the river. The few people up and about muttered and scowled when they saw them.

Matthew struggled to remember the kind and gracious city he had visited a few years before. There was little to remind him. The evidences of neglect were everywhere. Paint peeled from buildings and shutters hung free, creaking in the breeze. Fence posts lay where they had fallen, whole sections of the once proud, elegant structures now sagging to the ground. What had been carefully tended yards abloom with flowers, were now dusty, weedy spots. Trash and litter were everywhere, clogging the streets and covering the sidewalks.

Matthew felt a surge of pity for the people of the once proud city. They had paid dearly for the honor of being the capital of the Confederacy. The rather dubious honor had assured they would become a besieged city. That they had managed to survive this long was a miracle. His thoughts flew to Carrie. Was she still in the city? Were she and her father well? What had happened to his friend Robert? It was doing Matthew no good to try to block out the past. Everything he saw brought it to life, rising to taunt him. It was bad enough to be heading to prison. It was even more torture to be in the city which had once held such fond memories for him.

"It doesn't look much like I thought it would," Peter said quietly.

Matthew glanced over at his fellow journalist. "It's changed," he said. "Just like everything has been changed by this war." He knew his voice sounded bitter. He was losing his battle against despair.

"We're going to make it," Peter said. "We'll probably be exchanged in a few weeks. They won't keep us long."

Matthew nodded.

"You can't lose hope."

"I also can't survive on pipe dreams," Matthew reminded him. "No one will be happier than me if I make it out of this place again, but I'm not counting on it."

Peter stared at him in silence. "You don't sound like yourself," he said finally.

"We'll see how you sound after a few weeks in this place," Matthew countered. He didn't tell Peter of the months of endless nightmares he endured after his first prison stay. He had managed to put them all behind him, but in the last two weeks, they had again become a constant reality.

"Is that it?" Peter asked.

Matthew glanced up and nodded. "That's it." The building was the one of his nightmares. The three-story brick structure, once a tobacco warehouse, loomed over the street. He could see the faces of men peering from every window. As before, there was no glass to keep the rain and cold out. At least it was summer, he told himself grimly. He wouldn't be freezing for a few months. His heart caught as he remembered the coat Carrie had brought him the winter he had been confined. He had felt guilty being warm while he watched other men sicken and die, yet he was sure the coat had been the only thing that helped him survive... *Only to end up back here again,* he thought.

Libby Prison was as crowded as Matthew remembered. Hundreds of men looked up as he and Peter were escorted into the room after being registered in the office with the twenty others who would be held here.

"Welcome to Libby Prison."

Matthew forced a smile as he turned to look at the man standing close behind him. "Greetings from the outside world." He knew from past experience that the men confined here longed for any word of what was happening outside the four walls they were trapped in.

"My name is Captain Arthur Anderson."

"And I'm Matthew Justin. This is Peter Wilcher."

"Your commissions?"

"We're journalists."

A smile lit Captain Anderson's face. "Come on over here, boys. We've got us a couple of journalists. Now we can really find out what is going on out there." He pulled up a barrel and plunked down on it. "Talk."

Two hours later Matthew and Peter had answered all their questions. At least the ones they had fired at them so far.

"My turn," Matthew finally said. "How is the prisoner exchange going?" In spite of his determination not to hope, he was grasping onto the chance his time here would be short.

Anderson shrugged. "Hooker lost a lot more men than Lee at Chancellorsville. There has been exchange going on, but there are still a lot of us here. The Rebels like to hang on to the officers in case there is someone really important they want to exchange for."

Matthew felt his hope flicker. "I see."

"Come on, Matthew. They aren't going to keep a couple of journalists here," Peter argued. "We'll be out of here soon."

Matthew said nothing. The look on Anderson's face said it all. The rules of this war had changed. They were now being written as need dictated. There might be the need for a couple of Yankee journalists. As long as there was that possibility, they would be held. Their very novelty made them a valuable commodity.

"What's Belle Island like?" he asked. He wanted to take his mind off his own situation.

Anderson scowled. "It's like nothing you've ever seen. And nothing you ever want to experience. This is a grand hotel compared to what those men are enduring. There is precious little shelter, and never enough food. Those men are crammed in there like rats in a cage." His voice grew husky. "We watch them from the windows sometimes. You can see dark shapes tottering around. God help them if this war isn't over by winter. Having them out there then will be nothing short of murder."

Matthew watched the agony play over the man's face. Some of the men he commanded must be confined on the island.

"I'm the president of the Libby Prison Association," Anderson said finally. "It is my privilege to inform you of the rules of conduct we have established here." He smiled. "They're pretty simple really. We decided that when we finally get out of here, we will still be civilized gentlemen."

"Those of us who started that way," a listening man hooted. The room rang with laughter.

Matthew felt himself relax a little. The faces had changed since he had last been here, but the camaraderie remained the same. You could steal a man's freedom, but you couldn't steal his humanity. That was a choice that would always remain his. As before, Matthew determined to maintain his humanity.

"What happens if you need to go to the bathroom?" Peter asked quietly.

Matthew smiled, settling in his cramped position among the rows of men lying on the floor side by side, their feet towards the narrow center aisle. He had asked the same question. "You do your best to hold your bladder," he said. "It's almost impossible to get up without stepping on someone. It's not the best way to form friendships," he said dryly.

Peter was quiet, digesting this piece of information. "Do you really think we'll be here a long time?" His voice lacked its usual confidence.

"I won't be," Matthew said, his voice barely above a whisper.

Peter turned over to stare at him. "What...?"

"I'm going to escape," Matthew whispered. Then he turned his back to avoid any more questions. One day back in the prison had convinced him he would not willingly stay any longer than necessary. Every day would be spent waiting for the right opportunity.

Chapter Sixteen

Robert settled down at a rustic wooden table with a mug of ale in his hand. He leaned back against the plush cushions behind him and scanned the room. He had been in London almost a month now. He had become familiar with the streets, grown accustomed to the constant noise, and made many new friends, but nothing eased the ache in his heart for Carrie. He thought about her now as he took a sip from his mug. He tried to envision her—where she was, what she was doing. He frowned, once again feeling the frustration of not even knowing if she was safe. If she had written letters, none of them had reached him.

"What's the frown for, old man?"

Robert looked up as a cheerful voice broke into his thoughts. He smiled, relieved to have someone to take his mind off home. "About time you got here, Charles," he said, raising his mug. "I've been waiting for almost twenty minutes."

"I got delayed," Charles said casually, slipping into the chair next to Robert. "The weather is rather beastly, don't you think?"

"London weather is almost always beastly," Robert scoffed. "I can deal with it knowing I will be returning to the sunny South, but I don't know how you Londoners stand it."

"Oh, we get used to it," Charles grinned. "Besides, it gives us something to complain about." He took a large gulp from the mug of ale the waitress sat down in front of him and breathed a sigh of relief. "I spent enough time in your sunny South to prefer clouds to suffocating humidity and hordes of mosquitoes. I'll take London, thank you."

"To each his own," Robert responded. He leaned forward. "What did you find out?" Charles was more than a friend. The middle-aged man sitting next to him had spent almost a decade in both North Carolina and South

Carolina after he graduated from school in London. He had stayed long enough to develop a firm loyalty for the South. He owned several warehouses down by the waterfront that were stocked with tons of goods destined for the Confederate coastline.

Charles reached up and tugged off his tweed hat. His coppery curls shone under the light. Bright blue eyes regarded Robert thoughtfully. "I'm afraid it's not good news," he said.

Robert took another drink of his ale and waited. He made sure his face didn't reveal the sick feeling in his stomach. He never knew who might be watching.

Charles leaned forward, his voice dropping to a whisper. "Russell ordered seizure of the *Alexandra* today."

Robert felt his heart sink. The *Alexandra* was a boat commissioned by the South. It wasn't one of the boats he was here for, but he knew its reputation. Its capacity to not only run the blockade, but also play a large role in destroying the weaker vessels of the Northern navy, had inspired hope in the Confederate government. "But I thought Russell was going to look the other way?" he protested. "His foreign policy so far would indicate he doesn't want to get too involved in the blockade business."

"Things change. He seems to be paying more attention to the Foreign Enlistment Act of 1819."

Robert had done his homework by now. "The act prohibits the building and equipping of armed ships in British ports for the support of belligerents in a war in which Great Britain is neutral," he stated. "But there is no rule against the building of ships sailed from British ports and equipped elsewhere."

"Unless there is clear evidence these ships are intended for use in your civil war," Charles reminded him.

"And is there clear evidence?" Robert demanded. He had learned enough to know the American emissary sent over to negotiate the purchase of the two boats now in the Laird shipyard had covered his tracks extremely well.

Charles shrugged, taking another gulp of his ale. Loud music blared from the band, effectively covering their conversation. They met here often. It was a safe place to carry on business, and the food and drink were good. It was always crowded, so there was no reason they should stand out.

"What can I get for you chaps?" the waitress asked, poising her pencil above her pad.

Robert glanced up and saw her thick dark hair. Once again his heart ached for Carrie. "Beef pie," he said. Charles ordered the same, and the waitress moved away.

Charles leaned forward again. "Russell is getting nervous. He's afraid Northern privateers are going to start interfering with British commerce in retaliation. English shipping interests are starting to fear the same thing."

"And you?" Robert asked.

"I'm different," Charles replied. "I'm not in it for the money. I have a loyalty to the South these other men don't have. They've been eager to be involved as long as the money was good, but they aren't eager to jeopardize their other ventures. They have plenty of other ways to make money." He shook his head. "I'm sorry, Robert. That's the way it is."

"So what is Russell going to do?"

"I don't know. I don't think Russell does either."

"He knows about the two ships in the Laird shipyard?"

Charles nodded heavily. "My reports say he does. We've done our best to keep them a secret, but they are rather large," he said sardonically.

"So what do we do now?"

"We wait," Charles said. "It's all we can do. Russell ordered the seizure of the *Alexandra*, but the courts have to support him. They may decide to order her release." His voice held little confidence.

The waitress appeared with their food, and Robert picked at it listlessly. He had lost his appetite.

"Say, old man," Charles admonished him. "It's not the end of the world. We don't know for sure what is going to happen. In the meantime, there are still a lot of top-notch blockade runners already out there." He took a hearty bite of his pie. "I'm sending out six ships myself tomorrow."

Robert was too disheartened to think of anything to say.

Charles grinned and stood up. "I'll be right back," he announced.

Robert watched him as he threaded his way across the crowded room. He stopped in front of a woman with blond hair pulled back into a loose chignon. Even from here, Robert could tell she was very attractive. Charles talked to her earnestly for a few moments, and then she looked up across the room to where he was sitting. Moments later, the two were moving toward him. He stood as they approached the table.

Charles took the woman's arm as they reached the table. "Robert Borden, I'd like you to meet Suzanne Palmer. She's a fellow Virginian."

"Really?" Robert asked.

Suzanne stepped forward and offered a daintily gloved hand. "It's a pleasure to meet you, Mr. Borden."

"I haven't heard that accent since I left home," Robert laughed. "I'm convinced. Will you please join us, Mrs. Palmer?"

"Miss Palmer," she corrected him. "At least for another few months. I'm to be married in December to a wonderful Englishman."

"Congratulations," Robert replied. "I highly recommend it. I was married myself a few months ago."

Suzanne smiled. "And where is your wife? I would love to meet her."

"I'm afraid she is still in Virginia." For some reason he felt compelled to explain. "Carrie is working at Chimborazo Hospital in Richmond. Even though she hasn't yet attended medical school because of the war, her services are much in demand there."

"They wouldn't let her come?"

"She chose not to," Robert said honestly, somehow sure this woman with the direct eyes would understand.

Suzanne regarded him closely for a few moments. "And how do you feel about that?"

"I miss her, but I respect and support her decision. She's quite good."

Suzanne threw back her head and laughed, obviously not caring what anyone around her thought. "I like you, Robert Borden," she said. She turned to Charles. "Thank you for bringing me over here. May I join you for a while?"

"Certainly," the two men said in unison.

"What brings you to England, Miss Palmer?" Robert asked.

"Oh, the social life," Suzanne said airily. "The South is simply not the place to be now."

Robert gazed at her and smiled. He knew she was lying, and that she knew he knew. "I see," he said casually. "How long have you been in this invigorating city?"

"Almost six months." She beamed across the table at him. "I simply love London. It is so alive!" She laughed. "I'm sorry. Some people are a little put off by my enthusiasm, but I spent almost my whole life on a small Virginia plantation. Thankfully, I was able to escape and spent several years in Washington, DC, but even that is dull compared to London."

Something stirred in Robert's mind—a memory that tugged to be acknowledged. He looked at Suzanne more closely. There was something about her that seemed familiar.

"I'm afraid I've said too much," Suzanne said, a curtain dropping over her eyes.

Robert closed his mind to the memory, whatever it was. "No you haven't," he said. "I've never seen you before until tonight. You're a Southern damsel in distress who simply can't abide the idea of war, so you fled to London. I daresay there are many Southern women who would follow your example if they had the chance."

Suzanne smiled at him gratefully. "You are a true Southern gentleman, Robert Borden."

Robert smiled in return and signaled the waitress over. Once Suzanne had ordered, he turned back to her.

"Now tell me what it is you like so much about this city." He was fairly sure this would be safe conversation.

"Oh, everything," Suzanne exclaimed. "I've tried to answer that question for myself before. I can't decide if it's the Thames River, the London Bridge, Buckingham Palace..." Her voice trailed off. "Or maybe it's the people. I feel so much a part of the world when I'm in London. I have met people from so many different countries. They inspire me and challenge me."

Robert watched her eyes light with excitement and once more felt the familiar pang.

Suzanne, opening her mouth to continue, stopped suddenly. "Is something wrong? Am I gushing a little too much?"

"Certainly not," Robert assured her. "It's only that you remind me so much of my wife. I think you two would be good friends."

"From your description so far, I'm quite certain of it," Suzanne replied. "Tell me," she said, leaning forward, "do you mind being the husband of an independent, hard-headed woman?"

Robert laughed. "Nervous about how your husband will respond to you?"

Suzanne smiled demurely. "Perhaps." She laughed. "I'm afraid he knows full well what he's getting into."

"I don't mind," Robert said. "No, it's more than that. It's not that I don't mind, it's that I love Carrie the way she is. I wouldn't want her to be any different. I realize there are many men who would think me either foolish or stupid, but they are entitled to their opinion. I find Carrie refreshing and stimulating. I'm proud of who she is, and of who she is going to become."

"You don't feel threatened by her?" Suzanne prodded.

Robert looked at her closely. Perhaps she wasn't as confident as she had at first seemed about her upcoming marriage. "If I'm threatened by her, that's not her fault, it's my own. I realize it's not orthodox thinking, but I don't view her so much as a wife as I do my partner in life." He paused. "I must admit I didn't always feel that way. It took some time for me to change."

Suzanne smiled. "Thank you for being honest." She hesitated. "It's so wonderful to meet another Virginian. I feel like I belong in England, but it's always good to get a taste of home."

"Will you ever go back?" Robert asked.

"I might," Suzanne said evasively.

Robert realized he had blundered into uncomfortable waters again. He looked to Charles for help.

"I hear your future husband is involved in the cotton industry, Miss Palmer. How goes it these days?"

Suzanne relaxed visibly. "Things have been quite rough for the last two years. At first, no one thought the war would last very long, or that it would have much effect on the industry. America's crop in 1860 was the heaviest on record, according to Anthony. Most of it arrived here by the beginning of the war."

"Her fiancé owns several cotton mills in Lancashire," Charles explained to Robert.

Suzanne nodded. "The whole industry came almost to a standstill last year. Many of his workers and their families suffered greatly, especially during the last winter. The government stepped in to help them, but of course it wasn't enough. Things are improving, though."

"How?" Robert asked. "I can't imagine enough cotton is getting through."

"No. Once it became obvious the war wasn't going to end soon, the mill owners started looking for other sources. New supplies started coming in from Egypt and the East this spring. The crisis seems to have passed."

"For England," Robert muttered.

Suzanne gazed at him. "I feel the same way you do, Robert. I know the South counted on England's support because of their dependency on our cotton. It certainly caused distress for a while, but England has adjusted." She sighed. "I'm afraid England is going to stick to their policy of neutrality." She leaned forward and lowered her voice to a confidential whisper. "There are still ways they are willing to help, however."

Robert stared at her, wanting to ask what she meant, but knowing she wouldn't tell him. Suddenly, he was very weary. Charles' news, along with the latest on the cotton industry, had tired him. He stood abruptly. "It was a pleasure meeting you. I hope I will see you again."

Suzanne and Charles stood with him. "I'm sorry if I have upset you," Suzanne said.

"Not at all." Turning, he strode out of the restaurant. He took great gulps of air as he broke out onto Fenchurch Street. Fog swirled around him as he turned west. He needed time to think and to process what was happening. It seemed everything was falling apart.

Minutes later, he was crossing Thames Street. His footsteps echoed in the mist as he walked out onto London Bridge. Gas lamps glowed through the fog, causing the vapors to dance and swirl in protest against the invading light. Robert reached the center of the bridge and leaned against the railing heavily. The fog swallowed everything around him, but he could still hear water lapping against the pilings.

His surroundings matched his mood exactly. Loneliness battled with a feeling of utter futility. Without more powerful blockade runners, the South would lose the war. Every day, the dim hope England would eventually recognize them faded away even more.

"We may have lost the way of life we have cherished, but we won't have lost our souls. We won't have lost our ability to love and laugh. We won't have lost our ability to learn and grow."

Olsen's words reverberated through Robert's mind. It was almost as if the old man were standing beside him, urging him not to give up hope, exhorting him to find the things worth living for. Robert scowled, staring into the enshrouding mist. The fog wrapped a cocoon around him, separating him from the rest of the world, blocking out the muted noises and activities of London.

Robert didn't know how much time had passed before he stepped away from the railing, a peace permeating his heart. A sure realization gripped him. He thought he had hope before, but it had been a hope based on the evidence surrounding him. True hope—the hope he now grasped—was what came when you lost all *reason* to hope. It was a condition that defied all rationale and circumstances. It was the hope that sprang from your true reasons for living and for being.

Robert was sure of one thing now. His hope wasn't dependent on whether the South won or lost the war. His hope was based on his own ability to love, laugh, learn and grow. No outside force could ever take those things away from him. The whole crazy world might be spinning out of control, but those things would always be under his control.

Carrie stopped to wipe at the sweat pouring off her face. The end of September had definitely brought no respite from the brutal summer heat. She stepped over to the shade of a tree to cool off after the climb up the hill from her father's house. The weariness pressing down on her had become her constant companion. The summer had been just as she had envisioned. After the initial swell of wounded soldiers from Chancellorsville, there was a respite until Gettysburg. The thousands of soldiers from that awful battle now filled every available space in the city. Once again, the stench of death hung in the air.

"Carrie!"

Carrie turned as she heard her name called.

Louisa, her face flushed from the heat, hurried up to her. "Thank you so much for coming up on your day off. It means so much to Perry and me."

Carrie shook her head. "I don't know how you manage to stay so beautiful in all this heat. I feel like nothing more than a wrung-out washrag." She smiled. "Are you ready for the big event?"

"I think I am." Louisa giggled nervously and then clutched Carrie's arm. "Can you believe Perry and I are actually getting married?" "

"I'm so happy for you," Carrie said sincerely, marveling at the change in her and Louisa's relationship. Louisa had been at the hospital every day, taking care of Perry's every need. In spite of Dr. Wild's pessimistic outlook for the wounded soldier, he had recovered rapidly and was beginning to move around on his crutches. The first day he stood on his own, he and Louisa announced their wedding. It would be several more weeks before he would be well enough to be released from the hospital, but at least they would have the security of knowing they were married.

"You're sure Pastor Anthony wants to do our wedding?" Louisa asked for what seemed like the tenth time. "I was so awful to him that first day we met in the square."

"He's happy to do it," Carrie said. "He's not one to hold a grudge. He should be here any minute."

Louisa smoothed down her hair. "Are you sure I look all right? I never really imagined having my wedding in a military hospital."

"You look beautiful," Carrie said again, laughing. "And you're not getting married in the hospital. You're getting married out here under this tree."

"Can you believe you're going to be my matron of honor?"

"We've certainly come a long way."

Louisa stuck out her tongue playfully. "It goes to show that two people don't have to agree on everything in order to be friends." Her expression became thoughtful. "We still disagree on so many important things. I want the South to win the war. You wish the Union had never dissolved. I fully intend to have slaves again when this war ends. I know you hate the whole idea. You chose to stay here in Virginia when Robert left. I think you're crazy."

"When you put it that way," Carrie said slowly, "I'm not really sure I feel comfortable being your matron of honor."

Louisa's eyes widened, then narrowed as she saw the fun dancing in Carrie's eyes. "Oh, be quiet! I'm nervous enough without you trying to scare me to death."

They were both still laughing when Carrie heard wagon wheels approaching. "You won't be Louisa Blackwell for much longer."

Louisa clutched her arm suddenly. "Carrie, I have to tell you something. I'm so sorry I was so awful about you and Robert. I know I've said it before, but now that I'm getting married, I feel even worse about it. I never loved him. I only wanted him because it was obvious how much he loved you. I was horribly jealous. Will you forgive me?"

"You know I already have."

Louisa sighed. "I know." She moaned slightly. "I'm such a wreck. Why am I so nervous? It's not like this is a big wedding. My mother won't even be here to criticize things."

Carrie's heart swelled with compassion. Louisa's mother had not improved. She was finally taking a little food, but she still sat staring out the window, responding to nothing and no one. Her devastating losses had completely broken her. In spite of Louisa's words, she knew her friend was greatly burdened by her mother's condition and would have given anything if she could have been there to celebrate with her. She knew there were no words to ease her pain, so she simply squeezed her hand.

"Thank you," Louisa whispered, wiping at her sudden tears. She straightened. "I'm going in to get Perry. It doesn't matter who is or isn't with us today. The point is that when it's all over, we'll be married." Her voice became vehement. "And without a leg, he won't have to fight again. I'm not going to lose another man I love to some Yankee bullet."

It was mid-afternoon when Carrie made her way back down the hill. Louisa and Perry's ceremony had been simple but beautiful, their love for each other obvious. They planned to return to Perry's farm in Georgia when he was well enough to travel. As long as the war didn't follow him, it was over for the young man who sacrificed so much for his country.

Carrie's thoughts flew to Robert as she walked. Her thoughts were already with him constantly, but the wedding had accentuated them. The beauty of their wedding day rose to both comfort and taunt her. Their time together had been so short. She shook her head, knowing things would be no different until the war was over.

Janie was waiting for her on the porch when she reached the house. Carrie tensed, knowing by the look on her face that something was wrong. Visions of a relaxing afternoon fled. Carrie sighed and steeled herself. "What is it?" she asked.

"Your father came home a few minutes ago," Janie said hesitantly. "He seems very upset."

Carrie nodded, then climbed the steps. "Thank you."

"Carrie..." Janie reached out a hand. "What can I do to help? Your father—"

"Has changed," Carrie finished woodenly. "I know. I wrack my brain every night for some way to help him. Some way to give him hope."

"He has to find that within himself," Janie replied, gripping Carrie's hand tightly.

"I know," Carrie said. "In the meantime, I have to watch the man who has meant everything to me since childhood self-destruct." She shook her head and reached for the doorknob. She found Thomas pacing in the parlor.

He turned to her as soon as she opened the door. "Will the calamities in our nation never cease?"

Carrie moved over to sit down in the blue chair next to the window, hoping to catch some of the breeze kicking up. She had learned from experience that it did no good to try to respond to her father. She didn't know the right words to say, and he had no interest in hearing them anyway. He seemed only to want to vent the raging anger that grew in him daily.

Thomas turned and stalked across the room. "You know that the Federals have occupied Chattanooga, eastern Tennessee and Cumberland Gap?" He didn't wait for an answer. "They have succeeded in cutting

Richmond's main rail link with the West." He shook his head bitterly. "We have lost the Mississippi, now this."

He slammed his fist against the mantle and whirled toward her. "Davis detached Longstreet and twelve thousand men from Lee's Army of Northern Virginia. He sent them to reinforce Bragg, and to try to save what he can. Because they had to take a round-about route through the Carolinas due to the loss of the railroad, they missed it." He scowled ferociously. "They missed it!"

Carrie was confused. "They missed what?"

"The battle. Or at least they missed the part where they could have done some good and made a difference." Thomas snorted. "Some of them never even made it there." He paused. "For once, our General Bragg decided to fight instead of retreat. If you want to call it that," he said scornfully. "From all the reports we have received, the battle at Chickamauga was more like mad guerilla warfare on a vast scale. Each army seems to have bushwhacked the other. It seems all the science and art of war went for nothing."

Carrie decided not to comment that she saw no art in war. It would do nothing but add to her father's agitation.

"Bragg did at least succeed in pushing the Federal Army back. I'm sure the official reports will say it was a solid Confederate victory."

"It wasn't?" Carrie hated having to be so cautious with her father.

"Of course it wasn't," he snapped. "Bragg fought to the limit of his army's capacity for two days for the singular purpose of driving the Federals away from Chattanooga in an effort to regain our railroad. All he did was drive them right into it. Our general has won a victory he can't use."

He resumed his pacing. "Not only that, but he didn't finish the job. The battle at Chickamauga should have been nothing but an opening for him to finish off Rosecrans' army. Once again, he failed to finish what he started. From what we can tell, this was the most complete victory of the war, yet the Federals still have their army." Thomas' voice grew increasingly bitter. "And we have lost eighteen thousand more men," he growled.

Carrie whitened. How long could the South tolerate such horrible losses of life? How long would they continue to send their young men to death and mutilation? They must run out of available manpower sometime. Would there be any young men left in the South when the war ended? Would there be any to help rebuild the country?

Thomas continued to pace restlessly. "I fear it was our last chance. Bragg had one of the Union's strongest armies right where he wanted them, and he let them get away. We will probably never again have such a chance."

The bitterness and anguish in his voice tore at Carrie's heart.

Thomas whirled around to stare at her. "I fear the Confederacy is close to breathing its last breath." He took several deep breaths of his own and then stalked from the room.

Carrie gazed after him, once more feeling the sick helplessness she experienced in every recent dealing with her father. She could hardly believe this was the same calm, reasonable man who had taught her to think clearly. She had been so relieved when he started to work with the government—had been so glad to see the spark return to his eyes after her mother died. Now, his very involvement was sapping the life from him and turning him into a bitter old man before her eyes.

"Carrie?"

She looked up slowly. "Come in."

Janie eased in and knelt beside her, taking her hand. "I'm sorry."

"You heard?"

"Through the window."

Carrie fought the tears. "He's helped me so many times when I was so confused. Why can't I help him?" she cried.

"There will be a time when he's ready," Janie said. "Until then, there is nothing you can do."

"Except watch him self-destruct? Watch him become someone I don't even recognize?"

Carrie took a deep breath and changed the subject. "I'm going out to the plantation."

"When?" Janie asked, clearly surprised.

"I don't know yet," Carrie admitted. "I've been thinking about it for a while now. Everyone I talk to says we're going to be in for another hard winter. I keep thinking about all the herbs I have stored in the basement out there. We're going to need them this winter. Chimborazo is building up a fairly good supply of alternative medicines to see them through, but the black hospital simply doesn't have enough to make it. If we have the kind of winter we did last year, too many of them will die." She took a deep breath. "I have to do what I can to prevent it."

"But what about all the Union cavalry around the city? It's not safe to go out there."

Carrie shrugged. "I'll take Hobbs with me."

"How much can he do against a unit of cavalry?" Janie asked skeptically.

"Surely you agree I need to go?"

Janie hesitated. "Will you tell your father?"

"Tell your father what?"

Carrie jumped as Thomas walked back into the room. Her mind raced as she tried to figure out how to answer him. Gone were the times when they could reasonably discuss her radical ideas. She was quite sure how he would respond to this.

"Tell your father what?" he repeated.

"I'm going out to the plantation to bring back herbs," Carrie said calmly.

"And when do you propose to do this?" he asked, his voice too calm, his eyes flashing.

Carrie shrugged. "I haven't decided yet."

"I forbid it," her father boomed. "I forbid you to go out there. It is a foolish idea."

Carrie looked at him for a long moment, then stood and walked from the room.

Chapter Seventeen

Rose shifted John to her other hip and continued stirring the pot of grits simmering over the fire, singing to him softly. He cooed and gurgled, smiling up at her in delight.

"John looks just like his daddy," June said, steadying little Simon as he tottered across the room.

Rose gazed down at him lovingly. "He's going to be as big as his daddy," she said playfully. "He already weighs more than any baby I ever knew at four months." John laughed, bouncing up and down in her arms to signal his approval. "Whoa, little man. You're going to bounce right into the pot of grits."

John laughed louder, waving his arms and kicking his feet.

Rose finally gave up. "You finish the grits, June. He's going to end up in them sure enough. I'll watch Simon." Settling down on the chair next to the window, she put John down on his blanket. Seconds later, he was rolling around gleefully.

June began to stir the grits, watching him thoughtfully. "He's going to be walking long before Simon was."

"I hope I'm not supposed to be impressed by that," Rose groaned. "I see how much trouble you have keeping up with your active son. It's hard enough to try to keep John quiet while I'm teaching now."

"You know Mammy Sukie said she would watch him."

"I know." Rose continued to watch John. He was her constant delight. She cherished every moment she spent with him. And June was right. He was already the spitting image of Moses. Having him close made the ache of missing her husband a little more bearable. She hated the idea of being away from him when she taught, but she knew the day was coming.

"I wish their daddies could see these little boys," Rose said wistfully.

"Yes, well, it looks like it won't be happening anytime soon," June said. "We got to keep on living."

Rose looked at her sister-in-law sympathetically. Whenever she got that brisk, no-nonsense tone in her voice, it meant she was battling loneliness for her husband Simon, who she hadn't seen in over two years. "It's going to end someday," she said.

"I keep telling myself that." June sighed. "It's just that some days my heart is able to listen better than others." She turned and stared at her son and then turned back to the fire. "I reckon these grits are done. I've got to get a move on. I have a lot of washing to do over at the fort today."

"You're going to eat," Rose protested.

June shook her head. "I'm not hungry."

"You sit down and eat right now. You're working too hard, and you're not eating enough. I've been quiet long enough." John and Simon looked up in surprise at the stern tone in her voice.

"Eating seems to take more energy than I have," June admitted.

"You won't have any energy if you don't eat," Rose said firmly. "Winter is coming soon enough. We'll be forced to cut back what we eat then. You've got to take care of yourself now."

June sighed heavily as she dished up a large bowl of the steaming white grits and settled down at the table.

Rose watched her for a long moment. "You're hiding something from me," she said. "What is it?"

June stared down at her bowl. "You're crazy."

Now Rose knew she was right. She set her own bowl aside. "What is it? You know you'll have to tell me eventually." She scowled. "Is someone mistreating you over there?"

"Of course not," June said. "I wouldn't be putting up with how some of those soldiers treat our women. The soldiers I wash for are real nice."

"Then what is it?" Rose persisted, alarm bells ringing in her head as she saw fear tighten June's soft face.

"I didn't want to tell you," June said. "Sometimes I hate that you always be knowing what I'm thinking."

Rose made no effort to correct June's English. She reached forward and took June's hand.

June looked up finally. "You know those bunch of fugitive slaves that showed up a week or so ago? The ones from North Carolina?"

Rose thought for a moment. There were so many contrabands flowing into the camp now that it was hard to keep track. "There were about twenty men? They were coming to make sure the camps were safe, then they were going back for their families. I remember."

"They're gone," June said.

"They've gone back for their families? That's good," Rose replied, wondering what it was about this that was bothering June. "It will be good to get them back before it starts to get cold."

June shook her head, her eyes dark with anger. "They didn't go back to North Carolina."

Rose fought her impatience. "Where are they?"

"They done been sent up north," June said. "They've been sold."

"Whatever are you talking about?" Rose's heart began to pound. "What do you mean they've been sold?"

"Just what I said. Some of these soldiers here ain't any better than Southern slave owners."

"Why don't you tell me what's going on," Rose commanded, struggling to breathe evenly.

June seemed glad to get it off her chest. "Them twenty men were given a place at the fort," she said. "I reckon them Union soldiers knew what they were going to do with them all along. A few days ago, they loaded them on a boat and shipped them off." She paused. "They didn't seem real happy, but I guess they knew it wouldn't do no good to fight." She smiled briefly at Simon who had tottered over, and lifted him onto her lap.

"Yesterday," she continued, "I heard some of the soldiers talking. I don't guess they knew I was close enough to hear, or maybe they figured that since all I do is wash clothes, I was too stupid to understand." Her voice was more matter-of-fact than bitter. "They done sold those men as draft substitutes for rich white boys up north who don't want to fight."

Rose leaned forward in disbelief, shaking her head.

"It's true," June insisted. "I heard them say it myself. They are getting five hundred to a thousand dollars for each of those men. Once they get north, they get put into the army in place of those white boys who get drafted. I reckon they're making a lot of money."

Rose stared at her. "I can't believe General Butler is letting that happen."

"Oh, he doesn't know," June replied. "They are smuggling those men—hiding them away in those big boats."

Rose pushed herself away from the table angrily. "Well, I will certainly have a talk with the general." She turned to June. "I can't believe you were trying to keep this from me. Why?"

"Because you ain't got no sense," June said flatly. "Those soldiers are going to be real angry if someone stops their moneymaking scheme. I know most of the Union soldiers are gentlemen, but there be some that aren't. You know what kind of things they will do to someone who gets in their way. Especially if that someone be a woman." Her voice rose with fear. "I don't want nothing to happen to you."

Little John stopped his rolling on the blanket and looked up in alarm. Moments later, his wail filled the cabin. Rose scooped him up, cuddling him close. "You can't really expect me to do nothing," Rose said in disbelief.

"You can't get those men back."

"But I can perhaps stop it from happening to someone else," Rose snapped. "Those men came here thinking they would have a safe place when they escaped from their masters. They found no better than what they had run from."

"They were probably going to join up with the army anyhow," June said desperately.

"Listen to yourself," Rose said, trying to find patience in the obvious light of June's fear.

"I know what you're gonna say. You're going to tell me someone has to stand up for change or things will always remain the same."

"It's true."

"I know," June said, "but it seems like you're always the one to do the standing. I get so scared for you sometimes." She shivered. "Those soldiers are mean men. They wouldn't think twice about stopping some nigger woman who got in their way."

"I refuse to let fear stop me from doing what I think is right." Rose swallowed the butterflies swarming in her throat. "General Butler is a fair man. He was the one who first opened up these camps to contrabands. I can't believe he would let this continue if he knew."

"One man can't possibly control everything around him," June protested. "It's gonna keep happening. You know how it is. People don't care nothing about blacks except how much money they can make off them."

"And as long as people like you give up and look the other way while it happens, things aren't ever going to change." She leaned forward to squeeze June's hand. "I'm not going to be foolish, but I certainly am going to do something. At least I'm going to try. It's the only way I can live with myself."

"I wish I was as brave as you," June said quietly, "but I ain't." She paused for a long moment, shaking her head. "I remember when my daddy ran away and got hanged for it. They came after the rest of us—Mama and us kids."

Rose listened, her heart aching for the pain and fear radiating from June's eyes. Moses had told her this story.

"They whipped us all," June whispered. "Me, Mama and Moses still got the scars. Sadie was so small that she never walked right after that. And Carmen...she didn't survive her injuries." June paused. "I guess they whipped the courage right out of me."

"You've got plenty of courage," Rose replied, "but some people are meant to do more. Sometimes I wish I wasn't one of those people, but I am. The only way I can live with myself is to try to make a difference."

"Don't you get scared?"

"All the time," Rose admitted. She smiled. "My mama used to tell me there wasn't anything wrong with fear unless you let it control you. She used to tell me that brave people felt the same amount of fear as scared people, but they decided to ignore it and crash right through it." She leaned forward, her eyes burning. "Things aren't ever going to change for our people as long as we sit back and let it happen. We aren't the first people to be treated wrong in this world, you know. It's been happening since the beginning of time, I imagine. For some reason, folks always like to have someone they feel they have power over."

"Well, if it isn't going to change—"

"I didn't say things couldn't change," Rose interrupted. "I said it's been happening for a long time. It's the people who stand up and decide to fight for themselves that see change." She raised her head, the light of battle shining in her eyes. "Things have already changed so much. More and more of us are claiming our freedom. When this war is over, we'll all be free! It's happened because people have been willing to stand up and proclaim that things won't stay the same."

"You sound like a crusader," June said.

Rose sat back and laughed. "I guess I do." She sobered. "Our little boys are going to grow up in a different world than we did. They're not going to be slaves. They're going to have a chance to make something of their lives." Rose gazed down at John. "I intend to do everything I can to make sure he gets his chance."

"When you put it like that..." June murmured. She looked down at Simon for several moments and then straightened. "I'll keep listening at the fort. I'll let you know everything I hear." She stood, settled Simon on her hip, and reached for his blanket. "You be careful. I'm going to drop off Simon at Mammy Sukie's and get to work."

Rose watched her go, then began to bounce John on her knee absent-mindedly, her thoughts racing. A knock on the door interrupted her. "Come in," she called.

Deidre entered the cabin. "Good morning, Rose."

Rose looked at her closely. "What's wrong?"

Deidre sank into the chair June had vacated. "I got me something big to think about."

Rose waited quietly. She knew Deidre would talk when she was ready. John gave an unhappy whimper, and she shifted his position so she could feed him.

"They want to send me and the children north," Deidre announced.

"Who does?"

"The Freedmen's Friends Society. They think me and the children will have a better chance of a good life if we go north."

"From the sound of your voice, you don't seem too convinced," Rose observed. She had heard about the Society offering to ship ex-slaves north. She had received mixed reports. Some of the ex-slaves wrote back glowing letters describing their new lives, but other letters were full of homesickness and unhappiness.

Deidre shook her head. "They tell me the children will have the chance for a better education up there. I reckon that's a good thing. Me and Wally never got none down here." She sighed. "I wish I could talk to Wally about this."

"How do you think he'd feel?" Rose asked carefully. Wally had been gone for several months now, serving as a sailor on one of the navy's ships.

"He'd want what's best for the children," she said. "He'd also feel real bad about leaving our farm. I guess I would, too."

"Things are going to be different here when the war is over," Rose replied. "All the ex-slaves can't up and move to the north. Some of us are going to have to make our lives down here."

"You planning on staying down here?" Deidre asked, fixing her with a burning gaze.

"Moses wants to be a farmer," Rose said. "There is no better land than the South for farming, as far as he's concerned. There are going to be as many children here who need a teacher as there are going to be up north."

"It ain't gonna be easy," Deidre said. "If the North wins this war, there are gonna be a lot of mad white people around here. They ain't gonna take kindly to black folks trying to act like their equals."

"We *are* their equals," Rose said. "And I never said I thought it was going to be easy." She paused. "I used to think I wanted to live in the North. I thought it would be easier—that I would find less prejudice." She shook her head. "People are people, no matter where they are. Our race has a long battle in front of us. Wherever we live," she said. "The South is my home. We'll stay here and carve out a life for ourselves."

Deidre shook her head. "They ain't gonna like it if I tell them we don't want to go. Seems like they think it would be best." Her voice grew fretful. "I wish my Wally was here to tell me what to do."

"Well, he isn't," Rose said, marveling that this was the same woman who had so fearlessly delivered her and June's babies. "It's your responsibility to make the decision for your family. You have to do what you believe is best."

Deidre blinked at her and then straightened. "I reckon you're right," she said in a stronger voice. "You think my children can get all the learning they need down here?"

"I think it will take time for things to change," Rose said, "but I think that change will come. As long as there are enough of us willing to help make it happen."

Deidre sat taller. "I reckon I'll be one of those people." Her eyes suddenly shone with pride.

Rose breathed an inaudible sigh of relief. "Good. I would have missed you terribly if you had gone."

"One of these days, my Wally and I are going to load up a wagon and take our children back to our farm. We've been legally free for a while now. Soon we're going to be treated like we're free," Deidre said. "Things are gonna be different."

Rose stood and handed John to her. "Can you hold him while I bank the fire?"

Deidre looked down tenderly. "He's sound asleep."

"All it takes is a good meal," Rose agreed. "I guess it takes a lot of energy to grow as fast as he's growing."

Deidre nodded. "I thought we were going to lose both of you the night he was born," she said gruffly. "Ain't never had a baby come into the world as rough as your little John did."

"He's a fighter," Rose replied. "He's going to have to be," she added, staring at his glowing dark skin and curly black hair. "He has no idea what he's gotten himself into."

The streets were thronged with people as Rose wove her way toward the school. Even though it was the end of September, hot humidity still groped at her. Screaming children raced barefoot through the dusty streets, laundry flapped on clotheslines, and people's voices could be heard everywhere. As Rose passed one ramshackle cabin, she heard the voices of two women raised in heated argument. She frowned. The cloying heat and incessant overcrowding had stretched tempers to the breaking point all over the contraband camp.

"I told you I ain't gonna take it anymore!"

Rose turned as the door to the cabin flung open and the voices shrieked out into the road.

"You can get yerself right out of this here cabin!"

Two women appeared on the porch, grappling as they screamed at each other.

Rose sighed and started forward. Peacemaker had been added to her endless list of duties as the long summer wore on. She shifted John to her hip, trying to decide what to say.

"I said get out!" the larger woman yelled, giving the other a mighty shove that sent her toppling into the dust outside the cabin.

Within seconds, a crowd surrounded them, staring in fascination as the two women continued to scream at each other. Rose understood they were hungry for any kind of entertainment they could get, but she couldn't see the attraction of two women fighting like dogs.

"Let me have that boy," an urgent voice sounded in her ear.

Rose nodded and handed John to Mammy Sukie. "Thank you," she said gratefully. Then she stepped up to the woman sprawled in the dust and extended a hand.

"Don't you help her up, Miss Rose," the larger woman yelled.

"Now, Candice, you know I'm not going to leave Tonya down here," Rose said soothingly. "What's going on here, anyway?" She fought to keep the exasperation from her voice. She knew it wouldn't help.

"That Tonya done stole my one good dress for my little Angel," Candice said angrily. "She knows I done been saving it."

Tonya ignored Rose's hand and heaved herself up from the ground. "You a fool to be saving that dress," she retorted. "My little Fannie be walking around in a dress full of holes while you got that perfectly good one stuck away in a box."

"It's my Angel's!" Candice screamed.

Rose stepped between the two women before they went at each other again. "Why are you saving the dress?" she asked calmly. She was sure she knew, but if she could get Candice talking reasonably, things might simmer down.

"You know why, Miss Rose," Candice protested. "My little Angel almost died a few months back. If the fever takes her again, I won't have nothing good to bury her in if Tonya steals that dress," she said. "My little girl might not have had much, but she ain't gonna be put in her grave dressed like a rag doll." Her voice was stubborn.

Rose had grown used to this feeling. Whenever the barrels of supplies came from the north, the best clothes were snatched up quickly, never to be seen again. Rose had finally discovered the women were hiding them away for anticipated funerals. Nothing she said could change how they felt about it. She decided to try a different approach.

She turned to Tonya. "May I see the dress, please?" Her voice was kind but firm. Tonya hesitated and then handed it over reluctantly. Rose looked it over carefully and glanced up at Candice. "This isn't really such a nice dress," she lied. "I've got a lot better ones put away for funerals."

"What you talking about?" Candice asked.

"Just what I said," Rose responded. "I got several barrels of nice clothing a few weeks back. I took the best clothes and put them aside. That way, whenever we have need of some for a funeral, they will be there. I'm not so naïve as to believe we will get through the winter without someone dying." She paused, staring Candice straight in the eyes. "I also know how important it is for our children to be dressed well and warmly if they are to survive the coming winter. Hiding clothes from each other will only mean more children will die. Is that what you want?"

"Why, of course not!" Candice sputtered.

"I didn't think so," Rose said kindly. "I promise you that if something happens to your little Angel, she will have the right clothes for her funeral."

Candice stared at Rose for a long minute and then turned to Tonya. "I reckon you can have that dress," she muttered. She turned to go inside, but swung back. "And I reckon you can stay here."

Rose breathed a sigh of relief as the crowd melted away. She took John from Mammy Sukie's arms. "Thank you."

"Don't you get tired settlin' all these fights?" Mammy Sukie asked, her round face glowing with sweat, her compassionate eyes regarding her closely.

Rose shrugged. "Teaching is easier," she admitted. "I dream of the day when that will be all I have to do." She turned away. "I'm late, though. I have to be going."

The school was already full when she entered. Now that the camp was so crowded, they were teaching in shifts. Two hundred children, ages eleven through fourteen, were crammed into the building designed to accommodate about fifty. There was the expected amount of whispering and giggling, but for the most part, they were remarkably quiet. Two new teachers who had been sent down by the Missionary Alliance were standing next to the wall, waiting. Rose smiled at them warmly, remembering her first days in the camp. She placed John in his little crib and walked to the front of the building.

"Good morning."

It was late afternoon when Rose finished teaching. At least for that shift. By eight o'clock, the room would be crammed full of adults eager to make up for the years they spent with no education. Rose loved teaching them, loved watching them soak up knowledge like the ground during a spring rain.

"Can I watch John for a little while?" a small voice asked eagerly.

Rose turned and smiled. "I was hoping you would ask," she said in relief. Annie was one of her favorite students. The little girl standing in front of her bore no evidence of her brutal rape the year before by marauding Union soldiers. Her face and eyes beamed with confidence and joy. It had taken her a little while, but she had conquered her fears. Annie was determined nothing would keep her from school. She dreamed of being a doctor. Rose encouraged her every way she could.

She kissed John and placed him in Annie's willing arms. "I have to go over to the fort for a little while. Will you take him to my house in a couple of hours if I'm not back? June will be there by then."

"Sure thing, Miss Rose," Annie said brightly, catching the hand John was waving about in excitement.

Rose smiled. John loved Annie. They would be fine together. Gathering her things, she stepped out into the bright sunlight. It took her only a few minutes to walk to Fort Monroe. The sun was still shining, but a bank of clouds on the horizon predicted a late afternoon storm. Rose welcomed it. Rain was needed to cool things off—including the tempers flaring throughout the camp. It had been weeks since their last rain.

As Rose strolled toward the fort, she thought about her plan. She really had no idea if General Butler would see her. He was a very busy man, but she had to try. If he knew what was going on, she was sure he would try to put a stop to it.

The man working the desk looked up pleasantly as she entered the room outside General Butler's office. "May I help you?"

"I'd like to see General Butler, please."

A flicker of amusement shone in his eyes. "Do you have an appointment?"

"No," Rose admitted. "I will be happy to make one and come back later if necessary."

"What makes you think he'll want to see you?" the man continued, not unkindly. "The general has a lot of people who want to see him."

"I think he will want to hear what I have to say," Rose said. "It will only take a few moments."

"Well, why don't you tell me what you have to tell him? I'll make sure he gets the message."

Something told Rose to proceed very cautiously. "I would rather talk with him myself," she said courteously, realizing she had begun to tread on dangerous ground.

An angry spark appeared in the uniformed man's eyes. "You're one of those teachers over in the camp, aren't you?"

Rose saw no reason to deny it. "Yes."

"I thought so," he grunted. "You don't sound as stupid as the rest of them."

Rose flushed angrily but held her tongue. Her priority was gaining an interview with General Butler. "May I make an appointment with the general?"

"I reckon so," the man said. He flipped open the book lying in front of him. "I think he'll have some time around Christmas." He slammed the book shut and laughed.

Rose ground her teeth. She had not expected to find a man like this working for General Butler. "I see." She cast around in her mind for a way to accomplish her mission.

Suddenly, the door to General Butler's office swung open. He strode out, stopped, and looked at her. "Hello," he said graciously. He turned to the man at the desk.

"Where is Sergeant Creighton, Russell? I was expecting him ten minutes ago."

"I don't know, sir," Russell replied. "I haven't heard anything."

Butler frowned. "If he comes, tell him to come back tomorrow. I have something I need to take care of."

"Yes, sir," Russell said instantly.

Butler turned to leave the room, then spun back around and looked at Rose. "Have you been helped?"

Rose hesitated. "I was here to make an appointment with you, sir." She saw Russell frown over the general's shoulder.

"And when am I going to see you?" Butler demanded.

"We hadn't set up a time yet," Russell interrupted.

Butler turned and looked at him closely. "What is it you need, young lady?"

"A few minutes of your time," Rose said carefully.

"I have a few minutes," Butler said. "Come with me."

Rose flushed with triumph but sobered when she saw the glowering look on Russell's face. She tried not to make enemies. Especially with soldiers. "Thank you, sir," she responded, falling in beside him.

Butler was silent until they exited the fort and were walking across the grounds. "Who are you?"

"My name is Rose Samuels. I'm one of the teachers in the contraband camp."

"Trouble over there?"

"No, sir. At least not beyond what is normal. I'm afraid the trouble is here in your fort."

Butler ground to a halt and turned to stare at her. "What would you know about my fort?"

"I've heard things," Rose said. She had no desire to implicate June.

"What is it?"

Rose told him what June had said that morning. "I was sure you would want to know," she finished.

Butler turned to stare out at the bay. "You say these men were shipped north a day or two ago?"

"Yes, sir."

"I'll make sure someone is waiting for the boat when they land," he promised. "If they want to come home, they can. If they want to stay and fight, they can stay. But they won't be auctioned off," he growled. He shook his head heavily. "You realize there are many different feelings in the North about you people?" he demanded.

"Yes, sir. It's fairly obvious." Rose silently exulted that the captured men would be freed.

"I'll do what I can to make sure this is stopped," Butler promised. "You're a very courageous lady," he said.

"I'm only doing what should be done," Rose said. A group of soldiers passed. They stared at her closely but made no comment. Butler seemed not to take notice, but Rose pushed away a vague feeling of uneasiness.

"You have a husband?" he asked.

"He's serving in the army," Rose replied. "He started out as a spy. Now he is serving under Captain Jones."

"We'll win this war yet, Mrs. Samuels," Butler said. "You keep getting your people ready."

Rose opened her mouth to respond, but the general was finished. Nodding, he spun on his heel and walked rapidly away. Rose watched him go, satisfied she had done everything she could. Hugging her triumph close, she turned to retrace her steps back to the camp.

The clouds she'd seen perched on the horizon earlier were now boiling overhead. A streak of lightning flashed across the sky, followed by a deep rumble of thunder. Rose quickened her steps. If she hurried, she could make it home before the storm hit. She had almost reached the outskirts of the camp when a figure stepped out in front of her.

"Where you going so fast, miss?"

Chapter Eighteen

Rose stopped dead in her tracks, her heart beginning to pound. "Excuse me?"

"You hard of hearing?" the tall, lanky soldier snarled. "I asked where you were going so fast."

"Home," Rose said evenly, fighting to control the panic rising in her.

The soldier leaned against the tree. "I don't think so," he said casually, his hard eyes belying his tone of voice.

"Why not?" Rose snapped, suddenly angry.

The casual expression evaporated from the man's face. "Don't get uppity with me, nigger. It won't take much to show you your place." He turned toward the building behind him. "This the one you wanted?"

"That's the one," a deep voice answered.

Rose stared as Russell, the soldier from General Butler's office, stepped from behind the building. "What do you want?" she demanded.

"Not much," Russell shrugged, his eyes cold and uncompromising. "I'd like to know what you talked to the general about."

"That was between me and the general."

Russell scowled and stepped closer, grasping her arm tightly. "I intend for it to become between you and me."

Rose was confused. "Why? What difference could it make to you?"

Russell smiled coldly. "I suppose that's a fair question. I didn't like the things General Butler was saying when he stomped back into the office a few minutes ago. Me and the boys look after each other, you know. I need to know if someone is going to get in trouble."

Rose stared at him with a sinking heart. She glanced around to see if there was any avenue of escape, but she knew without looking she was trapped. She squared her shoulders. "Do you have some reason to be worried, Mr. Russell?"

"Don't get uppity with me, nigger," Russell growled. He gripped her arm tighter until she gasped with pain. "Tell me what you told the general."

Rose fought the desire to slap him in the face. She knew it would be the end of her. Desperately, she tried to figure some way to get out of her predicament. "I went there on behalf of some recent refugee slaves," she admitted.

"The boys having a rough time?" Russell sneered. "Having to work harder here than they wanted to?"

Rose bit her lip. She knew every male contraband was working for the federal government. Those who got paid were paid well below what the white soldiers received. "They were taken away to be sold on the auction block up north," she said. "They came here to escape slavery."

"I guess some folks can't escape who they are," Russell said. His eyes glittered angrily. "How'd you find out about those boys?" he demanded.

"I heard talk," Rose said evasively, envisioning the fear shining in June's eyes earlier that morning.

Russell gave her arm a cruel shake.

Rose bit her lip to keep from crying out and stared at him defiantly. She wouldn't give him the satisfaction of knowing how scared she was. She began to pray silently.

"I want to know where you heard the talk."

Rose shrugged. "I really can't remember." She cried out as his fingers bit even deeper into her tender flesh. She struggled to wrench free. The man who had stopped her stepped up and grabbed her other arm.

Russell thrust his face up to hers, his hot breath fanning her face. "I would encourage you to remember." He paused. "If you want to go home, that is."

Rose thought of John waiting at home for his evening feeding. She thought of June. She would never betray her friend. She shook her head.

Another crack of lightning ripped through the air, ominous thunder following close on its heels. Yellowish clouds swirled in a violent dance above their heads. A vicious wind kicked up, tossing the limbs above their heads as if they were mere twigs.

Rose continued to stare at Russell defiantly. If she gave into her fear and looked away, he would have won. He would have control. The silent battle continued as the storm raged over their heads.

"You ain't gonna get her to talk," the other man said. "This storm is gonna be a big one. We need to get out of here."

"She'll talk," Russell snarled, reaching up to touch her face. "She'll talk, or at least she'll give us some entertainment."

Rose stiffened. She refused to let him see her fear. *God, please help me,* she cried silently.

"Are you crazy?" the other man exclaimed. "General Butler will find out and then our gooses will be cooked for sure. It's bad enough we might get caught for sending them men north."

"Will you shut up!" Russell shouted, releasing Rose's arm as he spun to yell at the other man.

Rose resisted the temptation to run, knowing it would only infuriate him more. She didn't have a chance of outrunning him in her long skirts anyway. She longed for Moses to come to her rescue, but she knew it was impossible. He was miles away on the battlefield. Her mind raced to figure out some way to reason with the man, then abandoned the idea. There was no reasoning with someone like him.

The first big drops of rain began to fall, and lightning continued to fly overhead.

Russell turned back to her. "Get out of here." he snarled. "You're going to be lucky this time, but don't think it will last. I hear about you skunking on me and my friends again, and you can kiss your life goodbye." He paused, staring hard. "There's all kinds of ways to get rid of women like you. No one would ever know who did it. If you've got a husband and kids, you better think about it."

Rose kept her face impassive. She would reveal nothing to give him further ammunition.

The sky opened up in a torrential rain that obliterated the nearby buildings from sight.

Russell laughed and shoved her toward the camp. "Get out of here, nigger. I don't want to see you again."

Rose stumbled and fell, the dirt clinging to her wet dress. Springing to her feet, she glanced around. The two men had already disappeared. She took a deep breath and began to walk slowly toward home. It would do no good to run. She was already soaked through, and she needed the time to pull herself together before she reached the cabin. She already knew she wouldn't tell June about her encounter. It would only terrorize her more.

Now that Russell had disappeared, Rose let herself feel the full extent of her anger. She was angry that attempts to help her people resulted in situations like this. Angry there were so many bitter people full of hatred. Angry that men like Russell could make her people afraid of Northerners when there were just as many of them who were eager and willing to help.

I won't stop, she vowed. *I won't stop trying to change things.*

Matthew paced restlessly. His opportunity had come. If all went well, he would be free of Libby Prison in a few hours. His mind raced as he went over the plan he had so carefully calculated. It was certainly not foolproof, but it was the only real chance that had come his way so far. He was determined to take it.

"We're ready for the meeting, Matthew," Captain Anderson called.

Matthew nodded and moved in the direction of the crates that had been circled up in the far corner. He was one of the few who knew this meeting of the Libby Prison Association had not been called for the regular reason of discussing light topics or reading from books. The agenda today was much more serious. He felt sorry for the men who were to be singled out, although he knew they deserved it.

Captain Anderson cleared his throat as soon as the circle was full. "I hereby call this meeting to order."

Matthew watched as the men surrounding him tensed and leaned forward. It was obvious from Anderson's voice that something unexpected was about to happen.

"Would Colonel Tibbens and Lieutenant Flanagan step forward?" Anderson asked.

Only Tibbens stood. Flanagan stayed seated on his crate, his head between his hands. Tibbens stared at the other man, but neither one said a word.

Anderson's voice, when he finally spoke, was sharp. "It has come to the association's attention that the two of you signed a statement saying the prisoners have been receiving adequate food and clothing from the Rebels. Is that true?"

Tibbens stared at the floor, avoiding the eyes of his fellow prisoners. "Yes, I signed a statement to that effect. I felt it was correct."

"Traitor!" one of the men yelled.

Matthew watched. He had taken up his belt two notches since arriving at Libby Prison. He well understood the man's anger.

"I'm not a traitor!" Tibbens yelled back.

"Look at you," one of the other men yelled. "You've lost forty pounds since you got here." The anger in his voice faded away as he shook his head. "How are we ever going to make a difference here if our own members aid the enemy?"

Angry muttering echoed his sentiments.

Anderson gaveled the meeting back to order. "We have written a resolution condemning these statements. We have made it clear their statements are a gross misrepresentation of facts, and their inferences unqualifiedly false." He fixed the two offending officers with a glare. "If we could rid ourselves of your presence, we would do so most gladly. However, we're stuck with you. I'm afraid you won't find the rest of your stay here very pleasant." His voice was flat and hard.

"Traitors," several of the men muttered again, their faces hard, their eyes glowing.

Matthew continued to watch. His yearning to escape had only increased since the overcrowding worsened after the fighting at Chickamauga. Tension and hopelessness was at an all-time high since Jefferson Davis abruptly terminated prisoner exchanges. There was one final exchange happening today. A group of army surgeons was being released to help the Confederacy's critical need for their own medical personnel.

"You have a copy of our resolution don't you?" Anderson asked.

"I do," Matthew agreed. "I will make certain the Northern public becomes aware of the true situation here in the prison. Now that exchanges have stopped, I feel certain something will be done. I don't believe Lincoln will let things continue as they are."

"He'd better not," one officer muttered. "I don't know how much longer I can take this." He looked at Matthew. "Lucky devil."

Matthew didn't deny his statement. He was considering himself very lucky right now. It gnawed at him that it had taken another man's death to open the door of opportunity for him, but he was still eager to grasp it.

"This meeting is over," Anderson announced. He looked at Matthew. "Let's get you ready."

Two nights ago, Dr. Kenneth White had passed away, taken by the typhoid he contracted treating men on the battlefield. The planned prisoner exchange was known. Anderson had ordered the doctor's body to be hidden, and another man answered for him at roll call. So far they had been lucky. The guards were oblivious.

Matthew moved to a chair in the far corner for the transformation. He winced as the men came at him with dull razors and penknives, but he endured it stoically.

"Your own mama won't know you when we're done with you," Anderson laughed.

An hour later, the men held up a piece of tin for Matthew to see himself. His mustache had been shaved off and they had trimmed his beard close to his face. His shoulder length red hair had been lopped off to just above his neck. *What used to be red hair,* Matthew corrected himself. He stared at himself in amazement. One of the men had gathered soot and charcoal from the cook fires, and they had used it to darken his hair. From a distance, he resembled the tall, lanky doctor who now lay covered by boards in the back of the room.

"I always wondered what I would look like with black hair," Matthew muttered. Even his eyebrows had been darkened. Matthew was sure no one would recognize him. He grinned, then sobered. If his escape attempt worked, he knew the officers he was leaving behind were counting on him. They had chosen him to take the doctor's place because of his position as a journalist. They held on to the hope that public opinion could change their situation. He prayed he wouldn't let them down. He turned to tell them thank you again.

"Dr. Kenneth White. Dr. Marvin Gallagher. Dr. Stephen Lawing."

Matthew jumped as the roll call for the prison exchange began. They had completed the transformation just in time.

Anderson grabbed a slouch hat and crammed it on top of his head. "Have a good trip, doctor," he said.

Matthew exchanged a long look with him and then took his place in the line. His heart pounded as he waited, suppressing a shudder at the knowledge of how he would be treated if he were discovered.

"Let's go," the guard called.

Matthew took a deep breath and walked out of the room. He tensed as he passed the prison policeman, but he did little more than glance at them. Matthew sighed with relief as they cleared the prison door and stepped out into the warm sunshine. He lifted his face for a moment to feel the rays warm his white cheeks and then looked back down quickly. He was still not out of danger.

The guard ushered them east toward the canal and the waiting *Flag of Truce* boat. The other men around him grinned in happy excitement to be free. Matthew wanted to join in but knew it was still too soon. When the boat had pulled away from the dock and was steaming down the river, he would celebrate.

He began to relax a little as the group reached the waiting boat. Surely if they missed him he would know by now. He watched as the Confederate guard finished his check of the paper and ran a gaze over the assembled group. There was no cause for concern here. The guard had never seen Dr. White. He was checking to make sure the number of prisoners matched the number on his paper. All was going well so far.

"All right," the guard called, "get on board. Your vacation in the South is over."

Matthew joined the line of men filing onto the boat. He could feel freedom within his grasp.

"Stop that boat! Stop that boat!" A faint shout floated to them on the breeze.

"What the...?" the guard muttered, holding up his hand to stop the line.

Matthew felt his heart begin to pound again.

The shout was louder this time. "Hold those prisoners! Hold those prisoners!"

Matthew looked around wildly, searching for an avenue of escape. The guards pressed closer. There was no way out.

The whole group turned to watch the prison policemen racing toward them. He reached the line and grabbed Matthew's arm. "This man isn't a doctor," he shouted. "His name is Matthew Justin—a journalist from Pennsylvania. He's trying to escape!"

The four guards who had accompanied the doctors to the boat immediately surrounded him. Matthew forced a grin and held out his hands casually for the cuffs. "I guess the game's up, boys." He took a deep breath. "I almost won."

A guard stepped up close to his face. "You'll wish you had, Justin," he snarled. "If you thought you were uncomfortable before, you don't know anything. We have special treats for men who scorn our hospitality."

The rest of the doctors were silent as Matthew was led away, but he could feel their sympathy reaching out to him. *Tell the story*, he pleaded silently. *Tell the story.*

Men were crowded at the windows as Matthew was escorted back to the prison.

"What are you staring at?" one of the guards yelled. Shots rang out from his pistol, crashing into the walls and spitting out chips of brick. He laughed loudly.

When Matthew glanced back up, all the faces had disappeared. He took one final breath of fresh air before the darkness of the prison swallowed him again.

"Ever heard of *Rat Dungeon*?" one of the guards taunted.

Matthew fought to control the bile rising in his throat. His punishment for trying to escape was going to be confinement in the east cellar room known as *Rat Dungeon*. He wildly considered trying to break away and run for it, but knew he would be shot instantly. The guards would be happy for any excuse to kill a man who had almost outsmarted him.

It might be better.

Matthew fought the hopelessness threatening to engulf him. For a few brief minutes, he had almost been free. It would have been better to have never experienced it, he thought bitterly.

Don't let them win. Choose life.

Again, Matthew considered running and making himself a target. He was sickened by the thought of the dark hole teeming with rats where he would be served only bread and water. He himself had passed food down to the men unfortunate enough to be confined there.

Choose life.

The persistent voice would not be ignored. Matthew cast aside the idea of running and straightened his shoulders. He was not beaten yet. They would not keep him down in *Rat Dungeon* forever.

Somehow he would find a way to escape.

Chapter Nineteen

"Where to, Miss Carrie?" Spencer asked cheerfully.

Carrie took a deep breath and looked down the street. She wasn't expecting her father, but there was a chance he would come home early. "I'd like to go out to Poplar Street."

Spencer glanced back at her. "Out past the navy yards?"

"That's right," Carrie said. "And I'd like to go now."

Spencer stared at her for a moment, then picked up his reins. "Yes, ma'am."

Carrie settled back in the carriage, taking deep breaths of the air. Fall had finally descended on Richmond. While she welcomed the refreshing coolness, she also knew winter was close at hand.

Spencer drove down Broad Street, turned left on Eighteenth, then turned right on Cary Street. Carrie finally began to relax. Her father would have no reason to be in this part of town. She could imagine his anger and dismay when he found the note she left for him, but she was doing what she had to do. Janie would undoubtedly catch the brunt of her latest escapade, but her friend had agreed Carrie was doing the right thing.

Janie had promised to deal with Thomas. Carrie didn't envy her. She loved her father dearly, but he was no longer the same man. Every day seemed to deepen the anger and bitterness seeking to destroy him. She tried to conjure up images of her father when he was loving and reasonable, but they grew dimmer each day. She struggled to hold on to them—to hold on to the hope he would be that man again someday when the war was over.

She leaned forward. "You can stop here."

Spencer looked at her in surprise. "What's out here, Miss Carrie?"

Carrie was already swinging from the carriage. Hobbs, who was waiting for her on the side of the road in a wagon, waved.

Spencer looked from one to the other of them in confusion. "What's going on here? What are you doing here, Hobbs?"

"I'm going out to the plantation. My father has refused to let me go, so I'm afraid I've had to resort to other means."

"He don't know you're going?" Spencer asked in a shocked voice.

"He will when he gets home," Carrie assured him. "I left him a letter."

"It ain't safe," Spencer protested.

"Oh, for heaven's sake!" Carrie exclaimed. "You sound like my father."

"Ain't you heard them reports of Yankee cavalry around the city?" Spencer persisted. "You think they're gonna let you roll right through?" He glared at Hobbs, who shrugged.

"Hobbs agrees with you, if that makes you feel any better. But it doesn't matter. I'm going."

Spencer groaned. "I done heard you use that tone of voice before. I know there ain't no talking sense to you when you talk like that." He gazed at Hobbs sympathetically. "You be heading for a heap of trouble, man."

"All we can do is try," Hobbs replied.

"What's so all-fired important out there at that plantation? I don't reckon you got it in your head just to go out for a visit."

"Hardly." Carrie laughed, then sobered. "It's going to be a hard winter, Spencer. Without medicine, too many people down in the black section of town will die. There is no regular medicine to be found. Any making its way through the blockade is snapped up by the medical hospitals." She looked at him pleadingly, begging him to understand. For some reason, it was important to her. Maybe because her father had refused to even listen. "I have a basement full of herbs and plants at the plantation. It will be enough to last the winter." She took a deep breath. "I have to do what I can to try to save as many lives as possible."

"Even risk your own?" Spencer asked. "You're a good woman, Carrie Borden. You go on out to your plantation, and I reckon I'll pray for you every day."

Carrie hugged him impulsively. "I'm sorry to pull you into the middle of this, but I couldn't have Hobbs show up in the wagon. If Father happened to be home, it would have all been over."

Spencer nodded. "Ain't you taking anything with you?"

Hobbs reached over the seat behind him and held up two large bags. "I went and got them last night." He also reached down and held up a rifle. "We won't go down without a fight," he said.

"Lot of chance you stand against a bunch of Union cavalry. A man on a crutch, and a woman," he snorted.

"Who also happens to be a good shot," Carrie reminded him, holding up her own pistol.

Spencer shook his head. "Get on with you." He glanced up at the sun. "At least you'll be traveling mostly at night. Maybe that will keep the cavalry from finding you."

Carrie was glad when the sun sank below the horizon. They were several miles out of town and had not been challenged, but she yearned for the protective covering of night. She thought longingly of all the trails weaving through the woods that were unknown to all but the locals who used them. There was no way the wagon would fit on them. Their only choice was the main road, appallingly open and wide. She fingered the pistol in her waistband, wondering if she could really use it to shoot a Union soldier. She shuddered and turned her mind to other things.

Carrie could hardly wait to get home. Fall was always one of her favorite times of the year. Trees were turning in Richmond, but she longed for the wide-open spaces of the plantation, burnished by the gold, red and yellow leaves of autumn. She tried to relax enough to enjoy the canopy of colorful trees they were rumbling beneath, but she finally gave up. Every muscle in her body was strung tight in anticipation of Federal soldiers.

"What you thinking about over there?" Hobbs asked quietly.

Carrie knew it would do no good to talk about her fears. "I'm wondering if Sam and Opal and the kids are still there. Wondering how many of Father's people have stayed." She paused. "I've heard so many stories of plantations being destroyed. I guess I'm mostly hoping our home is still there." She heard a sharp crack and snapped her head up. She relaxed as a deer bounded across the road in front of them. "I don't know what I'll do if I have to go home and tell Father that Cromwell Plantation has been burned. I think it would completely kill him."

"He's living to go back there, ain't he?"

"I think so," Carrie mused. "He left the plantation to bury himself in politics after Mother died, but I think he dreams of going back every day now. The war has drained him. It's turned him old. I think he hopes the plantation will give him back some of what's been taken."

Hobbs nodded and concentrated on his driving once more. Carrie was content to be left with her thoughts.

It was past midnight when Hobbs turned onto the narrow drive leading to the plantation. Carrie sat straight in her seat, gripped by both excitement and dread. She yearned to speed up time and be there. Another part of her wanted to slow it down—to delay the discovery of her home destroyed.

"I reckon we outsmarted them Yankees this time," Hobbs said.

Carrie clasped her hands and leaned forward. A pale moon cast its milky glow over the pastures lining both sides of the road. She longed to glance over and see Granite cantering beside the fence. She smiled as she remembered how eagerly he would prance around the gate until she came and greeted him. At least she knew Granite was alive and well, stabled in her father's small barn until Robert came back from Europe. She had wanted to ride him out but knew the wagon was necessary to haul back all the bottles of herbs.

Carrie squeezed her eyes shut as the wagon approached the curve that would deliver them to the front of the house. She scolded herself for her fear but kept them squeezed tight anyhow. She couldn't bear the thought it might not be waiting for her.

"You can open your eyes, Carrie," Hobbs chuckled.

"Is it there?" she asked, keeping them shut.

"Yes. I reckon it's still there."

Carrie's eyes flew open before he finished speaking. "It's still here!" she cried. "Please stop," she commanded. When Hobbs obliged, she sat and stared. The glow of the moon covered any signs of neglect. Her father had always demanded the outside of the house be kept in sparkling condition, but three years of war had resulted in cracked and peeling paint. In the mystical light of the moon, though, it shimmered as if it wore a fresh coat of white. Towering oak trees stood silent guard, their limbs tossed by the breeze, swirling shadows over the house.

"It's beautiful," Carrie said softly, her eyes glimmering with tears of gladness. She had not admitted, even to herself, how devastated she would have been if it had been burned or destroyed. Her relief washed over her in great waves of happiness.

"Sure is dark," Hobbs observed.

"Well, no one was expecting us," Carrie laughed. "I was hoping we wouldn't wake them."

"Where you plan on us staying tonight?" Hobbs asked dubiously.

"There is an apartment above the barn. We can stay there tonight and let Sam and Opal know we're here in the morning." She glanced at the dark windows staring down at her. "If they're still here. It's been months since I was here last. A lot could have happened."

She saw the front door crack open a little, and a dark face peered out at them. She opened her mouth to call out but hesitated. What if Sam and Opal weren't still here? She had heard of plantation houses being taken over by runaway slaves. With most of the white plantation owners gone from their homes, there was little to stop them from doing what they wanted. She fought to control her pounding heart. She hadn't come this far to be afraid now. "Hello," she called.

The door opened wider. "Who be out there?" a gruff voice demanded.

Carrie grinned. "Sam! It's you! I was so afraid you wouldn't be here."

The door flew open all the way and a stooped figure walked out onto the porch. "That be you, Miss Carrie?"

"It's me." Carrie jumped down from the wagon and ran over to the wide steps leading up to the porch.

"Why, I'll be jiggered," Sam exclaimed. "What in the world you be doing skulkin' around at night, girl?"

Carrie turned back for a moment. "Go ahead and bring our things in, Hobbs. I don't guess we'll be sleeping in the barn." She raced up the stairs and gave the elderly black man a big hug. "It's so good to see you again."

Sam chuckled and stepped back. "You all right, girl?" he asked, his voice anxious.

"I'm fine, Sam," Carrie assured him. "We heard there are a lot of Union cavalry hanging around out here so we thought we'd have a better chance of making it here at night."

Sam nodded and pulled her into the foyer. "You be right about that, Miss Carrie. So far they done left this place alone. I guess we been real lucky."

"Have they been here?" Carrie asked as she looked around. The huge chandelier gleamed softly in the lantern light. The faint tick of the grandfather clock her father had shipped back from England filled the hallway.

"Yes, they been here," Sam admitted, trying to hold back a yawn. "They done wanted me and Opal and the kids to go off with them. Wanted to take us to one of them contraband camps." He shook his head. "We wouldn't go."

"And the others?"

"We be the only ones left," Sam said. "All the others took off 'bout a month ago. Them Yankee soldiers tole 'em if they took off, it would make it easier for the North to win this war. Said it would break their masser's spirit and hurt the South." He paused. "Most of the men went off to be soldiers and fight. I reckon the women be over 'round Hampton, but I don't really be knowin'."

"I expected it," she replied. "I hope they have good lives."

"Oh, I reckon some of them will be back when this war be over," Sam commented.

"Be back?" Carrie asked, startled. "Why would they want to come back?"

"This war ain't gonna last forever, Carrie girl. When it ends, somebody gonna be working this land. Don't matter much if it be the North or the South runnin' things. They gonna need somebody to work it. Them that left don't want to be slaves, but that don't mean they wouldn't mind workin' for a fair wage. This is home to some of them. All they've ever known. They'll be back."

"I hope there is something for them to come back to," was all Carrie said.

"I reckon time will tell," Sam said. "And me? I figure whoever ends up with this big place gonna need somebody to keep it going. I reckon I don't want to leave my home."

"But you worked before the war to help slaves go free," Carrie protested. "Don't you want to be free?"

Sam laughed. "Your daddy may have some papers saying he owns me, but it don't seem to be affectin' my life none now, does it? I be livin' my life the way I want to. I reckon I'll wait and see what happens when this war be over." He shook his head. "I ain't gettin' any younger. I done did my part in givin' others a chance. I figure I can live the way I want now."

Carrie gazed at the old man fondly. The lantern he held in his hand illuminated his wrinkled, leathery face and kind eyes. Silver hair gave him a distinguished air, and even though his shoulders were stooped, he held himself proudly. "It's good to see you again, Sam."

"You too," Sam said gruffly. "Now, let's get you and this fellow settled in. Your room be waiting for you like always."

"Thank you. How about putting Hobbs in the blue room?"

Sam turned around and looked at Hobbs closely for the first time. "You done give up some of that leg fighting?"

Hobbs nodded. "I'd have given up a lot more if it hadn't been for Carrie. She and one of those doctors saved it for me."

Carrie was embarrassed by the admiration she heard in his voice. "It was nothing."

Sam chuckled. "You ain't changed much, girl. Still not wanting to take credit for all the thin's you do."

Carrie turned away. "I'm glad we didn't wake Opal and the kids. I'll look forward to seeing them in the morning."

"They sho 'nuff gonna be surprised," Sam replied, his eyes twinkling. "I'll keep them kids quiet so you can sleep in."

"Don't you do any such thing," Carrie scolded. "I didn't come out here to sleep. I can't stay long, and I want to do as much as possible."

Sam held the lantern higher and peered at her. "Don't look to me like you been sleeping much no matter where you are." His voice grew stern. "If you wake up on your own, then so be it. But them kids gonna be quiet as church mice. They ain't gonna be the ones to add to them circles under your eyes."

Carrie smiled and climbed the stairs, warmed by his concern but still determined to get up early. There was so much she wanted to do while she was here. As she walked down the hall holding her lantern high, the memories swamped her. So much of who she was had been crafted within these walls, and on the vastness of the plantation. She shivered in anticipation, then yawned, fatigue pressing down on her.

Carrie turned the flame on the lantern higher as she entered her room. Nothing had changed. Her four-poster canopy bed still occupied the place of honor, its exquisite rose-bordered white coverlet glowing in the light. She stared at it sadly. The bedding had been a gift from her father. She swallowed her sudden longing for what had been and glided across the room to the large mirror. Setting the lantern on her dresser, she stared deeply into the glass. Knowing the mirror's ultimate secret—the opening it covered that led to tunnels under the plantation—did nothing to diminish the mystical allure it had held over her since childhood, when she would spend hours gazing into it and dreaming.

The mirror called to her now. Carrie sat down at her dressing table and pulled out the brush she kept there. Slowly, she unpinned her hair, watching it cascade over her shoulders. As she ran the brush through it, she gazed into the mirror imagining Robert behind her, looking deeply into her eyes as he reached forward to caress her face. The ache of missing him was a physical pain.

Abruptly, she stood and walked to the window. She threw it open and took in deep breaths of the cold, crisp air. She wouldn't be surprised if they had their first frost tonight. She stood there, straining to bridge the ocean that separated her from the man she loved, until she was shivering. She reached to pull the window shut but changed her mind. The fresh air would do her good. She gathered extra blankets from her wardrobe and piled them on the bed.

She was asleep before her head hit the pillow.

The sun was high in the sky when Carrie woke the next day. She yawned and stretched, feeling more rested than she had in months. Cool air washed over her face, making her burrow deeper into the mound of covers. She lay quietly, listening to the sound of birds and the wind whispering through the branches of her favorite oak sentinel stationed right outside her window. She could already feel the magic of the plantation working its way into her heart.

She had forced herself to deal with Richmond's crowded conditions, but her heart and mind yearned for open spaces. She only felt like herself when she had room to move and think and be. She couldn't be home for long, but she was going to make the most of it. She glanced around her room, brought to life now by the sun streaming in through the window. She glanced at the clock.

"Oh my goodness!" She sat up and threw back the covers. "No wonder the sun is so much higher than I thought it should be." Carrie moved to the window, glad there was no one to hear her talking to herself. If there had been frost the night before, the sun had been up long enough to melt it all away. Reaching over to grab a blanket off the bed, Carrie wrapped it around her closely and sank down on her window seat.

The view from her room was spectacular. Wave upon wave of gold, yellow and red spread out as far as she could see, an undulating sea of color banked by the shimmering blue sky. Small clumps of pine cast dark green splotches. A few clusters of fluffy clouds lumbered slowly, casting an occasional shadow over the land as they tried in vain to capture the sun.

Carrie's growling stomach finally forced her away from the beautiful scene. She dressed and braided her hair, content to leave it down today. She was home, and she wasn't going to allow protocol to determine her actions. Smiling into the mirror gaily, she headed for the muted sounds in the dining room.

"Miss Carrie!" Opal sprung up from where she was seated as soon as Carrie entered the room. "It's so good to see you."

"It's wonderful to see you, Opal. You haven't changed a bit," Carrie said warmly, giving the woman a big hug and then stepping back to inspect her. She wasn't too much older than Carrie, but the years of laboring in the fields had aged her.

"Get on with you!" Opal laughed. "I knows better than anyone that my dresses be tighter than they were the last time you were here."

"It's wonderful you and the children have enough to eat." She thought of all the children roaming the city streets with pinched faces and thin arms.

"Things still bad there?"

"They get worse every day," Carrie sighed. "I don't know what this winter is going to be like." She shook her head. "That's one reason I'm here. I've come for the herbs I stored in the basement." She frowned, a sudden fear gripping her. "They're still here, aren't they? The Union soldiers didn't take them?"

"They still be there," Sam reassured her. "Them boys talked about takin' them, but I heard them say they wouldn't know what to do with them no way. They be right where you left them."

Carrie smiled in relief. "Good." She looked around. "Is Hobbs still asleep?"

"I ain't heard not one sound from that room." Sam chuckled. "That boy sleeps like the dead."

"He needed rest," Carrie said. "I'm glad he's getting it." She turned to Opal. "How are the kids?"

"Just fine," Opal replied, her face lighting up with a proud smile. "Being out here has done them a world of good. They still miss their mama and daddy, but they're happy." She glanced out the window. "They should be here any minute. I sent them out to finish up their chores. Keeping them quiet has been some work." She laughed. "They been clamoring to see you ever since they found out you were here."

"I can't wait to see them," Carrie said. She had been glad to provide the children a place to live after their mother, Opal's cousin, had been killed in an explosion at the armory in Richmond. Their daddy was in prison after being captured for spy activity. Carrie's attempts to find out how he was doing had been futile. Castle Thunder, the prison where he was held, would release no information.

Carrie heard the sound of a door being pushed open and suddenly three children swarmed into the room.

"Miss Carrie," Carl, the youngest at eight, cried. "You really are here."

"It's good to see you, Carl." Carrie laughed. "Come here and let me see how you've grown."

Carl raced over and stood in front of her proudly, his muscular body held erect.

Carrie stared at him in amazement. "You've grown at least three inches since the winter."

"Yessum. Opal says my daddy isn't going to recognize me." A sudden frown puckered his face. "You reckon that's true?"

"Boy, you know your daddy is going to know you in a second," Opal scoffed. "He carries a picture of you in his mind that isn't ever going to fade."

Carl relaxed and grinned. Carrie reached out to give him a hug and then turned to smile at the other children. Eleven-year-old Amber and fifteen-year-old Sadie smiled in return.

"Hello, Miss Carrie," they chorused together as they rushed forward to give her hugs.

The next hour flew by as the three children regaled her with stories of their adventures on the plantation. "Where is Susie?" she finally asked. "I thought I would see her by now."

"I didn't think you would ever ask." Opal grinned. "Susie is married."

"What?" Carrie asked in astonishment.

"She met a young man who came through here as a runaway. All the way from North Carolina. Heard we would help him here."

"So she's gone?"

"Nope. She told that boy—his name is Zeke—that if he wanted to marry her, he would have to stay right here until her daddy got out of jail. She wouldn't even think 'about leaving until she knew he was okay and that the other kids had their daddy back." Opal paused. "They're living down in Rose and Moses' old cabin. I hope that's all right."

"Of course it is," Carrie said. "I'm so glad she's happy."

"What about you?" Opal asked. "Whatever happened to that Robert fellow? He ever come back?"

"I'm married, too," Carrie announced happily.

"Say what?" Sam exclaimed. "I think you better be tellin' us the whole story."

Another hour flew by while Carrie shared with them all that had happened since she last saw them.

"Well, I be real happy for you, Miss Carrie," Sam said. "I know you be missin' Robert somethin' fierce, though, ain't ya?"

Carrie nodded, tears springing to her eyes. She brushed them away impatiently. "It was my decision to stay. You'd think I wouldn't be a crybaby about it."

"Don't change the missin' none," Sam said compassionately. "How's your daddy be doing?"

"Not good," Carrie said sadly. She told them of the bitterness and anger consuming him. "He needs to come back to the plantation. Maybe he can find some peace here."

"You tell your daddy we be right here waitin' for him," Sam replied. "It won't be the same, his payin' us a wage and all, but we'll take the same good care of him."

"I'll tell him," Carrie said gratefully. She pushed away from the table. "I have work to do."

"You want me to help you box them herbs up, Miss Carrie?" Opal asked.

"No, thank you. I think I'm going to go down and sort through them. I've lost track of what is actually there. You can have Hobbs come down to help me after he's up and has eaten breakfast. Or lunch..." she said with a grin.

Carrie eased down the stairway into the basement. Cobwebs brushed her face and the air was musty. She had wanted to come down on her own for a reason. She was glad Opal hadn't pushed to help her.

Setting her lantern on the table, she ignored the rows of bottles gleaming at her temptingly. She wanted to do some exploring before Hobbs joined her. Carefully, she walked around the shelves lining the wall of the basement room. They stretched from floor to ceiling in what looked like an unbroken line. Close examination revealed nothing that would indicate a hidden opening to the maze of tunnels running underneath the plantation.

She reached for the lantern and held it high to illuminate the shelves better.

Her great-grandfather had been a crafty man. He concealed the door in her room so well no one would have ever guessed it was there. It was all that had saved her when the Union soldiers tried to capture her. Her ancestor would have hidden this opening just as well. The trick was to figure out what he had been thinking.

Carrie walked back and forth slowly, staring at the walls of shelving carefully. Maybe she had been wrong about her location when she was down in the tunnels before. She had been so sure that the crack of a door she saw in there led into this part of the basement, but maybe she had been turned around. She was about to give up when she suddenly noticed something. One brick along the outside of the shelves seemed to stick out a fraction more than the ones surrounding it.

Carrie set the lantern down and stepped closer. Putting her hand on it, she pushed. Nothing. It seemed to be solidly in place. She sighed in frustration. It was just her imagination. She turned to move away, then stopped. Time could have made the brick stick in place. Once again, she reached for the brick and tried to shake it back and forth.

Several minutes passed. The brick remained in place. Carrie was about to give up when she felt the mortar move under her hand. Her heart began to pound with excitement as the brick gradually became looser and looser. There was enough of it sticking out now to allow her to grasp it with her fingers. She smiled triumphantly when she pulled the brick out and raised the lantern to peer inside. Her grin widened when she saw the rope handle hidden cleverly in the recess.

"You were really something," she murmured to her long-gone ancestor. As she reached for the rope, she prayed it wouldn't disintegrate in her hands. She needn't have worried. The rope was still strong and supple. The brick had protected it all these years. She grasped it and tugged. Slowly, but with great ease, a portion of the long wall of shelves swung toward her smoothly.

Suddenly, she heard footsteps overhead. A quick glance with the aid of the lantern confirmed the existence of the tunnel sloping away gently toward the river. Carrie stepped back and swung the door shut again. She had just replaced the brick, shoving it firmly in place, when she heard Hobbs' voice overhead.

"You down there, Carrie?"

"Come on down, Hobbs," Carrie called. "I'm starting to work on the herbs."

Moments later, he was standing next to her, gazing in awe at the rows of bottles that stretched from floor to ceiling on every wall of the big room. "You sure did a lot of work," he whistled.

"I thought it might come in handy someday," Carrie said. "I'm glad I was right."

It was almost dark before Carrie and Hobbs finished carefully packing the herbs in crates to keep them from breaking. Sam helped Hobbs carry up the last box, then Opal called them in for dinner. Carrie ate hungrily. The long day of labor had been tiring, but she was satisfied with the results. Unless the black hospital was hit with something terrible, there would be enough medicine to make it through the winter.

"I'm going to spend the evening in my father's office," Carrie announced when she was finished. "I have some work I want to do there."

"What are your plans for tomorrow?" Sam asked.

"I'm going down by the river," Carrie announced. "I've done all the work I intend to do. Tomorrow I'm going to have fun."

Sam nodded his agreement and turned back to his paper. Carrie watched him quietly for a moment, noticing the intelligent shine of his eyes and the thoughtful crease of his forehead. How could people think blacks were an inferior race to whites? "You'd make a fine lord of the manor," she said.

Sam looked up and grinned. "Thank you, Miss Carrie. I reckon I would at that." He shook his head. "Won't be gettin' a chance to do that, but I reckon I could have if things had been different." He picked up his paper again. "You get on now."

"Yes, sir," Carrie said demurely. Sam's laughter followed her from the room.

Carrie stopped smiling when she entered her father's office. She lit the lanterns along the wall and stood quietly in the center of the spacious, elegant room, absorbing the essence of her father's presence. She could still feel him there. Could almost smell the aroma of his pipe. Could almost see him bent over the plantation record books, or brooding over a book. Could almost hear his ready laugh as she flashed in to talk with him. Tears welled in her eyes. She missed him. She missed the man who had encouraged her to be different from everyone else. The man who had cheered her on no matter what she did. The man who had taught her to be fair and never let bitterness rule her actions. What had happened to him?

Carrie shook her thoughts away and began to roam around the room. She didn't really know why she had come in here or what she was looking for. She had simply felt this strange compulsion. She had learned to listen to these quiet messages in her head. She walked slowly, her eyes scanning the bookshelves.

She stopped, a row of albums luring her. She reached out and grabbed the first thick volume, settled down in her father's plush chair, and opened it carefully. "Family pictures," she murmured in delight. She wasn't sure she had seen them before. Most of the pages were empty, but the first few held paintings of her mother and father when they were children and then grown up. She examined them closely, staring at the bright happy looks on both their faces. When those portraits had been done, neither of the confident people smiling up at her had had any idea their whole way of life would be shattered—that one would be taken by a sudden illness, leaving the other behind to deal with life.

Carrie blinked away tears as she absorbed the looks of youthful innocence on their faces. Her heart also grieved for the generation living now that had already been robbed of their youthful innocence by the war. Carefree smiles had long ago been replaced with worry and sorrow.

She continued to flip the pages slowly. Suddenly, her hand froze. She picked up the heavy volume and held it closer to the light, poring over the face staring up at her. Her hands shaking, she flipped the miniature portrait over. "Thomas Cromwell, the third." Not able to believe what she was seeing, she turned it back over again.

A sudden pounding of footsteps on the porch arrested her attention. The front door flung open, crashing against the wall. Seconds later Carl's young voice filled the hallway. "They're coming! The Yankees are coming!"

Carrie whitened and jumped up from the desk. Grabbing the thick volume, she slammed it shut and stuck it under her arm. She reached the hallway at the same time Sam did.

"What you talkin' about, boy?" he asked sternly.

Carl nodded his head excitedly, his eyes wide in his face. "I saw them, Mr. Sam. I was comin' back from fishin'." He gasped for breath. "They comin' here to the house. I heard them say so."

"Tonight?" Sam asked.

"I don't think so," Carl said, trying to catch his breath. "They set up camp a mile or so from here. They said they was gonna come before dawn and surprise us."

"What they comin' for?"

"I dunno," Carl said. "I heard 'em say something about looking for food."

"They aren't going to get any of my food," Opal snapped, walking up behind them. "Them soldiers got plenty. They aren't taking what I worked so hard for all summer. I aim to feed you children all winter, and I need that food."

Sam turned to Carrie. "You got to get out of here."

Carrie nodded quickly, her heart racing. "Get Hobbs."

"I'm here," he announced from the shadows. "I heard enough. I'll get the wagon hooked up." He turned and disappeared.

Carrie thought quickly. The rest of the children had gathered in the foyer and were staring in wide-eyed fright. "You don't have anything to worry about," she assured them. "Those soldiers aren't going to take your food." She began to give orders. "Amber, please go upstairs and pack my things, then bring them down to the wagon." She turned to Sadie next. "Please take care of Hobbs' things." Then she turned to Sam and Opal. "Come with me," she urged.

"You need to be gettin' out of here," Sam said anxiously. "Them soldiers might decide to come tonight after all."

Carrie shook her head decidedly, forcing away the image of all the boxes stacked in the wagons. She ached to think of something happening to the herbs, but she refused to leave Sam and Opal with the possibility of not enough food for the long winter. "Come with me," she repeated, breaking into a run. Somehow she knew she didn't have a minute to lose.

"Where we goin'?" Sam gasped as they reached the top of the basement stairs.

Carrie flew down the stairs, holding the lantern high, not bothering to answer. Moments later, she was smiling at the astonished looks on Sam and Opal's face. "No one is supposed to know about this," she said. "This tunnel is a Cromwell family secret." She paused to take a breath. "It's the only way I can think of for you to save the food. If you hurry, you can probably get most of it down here."

Sam and Opal edged forward to stare into the dark opening of the tunnel. Quickly, Carrie showed them how it worked.

Sam whistled. "Thank you, Miss Carrie. We'll make sure we hide all that food. And I promise you that ain't nobody here gonna be tellin' your family secret. Now you and Hobbs got to be gettin' on."

Carrie nodded, headed back up the stairs, and hurried outside. Hobbs was already waiting in the wagon. Amber and Sadie were just putting the bags in the back.

Carrie swung around to give all of them a fierce hug and then jumped up into the wagon seat.

"Good luck," Sam called softly.

"You too," Carrie called back, gripping the seat as Hobbs urged the horses into a brisk trot. She waved until she knew the darkness had swallowed them and turned back to stare hard at the road in front of her, her heart pounding.

"I'll get us out of here," Hobbs said just loud enough to be heard over the rumble of the wagon wheels.

Carrie stared out over the fields now barely discernible in the darkness. Her heart ached to have to leave the plantation so abruptly. She wasn't ready yet. She hadn't re-found all of her heart yet. Her mind flew to her special place by the river. Tears poured down her face as she realized her months of longing wouldn't be fulfilled.

Stop it, she told herself. *You got what you came for. Let that be enough.*

Hobbs cursed under his breath and sawed back on the reins.

Carrie, caught off balance, grabbed for her seat, barely stopping herself from flying out of the wagon. "What are you...?" Her words died as she looked up and saw a line of horses extended across the drive just past where it entered the main road.

She saw Hobbs move to grab his rifle but reached over and stopped his hand. "It's too late," she said quietly.

"You're a wise woman," the lead horseman said. "I would hate to have to put a bullet through your driver's heart."

"I would hate that, too," Carrie said, fighting to remain calm.

"Where are you going so late at night?" he snapped.

"Home," Carrie said simply. "I find I prefer to travel at night. I have been visiting all day."

"I bet," the soldier laughed. "I'm afraid you're not going anywhere, ma'am. Why don't you step down from that wagon?"

Chapter Twenty

Robert leaned against the railing of the British commerce ship, watching the skyline of London disappear with mixed feelings. His mission had failed. In spite of the court's order for Russell to release the *Alexandra*, with which he had complied, he had nonetheless put the two boats close to completion in Laird Shipyard under supervision early in September. A few weeks later the British government bought the two badly needed ships. It was rumored that Russell felt certain he had averted a crisis with the Union government and was proud of his actions.

Those same actions had made Robert's purpose for being in London obsolete. He had packed his bags and made arrangements for the first ship leaving England. Even though he regretted the outcome of the Confederacy's attempt to buy the blockade runners, he could not deny his excitement over reaching home and Carrie.

"Why, it's Mr. Borden, is it not?"

Robert spun around as the musical voice sounded over his shoulder. "Miss Palmer?" he asked with a smile.

"You remember me," she said in a pleased voice.

"I could never forget the only fellow Virginian I met in England," Robert responded. "How are you?"

"Rather anxious to get this trip over," she confided honestly. "In spite of the improvements made on the blockade runners England has managed to slip past their government, I still get nervous at the idea of running it."

"Understandably," Robert agreed. "I'm afraid I'm so eager to get home that I haven't given it much thought."

"Does your wife know you're on the way?"

"I will be the letter announcing my arrival." Robert grinned. "Are you going back to the South to stay, Miss Palmer?"

"Please call me Suzanne," she protested. "We're going to be on this boat for a while."

"And I'm Robert," he responded graciously. "Now, are you returning to stay?" He wondered what had happened to her fiancé but didn't want to ask. He was afraid it would be awkward.

"No," Suzanne said, gazing back longingly at the rapidly disappearing city. "I'm going back to take supplies to loved ones." Her look hardened. "I have received countless letters from friends and family in dire need of the basic necessities of clothes and food. The Union blockade is causing them to be quite destitute, I'm afraid. I'm happy to report, however, that there are dozens of barrels of clothing stored in the hull of this ship. I have the government's promise that the blockade runner I get on will run them through. I intend to make sure they get there." She smiled slightly. "Then I'm returning to London. I'll be married upon my return."

Robert looked at her in admiration. "You're a very brave lady."

"Poo!" Suzanne scoffed. "One does what they have to do in these times." She turned away from the railing. "I have some unpacking I need to do to get settled. Will I see you at dinner?"

"Certainly," Robert responded, glad to have agreeable company for the return journey.

Robert grinned broadly as the man directing passengers pointed him and Suzanne toward the *Phantom*. "This is the boat I came here on," he confided. "I don't think we have a thing to worry about. Captain Bueller is a first rate fellow."

"I'm glad to hear that," Suzanne replied. "I'll form my own judgment of him after he agrees to carry my shipment of clothes."

Robert laughed. He had grown accustomed to Suzanne's strong will. She reminded him more and more of Carrie. If all went well, he would be home in less than two weeks. He could hardly wait. Their trip from London had been uneventful. Suzanne had kept it from being deadly boring. They had been forced to prolong their stay in Nassau, but three days on the sunny little island had certainly not been a hardship. It was only Robert's impatience to get home that kept him from truly enjoying it.

"Good to see you again, old man," Captain Bueller boomed as Robert stepped onto the boat.

"The same," Robert responded sincerely. If possible, the captain was a little more wind-burned, but other than that he hadn't changed.

"So what do you think of our little town?"

"Little town?" Robert laughed. "I found London very interesting, but it could never hold my heart the way the South does." He turned toward Suzanne. "Here's a woman who feels differently, however. She's headed back to London as quickly as she can." Pulling Suzanne forward, he made the introductions.

"Welcome aboard, Miss Palmer," Captain Bueller said gallantly. "I hope you enjoy your trip."

Suzanne didn't return his smile. "I'll enjoy it much more when you have assured me the barrels of clothing I am accompanying from England will be on board your ship. Otherwise, I'm afraid I will wait for another boat."

Captain Bueller glanced at Robert and grinned. "Has trouble speaking her mind, doesn't she?"

Suzanne glared at him for a moment, then smiled reluctantly as she saw the fun dancing in his blue eyes. "So will you take my barrels?"

Captain Bueller nodded. "I was informed ahead of time of your mission." He peered at her closely. "You must be an important lady."

Suzanne shrugged. "No more so than the next person."

Robert watched her. Once again the feeling of having seen her somewhere before rose to taunt him. He thought about what Bueller had said. She must indeed be important for the English government to intervene in the matter of some clothing. *Who was she?*

Suzanne extended her hand. "Thank you so much, Captain Bueller." Now that her mission was assured, she was all politeness and charm.

Captain Bueller laughed affably. "Know how to get what you want don't you, ma'am?" He tipped his hat. "You're welcome aboard the *Phantom*. I'm hoping for a smooth trip."

"I just want to get there," Suzanne said. "I don't care if it's smooth or rough. I've seen it all." She smiled, turned on her heel, and walked to the front of the boat.

Bueller gazed after her for a moment and turned back to Robert. "Interesting lady," he said dryly.

"She's amazingly like my wife," Robert grinned. "You don't want to be the one standing in their way."

"I imagine." The captain changed the subject. "Was your trip a success?"

"No," Robert said. "I learned a lot about England, but I'm afraid I did nothing for the Confederacy. I'm glad to be returning home."

Bueller nodded. "We leave in one hour. Will you join me up front then?"

Robert was pleased. "Certainly."

He settled himself in short order, then joined the captain. "How are things?"

"Depends on what things you're asking about. I don't think your Confederacy is doing too well. I don't imagine you've heard anything about that fight down in Georgia. Chickamauga I think they called it."

"The news reached England just before I sailed," Robert said. "I understand it was a smashing Southern victory."

"Goes to show how much you can trust the papers." Bueller grunted, checking his instruments as he talked. "That battle cost the South way too many men. The North seems to have an endless supply of manpower, even if they aren't too keen on the draft. The South is simply going to run out of men at this rate."

Robert frowned. "Is there any good news?"

Bueller thought for a minute. "Winter is coming," he finally announced. "That should stop the fighting for a while. Give the South time to get ready for next spring."

"Joy," Robert muttered.

"You'll have to fight when you get home, won't you, old man?"

"Let's not talk about it," Robert said. "I'm going home to my wife. That's all I want to think about right now. You just get me through that blockade, or I'll be forced to swim it myself."

"Aye, if you were on some of the boats recently, that would be exactly what you would be doing, I'm afraid."

"What do you mean?"

"The Union Navy is stepping it up to destroy the blockade runners. It's always been a risk, but now it's getting downright dangerous out there."

"You thinking about giving it up?"

"Me?" Bueller laughed. "Why, I live for this type of adventure. There's nothing I like better than outsmarting those Yankees."

"Some of the commerce men don't seem to feel the same way."

"They're in it for money." Bueller shrugged. "I got enough money stashed away to last me the rest of my life. Some of these fellows have been spending it as fast as they get it. It's getting to the point where the risk is greater than the reward. We lost four ships last week."

"Four ships in one week!" Robert exclaimed. "What happened?"

"They weren't fast enough," Bueller said laconically. "A couple of them were sunk. Another two ran aground in an attempt to save the cargo. One was successful, the other's supplies were commandeered by the Union Navy." He scanned the horizon. "The *Phantom* won't have any trouble."

"Here's hoping," Robert replied fervently.

Bueller changed the subject. "I've seen our Miss Palmer somewhere before. What do you know about her?"

"Not much," Robert admitted. "We talked a lot on the way over from England but never discussed many personal things." He shrugged. "She's been in England a while. Engaged to marry an English chap when she goes back." That was all he said. He was reluctant to admit he felt he knew her from somewhere, too. She was obviously loyal to the South. Her secrets were her own to keep.

"I know I've seen her," Bueller repeated. "Maybe it will come to me."

Three days later, under the cover of night, the *Phantom* approached the shore of North Carolina. Robert was up top with Bueller, scanning the horizon for any sign of a Union blockade ship. The moon, when it popped out from the thick clouds scudding across the sky, was bright, but for the most part it stayed concealed. A brisk breeze had kicked up high swells that exploded as the low-built blockade runner forged through them at top speed.

"Not a Federal in sight," Bueller said jubilantly. "Chalk up another one for the *Phantom.*"

Robert breathed a sigh of relief, his pulse quickening as he realized how close he was to Carrie. Just a few more minutes and he would be on shore. A few more days and he would be home.

Bueller suddenly cursed and craned forward. "What the devil is that?" he muttered. He leaned forward to bark instructions into his speak tube, but before he could get any words out of his mouth, the swiftly moving ship swung hard to the starboard.

"What the...? Bueller cried.

Seconds later, Robert grabbed for the railing as the *Phantom* ran hard aground and shuddered to a stop. "What happened?" he yelled, stunned at the sudden change of events.

"I'd give anything to have the answer to that one," Bueller growled.

Robert peered forward. "Is that a Yankee boat in front of us?"

"That's probably what the pilot thought," Bueller snapped. "Actually it's one of our own boats. It's evidently in the same predicament we are now in. Our pilot must have thought, in his little pea brain, that our only course seemed to be to run for shore. He never even gave me a chance to give him orders." His voice was coldly furious. "I'll have his head for this!"

Flares flashed around them in the night sky. Robert jerked his head up.

Bueller glanced back. "There's your Yankee ship," he said.

Robert was about to ask him how he could sound so calm when they were about to be blown up, but he got his answer before he opened his mouth. From shore came the sound of tremendous explosions as the alert gun crews of Fort Fisher threw a barrage of shells at the attacking Federal ship. Minutes later, the ship reversed course and drew out of range.

"We'll have time to get out of here," Bueller said. He smashed his fist against the rail. "Without my boat," he added bitterly. Then he forced a grin. "I don't guess you can win at this game every time." He shook his head. "I just didn't expect it to end in such a humiliating way— run aground by one of my own men."

Suzanne Palmer appeared, her face white and anxious. "What is happening here?" she cried.

"I'm afraid it's going to take us a little longer than I thought to reach shore," Bueller replied. "I'm sorry for the inconvenience." The wind changed from a brisk breeze into a howling wind. Bueller grinned. "Looks like we got us a bit of a nor'easter as well. That should help keep the old chaps away."

Robert was staring at Suzanne. He had not thought her capable of expressing the raw fear he saw etched on her face. She gazed at him for a moment and then spun away in the direction of her cabin. She would be safest there, he knew.

The once mighty ship now groaned pitifully as the storm smashed the *Phantom* against the sandbar she was stranded on. White spray cascaded across the deck, drenching him in seconds. He shivered in the cold but was determined to see what happened. A few hundred yards away, the boom of breakers against the shore could be heard above the storm. Shouts of the ship's officers and crew added to the chaos. He looked down on the deck. Captain Bueller seemed to be everywhere at once, shouting orders, helping to secure things.

"Robert!"

Robert turned. "Why aren't you in your cabin, Suzanne?" he shouted above the melee.

"I have to get off this boat!" she cried. "Will you help me?"

"Are you crazy? Do you see what is going on out there? Besides, Bueller seems to be showing no alarm. I'm sure he is confident we will all get off before the Federals reach us." He reached forward to grab her arm. "Let me take you back below."

"No!" She wrenched free from his grasp.

Robert stared at her. What had gotten into her?

Suzanne took a deep breath and leaned closer. "I'm a spy," she cried above the storm. "I guarantee you the captain on that ship knows who I am. If they capture me, I'll go to prison."

Robert nodded his head slowly. "That's where I know you. I've seen your picture in the paper. You've been caught before. In Washington, DC."

"I spent six months in the Old Capitol Prison," Suzanne acknowledged grimly, her eyes glowing with fear. "I won't ever go back there." She grabbed his arm again. "You have to help me get off this boat. I'm your friend."

Robert stared down at the boiling water. He knew trying to manage this in a rowboat would be suicidal.

"Please!" Suzanne pleaded. She reached up and pulled a bag from inside her dress. "These are papers for President Davis. They are from someone very important in the English government. It is imperative he get them."

"Those papers aren't going to do him any good if they're at the bottom of the ocean," he yelled.

Suzanne glared at him and spun away. "I'll find someone else to help me," she cried. "And if I don't, I'll go myself."

Robert knew she meant it. It sounded like something Carrie would say. Grimacing, he lunged forward and grabbed her arm. "Hold on," he shouted. "I'll go with you."

Suzanne whirled and hugged him. "Thank you! I'll get my things," she hollered. Then she turned and disappeared.

"What was she doing up here?"

Robert turned to see Bueller walk up behind him. He still had hopes he could talk Suzanne into staying on the ship. "How long before we get off this thing?"

Bueller shrugged. "Tomorrow."

Robert hesitated and then explained the situation. "I told her I'd go with her."

"You're a fool," Bueller scowled. "Neither one of you knows anything about handling a boat."

"I know that as well as you," Robert responded, "but what am I to do? The lady is crazy enough to go on her own, and I can't send her off to die."

"So you go to die with her? I can see how that will help things."

"I'm ready." Suzanne appeared behind them.

Bueller turned on her. "Now look here, Miss Palmer. You've simply got to put this crazy idea out of your mind. I assure you this situation is much less perilous than it seems. The wind seems to be falling. The *Phantom* is firmly stuck on the bottom and is in absolutely no danger of cracking apart." He waved his arm into the night. "You don't have to worry about the Yankees either. They're not going to risk having the guns at Fort Fisher blow them apart." He took a deep breath. "Wait until morning. I'll send some of my crew with you. I assure you that you are much safer staying on board tonight."

Suzanne approached until she was standing inches from Bueller. She planted her fists on her hips and stared up at him. "Have you ever spent time in a prison, Captain Bueller?"

"No, I haven't."

"Then don't tell me I'll be safer if I stay on this boat," she snapped. "I know exactly what it will be like if I'm captured. Last time, they let me out after six months. I can assure you they won't be so kind this time." Her voice grew bitter. "My future husband tried to talk me out of coming. He told me it was much too dangerous. I wouldn't listen. Now I'm here, about to be captured by the Yankees, and all my barrels of clothes are probably taking on gallons of sea water." She shook her head angrily. "I was foolish."

"You're about to be foolish again," Captain Bueller snapped. "Is death preferable to possible prison?"

Robert watched her face closely, grimly realizing she would indeed choose death.

Suzanne turned away. "I'm quite capable of undoing one of those rowboats, Captain. I'm going, even if I have to go alone. I'm not simply going to sit here and wait for the Yankees to come get me."

Robert stared after her. "See what I mean?"

"You say your wife is like that. I pity you," Bueller grinned half-heartedly.

"I've never been in prison, so I don't know how adamant I would be about not going back. However, I've not even experienced it, and I don't find the prospect particularly appealing."

"There is no danger of that!" Bueller protested.

"Oh, you convinced me," Robert said readily. "You didn't do such a good job on Suzanne. I'm afraid I'm going to have to accompany her." He glanced out at the sea. "At least the wind is dying down."

"The surf will pound you to death."

"Perhaps," Robert said, trying to swallow his fear. "I guess we'll see."

Bueller stared at him and then extended his hand. "Good luck. I think you're foolish, but then I've been accused of the same thing many times myself. I've always come through. I hope you do, too."

"Thanks," Robert said gruffly, gripping Bueller's hand. "Good luck yourself. I hope I see you again." He turned and went in pursuit of Suzanne.

He found her standing next to one of the lifeboats, peering out into the darkness.

"Can we at least wait for the break of dawn?" he suggested. "Not even the Yankees are crazy enough to try to board this boat in the dark. As soon as the sky begins to lighten and we can see shore, we'll go," he promised.

"I thought Captain Bueller changed your mind."

"He did. But he didn't change yours, and I can't let you go alone."

Suzanne clutched the leather purse around her neck. "The Confederate government will thank you."

"We'll see," Robert mumbled.

The ocean was still gray and furious when Robert took a deep breath and began to untie the ropes holding the lifeboat.

Captain Bueller materialized out of nowhere and began to help. "You're really going to do this aren't you, old man?"

Robert nodded. There was nothing to say. He felt sick at heart and would have gladly followed Bueller's recommendation to stay on board if Suzanne had not been so afraid.

"Is this what you chaps call Southern chivalry?" Bueller asked.

"Something like that," Robert replied, trying to force a light note into his voice.

"Make sure you keep the bow pointed into the waves," Bueller ordered. "If you let this boat go broadside, you're doomed. The waves will swamp you in a second." He tugged at a stubborn piece of rope. "Start rowing before you even hit the water. That way you'll have a better chance to maintain control." He took a breath and continued to bark orders. "Keep Miss Palmer low and in the center of the boat. It should help stabilize it."

Robert listened closely, grateful for the instruction.

Bueller turned. "Do you know how to swim, Miss Palmer?"

"I do," Suzanne replied, staring down at the water surging angrily at the sides of the *Phantom*.

"What are you carrying in that bag around your neck?" Bueller asked.

Suzanne drew back. "I don't believe that's any of your business."

"No, ma'am, I suppose it's not," Bueller snapped. "Except that the way you're walking, that thing looks like it weighs a pretty amount. You end up in the water, and it won't matter if you know how to swim. You'll sink like a rock between that bag and all those clothes you're wearing."

Suzanne hesitated. "I'll be fine," she said. She glanced out at where the Yankee ship had attacked from. "Are we free to go now?"

Bueller nodded heavily and stepped away. "Good luck." He waved several of his men over. "I need your help in letting this boat down."

The crew stared at Robert and Suzanne as if they were certain they had lost their senses.

Robert stepped into the rowboat, steadied it against the side of the ship, and offered a hand to assist Suzanne. She hauled up her skirts and eased in gingerly, staring down at the rampaging water with wide eyes. "You sure you want to do this?" Robert yelled.

Suzanne glanced north. She set her lips and nodded curtly. "Yes."

"Lower us away, boys," Robert called cheerfully. "We'll see you on shore later."

"Dinner's on me tonight," Bueller yelled back. "If you make it."

"We'll make it!" Suzanne yelled defiantly.

Robert jumped to the oars and waved for Suzanne to take her place. Hunkering down low, she grabbed the sides of the boat and steadied herself. The boat was swinging wildly before it even hit the water, caught by the wind still gusting from the north. Just as Bueller had instructed, Robert began rowing before the boat touched the churning sea.

He gasped when the full force of the ocean struck the little boat. Throwing all of his strength into the oars, he somehow managed to pull the wooden boat away from the sides of the *Phantom*. He knew one solid hit would decimate the tiny craft. Sweat poured from his face as he grappled to keep on course for shore.

"Keep the bow pointed into the waves," he gasped, trying to remember all his instructions. His few times rowing on the calm James River had done nothing to prepare him for the battle he faced now. He glanced up for a second and saw Suzanne huddled in the center of the boat, her face white and strained. Somehow it helped to know she was terrified. He knew he was.

An incoming wave picked up the boat like it was nothing more than a toy and spun it around ferociously. Robert cursed and fought to bring it back around. Another wave surged under them and he felt the boat begin to tip. "No!" he shouted into the wind and pounding surf. He launched all of his weight into the oars until the boat began to turn back into the waves.

There was a slight let up in the wind, and Robert gasped as his muscles screamed and burned with pain. A quick look told him they were still at least a hundred yards from shore. In this maelstrom, it looked as if it were a hundred miles. He didn't know if his strength would hold up. It was taking all he had just to hold them on course.

"We have to make it!" Suzanne screamed above the noise. "Davis has to have what's in this bag."

"And I want to see my wife again," Robert shouted back, suddenly furious he let Suzanne talk him into something so foolish. "If the boat goes down, we'll have to swim for it!"

"I have gold in this bag," Suzanne hollered. "I won't make it."

Robert stared at her in astonishment for a brief moment. *Gold.* He shook his head grimly. If the boat capsized, she was doomed. He would never be able to haul all that weight.

The wind kicked back up and the waves surged even higher. Mountains of green-black water rose around them threateningly.

Robert threw his weight into the oars. For a wonderful moment, the little boat surged through the waves, headed straight for shore. Then, with no warning, a violent blast of wind caught them on the crest of a wave. The boat shuddered, hesitated, and swung broadside to the waves. Robert grunted as he hauled at the oars, but the boat was now moving at the mercy of the seas.

"God, help us!" he heard Suzanne scream as they careened down the side of the towering wave.

Robert looked up and saw the wall of water descending on them just before the little boat flipped, throwing him into the water like a rag doll.

The impact of the cold water left him breathless. He clawed for the surface and finally broke free, gasping and choking.

"Suzanne!" he screamed.

Nothing but rolling, churning water met his searching eyes. Another wave picked him up and sucked him back under. His lungs were burning when he broke through the surface. He knew he was weakening fast. If he didn't get to shore soon, the ocean would win. Once more, he fought the seas, pushing himself up as high as he could go, searching for any sign of Suzanne. He already knew what he would find. She never stood a chance with all the weight she was carrying. She had probably gone directly to the bottom.

Tears mingled with salt water as Robert turned toward shore and began to fight for his life. He lost count of the times the waves picked him up, churned him along the bottom, and spit him back out. He was about to give up and let the sea claim another prize, when he felt solid ground.

Staggering to his feet, the salt water gurgling in his throat, he stumbled onto the wet sand and collapsed. The waves pounded inches from his feet, but he was too exhausted to care. Robert had no fight left.

Chapter Twenty-One

Carrie stayed seated in the wagon and stared at the Union soldier coldly. "On what basis are you detaining me?"

The Union soldier hooted with laughter as he advanced toward her. "Allow me to introduce myself, ma'am. My name is Captain Pemberton." He smiled. "In case you can't see well enough in the dark, I am a Union soldier. From the sound of your accent, there is no doubt you are a Rebel. That makes us enemies," he said patiently, as if he were explaining things to a child.

"I am not an imbecile, Captain Pemberton," Carrie snapped. "You still have not explained why you have detained me. Or has the Union Army sunken so low that you have nothing better to do than stop defenseless women in the middle of the night?" Carrie swallowed to control the tremor in her voice. She knew she was playing a dangerous game. She was also determined to let Sam and Opal have all the time they needed.

"Riding around with an armed guard hardly makes you a defenseless woman," the captain said, amusement tingeing his voice. "Are all the Rebel women as spirited as you are, Miss Cromwell?"

Carrie gasped. How did he know who she was?

"Ah, so I was right," Pemberton said triumphantly. "I was merely taking a wild guess. My reports simply say this plantation is owned by the Cromwell family. Beyond that, we know little."

Carrie breathed a sigh of relief. They didn't know her father worked with the government. Whatever their plans were for her, it was best that they not have that tidbit of information. They also didn't know she was married. Somehow she knew it wouldn't help them any if they were to know her husband was a Confederate captain. She prayed Hobbs would stay quiet.

"We do know that no one but slaves have been on this plantation for months. Why have you come home, Miss Cromwell?" Pemberton asked.

"To visit," Carrie said calmly. "I've already told you that."

"And I'm Abraham Lincoln," Pemberton said. "Miss Cromwell, I'm afraid I'm losing my patience. In spite of your low opinion of me, I don't enjoy accosting women in the middle of the night. I'm simply doing my job, and you're making it difficult."

One of his men edged forward toward the wagon. "Hey, Captain. They've got this wagon loaded with something. Looks like it's completely full."

Pemberton trotted forward, stared at Carrie, and tilted his head. "Care to tell me what you're transporting, Miss Cromwell?"

Carrie bit her lip. There was nothing to stop the soldiers from discovering for themselves what was in the crates. "Herbs," she said.

"Herbs?" Pemberton echoed. "You're roaming around in the middle of the night with a wagonload of herbs?" His voice sharpened. "You must take me for a fool." He turned to his men. "Break open one of those crates."

"Please be careful with them," Carrie pleaded. "Those herbs are very important."

The man who spotted the crates pried the lids off one of them. He held up a bottle in the darkness. "There's not anything but a bunch of bottles, Captain. It's too dark to see what's in them."

"Bring a lantern up here," Pemberton ordered.

A match flared, and the steady light of a lantern illuminated the road.

Carrie took a close look at her captor. She was surprised. His deep voice indicated a much larger man, but the man sitting erect in his saddle was scarcely taller than her. He didn't look to be much older either. Dark brown hair topped a rough-cut face. His face was firm, but his eyes weren't unkind.

Pemberton reached for the bottle and held it up to the light. "What in the ...?"

"They are herbs, Captain, as I said. I wasn't lying to you. Every crate contains the same thing."

"Why?"

Carrie decided to be honest. The captain's question seemed to be one of genuine interest. She could admit it must look suspicious for a woman to be traveling at night with such a strange load. "They are medicine, Captain. At least, they will be when I have a little more time to make my mixtures and potions."

"Sounds like a witch doctor, Captain," one of the men called nastily.

Carrie felt her temper rising. "Your blockade has made getting medicine almost impossible," she said. "We have learned how to improvise."

"Hey, Captain, you ain't gonna let this stuff get through to them lousy Rebel soldiers are you?"

Carrie felt Hobbs stiffen beside her. She wanted to warn him to stay calm, but all she could do was reach over and touch his leg.

"This medicine isn't for soldiers," Carrie said honestly. "It will be taken to the hospital for black people in Richmond."

Captain Pemberton stared at her. "You really expect me to believe that?" he scoffed. "What do you take me for? I know better than to think you Rebels care enough about black people to do that."

"I'm afraid there's a lot you don't know," Carrie said. "Not all people are the same." She glanced around. "Now, I have shown you what I'm carrying, and I'd like to be on my way."

"She's gonna take these things to them soldiers," another of Pemberton's men called. "Besides, we can't let things go into Richmond."

"My man is right, Miss Cromwell. Please step down from the wagon. I'm afraid this is now Union property."

"You bunch of dirty Yankees!" Hobbs suddenly cried. "You're messing with the wrong woman. Her father is important in the government."

Carrie groaned as the sardonic look in Pemberton's eyes changed to one of cold rage.

"You would have done better to keep your driver quiet, Miss Cromwell," he said. "You really should have more control of him." Pemberton turned to Hobbs. "Get down out of that wagon."

In response, Hobbs grabbed the reins and lashed at the horses furiously. "Get on!" he cried. The horses, startled, surged forward but got less than a dozen feet before they plunged to a halt, surrounded by Union cavalrymen. Hobbs cursed and reached back quickly, pulling the rifle out and firing before it was even aimed. The shot careened harmlessly into the dusty road.

The butt of a rifle appeared from the dark, smashing into Hobbs' head with a sick sound. Hobbs stiffened and slumped against Carrie.

"Tie him up," Pemberton ordered. "Then throw him into the back of the wagon on top of the crates. We'll take care of him later." He turned to Carrie and regarded her thoughtfully. "And just who is your father, Miss Cromwell?"

Carrie stared at him defiantly.

One of the men edged forward. "I bet I could convince her to talk," he laughed, pulling a whip from the back of his saddle. "Why don't you give me a go at her, Captain?"

"Quit showing your ignorance," Pemberton snapped. "Put that thing away."

The man backed away and recoiled his whip. "Her driver tried to kill one of us," he muttered.

"Then her driver should pay," Pemberton said. "And he will."

"What are you going to do to him?" Carrie asked as Hobbs was dumped unceremoniously into the back of the wagon, his head hitting one of the crates with a crack.

"We aren't equipped for prisoners," Pemberton said. "We are on a raiding mission. I'm afraid he will just be in our way."

"One bullet will take care of him," a soldier said casually, riding up to the back of the wagon and pulling out his pistol.

For one wild moment, Carrie thought of pulling out her own pistol.

"Leave him be," Pemberton ordered. "I'll let you know what I decide to do with him. Whatever it is, I want him to wake up first and tell us who Miss Cromwell's father is. I have a feeling that information could be useful to us."

Pemberton turned back to Carrie. "We will take you back to your plantation. I know that's not quite the home you had in mind to return to tonight, but I'm afraid it will have to do." He edged closer and held out his hand. "And you can hand me that pistol. I'm afraid if there's any more shooting tonight, my boys aren't going to respond as kindly as they did to your driver."

Carrie handed it to him silently, her mind racing to figure a way out of her current predicament. What would they do with her and Hobbs? Now that they knew her father was someone important, her situation had become more precarious. She shuddered at the thought of what they would do to Hobbs. Her anger at his impulsive actions had died when they knocked him unconscious and threw him in the back of the wagon. How much more would he have to pay for his actions?

The house was dark when the wagon, now driven by one of Pemberton's soldiers, rolled down the drive. Carrie knew Sam and Opal were peering out the windows at them.

"Anyone home?" Pemberton asked. He sighed when Carrie shrugged. "You can make this hard on yourself or easy, Miss Cromwell." He shook his head and motioned to his men. "Search the house."

"There are only some of my father's people," Carrie said. "They are no threat to you."

"I thought we came here and let all the slaves go earlier this year?" Pemberton asked in astonishment. He glared at Carrie. "What did you do? Buy some more?" He shook his head in disgust. "You people are really something."

Carrie bristled at the arrogance oozing from his voice. Exhaustion was beginning to wear her temper thin. "The people in that house have been with my father for years. They know they are free to go at any time. They have chosen to stay here."

"And where may I find your father, Miss Cromwell?" Pemberton snapped. "Something tells me he's not here taking care of his slaves."

Carrie shrugged, and then she raised her voice, hoping to stop any damage to the house. "Sam and Opal," she called. The soldiers stomping up the stairs stopped and turned around. "Come on out," she yelled. "They know you're the only ones in there." *Hide the kids in the tunnel,* she pleaded silently, hoping they would pick up on her cue. There was no reason to put the children at risk.

Slowly, the door to the big house opened. Sam and Opal stepped out.

"You be all right, Miss Carrie?" Sam called.

"I'm all right, Sam."

Pemberton swung down from his horse. "I guess we'll make your house our headquarters for a while," he said pleasantly. "I think it will suit us just fine."

"Do you always show such disregard for others' property?" Carrie asked.

"I'm your enemy, Miss Carrie Cromwell. You will do well to remember that," Pemberton snapped. "It would not take much more to push me to my limit. I can be most unpleasant if I choose to be."

I bet you can, Carrie thought.

A sudden clatter from down the road caused her to snap her head up. Two horses galloped up to the porch, their sides heaving. "Captain Pemberton!" one of the men called.

"What is it?"

The man swung down from his horse. "We ran into a Rebel ambush a few miles back." He paused. "Your brother was shot."

"How bad?" Pemberton asked sharply.

"He's hurt pretty bad," the soldier responded. Suddenly he noticed Carrie and the wagon. "What's going on?'

"Where is Clifton now?" Pemberton snapped, completely ignoring the question.

Carrie felt a stirring of compassion for the man who claimed to be her enemy. The anguish in his voice was obvious.

"A few miles back," the soldier responded. "We were afraid to move him."

Pemberton whirled toward the men on the porch. "Get down here and unload this wagon. Be quick but don't break anything. Those crates could be valuable." The look he shot Carrie clearly revealed he didn't believe her claim that all the crates were full of herbs.

Carrie breathed a sigh of relief. She didn't care about his reasons, as long as they weren't destroyed.

Within minutes, the wagon was empty. Hobbs lay motionless on the ground where they had dumped him. Carrie stared at him, wondering if he was still alive, then exchanged a long look with Sam and Opal.

"Take the wagon and bring Clifton back here," Pemberton snapped. He cursed and slammed his fist into his other hand. "Fine time to be without a doctor," he growled.

Carrie was sitting with Sam and Opal in the parlor when they heard the wagon return. Not a word had been spoken since Pemberton ordered it away. He had done nothing but pace back and forth in the parlor. Carrie watched him silently, longing to check on Hobbs still laying out in the dark under guard.

"Keep an eye on them," Pemberton snapped as he turned toward the front door.

A few minutes later, he strode back in, followed by four men holding a crude litter. A young man, covered with blood, was stretched out on it. Carrie grimaced at the deep crimson splotch covering his chest. Another red area was growing on his right pants leg.

"Where can I put him?" Pemberton asked.

Carrie sprang to her feet. "There is a small room off the kitchen."

"Find a better room than that," Pemberton ordered one of his men.

"I don't care where you put him, Captain, but he will be closest to hot water from the kitchen there," Carrie said. "Your brother needs medical attention."

"I realize that, Miss Cromwell," Pemberton said furiously. He ground his teeth. "Where in the world am I going to get someone to help him?"

Carrie looked at the fear on his face. Obviously, he and his brother were very close. "I can help him," she said.

"You?" Pemberton asked contemptuously. "What are *you* going to do? Pour herbs on him?"

Carrie smiled gently, calm now that there was a need. "I serve as a doctor in a Confederate military hospital," she explained. "I can help your brother."

Pemberton stared at her in disbelief and then turned away. "Find him a room," he ordered again.

Carrie stepped forward and grabbed his arm. "If you want your brother to live, you will let me treat him," she said, amazed at her own audacity. "If those bullets aren't taken out soon, he will die. It won't take long for infection to set in."

Pemberton wrenched his arm away but stared down at her.

Carrie returned his gaze and motioned toward his brother. "He needs help now."

"Why would you help him?"

"In spite of your low opinion of me, not all Southerners are alike," Carrie replied. "I hate this war, but I most certainly do not hate Northerners. Your brother is very badly wounded. I am committed to helping people. It's that simple."

Pemberton's eyes burned into her for several long moments. "Put him in the room beside the kitchen," he barked.

Relieved, Carrie turned and began to give her own orders. "Opal, put a large kettle of water on to boil. Sam, bring me a supply of rags." They stared at her in amazement and then sprang to do her bidding.

Carrie's mind flew to Hobbs lying out in the dirt. She turned to Pemberton. "I have only one request," she said, realizing it was a huge gamble. The captain was already distraught. She didn't want to send him over the edge.

Pemberton whirled. "What is it?"

"I want my driver brought in and put in the room beside your brother. He might die if left out there. I don't know how badly hurt he is."

"He might die anyway," Pemberton said.

Carrie stared at him, willing the spark of humanity in him to flare into flaming life.

Pemberton nodded. "Go get him."

Taking a deep breath, Carrie decided to push further. "If I save your brother's life, I want your promise you will not kill my driver." She shuddered at the bargaining she was doing with men's lives.

Pemberton thought for a moment and then nodded curtly. "And if he dies, your driver dies, too."

Carrie nodded slowly, realizing with a sick feeling that the game she had decided to play had very high stakes.

She jumped into action, hurrying back to the room where they had deposited the wounded soldier.

Opal came in with the first pot of boiling water. "Still had some hot on the fire from supper," she whispered, reaching out to squeeze Carrie's arm.

Carrie turned to Clifton. She cut away the clothing around his chest wound. That was the one that would need attention first. Her lips pressed together tightly as she stared at the gaping wound. "Have one of your men get the bag under the front seat of the wagon. It has a few medical supplies in it." She heard running feet, and less than a minute later it was in her hands.

Carrie pulled out the instruments she needed, turned up the light on the two lanterns beside the bed, and went to work, praying silently. Clifton was already in shock, his pulse dangerously low.

"Captain Pemberton, I'm going to need your help."

"I'll do anything," he said promptly, all the arrogance gone from his voice. Carrie glanced up. He was staring at his brother's white face, his own face pinched and strained. "Hold this cloth over the wound on his leg. The bleeding has to be stopped." He nodded and stepped forward, doing as she directed. Carrie picked up the forceps and leaned over Clifton's chest.

"What are you doing?" Pemberton snapped.

Carrie sat back impatiently. "I have to take the bullet out."

"What about chloroform?" Pemberton growled. "You aren't just going to operate on him."

"It's happening all over the South," Carrie said. "I'm afraid your blockade has made it almost impossible to get the drugs we need. I would gladly use it if it were available," she said harshly. She softened at the look of pain on the captain's face. "He won't feel a thing," she said more kindly. "He's completely unconscious. He will hurt afterward, but he won't feel the operation."

Pemberton gazed down at his brother's face and nodded.

Carrie bent back to her work. It took almost thirty minutes of deep probing for her to finally locate the bloody bullet concealed deep in his chest cavity. Thankfully it had gone in far enough away from the heart and lung not to do damage there. As she carefully sewed the wound shut, she prayed. Chest wounds were the most dangerous. If infection set in, there was no possibility of amputation to save his life.

She went to work on the leg wound next. The bullet had not gone as deep, so it took her only a few minutes to remove it. The torn and ragged skin surrounding the wound was another matter. There was no way she could sew it up.

She turned to Opal who was standing close by. "Bring me some flaxseed and red pepper." She paused. "And please bring me some of the red oak bark decoction I made. She glanced up and spoke to the captain before he could ask his question. "They are herbal remedies, Captain Pemberton. They have proven to be quite effective against infection and gangrene."

For once, Pemberton didn't react. Carrie turned back to Clifton, using the rags and hot water to clean all the other wounds on his body. His color seemed to be improved now that all the bleeding had stopped, but his breathing was still shallow and fast, and his skin still clammy. Carrie prayed he would live—not just for himself, but for Hobbs as well. Her mind flew to him. What would she find when she was done with the captain's brother?

Opal returned, and Carrie carefully applied the herbal poultices to Clifton's wounds. When she was done, she covered him carefully with several blankets and stepped back. "That's all I can do," she said.

"Is he going to live?" Pemberton asked anxiously.

"I certainly hope so, but only time will tell. Have one of your men keep an eye on him. If he moves or wakes up, let me know."

"Where do you think you're going?" Pemberton growled. "My brother still needs you."

"There is nothing more I can do for him right now," Carrie said. "But there is a young man who also needs my help." She took a deep breath. "I believe that was our agreement."

Pemberton nodded curtly. "My brother better live."

Carrie felt another surge of compassion at the pain on his face. She stepped forward and laid a hand on his arm. "I hope he does, Captain. This war has already claimed too many lives. Your brother looks like a fine man."

"He is," Pemberton choked, his defenses falling away. "He saved my life up at Gettysburg. I owe him the same."

"I'll do my best," Carrie promised. Then she turned and left the room.

She found Hobbs lying just as still as when she had last seen him. The two soldiers guarding the room stared at her but made no comment. Carrie ignored them and examined Hobbs' head carefully. She breathed a sigh of relief when she found no cuts. There was indeed a huge lump on his head, but upon closer inspection, she realized his breathing was steady and deep. He would have a raging headache when he woke, and he would probably be disoriented, but he would recover. Carrie covered him with blankets and returned to Clifton's room.

"Anything?" she asked, when she entered the room.

Pemberton shook his head heavily. "Nothing." He looked up. "How is your driver?"

"He'll live."

"If my brother lives."

"Right," Carrie snapped, leaning over Clifton. She was encouraged. There was even more color in his face, and his breathing was a little steadier. She glanced up at Pemberton. "Are you hungry?" He nodded abruptly. "I'll get you some food."

"Don't bother to try anything," Pemberton replied. "Your driver's life is dependent on my brother's, you know."

Carrie was tired of playing games. Exhaustion dogged every movement. "Look, Captain Pemberton, even if my friend weren't lying in the other room, I would still do my best for your brother. He is a human being. He is an American. That still means something to me."

Pemberton sat up straighter in his chair. "You're a Unionist? Why didn't you say so?"

Carrie shook her head. "I didn't say I want the North to win. Quite frankly, I'm confused about the whole mess. I don't think this war should have ever started. It's done nothing but multiply the problems in this country. All I know is that too many men are dying or being horribly wounded. I want it to end. Whether I end up living in the United States or the Confederate States of America means little to me right now. I want the killing to stop."

"Why are you in the South, Miss Cromwell? You don't believe in slavery do you?"

Carrie looked at him. For the first time she felt they were communicating as two individuals. "No, I don't," she agreed. "If I had my way, every slave would be free, but," she continued, "the South is my home. My father is here. My..." She broke off, shocked to realize she had almost told the captain about Robert. She turned to leave the room. "I'll go get some food."

A broad-shouldered soldier blocked her way. He was holding papers in his hands. "I found out who her father is, Captain Pemberton, sir."

Pemberton pushed away from the wall, but his voice lacked any real interest. "Who is he?"

"He works in the Virginia State government. He's one of Governor Letcher's top men."

"That true?" Pemberton asked Carrie.

Carrie looked at the papers the soldier was holding. What good would it do to deny it? "Yes," she said.

"We'll take her back north, Captain," his man said eagerly. "I reckon she'll be a real prize in the prisoner exchange game."

"She's a woman," Pemberton snapped.

"Yes, sir," the soldier agreed. "I reckon that will make her even more valuable. The Rebels aren't going to want anything to happen to her. Especially not with her daddy being a bigwig."

Carrie had heard enough. She moved past the soldier and headed for the kitchen. There was nothing she could do. She might as well eat. The idea of waiting for the right time to escape through the tunnel had entered her mind, but she cast it aside. She would never leave Hobbs.

Opal was stirring a pot of soup over the stove when she entered the kitchen. "You okay, Miss Carrie?" she asked.

"I'm fine," she said wearily. "Hungry."

"I'll fix you something."

"Take something to the captain first," Carrie replied, sitting down and letting her head drop on the table.

Sam walked into the room as Opal was leaving. He sat down next to her, watching the soldiers standing next to the door. Carrie stared at him, knowing he would interpret the question on her face.

The children?

Sam nodded comfortingly. *They be fine*, his eyes said.

Carrie dropped her head back down. She was confident the Union soldiers would not harm Sam and Opal. When they were gone, the children could come out of hiding. She didn't really think the soldiers would harm the children, but there was no sense in taking a chance.

Carrie didn't know when Opal put a bowl of soup in front of her. She was sound asleep.

Two days later Clifton was still unconscious. Captain Pemberton refused to leave his room, demanding his meals be brought to him there. Carrie had a bed moved in for him. She checked Clifton every thirty minutes, even though she knew there was nothing more she could do for him. Only time would tell if his body was strong enough to pull him through. Hobbs was conscious, still suffering from a headache and under constant guard by the soldiers assigned to him.

Carrie sat on the porch swing, gazing out over the fields. At least she hadn't told her father when to expect her back. *Within the week*, she had told him in her letter. She frowned, realizing she could be well on her way north before anyone sounded the alarm. She had struggled for the last two days to keep her mind away from the idea of going to prison. *For smuggling contraband*, one of the soldiers told her.

In spite of her best efforts, images of Matthew during his stay at Libby Prison came into her mind. She could see him, terribly thin, with that look of deep sadness in his eyes. She shuddered at the idea of being locked up. Thank goodness Matthew had been released.

"Miss Carrie!" Opal ran out onto the porch.

"What is it?" Carrie asked, alarmed. The soldiers sitting nearby sat forward.

"It's the captain's brother. He's woken up!"

Carrie smiled and ran into the house. She slowed as she approached the patient's room. Captain Pemberton stood by the bed, grasping his brother's hand.

Clifton raised his eyes slowly and stared around, puzzled. His gaze fell on Carrie. "Where am I?" he whispered.

"You'll have plenty of time for questions later," Carrie said soothingly. "How about something to drink?" She reached for the pitcher of fresh water she had been keeping by his bed.

"Thirsty..." Clifton agreed.

Carrie held the water up to his lips while the captain supported his brother's shoulder. Carrie glanced up at the captain. She saw the first look of hope in his eyes when he looked up and smiled slowly. Carrie motioned for him to lay Clifton back down. "We'll take it slow and easy," she said.

Clifton nodded slightly, then closed his eyes.

Carrie set the water pitcher down. "He's asleep," she said gratefully. "That's all he needs now."

"He's been asleep for over two days," Pemberton exclaimed.

"This is a healing sleep," Carrie explained, pulling the bandages back again to make sure there was no infection. She sighed with relief when she saw no angry red spots spreading out from the wounds. "He's going to be fine, but it will take some time."

"You're sure?" Pemberton asked anxiously. "You're not just saying it?" He held up his hand before Carrie could answer. "I'm sorry. I didn't mean that."

Carrie looked up quickly. It was almost friendliness she heard in his voice.

Pemberton sank down on the chair next to his brother's bed. "Thank you," he said. "I know you saved my brother's life. You didn't have to."

"You're welcome," Carrie replied. She looked down at Clifton's peaceful face. "It will be several weeks before it's safe for him to travel again."

Pemberton frowned. "I figured that. I'm expected back at Fort Monroe with my men in four days." He glanced at his brother. "Would it be safe for him to travel in the wagon?"

"I wouldn't recommend it," Carrie said. "He's had quite a shock. Infection could still set in if we're not careful. I would hate to lose him after all he's been through."

"He'll stay here," Pemberton said. He grew quiet, obviously in deep thought.

"He'll be fine here, Captain," Carrie said. "Opal and Sam can look after him."

"What about you? You're the one who's saved his life," Pemberton protested.

"I assumed I was my way to a Union prison," Carrie replied evenly.

Pemberton stared at her and nodded. "Yes," he murmured. He stood and turned toward the window, staring out of it for several minutes. He swung back around. "Got any ideas for an escape?" The corners of his mouth twitched.

Carrie smiled slightly. "I might."

"I figured as much," Pemberton said with a sudden, boyish grin. "I suggest you plan them for tonight," he said softly, glancing behind him to make sure none of his men heard. "I'll call my men into a meeting around eight o'clock."

Carrie's mind raced as she realized Pemberton was offering her freedom. "And Hobbs?" she asked.

"You'll come back and care for my brother when we're gone?"

"I promise," Carrie replied.

"Hobbs, too," Pemberton promised. "You'll have to move fast."

"We'll disappear so fast even you'll be surprised."

Carrie breathed a prayer of thanks for the tunnel.

Pemberton was as good as his word. At eight o'clock, he called all his men together for a meeting in the parlor.

"What about the prisoners?" one of his men protested.

"I don't think they're going anywhere," Pemberton said.

"I'll stay and keep an eye on them," the soldier said. "Tommy can tell me about the meeting."

Pemberton pulled himself up erectly. "I'm calling a meeting, Private. That's an order," he said coldly.

The soldier grumbled under his breath but followed Pemberton from the room. Carrie waited until the door to the parlor had swung shut, and then she sprang into action. She ran into Hobbs' room, put her finger to her lips, and motioned for him to follow her. He leapt up, an unspoken question gleaming in his eyes.

Carrie could hear Pemberton's muted voice as she and Hobbs made their way down the hallway. She ducked into the kitchen long enough to stuff a bag with some food, and she continued down toward the basement. Hobbs was right on her heels.

Carrie stopped for a moment to assure herself the rumble of voices was still coming from the parlor, then eased the door to the basement open and ran down the steps lightly.

Hobbs caught up and grabbed her arm. "What are you doing?" he whispered urgently. "This is the first place they'll look."

"Not where we're going," Carrie said. She lit the lantern and approached the now empty shelves. It took her only a second to remove the brick and yank at the rope.

"A tunnel," Hobbs whispered in awe.

"After you," Carrie said, laughing at the look on his face. "Welcome to the Cromwell family secret." She waited for him to duck into the tunnel and then pulled the door shut. "This lantern will come in handy," she said.

Carrie quickly explained what had happened with the captain.

Hobbs slumped against the wall in relief. "I ain't going to prison?"

"Not right now, anyway," Carrie replied.

"Is this where Opal's kids are?" Hobbs stared around in astonishment. "This is quite a place."

"One of my ancestors built it," Carrie explained. "I'll tell you the whole story later. And yes, the kids came through here. They probably went around and down to the slave quarters to warn Susie and Zeke. I'm sure all of them are safe." She turned away and tugged at Hobbs' sleeve. "Come on," she said impishly. "I don't want to miss any of the fun."

"What?"

Carrie pressed a finger to her lips. "Quiet. I'm not sure how much can be heard from in here." She turned and began to walk toward the center of the house, following the slight incline. It was only a few minutes before they could hear muted voices.

Then Pemberton's voice rang above the rest. "This meeting is over."

Carrie grinned. "It should only be a minute more," she whispered.

It was less than that when a shout was heard. "They're gone! The prisoners are gone."

Pemberton's voice was calm. "They can't have gone far. You men go outside and round them up. The rest of you stay here and search in case they were foolish enough to try to hide in the house."

Carrie listened closely, glad she had indeed had an escape plan. In order for Pemberton to save face with his men he would have to do everything possible to find her.

She gestured to Hobbs. "Let's get out of here."

Chapter Twenty-Two

Robert finally staggered to his feet. He didn't know how long he had lain there, but the tide had receded, leaving at least twenty feet between him and the still angry sea. He stared out at the water sadly. It was impossible to imagine Suzanne Palmer, so full of life and energy, dead at the bottom of the ocean. He knew her body would wash up eventually. Taking a deep breath, he turned and began to trudge toward the right. The least he could do was try to locate her body to assure a proper burial.

He kept glancing out to sea as he walked. There was still no sign of movement from the stranded *Phantom*, but a sudden movement from the left caught his attention. He stopped and stared in that direction, straining his eyes to identify what was out there. His questions were answered when the loud report from a cannon rolled toward shore.

The Yankee gunboat was back! The sound of the first shot had not died away when the big guns from Fort Fisher began a steady booming. The Union boat managed to stay out of range of the fire, continuing her own steady shelling. Most of the shots fell far short of the *Phantom*.

As Robert watched the sky began to clear, the mist lifted from the water. Suddenly, his view of the battle was unobscured. He frowned as he watched the Yankee shells land closer and closer. The Union boat edged nearer, seemingly daring Fort Fisher to hit it. So far it was winning the bet. Robert frowned. Bueller had better get his men off that boat. The Federals meant business.

There was a brief lull and then the shelling resumed on both sides. Suddenly, as Robert watched, the *Phantom* seemed to leap forward in the water and then shuddered to a halt, lower than she had been previously. The blockade runner had been hit. Moments later, smoke poured forth from the ship, more and more plumes rising up into the air. Robert was certain Bueller had ordered the boat fired. His attempt to break the blockade had failed this time, but Robert knew he would not walk away and relinquish his cargo to the North. Soon Robert could see flames licking from the boat.

He continued to watch. Bueller would have to get his men off soon. The entire boat could blow at any minute. As if beckoned by his thoughts, a swarm of men appeared and began to crowd toward the remaining rowboats. Moments later, three boats bobbed free of the burning wreck. The ocean, calmer now, granted them passage.

Robert was waiting on shore when the first rowboat scraped onto the sand. He helped haul it clear of the water and then turned to the next one.

Bueller stepped out onto the sand and grasped his hand. "I'm sorry," he said, his deep voice full of pain.

"You saw?"

Bueller nodded. "She never even tried to swim. The ocean swallowed her in a second."

Robert flinched. "She was carrying gold in her leather purse."

"She didn't stand a chance," Bueller said sadly. "I wish to God she had listened."

"Me too," Robert said woodenly. He waved his hand toward the burning boat. "I'm sorry about the *Phantom*."

Bueller glanced out to sea and shrugged. "It's a boat. It can be replaced." His face became pensive. "She gave me a lot of great adventures."

Robert stood with him, gazing out to sea in silent tribute to the two—a beautiful lady and a graceful boat— claimed by forces more powerful than they. The passions of the war had claimed still more victims.

Robert finally turned away. "We have to find her body."

"I'll send my men out," Bueller said. "There will be troops swarming all over this area soon."

"Why?"

"They'll wait for the boat to quit burning and then salvage what they can. There will still be things worth retrieving. The fire is more a ploy to keep the Federals from having the boat. She won't be worth fixing." His voice turned fierce. "She might never make another run for the Confederacy, but I'll be blamed if she is going to be used against us." He sighed heavily and turned, walking away toward the dunes. "Dinner is on me tonight," he called back cheerfully.

Robert stared after him. How could Captain Bueller be so morose one moment and so jovial the next? The realization came to him suddenly. The man had suffered great loss, but he still had the things most precious to him. He would find another boat, and he would continue to have his adventures at sea.

Robert turned for one more look out at the ocean. "Goodbye, Suzanne," he called softly. "You lived what you believed. You died for what you believed. May you rest in peace."

It was two weeks before Carrie asked Sam to deliver Clifton Pemberton to Fort Monroe. He had healed rapidly and was strong enough for the journey. Carrie waved goodbye to the man who had become her friend, then turned to Hobbs. "Let's go home." Now that her duty with Clifton was over, she was anxious to return to Richmond.

"Your father is going to be real glad to see you, Miss Carrie."

"If he's still speaking to me," Carrie said. "At least Sam was able to send word in that I was all right."

Hobbs clucked to the horses, urging them into a trot. "I reckon we'll make it this time."

"We better," Carrie replied. "Clifton assured me that all cavalrymen have been pulled away from Richmond for a while. He received word from the captain that we shouldn't have any trouble. I hope he was right."

Carrie glanced back with satisfaction at the crates of herbs stacked securely in the wagon. She knew Pemberton had been hard-pressed to keep his men from destroying them. They had been eager to seek vengeance for her and Hobbs' escape. Her respect for him as an officer had grown when she realized how skillfully he must have handled his men. She and Hobbs had waited in the tunnel for two days before Pemberton disappeared with his troops. Then she kept her promise to care for Clifton until he was well enough to travel.

Carrie turned her face toward the setting sun and breathed a sigh of relief. She was going home. In spite of all the longing she felt for the plantation at times, right now her heart was in Richmond with her father, with her patients, with Robert. Richmond was where he would come when he finally returned from England. She would be waiting for him.

Thomas was waiting on the porch when Hobbs brought the wagon to a stop. "You go on," Hobbs urged. "I'll make sure the wagon is safe in the barn. We'll take the herbs to the hospital tomorrow."

Carrie leaned over to kiss his cheek and then jumped from the wagon.

Her father stepped from the porch and caught her up in a fierce hug. "Carrie..." he whispered. "Carrie..."

Carrie reveled in the feel of his warm arms for a long moment and then stepped back. "You're not mad?"

"I've felt every emotion in the book," Thomas said. "Mostly regret." He took her arm and led her up the stairs. "Let's go inside. We have much to talk about."

Carrie looked at him closely and her heart leapt with gladness. She had not seen that look on his face in a long time. Something had erased the bitterness and anger, and replaced it with love and understanding.

Thomas led her to a chair and settled down in the one across from her. Several minutes passed while he looked at her, his eyes devouring her face. "I'm sorry," he said.

Carrie started to speak, but her father held up his hand.

"Please let me say what I need to."

Carrie nodded and sat back in the chair, enjoying the warmth flickering from the small fire. The whole house had a different feel.

"I was a fool," Thomas said simply. "I have accepted that. I hope you can forgive me."

Carrie waited, knowing he wasn't done.

"I have allowed my feelings about the war and about my country to totally consume me. For so long, I fought to keep them under control, to balance them against the rest of my life. I should have known it couldn't be done. When you once let bitterness take up residence in your heart, it quickly poisons your whole being." He paused. "It even poisoned my relationship with you."

"I love you," Carrie protested.

"I know," Thomas said. "I have thanked God for that every day. I don't know what I would do without that knowledge. I think, in the end, it's what saved me." He took a deep breath. "When I got your note saying you had left, not telling me before..." His voice trailed away.

"I'm sorry," Carrie said contritely.

"Don't be," Thomas said quickly. "I deserved for you to leave that way. I never gave you a chance to talk about it. I mandated what you were going to do like an overbearing oaf. I began to realize that day what I was doing. It took me longer to finally face it." He leaned forward. "Will you please forgive me?" he implored her.

"Of course." Carrie jumped up and wrapped her arms around his neck. "I'm glad to have my father back. You look like the man I love again. I'm glad." She paused and searched his face. "What have you done with all your feelings?" she asked quietly.

"That is a fair question, and one I expected you to ask." He took a deep breath and gazed into the fire. "I don't know what I will do if the South loses this war." He shook his head. "I suppose I should say *when* the South loses this war."

"You think there's no hope?"

"It's only a matter of time. We have the will to win, but we simply don't have the resources. Even when we win battles, we do so at unbelievable expense. Soon, there will be no men to fight the war." His voice wasn't bitter. It was matter-of-fact. "But that isn't what's important. I have allowed myself to believe my whole life will be over if we lose."

"You no longer feel that way?"

"My whole life will be drastically changed, but it won't be over. I will still have you. I will still have a son-in-law. God willing, I will someday have grandchildren." He looked up at her. "I watched my father become a bitter old man. He was too consumed with his own regrets to be any good to anyone else. He was never the kind of grandfather to you that I wanted him to be. I don't want to ever be like that." He walked over to the fire and turned to her. "No matter what happens, I still have a lot to live for."

"I'm so glad you know that," Carrie said, tears glimmering in her eyes. Once again, she rushed forward to give her father a hug. "I love you. And I'm so proud of you."

They stood quietly for a long time. Carrie had truly come home. She would tell him everything that had happened, but for now, she was content to be there.

Two days later, after delivering the herbs to the black hospital and checking on all her patients, Carrie walked to the room Pastor Anthony claimed as his office and knocked on the door.

"Come in."

Carrie took a deep breath, clutched the book under her arm more tightly, and walked in.

"Carrie," Pastor Anthony said, "I hoped you would have time to drop in before you left. We have missed you around here so much."

Carrie briefly outlined the events of the last few weeks. "It's good to be back," she finished.

"How are all the patients?"

"Doing well."

"Did you find somewhere to store all the herbs?"

"Yes."

Pastor Anthony regarded her closely for a minute. "What's really on your mind? You didn't just come in to chat, did you?"

By way of explanation, Carrie opened the book to the page she had marked and placed it in front of him. Pastor Anthony stared at it wordlessly, his face becoming tense and drawn.

"I found this while I was home," Carrie said. She waited.

Silence gripped the room for a long time. When Pastor Anthony spoke, his voice was hoarse. "I should have known this would happen. From the first day...when I realized who you were. I should have seen it coming."

"You've known all this time?" Carrie cried. "Why...?"

"Jeremy doesn't know," Pastor Anthony said, looking up quickly.

"He doesn't know he's half black? He doesn't know where he came from?"

Pastor Anthony shook his head.

Carrie sat back, staring at him. Finding the portrait of her grandfather made her realize why Jeremy Anthony looked so familiar. He didn't just resemble her grandfather. He was the spitting image of him at that age. The pieces had all clicked into place when she remembered Jeremy was adopted.

"Why don't you tell me the whole story?"

"Can't we leave it alone?" Pastor Anthony asked.

"Jeremy is my uncle. He is my best friend's—my aunt's—twin brother. I can't leave it alone. I want to know what happened."

Pastor Anthony sighed. "I guess you can fill in some pieces for me, too. Why don't you start?"

Carrie willingly told him the story of how her grandfather had raped Old Sarah. "When the babies were born, one was white—your Jeremy—and one was black. My father decided the only way to protect my grandfather was to get rid of the white baby." She took a deep breath. "So he sold him. Two years ago, I found a letter in his ledgers from an orphanage saying the wife of the man who owned Jeremy couldn't stand to see him in slavery so she had brought him there. All she said was that he was adopted by a white family who would take good care of him."

"We did," Pastor Anthony said softly. "We loved him like he was our own."

"That's obvious," Carrie said. "He was a very lucky boy."

"I didn't find out until he was a few years old that his mother was black." Pastor Anthony picked up the story. "The woman who ran the orphanage had a pang of conscience and decided my wife and I should know. My wife demanded we not tell Jeremy. She said it would only confuse and upset him. She was so adamant, that I agreed."

"Did you know Jeremy had a twin sister?"

"No," Pastor Anthony said. He shrugged. "I don't know if it would have made a difference. I don't know what I would have done. My wife was so determined that Jeremy be raised white." He swung around in his chair and stared out the window. "When I realized who you were..." He sighed. "One day, when Jeremy was a teenager, I realized he would probably start asking questions someday. I went back to the orphanage and managed to look at their records." He smiled slightly. "Being a pastor can have its advantages at times. I discovered Jeremy had come from your plantation," he continued. "I learned as much about your father as possible."

"You thought it was my father?" Carrie cried.

"I didn't know *who* Jeremy's father was," Pastor Anthony explained. "I was only told he was fathered by a Cromwell. By then, your grandfather was dead. It was not unusual for white owners to sleep with their slaves. I suppose what was unusual was that he fathered a white child." He paused and then added quickly, "I have not judged your father for what I thought were his actions. I am simply grateful to have Jeremy in my life."

"Jeremy has never asked where he came from?"

"Not since I discovered the truth," Pastor Anthony responded. "Oh, he used to ask questions when he was little, but we would tell him we were the luckiest people in the world to have been able to choose him. That seemed to satisfy him. After a while, he quit asking. There's no real reason he should have to know."

"He could have a black baby," Carrie said quietly.

Pastor Anthony whitened. "Yes, I know. I've thought about that. I guess I decided we would cross that bridge if and when we came to it."

Carrie leaned back in her chair and stared at him. "You have given your whole life to helping the black people in your congregation. Why are you ashamed to tell your son he is half black?" She was genuinely puzzled.

"You know the answer to that," Pastor Anthony said. "Most white people believe the Negro race is inferior to them. For two centuries, they have used that belief to justify slavery and discrimination. I didn't want that for my son. I didn't want for him to have to labor under that burden."

"But things are changing. Surely you believe that slavery is going to end? Even if the South by some miracle wins this war, the power of slavery has been broken."

"Slavery perhaps," Pastor Anthony agreed, "but not discrimination. I have watched what is happening in our countries. I am still able to get my hands on Northern newspapers. There is a cry to abolish slavery, but the vast majority of our country still believes blacks are inferior. They don't want them to be slaves, but they certainly don't consider them their equals." He rubbed a hand over his face wearily. "You've met Jeremy. He is extremely intelligent. Doors of opportunity are swinging wide for him. At such a young age, he is already highly respected in the area of finance. He has his whole life ahead of him. Why burden him with something he had nothing to do with?"

"But what if he could make a difference in how people view blacks? People would begin to realize their perceptions of blacks are wrong," Carrie insisted. "You spend every day fighting for the rights of black people. Why deny your son that chance?"

Pastor Anthony's eyes flashed, but his voice remained calm. "People look at me and accuse me of being a rather eccentric, do-gooder white person. They would look at Jeremy with scorn. Everything would be different for him. I won't do that to him."

Carrie was silent for a long time. "Would you like to know about his twin sister?"

"If she's anything like my son, she's very special," Pastor Anthony responded.

"She's the most special person I know," Carrie agreed. "She's very beautiful and as intelligent as Jeremy. For years, she taught the people on our plantation to read and write. Her school was a little clearing in the woods where she could hold her classes in secret." She chuckled. "She wasn't going to let a little thing like the law stop her from doing what was right." She paused, remembering. "She's my best friend," she said softly.

"She's married now," Carrie continued after a moment. "I helped her and Moses, her husband, escape a couple of years ago."

"They're the ones I set up the Underground Railroad escape for?" Pastor Anthony gasped, leaning closer.

Carrie nodded. "Your lives are connected in more ways than you know. I received one small note saying they made it to Philadelphia, but I haven't heard from her since then. Moses helped me escape the plantation when the Union soldiers came there that following spring. The last I knew, he was a spy for the North." She paused. "Both of them are committed to doing whatever they need to do to help their people be free."

"And you think I'm wrong for not giving Jeremy the opportunity to decide for himself what he will do with the truth that he's half black?"

Carrie thought for a long time and then shook her head. "I don't know what I would do if I were in your position. I can think I would know, but I can't really. I don't know how I would feel if it were my child." She looked up imploringly. "But don't you see? I can handle the fact that Jeremy doesn't know who he is. It doesn't really matter to me whether he knows we're related or not. But he has a twin sister out there who wants more than anything in the world to find her brother. Her mother and father are both dead. He's all the family she has left."

Pastor Anthony shook his head. "He's all the family I have left, too. It is better they not know."

"Better for whom?" Carrie asked. "Better for Jeremy perhaps, but certainly not for Rose."

"How did Rose find out? The records I read indicated the mother had agreed never to talk about Jeremy's birth."

"Sarah kept her secret until just before she died," Carrie said, her eyes misting as she thought about Sarah. "Then she decided Rose had the right to know the truth about her life—about who she really was." She paused. "Sarah had no idea what happened to her baby boy. All Rose knew was that she had a twin. It wasn't until much later that we found the papers saying he had been adopted." She stared up at Pastor Anthony. "She vowed then that when the war was over, she was going to come back and find her brother."

Pastor Anthony blanched. "I hope she doesn't do that." He looked scared for a moment but shook his head. "She won't find the records. They have very strict rules about not letting people see them."

Carrie stared at her friend in amazement, struck by the fear and determination she saw on his face. "Jeremy has every right to be proud of who he is," she said. "His mother was a wonderful woman—the wisest woman I know."

"His mother was my wife," Pastor Anthony snapped. He put his head in his hands. "I'm sorry, Carrie. I have no right to speak to you like that."

"I could tell Rose myself," Carrie reminded him gently.

Pastor Anthony nodded his head heavily. "I know." He peered up at her. "I'm asking you not to do that."

"You're asking me to put myself in a very difficult position. I care for you deeply, but I love Rose."

"We are not the only two people involved in this," Pastor Anthony reminded her. "There is also Jeremy." He paused. "And there is your father to consider."

"Excuse me?"

"Your father made what I assume was a very difficult decision in order to protect his father. The truth now could do little but embarrass him."

"My father feels very badly about what happened."

"Would he want the truth known?"

Carrie stood abruptly. "I'm not sure what I will do," she said shortly, "but regardless, I don't have to worry about it now. Rose lives in a foreign country." She was both disappointed and angry at Pastor Anthony's response. Mixed in with those feelings was deep compassion. She turned to leave but swung back around. "I think you are underestimating your son, Pastor. I think he has enough courage to face the truth about his life." Not waiting for a reply, she walked out, closing the door behind her.

Matthew shuddered as another blast of cold air whipped through the dark, dingy cellar. He thought longingly of the coat Carrie had brought him before, pulling the tattered remains of his clothing tighter in a futile attempt to get warm.

"You all right, man?"

Matthew glanced up wearily. "Yes."

"You ain't lookin' so good."

"You see how you look after you've been down in Rat Dungeon for two months," Matthew replied, shuddering in the cold. He raised his eyes to study the newest addition to their little group. Josiah looked to be in his mid-thirties. "What did you do to end up here?" he asked, not because he cared so much, but because talking would help pass even a few minutes.

Josiah shrugged. "Just got brought in yesterday. My men and I were ordered to do some raids out in the countryside near Fort Monroe. Ran into a nest of Rebels. Most of my men got away, but me and Sammie weren't so lucky." He nodded his head toward another man leaning against the wall, his knees drawn up tight to his chest.

"Being black is all it takes to put you in Rat Dungeon," another man volunteered bitterly. "These white Rebels don't take too kindly to black men coming down here to fight. They think we're nothing but animals, so they figure this hole is the right place to put us."

"What put you here, man?" Josiah asked Matthew. "You don't look too black." The hole rang with weak laughter.

Matthew glanced down at his thin body. "This was my reward for trying to escape."

"You tried to break out of here?" Josiah asked in amazement. "I've heard it can't be done."

"I almost made it," Matthew said grimly. He doubled over as a spasm of coughing seized his body.

"How long they gonna keep you down here?" Josiah asked.

Matthew shrugged. He had thought he would be out by now. He had seen other men come and go. His position as a journalist must have made him more of a threat than he realized. He gazed around at the ten men sharing the hole with him. Five of them were black soldiers whose only crime was that they were the wrong color. The other five were officers sent down for not following the rules. If things went as they normally did, they would be gone in a few days, back up to the relative airy openness of the upper prison.

"They're bound to let you out soon, Matthew," one of those men urged now. "They won't keep you down here forever. Captain Anderson has been talking to them."

Matthew turned away. He had survived by not counting on being released. The daily rise and plummet of his hopes when he expected to be freed any day had almost destroyed him. It was better to concentrate on staying alive. That was all he had the energy for. That, and planning his next escape attempt.

His resolve to escape had hardened into blind determination as the long days and nights crept by. The diet of bread and water had reduced him to skin and bones, but daily exercise kept him from becoming weak. The constant torture of rats running around his feet had almost driven him to madness, until he learned to block out the reality of their presence. Snatches of communication with the upper prison as they pulled back boards to drop down tiny morsels of food reminded him there was still a world outside Rat Dungeon.

It was almost dark when Carrie climbed the stairs to her house. A chill wind was blowing, making her pull her cape around her more tightly. She considered sitting in the porch swing for a while but decided the warmth of the house was more appealing. Her stomach growled, reminding her she hadn't eaten since morning. She hoped May had set aside some food for her.

"Hello, Mrs. Borden."

Carrie jumped as a deep voice sounded from the shadows. She gasped, her heart pounding, hoping against hope that her hearing hadn't deceived her. "Who's there?" she called cautiously.

"You don't recognize your husband's voice anymore?" Robert laughed as he emerged from the shadows. "I have indeed been gone too long."

"Robert!" Carrie cried, running into the arms he held wide.

"Hello, my love," Robert murmured, his voice thick with emotion. His lips lowered to cover hers.

Time stood still for Carrie as her body melted into his. She pressed against him, all the longing she felt for six long months finally expressed. Thoughts of everything else flew from her mind as she kissed him eagerly.

She finally pulled back and reached up to touch his cheek. "I always have to convince myself you're real," she said joyfully.

Robert picked her up and swung her in big circles. When he finally put her down, she was deposited on his lap in the porch swing. He held her gently, staring into her face. "I missed you." He peered closer. "You look tired."

"I'm not anymore," Carrie smiled. "There is so much to talk about. I want to know all about your trip. I want to tell you what has happened here."

Robert put a finger to her lips. "We'll have plenty of time to talk." He pulled her closer. "I have to admit I had something else in mind for tonight. I've been waiting out on this freezing porch for two hours."

Carrie blushed as she met his burning gaze. "I can think of somewhere you might be warmer," she said coyly.

Robert grinned. "That's more like it, Mrs. Borden."

Carrie clapped her hand to her mouth. "Janie," she whispered. "We're sharing a room again."

"Not as of a few hours ago," Robert said smugly. "I have it all taken care of, my love. I even have food up there. I know my wife."

Carrie held out her hand. "Lead the way, Mr. Borden."

Chapter Twenty-Three

Rose was just leaving school when Annie came racing up the road, her eyes bright with excitement. She knelt down to the little girl's level. "Is something wrong?" she asked anxiously. Things seemed to have calmed down in the contraband camp with the arrival of cold weather, but there were still occasional flare-ups of temper.

Annie shook her head, trying to catch her breath. "Miss June sent me over. Someone came and said there's something for you on the ship that just came into the harbor." Her voice was as excited as her eyes. "You reckon it's some new clothes? Remember, you said I could have a new dress when more came."

"I remember." Rose laughed, relieved to know the reason for her hurry. Thoughts of John injured or sick had frightened her. She patted Annie's head. "I'll let you know what was on the ship when you get to school tomorrow. Now get on home. Your mama will be worried sick about you."

Annie nodded and dashed away, her black pigtails bobbing behind her. Rose watched her for a moment, then turned and walked back into the school. She found Marianne Lockins still seated at the desk. "There is a new shipment that has arrived. I'm going down to the waterfront to get it."

Marianne smiled her pleasure. "Do you think it's from your Aunt Abby?"

"It must be," Rose replied, as eager to receive the letter she knew would be with the barrels as she was to get the clothes. "She told me there would be some on the way soon. That was over a month ago."

"That woman is amazing," Marianne said. "She has singlehandedly sent more clothes down here than all of the organizations who help us combined."

"She is quite a woman," Rose agreed. "When there is something to be done, it's better to get out of her way. She moves too fast for most people to keep up with. Her latest letter said there were contributions being sent from six other states."

"Six other states!"

Rose nodded. "Aunt Abby is collecting signatures for the petition to abolish slavery completely. Every time she makes a contact, she tells them about the camp. She said clothes and supplies have been piling in from everywhere."

"Do you want some men to help you?"

"No. General Butler promised the assistance of his men when the barrels got here. I'll have them delivered to the school. We can use it as a headquarters to distribute everything."

Marianne nodded and turned back to her work.

Rose hugged her coat around her as she strode briskly down the road. Virginia had enjoyed a wonderful Indian summer that had stretched far into the fall, but it had finally retreated to allow winter in. The sky was clear and bright, the air cold. If it hadn't been for the increased threat of disease throughout the camp, Rose would have welcomed it. The thick humidity of the coastal summers always drained her.

In spite of the beauty of the day, Rose frowned. How many people would die this winter? How many children would be claimed by the ravaging diseases that always swept through the camp when cold weather descended? Rose knew she should be grateful. She had heard reports of the conditions of other contraband camps. She knew the numbers of runaway slaves all over the South had swelled way beyond anything the government was prepared to handle. Everywhere, people were starving and dying. Yet, still they came.

Rose gazed out to sea as she walked, bewitched as always by the sparkling water stretching out as far as she could see. Flocks of gulls dove and twisted over her head, calling to each other loudly. *Delighting in their freedom*, Rose mused. *Just like my people*. She prayed the war would end soon so the job of rebuilding the country could begin. She knew the mighty power of the North was being poured into the war effort—into crushing the South into submission. Not until that had been accomplished would they turn their attention to the tens of thousands of blacks suddenly homeless and penniless. It was up to people like her, and Marianne, and Aunt Abby to stand in the gap until better times came.

Rose arrived at the wharf and presented herself to the soldier checking cargo off the large ship bobbing among the swells. "I believe there is a shipment for the contraband camp."

"That there is," the soldier said pleasantly. "I've got some fellows lined up to haul it over for you. Are you Rose Samuels?"

"I am."

"Then this letter is for you." He smiled. "I think this one is, too."

"Two letters?" Rose was confused. The handwriting on the first was clearly Aunt Abby's. The second letter revealed one she didn't recognize. Her heart began to pound with fear. Something must have happened to Moses. This must be notification from the government. She stared at the white envelope in horror. She was afraid to open it. Afraid to have all of her hopes and dreams destroyed.

The soldier was watching her closely. "Aren't you going to read them?"

"I'll wait," Rose said, straightening her shoulders. "I want to make sure all the barrels are sent over."

"Oh, all the barrels are already off the ship," the soldier assured her. I checked them myself. Why don't you go ahead and read your letters?"

Rose looked at him closely, sure she saw a hint of laughter in his eyes. What was going on? She glanced at the unfamiliar handwriting again. Her stomach tightened in rebellion. She shook her head. "I'll open it when I get home."

"Mrs. Samuels, I really think you should open it now," the soldier persisted.

"Why?" Rose demanded, fear making her irritable.

The soldier stared at her for a moment and then shook his head. "I told him it wouldn't work," he muttered.

"Told whom what wouldn't work?" Rose was hopelessly confused. Over the soldier's shoulder, she could see a large mountain of barrels being loaded into several waiting wagons. Every man was black, and dressed in Union blue.

The soldier shook his head again and turned toward the building behind him. "You better come on out," he called. "I told you she wasn't going to fall for it."

Rose stared at the building, her indignation growing. Who was playing this strange game with her? Her heart skipped a beat. Was this part of Russell's plan to get even? She stiffened and sucked in her breath.

A towering form stepped from the building. "She's a hard one to pull something over on." He chuckled. "I've known that a long time."

Rose stood, rooted by her shock. "Moses," she whispered, staring in disbelief.

Moses laughed loudly and swept her up into his arms. "Rose."

Moments later, they were surrounded by a swarm of men. Moses stopped spinning her around and set her down gently. "Rose," he said proudly, "I'd like you to meet my men."

Rose stared at the smiling faces in astonishment. "You were all loading the wagon."

"Yes, ma'am," one of them said with a grin. "We told Moses we didn't want to miss out on the excitement. He's done been plannin' this surprise all the way down here."

"And I messed it up," Rose cried. "I'm sorry." She looked up at Moses, secure within the circle of his arm. "How did you know I would be down here?"

"I didn't," Moses replied. "Not until I realized this ship was stuffed with supplies from Aunt Abby. Then I knew I could lure you down." He shook his head. "It almost worked," he said. He looked at his men. "Excuse me," he said gruffly.

Seconds later, Rose was swept up into his arms and kissed soundly. In spite of her embarrassment, she kissed him back fervently, overjoyed to have him there. His men's cheers rang in the background.

"What are you doing here?" she asked after he had put her down and she had regained her breath.

"My men and I have some work to do," he said, grabbing her arm. "I'll tell you all about it." He turned to his unit. "Finish taking the supplies over, then get settled in. We leave in two days."

"You have to leave so soon?" Rose asked.

"Yes, but I'm not going far. I should be back here by Christmas. This year, I get to spend it with my family." Moses' voice was husky.

Rose smiled up at him. "There is someone waiting to meet you," she said softly. "He's becoming quite a big boy."

"If he's like his daddy, that boy is going to be a tree," one of the men called.

Moses swung Rose up into his arms and strode down the wharf. His men cheered and whistled.

Rose stared up at him. "What are you doing? I'm perfectly capable of walking."

"Probably are," Moses agreed, "but I want to keep you close to my heart."

Rose was quiet after that, enjoying the feel of Moses' strong arms and pounding heart.

It was past midnight before Moses stood up again. He gazed down at his sleeping son, who was snuggled into his arms. "My son," he said in awe. "He's beautiful."

"As handsome as his daddy," Rose said quietly. Her weariness was forgotten in the joy of seeing John and Moses together. She blinked back tears as she watched the tender way Moses held and looked at his son. She had waited so long for this moment.

June had been thrilled to see Moses. The three of them talked for hours while little John and Simon had played on the floor in front of the fire. When John got sleepy, Moses scooped him up in his arms. John had slept contentedly for the last several hours.

"You want to put him to bed?" Moses whispered.

"I think that's your job tonight," Rose whispered back.

Moses smiled and carried John over to the small mattress on the floor, where he laid him down carefully.

"He's not going to break." Rose said with a quiet laugh.

Moses stared down at him with the same awestruck expression he had been wearing all night. "He's kinda big, isn't he?"

"He's bigger than the other boys his age," Rose agreed. "He's almost as big as some of the two year olds." She shook her head. "He gets heavier every day. He'd better start walking early, or soon I won't be able to carry him."

Moses looked up. "Aunt Abby sent a stroller."

"What?" Rose asked in disbelief.

"She told me she thought he would be big, so she sent a stroller."

"I can't use it," Rose said. "I would feel bad having something the other women couldn't hope to."

Moses nodded. "That's what I told her," he said, looking at her lovingly. "She said she would send it anyway."

Turning, he swept her up into his arms. "So, now that everyone's asleep..." he said huskily.

Rose smiled up into his eyes and lifted her arms. "I thought you'd never ask."

Moses left Fort Monroe early in the morning two days later. He hated to leave Rose and John, but at least he knew he would be back within three weeks. He could bear it that long.

"You be knowin' this land round here pretty good?" Pompey asked, riding up next to him.

"Pretty good," Moses agreed. He could still hardly believe he had been given command of twenty men on horseback and instructed to raid at will through the Confederate countryside.

He led his men a few miles from the fort and called them together. He gazed at them proudly. They were veterans of several battles now. Gettysburg had strengthened and sharpened them. He would trust his life with any of them. "I haven't told you all the reason we're here," he began.

"Me and the men figured you be holdin' something back," Pompey replied knowingly. "We be goin' after men, ain't we?"

"How'd you know that?" Moses asked, astonished.

"We hear thin's," Pompey said. "We done heard 'bout them raidin' parties sent out to get more of us coloreds to fight. Them slaves took one look at some of them white men and hid. I'm afraid they done heard some bad thin's 'bout how the Union treats coloreds."

"Some of it is true," Moses said grimly.

"Yes," Pompey agreed, "sometimes it be just like bein' a slave. Only one thin' be different." He paused, grinning. "When this be all over we be free for good. Then we gonna make thin's change in this country."

"We just got to keep fightin'," Mort chimed in. "I reckon we can get some men around here to join up with us."

Moses nodded. "I told Captain Jones we would. I told him he could count on you men." He watched as they straightened, looks of pride on their faces. He had grown to love these men fiercely. He longed for the day when they could all stand together with white men, equally. The day was still far off, but it was getting closer. At least legally. He knew it would be much longer still before the attitudes of people's hearts changed.

Pompey seemed to be reading his mind. "You reckon white folks will ever think we not be less than them?"

"I hope so," Moses replied. "They've got to change a lot of their thinking. It's going to take more than a sheet of paper saying we're free for white folks to see us the same as them. This war is only the beginning for us. Once we win our freedom, the real battle will begin. And I'm afraid it will last a lot longer than this war."

"I reckon that be true," Pompey agreed, "but I also reckon thin's will get better."

"They'd better," Moses replied as he gathered up his reins. "If not, we're all wasting our time."

Moses led his men down a dirt road heading east on the finger of land that went inland from Fort Monroe. It was the same road he and June had followed when he helped her escape. He much preferred the circumstances now. The air was cold, but it was dry and clear. There were no bugs to harass his men, and there was a plentiful supply of wood to stay warm on the coldest nights. Moses reveled in the feeling of freedom. For the first time there were no white officers around to throw subtle digs and sarcasms. It was just him and his men. He threw back his head and laughed.

His men entered into the spirit quickly. Songs poured forth as they rode underneath the canopy of live oaks spreading out over the trail. Towering pine trees lent their own splashes of green among the leafless oaks and maples.

"Hey, Moses," Mort called out. "You done heard the new song them white soldiers wrote? That one they call 'Sambo's Right to Be Kilt.' "

Moses shook his head. "Sing it for me," he called back.

Mort willingly broke into song, several of the men joining him. Their voices echoed through the trees.

> *The men who object to Sambo*
> *Should take his place an' fight*
> *And it's better to have a naygur's hew*
> *Then a liver that's wake and white.*
> *Though Sambo's black as the ace of spades,*
> *His finger a trigger can pull,*
> *And his eye runs straight on the barrel-sights*
> *From under his thatch of wool!*
> *So hear me all, boys, darlings, —*
> *Don't think I tippin' you chaff, —*
> *The right to be kilt I'll divide wid him,*
> *And give him the largest half!*

"What you think of that song?" Mort called when the voices dropped away.

"I think that the black man would have fought for his freedom long ago if given the chance," Moses called, swallowing his anger. He knew many white men were all for the black man fighting. What their motivation was—whether he thought the black man was capable or simply a good substitute for white men—didn't really matter. The white people who disagreed were quickly being shown how wrong they were. The black soldiers recruited by the army were fighting hard and fighting well. Their critics were being silenced.

The first plantation house Moses and his men approached was obviously empty. Shutters banged against the peeling paint and the front door swung open freely. Moses motioned for silence and edged forward cautiously. Now was not the time to get careless. The blue of their uniforms would be a welcome target for any loyal Rebels in the area. Add the blue to the color of their skin, and Moses knew that any of his men would be hanged on the spot. The singing was over. They were far enough away from the fort to be well entrenched in Confederate territory.

Moses lifted his pistol from his waistband and eased up onto the porch. He heard nothing. He motioned for his men to join him. Moments later, they were standing in the foyer of the forlorn house, looking around at the deserted opulence. It was obvious no one had lived in the home for a long time. A thick layer of dust covered everything. Cobwebs filled corners and lampshades.

"Looks like these people up and run," Pompey whistled.

"They probably found out their house was in the wrong place," Moses said. "McClellan brought his men right through here a year and a half ago. From what I heard, Rebels cleared out as fast as they could. Left everything and haven't come back. Most of them are in Richmond, I imagine."

"We get to tear things up?" one of his soldiers called.

"Those are our orders," Moses replied, wishing it wasn't so. The idea of destroying such a magnificent place didn't sit well with him. On the other hand, he understood that if the South was to be broken, their morale would have to be destroyed. With the grand plantations decimated and all the slaves missing, there was no way they could return to their former way of life.

Moses gave directions for ten of his men to demolish the inside of the house, then took the rest and headed in what he thought was the direction of the slave quarters. "I don't really expect to find anyone," he confided to Pompey. "This place is so close to Fort Monroe that any slaves wanting their freedom would have taken off long ago." A quick inspection of the ramshackle buildings proved him right. No one had been on this land in a long time.

Moses gazed around, envisioning the land lush and green with crops. He would love to have the chance to bring it back to life and see it planted with tobacco and corn and grain. His eyes swept the fields, his longing to be a farmer intensifying. Someday, when the war was over, he would return to claim a piece of the South as his own. He would make it bloom again. The destruction would end sometime. Then the rebuilding would begin. He was eager to be a part of it.

Moses motioned for his men to remount and retraced their steps to the house. He could hear the sound of breaking furniture and tinkling glass. His men were doing their job with gusto. He called for them, and they appeared on the porch, their faces creased with grins.

"We be havin' a real good time," one of them called. "Feels real good to have the power for a change."

Moses opened his mouth to rebuke him but stopped. He understood how they felt. All their lives they had lived in awe of the *big house*. They had looked and longed, then returned to their tiny shacks knowing they would never have a chance for such a life. Most of his men had escaped from slavery with the scars to prove it.

"Fire it," he said abruptly, turning away. He would follow orders, but it didn't mean he had to like it. Minutes later, flames were licking from the stately home. Great clouds of dark smoke rose into the air.

"Let's go," he ordered his men. If there were any Confederates in the area, they would be drawn to the smoke like moths to a flame. He didn't intend to stick around and wait for them. Ignoring the open road, Moses urged his horse into a nearby stand of woods, working his way north and east. Their mission had begun. From now on, secrecy and quiet would be the keys to their survival.

Two weeks later, Moses' men had good reason for the quietly jubilant looks on their faces. They had increased their number by almost fifty. Ten plantation houses had been destroyed, and they had filled wagons with goods from the plantations and hidden them in the woods. They would be driven back to the fort when his men returned from their mission.

Moses knew they would have to head back soon. Their number had grown so large it was becoming harder and harder to stay quiet and invisible. Always present in his mind was the knowledge that if any of his men were caught they would be instantly hanged for treason. As the number of black soldiers increased, so did the South's anger.

"What we be doin' today?" Pompey asked as he strolled over and settled down next to where Moses sat on a log, staring out over the James River.

"We have one more stop to make," Moses said quietly. He knew he was only a few miles from Cromwell Plantation. He couldn't squelch the urge to see if any of his old friends were still there. None of his men knew where he had come from, and he should probably just swing a wide berth around the whole place, but he couldn't bring himself not to visit.

Pompey looked at him curiously but heaved himself up. "I'll get the men ready."

The sun was hanging low on the western horizon when Moses broke out of the woods behind the slave quarters at Cromwell. He gazed around. The place seemed to be deserted. Then he glanced over at the cabin Carrie had built for Rose and him and stiffened. He held up his hand for silence as he watched the wispy plume of smoke curl up from the fireplace.

Moses swung down from his horse and advanced on foot, looking around carefully. If Cromwell was now deserted like all the rest had been, there was no telling who was in the cabin. He was almost to the tiny porch when the door burst open.

"What you doing here?" the man staring at him exclaimed. Then he peered more closely at Moses. "You be a Union soldier?"

"Yes," Moses said simply.

"What you be doing here?"

Moses tried to decide how to answer. He didn't know who this man was, so he couldn't be one of Marse Cromwell's old slaves.

"We be recruiting slaves for the Union Army," one of his new recruits called loudly. "You gonna be a man and join us?"

"I reckon I be a man whether I fight for the Union or not," the man replied.

Moses liked him instantly. He waved his hand for silence and shot a withering look at the man who had spoken before he turned back. "May I ask your name?"

"Who's asking?" came the even reply, the eyes dark and cautious.

"My name is Moses Samuels. I am a United States soldier," he said.

"You really be recruiting soldiers?" the man asked.

"Yes." Moses prayed this man wasn't a Southern sympathizer. He had heard stories of blacks turning other blacks in. He knew their rewards were high. "You the only one on this plantation?" he asked.

"Maybe," Zeke said carefully, his eyes guarded. "What's it to you?"

Moses realized he was getting nowhere. He didn't see any danger in letting his men know the truth. "I came from here," he said. "I'm looking for my friends."

"Do tell!" he heard Pompey exclaim behind him.

Zeke stepped further out. "You said your name be Moses?" He paused, staring at him. "You be Rose's man?"

Moses smiled. "Yes."

"I done heard lots about you," Zeke said, smiling genuinely now. He nodded toward the big house. "Sam and Opal still be up there. Them kids, too. All but Susie," he said. "She be my wife now. We're living down here in your old cabin."

"You gonna be a man and come fight with us?" the same new recruit shouted.

Moses whirled around and glared at him. "That will be enough," he ordered. "I gave clear instructions everyone was to remain quiet." He strained to remember the man's name. Finally it came to him. *Saul.*

Saul returned his gaze defiantly but fell silent. Moses frowned and swung back to Zeke. He was afraid Saul was going to cause trouble. Most of the new recruits were compliant, but Saul was different. "I'm sorry," he said.

Zeke shrugged. "That man could be trouble," he observed. Then he motioned in the direction of the big house. "Sam and Opal be up there." He turned and re-entered his house, closing the door behind him.

Moses smiled. He would love to have this man with him. His quiet confidence bespoke a natural leader. Somehow he knew without asking that Zeke had already considered fighting and decided against it. Moses hadn't forced anyone to join them, and he wouldn't start now. He turned back to his men. "Take a rest," he ordered. "I'll be back."

"Where you goin'?" Saul called.

Moses ignored him and swung up onto his horse.

He was starting to ride off when Saul challenged him again. "Ain't you gonna let us take care of this house, too?"

Moses spun away and began to trot up the trail. Saul's next words stopped him.

"I guess our mighty leader ain't so mighty after all," Saul sneered. "I know something about this here plantation. I been here before. It be bigger and grander than all the rest we done fired so far. I reckon it's got a lot of things the Union would like to have. The rest of you boys gonna sit back and let Moses steal from the Union?"

Moses tensed and swung around. He had sensed a showdown with Saul would come eventually, but he had hoped it wouldn't be so soon. He was thankful none of the new recruits had been issued firearms. He glanced over at his men. Without exception, they were staring at Saul with seething anger. He knew a single word from him would result in Saul's containment.

He inspected the new recruits. Most of them were glancing back and forth from him to Saul, uncertain as to what they should do. Moses knew they were good men, but they were used to being controlled by whomever had the most power. Until they learned to believe in themselves, they would believe in the strongest one around.

Moses locked eyes with Saul and rode forward slowly, not stopping until he was directly in front of the sneering man. "I don't take kindly to being called a thief," he said.

"Then you shouldn't act like one," Saul said. "Cromwell Plantation ain't no different than any of the other ones. It ought to burn, too."

"You would burn a house full of black people?" Moses was thankful Sam and Opal were still living there. "I would much rather be accused of being a thief than a murderer of my own people." His voice grew sharper. "They're living the life all of us wish we could live. So should I destroy the house they are living in, forcing them to return to the squalor of the slave quarters?"

"Let them fight for their freedom the way the rest of us are," Saul protested. "Why should it get handed to them? Is the man living there a coward?"

Moses smiled coldly. "You're letting your ignorance show, Saul. The man you are accusing of being a coward is almost seventy years old. The woman had her freedom granted to her, then returned to care for children who have been left homeless because their daddy is in prison for spying for the Union." He saw no reason to add that Carrie Cromwell was also one of his closest friends. He paused and looked around. He clearly had the agreement of everyone there. "I won't touch one piece of that house," he said.

Saul glanced around, realizing he had lost any support his challenges might have initially brought him. His eyes narrowed with fury. His face took on a caged look.

Moses watched him closely. He had known the humiliation would either cow him into submission or provoke his anger even more. It was obvious his years in slavery had left him bitter and vengeful. If his energy could be channeled, he would be a valuable soldier. If he was incapable of following orders, he would be no good to anyone. His presence in the army would give credence to the whites' criticisms that blacks wouldn't make good soldiers.

"I'm ordering everyone to stay here," Moses repeated firmly. Then he turned and urged his horse into a trot. He sensed Saul's movement before he heard Pompey's warning shot. Whirling, he had his pistol out before Saul got within five feet. He fired quickly, three shots in rapid succession. Saul jolted to a stop, staring at him wildly.

"I won't aim for the dirt at your feet next time," he said coldly. "White people already think you're a fool," he continued scornfully. "Don't give them any more reason to know it's true. You've got a choice. You can either decide to follow orders and be a soldier, or you can turn around right now and go back to where you came from. In case you don't know it, we have a war to win. I refuse to waste my time on men like you." His voice rang loudly in the clearing.

Saul cursed and turned toward the woods. Moses watched him go regretfully and turned to Pompey. "Send several men after him," he said quietly. "I want to make sure he really leaves the area. I won't have something happening to the house."

"Yes, sir," Pompey said quickly, springing into action.

Chapter Twenty-Four

Moses turned to ride off, secure in the support of his men. Minutes later, he rode up to the porch of the house. "Anyone home?" he called loudly.

The door opened, and Sam strode out onto the porch. "Glory be!" the old man exclaimed. "Moses, what you doin' around here?"

Moses jumped off his horse and embraced the old man. "Had to come tell you I'm a daddy," he said with a grin.

Sam's eyes filled with tears. "My Rose girl done had herself a baby?"

"A boy. His name is John."

"John," Sam repeated. "Her daddy would have liked that." He nodded. "Yes. He would have liked that."

"Rose wanted me to tell you that she is doing well and misses you." Moses saw joy spring into the old man's face. Rose had been like a daughter to him. Sam had vowed to her daddy that he would look after her when John was sold away in order to keep Rose's twin a secret. "She's not far from here, Sam. She's teaching in the contraband camps."

"I knew that girl was some kind of a teacher," Sam said proudly, staring off in the direction of the ocean. He turned back to Moses. "What you really be doin' here, boy?"

Moses explained his mission briefly.

Sam listened, both frowning and nodding. "I reckon it's got to be done," he said, "but I sure do hate to see all them pretty places burned up. It's gonna make it right hard for folks to live when this thing be over." He paused, staring at Moses. "Right hard for all of us."

Moses knew he was saying more than his words were. "What do you mean?"

"Them houses can hold either white or black people," Sam said. "It's more than that, though. Lots of the black people runnin' away are gonna want to come back to what they know. They's gonna want to farm like they done all their lives. If all the plantation owners ain't got no homes left, they ain't gonna be able to farm their land. They ain't gonna have no money to pay no workers." He shook his head. "The hard times gonna keep coming, Moses boy. This war gonna end, then all the ex-slaves, they gonna have to leave them contraband camps. I've heard talk of the hard times they been havin', but I don't think the end of the war gonna necessarily make things better." He stared out at the fields. "This country done got a lot of hurting to do yet. You mark my words."

Moses nodded. Sam made sense. He had already thought many of the same things himself. "I'm just following orders," he said lamely.

"You got to do what you got to do," Sam said. "Them people up in the North might be right. Might be the only way to make the South quit fighting this war. It's just a shame, that's all."

"I wish Rose could see Carrie," Moses said, changing the subject. "She misses her something awful. There aren't that many miles between here and Fort Monroe, but they might as well be hundreds of miles apart."

"Things ain't gonna stay this way forever," Sam said.

"Whose voice I hear out there?"

Moses stood up when Opal came running out onto the porch. "I had to stop in and say hello to my favorite cook," he said, grinning.

"Moses! Why, ain't you a sight for sore eyes. How'd you know I just pulled some apple pies out of the oven?"

"I followed my nose all the way from Fort Monroe." Moses leapt up onto the porch. A sudden shout in the distance made him step to the edge and peer toward the slave quarters. He waited for several minutes, but when he didn't hear or see anything more, he turned back toward Opal. "I figure I got enough time to sample them for you before my men start wondering where I am."

"Like I need you to tell me my pies are the best in Virginia," Opal scoffed, her eyes twinkling. "Get on in there before they get cold."

"Yes, ma'am," Moses responded. "I always follow orders."

Laughing and talking, the three moved into the house. Moses stopped inside the foyer and gazed in the direction of his men once more. Pushing down a sudden feeling of uneasiness, he turned and went in search of his apple pie.

Moses demolished a huge piece before he was willing to talk again. "Best pie I've ever eaten," he announced. He paused. "Well, I think it is, anyway."

Opal bristled instantly. "Who you know can make a better pie than me?"

Moses shook his head. "I'd have to think about that now," he mused, staring down at his empty plate. "Maybe if I had another piece I might be better able to recall."

"Get on with you, Moses," Opal snorted. "I should have known you be playing me for a fool." Her face wreathed in smiles, she dished him up another large piece.

Moses grinned and turned to Sam. "You heard anything from Carrie recently?"

"Miss Carrie done been here," Sam announced. "She ain't been gone that long."

"Carrie was here?" Moses asked, amazed. "Why didn't you tell me sooner?"

"You been too busy stuffin' your face with Opal's pie," Sam said. "I reckon you be wantin' to know how she's doin'."

Moses listened as Sam filled him in.

"Then she went and married that Robert man," Sam finished. "I figure she's real happy."

Moses leaned back in his chair. "Robert's alive? He made it?"

Sam stared at him curiously. "What you talking about, boy? You ain't makin' no sense. How'd you know about Robert bein' bad off for a while?"

"I found Robert on the battlefield after Antietam. He was shot up pretty bad. I didn't figure there was any way he could make it. I was going to take him behind Confederate lines, but decided to take him to some folks

I had passed by that day." He paused, remembering. "I was sure I was crazy at the time."

"Carrie said he got real close with the folks who took him in."

Moses stared at him dubiously. "Robert got real close to some black people?"

Sam grinned. "That Robert boy done a lot of changing. The good Lord answered our prayers like we asked him to. Carrie said Robert done come home a new man."

"And Granite? I found him on the battlefield near Robert. He didn't look so good."

"Granite is in a stall behind Marse Cromwell's house right now," Opal chirped.

Moses shook his head disbelievingly and sat back. "I'll be quiet. You fill me in on everything."

Sam opened his mouth to speak, but his head jerked around as the sound of shattering glass filtered into the kitchen.

"Jesus, help us!" Opal screamed.

Moses leapt up and dashed in the direction of the sound. He ran into the parlor, just barely catching a glimpse of Saul's face at the window before it ducked from sight. Seconds later, another large stone came hurtling through another pane of the window. Moses spun from the room when a heavy thud grabbed his attention. He whirled around in time to see a flaming pine knot hurl through the broken glass, landing on the carpet inches from a chair. Springing forward, Moses grabbed it and threw it in the fireplace.

He turned again, almost running into Opal. "You stay here," he said. "Toss whatever he sends in into the fireplace. I'll get him."

"Who is that crazy man?" Opal asked.

"Tell you later," Moses snapped, sprinting from the room.

Sam made it to the front door before he did. Before Moses could open his mouth to yell a warning, Sam flung open the front door and stepped out.

The report of a gun split the quiet air.

Moses saw Sam slump to the porch. He grabbed his pistol from his belt and edged forward cautiously.

Somehow Saul had managed to get a firearm. It would help nothing for him to run out and get shot himself. Somehow, he had to bring things back under control.

Moses approached the front door cautiously. A wild laugh rose through the air as another bullet slammed into the door frame inches from Sam's head. Loud shouts sounded in the distance. Moses knew his men had heard the shots and were on their way to the house, but he couldn't wait for them. Sam could be dead by then.

He started forward once more, just as he heard the sound of more tinkling glass. Moses leapt over Sam, firing his gun before he even hit the porch. Saul whirled around from his newest attack on the house, his face twisted and crazed. The firing of the gun seemed to have thrown him off guard, but he recovered quickly. Sneering with hatred, he whipped his gun up.

Moses fired twice and then threw his body across Sam's to protect the old man. He lay there waiting for the next bullet, but only silence greeted him. He looked up to see Saul sprawled on the grass underneath the window. Opal was staring down at him through the broken glass.

"You're some kind of shot," she said, glaring down at Saul with a look of disgust. "Where did that crazy man come from?"

The sound of hoofbeats exploded into the quiet, and the yard was soon swarming with Moses' men. Pompey jumped down from his horse and raced to where Moses sat on the porch.

"You all right?" he gasped.

"What happened?" Moses snapped, his heart still pounding wildly.

"That Saul is sho 'nuff crazy," Pompey said sadly. "Me and some of the boys went after him, like you tole us. He was waitin' in the woods a ways back, hangin' from one of them trees like a possum. He jumped down on Mort and knocked him out cold. Before we could even move, he grabbed Mort's gun and took off running." Pompey took a deep breath. "We went after him, but he disappeared so fast it was plumb scary. We been lookin' for him ever since. Then we heard the firin'. We got here as soon as we could. You sure you be all right?"

"I'm fine," Moses said. He turned back and looked down at Sam. "It's him I'm worried about." He motioned to two of his men. "Get him in the house."

Sam's eyes fluttered open. "You sure be a big man, Moses," he whispered hoarsely.

"What?" Moses asked, confused but overjoyed to know Sam wasn't dead.

"That man's bullet knocked me down sure enough, but I was ready to get back up. At least until you jumped on top of me." Sam forced a grin. "You get him?" he asked.

"I got him," Moses said, suddenly aware he had killed one of his own men.

Pompey interpreted the look on his face. "You couldn't have done anything else," he assured him. "That Saul was a bad one."

"Saul?" Sam asked. He gasped in sudden pain when he moved.

"Sam!" Moses exclaimed. "Where did he get you?"

"In the arm," Sam scoffed. "It knocked me off balance. That's why I fell."

Opal stepped out onto the porch then. "I'll take care of him," she said. "I ain't Miss Carrie, that's for sure, but I reckon I done watched her enough when she was here to know how to take this bullet out." She pulled back Sam's sleeve. "Ain't even in there very deep," she said with satisfaction. "Let's get him inside."

"Wait," Sam insisted. He leaned forward to get a better view of the man lying on the ground.

Mort looked up from where he was examining Saul. "He's dead," he announced. "Good shot, Moses."

Moses stared, not able to believe he had killed one of his own people, even though he knew he hadn't had any other choice.

"That be Saul from Riverside Plantation?"

"You know him?" Moses asked in amazement.

"He's been here before," Sam said. "I ain't never met a man so ate up with hate in all my life. He got treated bad, sho 'nuff, but that weren't all of it." He paused.

"Lots of us been treated bad, but it didn't make us crazy. It made us determined to change thin's. Saul didn't want to change nothin'," he said sadly. "He just wanted to kill thin's." He stared down at the dead man with hard eyes. "It's better this way, boy," he said to Moses softly. "Trust me. It's better this way."

Moses nodded and pushed himself up. "Let's get you inside, Sam." He looked at Opal. "You sure you can do this?" He took comfort from the confident shine in Opal's eyes. Then he turned to his men. "You'll find some glass in the barn," he said.

"I reckon I can fix them windows right quick," one of his men said.

"Good. We've made enough noise around here to raise every Rebel soldier within ten miles. Fix the window, then we've got to get out of here. I don't intend to lose any more of my men."

Moses followed Sam, carried by some of his men, into the house. He waited until only he and Opal were in the room. Then he looked down sadly. "I'm sorry," he said. "This is all my fault. I shouldn't have come here and put you in danger."

"Nonsense," Sam snorted. "Sometimes thin's happen. You can't go tryin' to be responsible for all that goes on in this world, whether it be good or bad. You just got to deal with it the best you can." He reached out his good arm and laid his hand on Moses'. "You saved my life," he said. "That's the thin' you got to remember." His hand fell away weakly. "Now get the rest of your men out of here. You still got a job to do. You go do it."

"I hate to leave you."

"Sam is going to be fine," Opal said. "You ain't got a thing to worry about. This ain't nothing more than a flesh wound."

Moses gazed at her and nodded. "Take care of yourselves."

Thirty minutes later, the windows fixed and Saul's body covered in an unidentified grave, Moses led his men away from Cromwell Plantation. In two days, they would be back at Fort Monroe. His mission was over.

Chapter Twenty-Five

Christmas Day dawned cold and dreary. Scattered snowflakes the night before had teased children into believing there might be a white Christmas, but they had subsided, seeming to know only the young would welcome them. The skies were overcast and heavy in Richmond, but the ground remained dry. The wind blew hard from the north, keeping most people huddled around the small bits of wood they were hoarding to keep their fireplaces warm. The pinched look of hunger already rested on many faces. Anxious eyes peered out from scarf-covered faces. It might be Christmas on the calendar, but gifts of any kind were scarce. The third year of the blockade had slowed supplies to a bare trickle. All the people of Richmond wanted was to find a way to stave off starvation. Some of them already knew they were asking too much.

Carrie hummed to herself as she hovered over the dining room table, putting on the last touches of greenery. There was little in the house to suggest Christmas was here, but at the last minute she had run outside and denuded the magnolia of just enough of its waxen leaves to decorate the table. There would be little to remind them of Christmases past, but they still had much to be joyful about.

Thomas put an arm around her. "Merry Christmas."

"Merry Christmas," Carrie said. She finished placing the last sprig of magnolia on the table. "Can you believe we're all together for Christmas?" She glanced over his shoulder and gasped. "It's snowing," she cried in delight. She clapped her hands together like a little girl and ran to the window to stare out at the huge flakes descending on the city.

"Not everyone will be as excited as you," her father responded wryly. "You have loved snow since you were a child."

Carrie continued to stare out the window. "I know snow is not welcome in the city right now. I know more people will suffer, but I can't help wanting there to be snow for Christmas."

"It's wonderful," her father insisted. "Enjoy your snow. Heaven knows there are too few things to enjoy around here." He kissed her on the cheek and moved away to settle down in his chair by the fire. He leaned his head against the back of the chair for a few minutes and picked up a paper from the stack he kept beside it.

Carrie watched him lovingly. A shadow of worry still lingered in her father's eyes, but the bitterness and rage were gone. He seemed to simply be waiting for the inevitable, working as hard as he could to hold it off, but under no illusion that it would not someday become reality. Carrie knew he would be heartbroken if the South lost the war, but she was now confident he would survive.

Robert came downstairs then, looking well-rested. Carrie kissed him and waved him over to the fire. "I'm almost done here. You and father can play lords of the manor."

"Oh, I fully realize that's only a game." Robert chuckled. "I have never been particularly overwhelmed by my wife's submissive nature."

"As long as you enjoy the game," Carrie said, her eyes sparkling with fun.

Robert swatted her on her behind and strolled over to the fire. He held his hands out to warm them, then settled in the chair next to her father. "Are we on a limited range of topics this morning?" Robert asked.

Carrie glared at him while she considered his question. Finally, she shook her head. "I suppose it would do no good to ask you not to talk about anything relating to the war. I realize it consumes everyone. And I suppose it helps," she added thoughtfully. "I only request we not talk about it during our meal. For one hour, I would like to pretend there is peace on earth and goodwill among men."

"You have a better imagination than I do," Thomas said.

Robert smiled and picked up a paper. He held it, but continued to stare into the fire. "I know there are many people suffering from the cold, including the soldiers bivouacked in their winter quarters, but at least the fighting has stopped for now."

"There are very few men left in the hospital," Carrie agreed. "Most have been released to go home. That's the only reason Janie was able to visit her family in North Carolina. I'm so glad she could," she said. "It's been three years since she's seen them. I'm sure they are having a joyous Christmas."

"She's probably eating better than we are here," Robert observed. "One thing I discovered running the blockade is that Richmond is suffering far more than other Southern cities. No one has it easy, but food is much easier to come by if you don't happen to live in the capital."

"We have plenty," Carrie said, hiding her smile. She hadn't yet told her father and Robert that Opal had filled several boxes with supplies from the plantation so they could have a special Christmas. Carrie had been hoping then that Robert would make it home from England in time. May was hard at work in the kitchen now. Tomorrow it would be back to simple fare, but for today, they would feast.

The dark, gray day did nothing to diminish Carrie's happy mood. "I invited Doctor Wild and Matron Pember over for dinner," she said.

Her father looked up, startled. "And what exactly are you planning on feeding them, dear?" he asked.

"Oh, they're used to not having much," she responded. "It will be nice for them to have somewhere to go. They both appreciated the invitation." She looked up to see Robert watching her closely.

"There's something in your eyes," he murmured suspiciously. He folded his paper and laid it aside. "You're hiding something, Carrie Borden."

Carrie shook her head. She should have known she couldn't pull one over on Robert. "Don't be silly," she chided him. Then she turned toward the kitchen. "I have work to do," she threw over her shoulder.

Robert shook his head. "Time will reveal all," he called, picking his paper back up.

Carrie stuck out her tongue and ducked into the hallway. She waited several moments to make sure her husband wasn't following her, before she slipped down the hallway toward the kitchen. She entered it quietly, pulling the door shut behind her.

May looked up with a grin. "I reckon you's gonna have a feast fit for a king," she grinned. "I ain't had good things like this to work with for quite a while now." She shook her head. "That Opal out on the plantation sure be a lucky woman."

Carrie leaned against the table and sniffed the air. "I'm not sure how we're going to keep this a secret with all these good smells."

May jerked her head toward a pile of rags in the corner of the kitchen. Her hands were covered with flour from making biscuits. She ran one hand over her shiny face, leaving a white streak. "You can stuff them things under the door. That ought to keep most of the smells trapped right here."

Carrie jumped to comply. "You're a smart woman," she said.

"I reckon that be true," May responded.

Carrie laughed and edged over to pick off a piece of biscuit dough. "I don't know why you bother to cook them," she grinned. "They're better raw."

May grunted and swatted at her hand. "Get on with you, Miss Carrie. I gots enough work to do without you in here deviling me!"

"Didn't Opal put some carrots in those boxes?" Carrie asked.

"Might have. Why?"

"Well, it's Christmas." Carrie smiled. "I thought—"

"You ain't giving none of our good food to that horse of yours." A minute later May snorted and reached into a box. She fumbled around for a minute and came up with a plump carrot. "Now get out of my kitchen," she scolded.

Carrie grabbed a coat from beside the door and ducked out into the raw day. She stood for a moment, staring up into the gray sky, and took deep breaths. The whole country might be in the grip of dark chaos, but for this day, she was going to put it out of her mind. It was Christmas. She turned and headed toward the stable.

Granite nickered a greeting before she had even opened the door to the barn. "Can't sneak up on you can I, old boy?" Carrie called.

His massive gray head rested on her shoulder while he munched contentedly on his carrot. "I know you're not getting enough to eat," she said, "but we're doing the best we can." He didn't look poorly, but he also didn't have the gleam he once had. Getting feed for him was every bit as difficult as obtaining food for the people in their household.

Carrie stroked his head, talking to him softly until the cold began to penetrate her clothing. "Merry Christmas," she called once more as she closed the door to the barn.

Carrie was overwhelmed by the delicious smells that blasted her when she entered the kitchen. Within minutes, the warm, moist air had chased all the chill from her shivering limbs. She stood still for several moments, breathing in the aromas, before May looked up and saw her.

May jumped slightly. "Girl, you always sneaking up on people like that?"

Carrie laughed and moved forward. "What else have you got for me to sample?"

May scowled and held up her rolling pin. "I'm going to give you a sample of something, sho 'nuff, if you don't get out of my kitchen."

Carrie leaned forward to kiss the startled woman on her hot cheek and slid out the door before May could recover enough to say something.

Robert and her father were deep in discussion when she reentered the parlor.

Robert glanced up. "You smell good," he commented.

Carrie shrugged. "Must be the hay from the barn. I went out to visit Granite." She was relieved when Robert nodded and turned back to her father. She really wanted the meal to be a surprise.

"Bragg never stood a chance against Grant," Robert said, frowning.

"I knew things were going to end that way. When Bragg beat back the Union Army at Chickamauga, he should have finished the job. Not that he necessarily could have," he said. "Oh, people screamed and hollered that he wasn't the man for the job, and maybe he wasn't, but the truth of the matter was, he didn't have the resources to finish what he started."

"But to lay siege to Chattanooga when the Union retreated there, and then sit and watch them gain strength while he got weaker?"

Thomas nodded in agreement. "There have been many people who tried to convince Davis that Bragg wasn't the man for the job. Our illustrious president did what he wanted."

"And now he's paid the price," Robert stated, shaking his head. "That Union general, Grant, seems to be rather effective."

"Rather," Thomas agreed dryly. "It was when he took over the Union Army in Chattanooga that things started to change. The assault he led on November the twenty-fourth was impressive."

"I've talked to a couple of men who were there. They said the Confederate position on Missionary Hill was so strong defensively it could have been held by a single line of skirmishers. When our men saw twenty thousand Union soldiers surging up that hill, though, they panicked. The fellow I talked to said they turned tail and ran."

"Luck or skill," Thomas replied, "it doesn't really matter. In the end, Grant was in sole charge of Chattanooga. I think it is fair to say Tennessee has probably been lost for good."

Carrie stared at him. His voice was amazingly matter-of-fact.

Robert nodded grimly. "I heard some men talking while I was in town the other day. They were foolish enough to say they thought the Confederacy was as well off now as it was at the beginning of this year."

"And what do they base such a ridiculous assumption on?" Thomas barked. "Those men must have blinders on."

"I agree," Robert replied. "From what I could tell of their conversation, they were basing their remarks on the area between Richmond and Washington. They contended that the rival armies had neither advanced nor retreated, in spite of the Union's greater power. They were boasting that the Union's cry of *On to Richmond* always meant either a bloody beating or a shameful blunder for the invaders."

"Did you remind them there is more to the Confederacy than the relatively small amount of land between Richmond and Washington?"

"I didn't figure it would serve any purpose to try to reason with men who were obviously ignorant."

Carrie moved forward with hot coffee and refilled both their cups. Her father smiled at her gratefully, took a sip, and resumed talking.

"The truth of the matter is that the government is almost bankrupt. We have an over-inflated currency and a grossly inadequate tax system." He took a deep breath. "We have no foreign affairs worth mentioning. Most of the other countries have decided after this summer that we will inevitably be defeated and pulled back into the Union fold." He stopped and stared into the fire. "Add to the fact that we have lost cities, rivers and whole armies this summer. No, I'm afraid that at the end of this year, we have nothing but trouble to look at." He grimaced. "I fear what will happen when winter is over."

"Do you think it can possibly continue?" Carrie asked.

"Oh, it will continue," Thomas replied. "I heard President Davis' speech to the congress a few weeks ago." He picked up a paper. "Let me read you what he said." He cleared his throat.

"'*The Northern government refused even to listen to proposals for the only peace possible between us—a peace which, recognizing the impassable gulf which divides us, may leave the two peoples separately to recover from the injuries inflicted on both by the causeless war now being waged against us.' "*

Thomas stopped and looked up. "After having said that, he finished with this: *'We now know that the only reliable hope for peace is in the vigor of our resistance.' "*

Robert looked at Carrie. "Davis believes there is no conceivable way to bridge the gap between the North and the South. Therefore, his only hope is to fight as hard as he can. To believe that somehow our armies can be made strong enough to keep the battle line from breaking."

"What do you believe?"

Robert shrugged. "I've thought a lot about it. I've come to agree with your father that the defeat of the South is inevitable. I have to believe that somehow the gulf separating the two halves of our country can be bridged." He shook his head. "I don't know how it's going to happen."

Abby bustled about the kitchen of her handsome house, flushed from the heat pouring from her stove. She had invited several friends over for Christmas dinner, promising a feast. The aromas wafting through her house were testimony to the success of her efforts the last two days.

Abby had welcomed the flurry of activity to take her mind off Matthew. She had heard nothing since a brief notice from his office early in the fall that he was once again in Libby Prison, and that all prisoner exchanges had been halted. She vividly remembered his stories from his first confinement. The last few days she felt a heavier burden every time she thought of him. Not knowing was driving her mad. What was he being forced to endure? She shuddered, turned to stare out the window, and whispered a prayer for him. After long minutes, she turned away. She had company coming.

Abby checked the last of her pies baking in the oven and hurried into the dining room to put the finishing touches on her table. Greenery was abundant, and candles lent a soft glow throughout the room. She had turned off the lanterns for this meal, preferring the ambience of candles. A crackling fire blazed in the fireplace. A small tree in the corner cast a delightful fragrance through the room.

She had just completed her preparation when the doorbell pealed. Abby whipped off her apron, stuffed a loose hair back into her bun, checked the mirror to make sure there were no smudges on her face, and walked to the door.

The house was soon full of the laughter of ten young women. Abby gazed at them fondly. All of them had been invaluable in her efforts to collect the petitions she had vowed to accumulate in Philadelphia. All of them were also childless, with their young husbands off fighting for the Union somewhere. Abby had been planning this meal for them for over a month. It was her way of saying thank you. It was also her way of helping ease the pain of a day designed for family.

"I got a letter from my husband," one stunning young redhead said. Then she frowned. "It was wonderful to hear from him, but it must be simply awful to be stuck in tents during this horrid weather. This war simply has to end soon."

"President Lincoln is sure it will," another, rather plain-looking blonde, said eagerly. "He's already talking about reconstruction. It makes the work we're doing even more important. One of the results of this war simply must be that all of the slaves are set free."

"They need to have the vote. That's the only way things are going to change."

"Well, certainly, but what about us? We need to have the vote. If we're going to spend all this time fighting for equality for blacks, surely there is nothing wrong with wanting it to extend to ourselves. I think we're passing up the best opportunity we will have in what might be a very long time. Right now, the whole country is looking toward change. They are actually considering the vote for black men. Not too many years ago, that would have seemed completely impossible. The whole country is going to be in turmoil when this war finally ends. All their energy is going to be spent rebuilding the country. Very few people are going to want something else major thrown in their faces. Asking them to consider women's right to vote will guarantee they block their ears."

"Surely it won't be that bad," another woman protested, even though her voice didn't sound as if she believed it herself. "Our country can only stand so much right now. What do you think, Mrs. Livingston?"

Abby gazed around at the group of women looking at her. "I'm afraid you're right, but I guess there is also some truth in what the people say who think we should shelve women's rights during this time." She shook her head. "Having said that, I want to say again that I think women are missing the best chance for equality they will have in a long time."

"Then why don't the leaders of our movement insist on pushing it through?" the blonde woman pressed. "Surely they aren't afraid? I've never seen such bold women in my life."

"They're not afraid for themselves, certainly," Abby agreed. She paused, searching for the right words. "It's rather difficult to explain." She stopped again, gathered her thoughts, and continued. "Whenever change is introduced, especially if it is great change, there is always pain associated with it. Human beings seem rather to be creatures of habit. It is difficult for them to break out of old ways of thinking and doing things. They resist it. The forcing of change is painful. Our country will experience great turmoil. This war is hardly the answer to our problems. It's really only another piece of them. A rather large piece," she added.

"But you can't back away from the pain," Abby continued. "Choosing to forge into change—choosing pain over security—takes a great deal of courage. Unfortunately, the number of people willing to do that is far fewer than those who embrace habit." She shrugged. "The leaders of our movement had to consider that. They chose to fight for freedom for the black people. Theirs is by far the greatest injustice." She stood. "Our time will come," she said strongly. "Our time will come."

Abby looked at the serious expressions on the faces of her guests and suddenly smiled. "Come on! It's Christmas. I won't allow morbid faces in my house." She clapped her hands and headed toward her piano. "I think we have just enough time for some songs before the ham is done. Can I interest anyone?"

Dismal expressions dropped away as smiles of anticipation replaced them. Soon, song echoed through the house. Abby sang for Matthew.

Matthew woke from a fitful sleep and rolled over to check the marks on the wall. He frowned as he stared at the straight little lines. He counted them, then counted them again. "Christmas," he muttered thickly.

"Yeah, Christmas," one of his hole-mates said sarcastically. "Merry Christmas, Matthew."

Matthew stared at him woodenly. He had fought as hard as he could to keep despair from gripping him, but he could feel it tightening his grasp. The constant aching cold and the gnawing hunger were wearing on him. He blinked his eyes to keep visions of happier Christmases from haunting him. Rat Dungeon was his only reality. Dreaming of the outside world would push him over the edge.

He heard the sound of clumping feet. Pulling himself up into a sitting position, he waited for the guard to open the tiny hatch above them. The bread morsels had become harder and drier, but he knew they were the only thing between him and death. Sometimes the guard dropped them in, not caring if they fell on the damp floor and were whisked away by the rats before the prisoners could get them. Matthew had learned to wait and reach for them as soon as the guards approached.

Without one word from the outside world, Matthew knew the war was going badly for the Confederates. The guards' tempers seemed to worsen on a daily basis.

Matthew was crouched below the door when it swung open.

"Matthew Justin!" the guard called.

Matthew jumped and gazed up. "Yes?"

"Merry Christmas," the guard said sarcastically. "You're out of here."

Matthew stood in stunned silence, afraid to believe his ears.

"Hey man!" one of his fellow prisoners called. "They're talking to you. You're out of here. You better move before they change their minds."

Matthew glanced back at the man speaking and nodded numbly, sudden tears springing to his eyes. The door behind him swung open and the guard motioned him forward. Matthew raised his head high, a symbol he hadn't been defeated, and walked steadily from the hole. The cheers of his fellow prisoners followed him.

Matthew drank in the relatively fresh air of the upper prison. Just before he reached the door that would take him to his original floor, the guard stopped him, twisting his arm cruelly. "I wouldn't entertain any more ideas of escaping," he said coldly. "Next time they might never let you out."

Matthew stared at him evenly and nodded. He wanted to spit in his face, but it was better to let his captors think he had been cowed into submission. That way they wouldn't be watching him any more closely than they would be already.

Captain Anderson was waiting for him on the other side of the door. "Matthew!" he exclaimed, clasping his hand warmly.

"Good to see you," Matthew said, trying not to notice the look of horror on Anderson's face. He could only imagine what he looked like after three months in Rat Dungeon. "Got some scissors?" he asked. "I have a feeling I need a haircut."

Anderson laughed and motioned to the other men. "Rat Dungeon didn't break him," he called out jubilantly. "I told you he was a bigger man than that!"

The other men rushed forward to grip his hand or give him a hug. Matthew choked back tears at the warm display of affection. Finally Peter, who had been waiting at the back of the men, stepped forward and embraced him. "You ready for Christmas dinner?" he asked.

"Christmas dinner?" Matthew echoed. "You mean you have more to eat than bread and water?"

"It's nothing exciting, but they did give us portions of meat and beans," Anderson said. "We all saved you some."

Matthew found himself staring down at a plate heaping with hot food, his eyes blurred with tears. He paused for a moment to give thanks. Then he began to eat ravenously.

Dr. Wild and Matron Pember had been there for almost an hour, laughing and chatting with Thomas and Robert in the parlor.

"I feel terribly lazy," Matron Pember called. "Isn't there something I can do to help?"

"Not a thing," Carrie called back. "You just need to enjoy yourself." It thrilled her to do something for the person who had made her first days at Chimborazo more bearable. To say she had been overwhelmed would be putting it mildly.

Carrie dashed back in the kitchen and saw May nodding her head. "I can call them to the table now?" she asked excitedly.

"Yes, ma'am," May said, reaching for a fresh apron. "Everything be ready."

"Not quite," Carrie said as she strode across the room.

"What you be doing, Miss Carrie?" May asked, startled.

Carrie ignored her and pulled two large plates out of the cupboard. She moved from pot to pot until the plates were almost overflowing with food. "These are for you and Micah," she said, smiling. "That army out there might eat all of it. I intend to make sure you two eat as well as we do. If I had my way, you would come out there to join us."

May stared at her and then broke into a cackling laugh. "Won't that be the day?" she exclaimed. "Marse Cromwell would fall over dead."

"Probably," Carrie agreed, "but the day is coming." She put her hand on the door and looked back. "Merry Christmas, May."

"Merry Christmas, Miss Carrie," May said timidly, her eyes glowing. "You be a fine woman."

Carrie smiled, moved through the dining room and into the parlor, where she clapped her hands. "Time for dinner," she announced.

Thomas was apologizing before he even stood. "I'm sorry we can't offer you more of a Christmas feast," he said to Dr. Wild.

"Think nothing of it," Dr. Wild protested. "It's simply wonderful to have such a hospitable home to spend the day in."

Robert sidled up to Carrie. "You look like the cat that swallowed the canary," he accused. "What are you up to?"

"I have no idea what you're talking about," Carrie protested innocently, batting her eyes at him.

"Yeah, right."

Carrie indicated where everyone was to sit and reached for the bell to summon May. It had barely tinkled before the door swung open. May strode in, carrying a tray holding a large, succulent ham. Close behind her was Micah with a plate piled with roasted venison and turkey. Carrie grinned as she watched the mouths of those surrounding the table drop open in amazement.

She could barely keep herself from jumping up and down when May wheeled, disappeared, and seconds later walked out bearing plates full of green beans, carrots, peas, okra, and sweet potatoes. Micah pulled the same disappearing act before strutting out with three different kinds of pies.

Still, no one had spoken a word. They were too busy staring at the table almost groaning under the sudden weight of so much food.

"Merry Christmas!" Carrie finally cried. "Merry Christmas!"

May and Micah smiled, ducked their heads, and stepped back into the kitchen for their own Christmas feast.

Thomas was the first to find his voice. "Where in the world did all this food come from?"

"I brought it back from the plantation," she explained happily. "Opal and Sam were determined we would have a good Christmas. I barely fit it in the wagon with all the herbs, but Opal wouldn't hear of me leaving without it."

Robert was still staring at her, shaking his head. "You will never cease to amaze me," he murmured.

Carrie blushed with pleasure and waved her hand over the table. "I suggest we eat while it's still hot."

Laughing and talking, the five of them heaped their plates.

It was past dark when Carrie leaned back, groaning. "I've eaten more today than I have in the last two weeks put together."

"I'm in agony," Dr. Wild agreed with a broad smile. "I will enjoy every stomach pain I have later."

"I think that's the best food I've ever eaten," Matron Pember enthused. "I hope your help received some of this."

"I filled their plates first," Carrie assured her. She stood to her feet, swaying dramatically. "If we can stumble our way into the parlor, I think this would be a wonderful time to sing." She headed in that direction. "Matron Pember is going to play for us."

"Me?" Matron Pember gasped.

"Yes, you," Carrie responded. "Don't pretend you can't. One of the days you sent me into your office, I saw the clipping your sister sent you. I couldn't help but notice the headline. Why didn't you ever tell me you used to be a concert pianist?"

"That was quite a long time ago," the matron protested.

"Not that long ago," Carrie shot back. "Of course, if you think the meal didn't warrant it..."

Robert shouted with laughter. "Trust my wife to get what she wants, no matter what it takes."

Matron Pember laughed, too. "I'll not do it for the meal," she protested. "I believe that closely resembles blackmail."

Carrie shrugged carelessly. "Whatever it takes."

"I'll do it because the idea of sitting in front of fine piano is a delight I won't pass up. I may be a bit rusty. Y'all will have to bear with me."

Carrie pulled up a chair next to the fire, listening to the matron play. If this was rusty, they were in for a bit of heaven when she got warmed up.

Matron Pember swung around. "I thought we were going to sing," she accused laughingly. "I'm not going to just give a concert."

Thomas stepped up to the piano and began to sing, his strong tenor floating through the house. Seconds later, everyone joined in.

Carrie blinked back tears of happiness as she sang, her arm linked through Robert's. They might live in a world wracked by war, but for this one day they had pushed the horror back.

Matthew was awake long after the rest of the men had gone to sleep. He was relishing his release from Rat Dungeon too much to let go of the delicious sensation. They had played cards and chess all afternoon, and Matthew listened eagerly as the men answered his rapid-fire questions, catching him up on the world as much as they could.

Captain Anderson rolled over carefully. "You still awake?" he whispered.

"Yes."

"Think you can get out of this line of men without stepping on anyone?"

Matthew was curious at the urgency in his friend's voice. He stood and eased carefully through the men surrounding him.

He and Anderson huddled at the far back of the room. They talked quietly for over an hour, glancing at the sleeping men occasionally to make sure no one else was listening.

Matthew was trembling with excitement when he crawled back under his thin blanket. He didn't even feel the cold as he hugged the secret Captain Anderson shared close to him. If all went well, he would be out of there in little more than a month.

Chapter Twenty-Six

Matthew sat next to the window, ignoring the cold blasting his face and inadequately clothed body. He gazed down until he located the street sewer that had inspired Anderson's plan of escape. He shook his head admiringly. The captain was an amazing man. It was clear that both of them shared the same burning passion to escape and reclaim their freedom.

"It's almost dark," Anderson said quietly.

Matthew nodded. He had been watching the sun for several hours, silently urging it to hurry its course across the sky. He lived for the night hours now. It was only when all the prisoners were sleeping that they could engage in their work. It was simply too risky to let all twelve hundred prisoners know of the escape route they were devising. Secrecy was paramount to the success of their plan.

Anderson looked around carefully and leaned closer to Matthew. "We need help," he stated flatly.

Matthew breathed a sigh of relief. He had been thinking the same thing, but hadn't thought it was his place to suggest it. It was, after all, the captain's escape plan. "I agree," he said. "Peter will keep his mouth shut."

"So will Wilson," Anderson said.

They selected fifteen men they believed they could count on to keep the secret, and then Anderson nodded and walked away. Neither man could do anything to arouse suspicion. Even being seen talking for an extended period of time was sufficient reason to have the guards watch you more closely.

Matthew turned back to his window, thinking of what they had accomplished so far. Anderson had been waiting for him to be released from Rat Dungeon. They had started work the next night, Matthew insisting he was strong enough. His enforced discipline of exercise in the black hole paid off. He was not as strong as before his imprisonment, but he was still capable of keeping up with Anderson.

Anderson had waited until everyone was asleep, then motioned for him to follow. Minutes later, they slipped into the kitchen and were standing in front of the fireplace. "This is it!" Anderson whispered excitedly. "If we can put a hole through the brick wall here, it will give us the access we need."

Matthew had looked at it doubtfully but helped shove one of the stoves away from the fireplace. Then, using only a knife Anderson had managed to acquire, they began chipping away at the mortar on the bricks. Their progress was excruciatingly slow, but neither man complained. At least they were doing something. Any activity was better than merely sitting, waiting for fate to deal its hand.

The night before, after five nights of chipping, the hole had been enlarged enough. Anderson ripped a board from one of the benches and slid it through the hole. Matthew shuddered as he recalled his horror of dropping down into Rat Dungeon. Amazingly, it was empty now, all the men either released or transferred to other prisons. He cringed when the familiar squeal of rats blasted him, but he had tightened his lips and had helped Anderson decide where the tunnel would begin.

Matthew began to relax when they decided other men would be joining them. Secrecy was still paramount, but it was encouraging to know others would be helping with the back-breaking work. It made the beacon of freedom shine brighter.

Peter appeared in front of him. "You realize what day this is?"

Matthew thought a moment and then shook his head. His mind was full of nothing but the escape attempt.

"It's New Year's Eve," Peter said, his eyes flicking toward the window. "Makes me think of all the parties back home. Man," he said, shaking his head, "I'd give anything to get out of this place and line up for a good tongue-lashing by my editor."

"Your chance may come sooner than you think," Matthew said, dropping his voice to a whisper and looking around to make sure no one was paying attention to them. Briefly, he explained the plan. Peter's face lit with excitement, and he nodded his head. "Count me in," he whispered.

New Year's Eve descended on Richmond with a driving storm of wind, snow and sleet. Matthew huddled close to the men stretched out beside him, searching for any body heat available, trying to control his shivers. He longed for the men to fall asleep so the group of conspirators could slip away. At least he was warm when he was digging.

"Midnight!" the guard rang out in his sing-song voice.

The song started down at the far end of the room, immediately picked up by every man until their voices rang through the night in brave, unified defiance.

> *O say can you see, by the dawn's early light,*
> *What so proudly we hailed, at the twilight's last gleaming,*
> *Whose broad stripes and bright stars through the perilous fight*
> *O'er the ramparts we watched were so gallantly streaming?*
> *And the rocket's red glare, the bombs bursting in air,*
> *Gave proof through the night that our flag was still there.*
> *O say does that star-spangled banner yet wave*
> *O'er the land of the free and the home of the brave?*

Matthew smiled through his tears. The pride he felt for his country was so fierce he could sense it gripping his body. The cold was forgotten as the song rose in the frigid air and floated out over the streets of Richmond. Song after song burst forth from the men, their patriotic fervor defying the reality of their imprisonment, until finally their voices faded away.

1864 had begun.

One week later, Matthew took a deep breath and squirmed into the tight confines of the tunnel. He was face down in the narrow passage that afforded just enough room for him to crawl forward on his stomach. Dirt and grime caked his hair and face. It was his turn to pass dirt back to the men waiting behind him. Anderson had ordered the men to break up into teams of six each. No one could stand more than a few hours in the stench-filled passage.

Matthew crawled forward until he reached the end of the tunnel. So far, they had managed to dig twelve feet toward the sewer line. The work was back-breaking, made more difficult by the low level of oxygen. Within minutes, Matthew was gasping for air. He knew several men were standing at the edge of the tunnel, fanning air toward him, but none of it seemed to be reaching him.

Laboriously, he hacked at the dirt in front of him with the knife. When enough had broken away, he loaded it into the dirt carrier and passed it back to Peter, who was stationed behind him. Their "dirt car" was a wooden spittoon with holes through each end, opposite each other. Ropes had been passed through the holes.

Peter touched him on the leg to signal he had gotten it and then tugged on the rope, signaling the next man to pull it back. Matthew continued to hack away. Minutes later, he felt Peter touch his leg again and reached back for the now empty box. The long night would pass this way.

Matthew was sweating and panting for breath when he felt the earth suddenly give way in front of him. He gasped and leaned forward. They had broken into the sewer! A rush of excitement gripped him and he craned his head back to tell Peter they had reached freedom. At the same time he opened his mouth, a gushing wall of sewer water surged through the hole.

Choking and spitting, Matthew struggled to wriggle his way backwards. He could feel Peter fighting just as hard, but the water continued to rush forward. Matthew fought to keep his head above the swirling water, all the time trying to move backwards. He lost track of time, shuddering violently as the cold, putrid water encased his body.

Finally, he felt his feet gripped. With one hard yank, he was pulled out onto the straw floor of the cellar. Too exhausted to move, all he could do was open his mouth wide, trying to pull in air. He knew how close he had come to drowning. The rest of the men gathered around him, staring down into his face. Their expressions were ones of grim concern, but no one could say a word, for fear they would be heard in the hospital room on the other side of the wall.

Matthew rolled over, wishing he could gag up the water, feeling violently ill. He motioned toward the board leading up to the kitchen. The watching men picked him up and carefully passed him up to the kitchen. Once there, Matthew staggered forward to a bucket and gagged up the sewer water he had swallowed, promptly throwing up all he had eaten that day. Weak and sweating, he leaned against the kitchen wall, gasping for breath.

"Go back down and close up the hole," he finally ordered. "We'll have to find another way."

Cold rain slashed at the windows as Opal stood staring out into the darkening sky. The ping of the water against the glass made her shiver. She was glad for shelter on such a forbidding night. Rubbing her hands together, she turned to throw more wood on the fire and peered into the oven to check on her loaves of bread.

"Sure does smell good in here," Sam said as he opened the kitchen door and strode in, shaking water from his hat. "It's a brute out there tonight. All the kids in?"

"Yes, I just finished feeding them. They're in the parlor doing their studies."

Sam peered into the oven and grinned with appreciation. "Somethin' be botherin' Zeke," he said, turning back toward her.

"I've noticed the same thing." Opal frowned. "It's like he's—"

"Restless," Sam finished. "That boy ain't been the same since Moses been through here."

"Something's been bothering Susie, too," Opal observed. "She's been awful quiet."

"She knows somethin' is eatin' at her man," Sam said. "Can't help but eat at her some, too."

"What should we do?"

"Do?" Sam asked. "Why, we ain't gonna do nothin'. They be grown folks, them two. They gots to work out whatever be botherin' them on their own."

Opal nodded and turned back toward the window, staring in the direction of the slave quarters. Susie had become like a daughter to her, as well as a close friend. She would give anything to take away the burdensome look she'd seen hounding Susie for the last few weeks. A sudden flash of movement made her stiffen and swing away from the window. "Someone is out there!" she whispered, motioning to Sam wildly.

Sam scowled, hauled himself up with a grunt, and edged toward the back door. Before he could reach it, the door swung open. Opal jumped back in alarm just as Susie and Zeke, dripping with water, dodged into the kitchen.

"What a storm!" Zeke said, moving instantly toward the fire.

"You done scared the sense out of me!" Opal cried.

"Why?" Susie laughed. "Isn't anybody but us going to be out on a night like tonight. This weather isn't fit for man nor beast." She sniffed and moved closer to the stove. "Is that your bread I smell cooking?"

"Should be ready in about fifteen minutes," Opal acknowledged. Her dream of owning her own restaurant hadn't diminished. It warmed her heart that people liked her cooking so much. One day, when this war was over and the children's daddy was free, she would head north and start her own little place.

Sam leaned back in his chair. "You didn't come dashin' through that storm just to see if Opal be makin' bread," he said. "What you really be doin' here?"

Opal realized Sam was right. She looked at Susie expectantly. "What are you two doing here?" she repeated.

Susie exchanged a look with Zeke and sat down at the table.

Zeke moved away from the fireplace and joined her. "I reckon we do have a reason to be here," he admitted, smiling shyly. He gulped down some of the hot coffee Opal set in front of him. "I reckon we're gonna be movin' on from here."

Opal gasped and leaned forward. "What are you talking about?"

Susie reached out and took one of Opal's hands. "Zeke has been real restless for a while."

"Since Moses was here," Opal said.

Zeke shook his head. "I was feelin' it even before Moses came through." He glanced at Susie.

"Zeke wants to serve in the army," Susie said, her voice firm in spite of the fear in her eyes. "He wasn't saying anything because he knew how strongly I felt about staying here until Daddy gets out of prison."

"You changed your mind?" Sam asked.

Susie frowned. "I wouldn't say I've changed my mind. It's just…" She hesitated, searching for the right words. "This war is dragging on longer than anyone thought. Zeke and I figure the Union needs all the black soldiers it can get to help win it."

"I ran away from North Carolina to join up with the army," Zeke explained. "When I met Susie, things changed."

"Women have a way of doin' that to a man." Sam chuckled knowingly.

Susie turned back to Opal. "I want to go with him," she said earnestly. "It could be a long time before Daddy gets out of prison. The children are growing up. They're happy here with you."

"And you're not," Opal said. She smiled gently. "You want something more?"

"Am I being selfish?" Susie cried. She leaned back, taking a deep breath. "I want to make a difference, like Zeke. When I was in Richmond, I helped with the spying. I felt like I was doing something." Her eyes brightened. "From what I hear, I can be of help in the camps. That's where I'll stay until the war is over. I can help Rose and still be close when Daddy gets out of prison. Then all of us can figure out what to do."

"You ain't being selfish," Opal said, squeezing her hand. "I been seeing the restless spirit growing in you every day."

"But what about you?" Susie asked. "You want to start your restaurant."

Opal shook her head. "There's a time for everything, Susie. Right now it's my time to be mama to three young 'uns. I promised your mama. Besides, I love those kids like my own. My time to own a restaurant will come someday." She looked up at Susie with shining eyes. "Right now my job is here."

"You're not mad?" Susie whispered. "You aren't going to be mad if we leave?"

"All of us have to do what we have to do. I can't go fight with the soldiers, and I don't reckon I would be of much use to Rose in her school." Opal chuckled. "I'm going to stay here and do what I do best." She stood up and walked over to put a hand on both Susie and Zeke's shoulders. "I'm right proud of you two. All of us working together are going to win freedom for our people."

"When are you leaving?" Sam asked.

"In a few days," Zeke replied. "We didn't really set a time. We wanted to talk with y'all first."

A sudden banging at the door made all of them jump.

"What in heaven's name?" Opal cried, springing up from the table.

Zeke leapt up at the same time and edged over to the door slowly. "I locked it behind me when I came in," he muttered.

Sam strode past him. "Land sakes," he said. "Ain't no army roamin' around on a night like tonight. Whoever it is, it be someone in trouble." He grimaced. "We ain't leavin' someone outside on a night like this."

Opal grabbed her throat with her hand as Sam unlatched the lock and flung the door open. She peered forward, her eyes wide with fright as the door swung wide.

"Good Lord," Sam muttered as he reached out and grabbed the arm of the swaying man in front of him. Seconds later, the soaking form was huddled up next to the fire, gasping for breath.

Opal moved over closer. "He ain't nothin' but a boy," she cried, compassion replacing her fear. She noticed the blood stain on his jacket. "And he's been hurt."

The boy finally gained enough control of his breathing and trembling limbs to look up. "Is this Cromwell Plantation?"

"Why you want to know?" Sam asked, motioning silently for the others to follow his lead.

Opal handed the boy a hot cup of coffee, and he gulped it greedily. The aroma of the bread told her it was done, and she turned away to lay the golden loaves on the table. She smiled when the boy looked at the bread wistfully. "We'll find out what he wants in a minute," she said.

A few minutes later, thick slices of bread lathered with wild grape jam were laid in front of all of them. Opal clucked her tongue as the boy demolished his in seconds. Without comment, she cut him another piece. Only when it was gone did the starved look start to fade from his eyes.

He leaned back and stared around at them. "My name is George Andrews. I'm from Richmond."

"You're a long way from home," Sam replied.

"Yes, sir," George said politely.

Opal looked at him closely. You didn't find many white boys who were polite to old black men.

"Mrs. Hamilton said if I ever got in trouble, that I would find help at Cromwell Plantation."

"You know Mrs. Hamilton?" Susie cried. "I used to work for her."

"Are you Susie?" George asked in relief. He turned. "You must be Opal. You're the one taking care of Fannie's kids."

Opal grinned. This white boy was a friend. "What you doing out on a night like tonight? Mrs. Hamilton trying to get you killed?"

George shook his head ruefully. "Mrs. Hamilton thinks I'm already at Fort Monroe. I have a message for General Butler."

"No more messages inside eggs?" Susie asked with a grin.

"This message is so important she wanted it hand delivered." His face whitened and he grimaced.

Opal sprang up. "Listen to us!" she cried. "We're throwing questions at this boy while he's hurt." She hurried forward. "Let me take a look at that. What happened?"

George shook his head and motioned her away. "I'll be fine," he insisted. "At first I thought some Confederate soldiers got me, but I really think it was a hunter. I saw somebody peering at me through the bushes, then they turned and left."

"They just left you there to die?" Opal asked.

"It was better that way," George said. "It's most important that no one get this message but General Butler." He paused. "I laid there for a while, then got my bearings and came here. It took me a while."

"What you want us to do?" Sam asked.

George took a deep breath. "This message has to get to General Butler. Can one of you take it there?" His gaze settled hopefully on Zeke.

Opal was bursting with curiosity to know what the letter said, but she knew better than to ask. Most likely George didn't even know. His next words confirmed it.

"I don't know what is so all-fired important in this letter, but Mrs. Hamilton seemed to be in a big rush to get it to the general. From the little she told me, I gathered it had something to do with all the Union prisoners held in Richmond. A big stink is being raised up north about it."

Opal gasped, exchanging excited looks with Susie.

"How old are you?" Sam asked.

George pulled himself up taller. "I'm thirteen."

"You know what you're doing could get you hanged?"

"I know," George said. "I was born in the North. I lived there till just before the war started, when my father was called here on business. My mother and father are strong Unionists. So am I."

Opal stared at him. The eyes staring back at them were the eyes of someone who had counted the cost and knew what he was doing. She shuddered suddenly. Mere boys were becoming men long before they should. She was sad, yet filled with admiration for the determined lad in front of her.

Zeke stood and held out his hand. "I'll take the letter," he said, glancing at Susie. "My wife and I were just leaving for Fort Monroe."

"But you said it would be a few days," Opal protested, knowing it was futile before she even said anything. She had thought she would have a little time to get used to the idea of Susie not being around.

"You heard the boy," Zeke replied. "The letter needs to get there soon." He turned to Susie.

Susie nodded. "We'll leave in the morning."

In spite of the near-disaster in the first tunnel they attempted, Matthew's heart pounded with excitement when he an Anderson made the first cut for where their second attempt would be. They were still in Rat Dungeon, but they decided that if they moved several feet to the right they could bypass the lower part of the sewer and hit it where it started to ascend up the street. That way they could dig in at a higher angle and avoid the same catastrophe they almost encountered earlier.

Matthew looked back over his shoulder and gave the thumbs up signal to the men who were watching them expectantly. Wide grins were his response. In spite of the previous disappointment and the ongoing stench of the cellar, the men's spirits were still high. Matthew knew how important it was for them to stay that way. No one could stand the conditions they were laboring under for long if hope wasn't shining brightly in their hearts—beckoning them on to the glorious freedom that waited on the other side of Libby Prison's walls.

Matthew and Anderson attacked the wall eagerly. The men behind them grabbed the boxes of dirt they sent back, spreading them under the mound of straw on the floor to hide it from the guards' roaming eyes. In spite of the horrendous conditions, Matthew knew it was the best protection they could have hoped for. None of the guards were eager to come near Rat Dungeon. Now that it held no prisoners, they had no reason to come there at all.

The ground was soft and relatively easy to dig. Three nights passed, and they had already dug almost two feet into the new tunnel. At this rate they would be out soon. Anderson labored beside Matthew, using the half trowel one of the men managed to steal. Matthew grinned and jabbed his knife in especially hard.

"What?" he muttered under his breath. He jabbed again, striking into the same hard surface. Touching Anderson's shoulder, he motioned toward the impenetrable spot and raised his eyebrows.

Anderson shouldered him out of the way and leaned closer, digging quietly with his trowel. Finally he turned, a look of deep frustration on his face. He shook his head and motioned for Matthew to back out.

All the men were once again assembled in the kitchen. Anderson took a deep breath. "I'm afraid we'll have to dig another tunnel, men. We've run into wooden timbers so thick we have no hope of cutting through them." He managed to smile through the grime covering his face. "We'll find another one. I know there is a way out of here."

Matthew watched as the listening men silently turned away and trudged back to their places on the floor. He exchanged a long look with Anderson, knowing they had seen the same thing. The latest failure was more than the exhausted men could take. Together, they had watched the hope in their eyes flicker and die.

Anderson watched them go. "They need a break," he said.

"We're still with you," a voice announced quietly.

Matthew spun around and grinned when he saw Peter and another man named Sprinkler standing behind them.

Sprinkler, a lieutenant, had been in Libby Prison for ten months. "I'm getting out of here," he said firmly, his green eyes glowing with determination.

Anderson nodded. "We've got time to look for another place to dig," he said with satisfaction.

Soon, the four men stood once more in Rat Dungeon. Holding their one meager candle high enough to shed its dim flickering light on the walls, Matthew walked along the perimeter of the dungeon. Suddenly, he stopped at the northeast corner. "Why didn't I see it before?" he whispered, motioning to the men to join him.

They stared at him, puzzled. Matthew jerked his thumb toward the board leading to the kitchen. When they were huddled around him again, he told them his plan. "I've been studying everything through the window," he began eagerly. "The ground is eight or nine feet higher outside where I showed you than it is by the canal."

"So?" Anderson murmured. "We can't get to the sewer that way."

"We aren't aiming for the sewer." Matthew spoke fast before Anderson could interrupt. "We're going to tunnel all the way under the street until we reach the other side of the fence we can see from the windows. There is an empty lot on the other side of it. No one will be able to see us there when we get out."

"Do you know how far that is?"

"At least fifty feet from what I can tell," Matthew replied. He leaned forward eagerly, certain his plan would work.

"Fifty feet!" Peter exclaimed.

"What's fifty feet?" Matthew asked quietly. "We have nothing but time. We can either admit defeat or do what it takes to get out." Silence was the only response.

Matthew took a deep breath. "Does anyone else have a better idea?"

Anderson grinned and slapped him on the shoulder. "By Jove, I think it will work. You know, for a journalist, you're not so bad." He leaned back and stared at Matthew appraisingly. "You're a lot smarter than you look," he said.

Peter and Sprinkler joined in the almost inaudible laughter.

Anderson stood. "We all need to get some rest. I predict the rest of the men will come back in with us when they see how well the new tunnel is going, but it's up to us to carry on the work for a while."

"We're still better off than when we started," Matthew commented. "There's four of us instead of two."

All four men reached out and grasped hands in the center of their small circle. They gazed at each other with determined faces and headed toward their beds. Tomorrow was a new day.

Chapter Twenty-Seven

Carrie straightened up from examining one of her patients. She smiled warmly. "I think you're ready to go home."

"You're not kidding me?" Private Abner Scroll asked eagerly. "I can really go home?"

"Really," Carrie said. "You've healed very well. You're walking well on your crutches. I see no reason you can't go home." She paused. "You know it will take you some time to get your strength back."

"Yes," Abner mused, grinning. "But I reckon I'll be able to put a crop in this spring. Ain't got to do that for the last three years." His grin broadened. "I reckon my wife and kids will be right glad to see me."

"I imagine so," Carrie agreed. "They've only written you letters almost every day," she teased. She was quite certain it had been Abner's family who helped him pull through. Whenever the discouragement seemed to settle on like a dark cloud, he pulled out his thick sheaf of letters. Carrie thought fleetingly of the big stack of letters she still had from Aunt Abby from before the war. Their warm encouragement was still a balm to her soul when she teetered close to despair.

Abner lay back against his pillows, his eyes bright with excitement. "When can I leave?"

"I think there is a train heading up into the mountains in a couple of days. As long as the tracks stay free from snow," Carrie replied, "I see no reason you can't be on it." She wanted to ask him how he planned on planting a crop with one leg but didn't. She knew that raw determination could achieve many things. "We'll miss you around here, Abner."

"Indeed we will," a cheerful voice said. Dr. Wild strode up and reached out to grasp Abner's hand. "You're a very lucky man, Abner. I really didn't think we were going to save you last summer. You were closer to death than any man I have seen come through here and make it. I guess God still has something for you to do."

"Yes, sir," Abner said solemnly. "I think about that a lot. I been asking God every day what my future is going to be like." He paused, a thoughtful expression on his face.

"And what has God told you?" Dr. Wild asked.

Abner looked at both of them with deeply serious eyes. "I reckon God told me that the best way to predict your future is to go out and create it yourself."

Carrie stared at Abner, struck again by the wisdom of the young farmer. "Create it yourself..." she murmured.

"Yes, ma'am," Abner said. "I was lying here one night feeling right sorry for myself, having lost my leg and all. I didn't see that I could have no kind of future." He paused. "I was kind of wishing God had done taken me on that battlefield. I figured I wouldn't be nothing but a burden to my family."

"They would never feel that way," Carrie protested.

"No, ma'am," Abner agreed easily, "but I did, and my feelings were the ones I was listening to. Anyway," he continued, "I kept asking God what my future was gonna be like, but I wasn't getting no answers." He took a deep breath and grinned. "That's when I finally began to understand. God was telling me I would create my own future. That I didn't have to lie around and wait to see what would happen. I had to take charge of things."

"So what are you going to create?" Dr. Wild asked.

"I'm a farmer," Abner said. "I reckon to keep on farming. And I'm a daddy, so I reckon I'm going to be the best daddy I can be. And I'm going to be the best husband to Ardith I can be." He looked up and grinned. "One day, I'm going to have one of the biggest farms in western Virginia. You remember that."

Carrie nodded, a lump in her throat. "I believe you, Abner. I believe you."

"I'll be watching," Dr. Wild promised. He turned to Carrie. "When you are done here, may I see you a few minutes?"

"I was just getting ready to leave," Carrie said quickly. She reached over to grasp Abner's hand one more time and then followed Dr. Wild to his tiny, immaculate office.

"If you are free this afternoon, I would appreciate your help with something."

"Certainly," Carrie replied. "The hospital is almost empty now. I have plenty of time. What is it?"

"Belle Island Prison," Dr. Wild said grimly. "I've heard about the conditions over there. Dr. McCaw has asked if I will go over to deliver medical care. I would appreciate it if you would join me."

Carrie gripped the seat tightly to keep from crying out in horror as the hospital carriage rumbled across the bridge leading to Belle Island. She gazed out over the prison camp located on the extreme lower end of the island. Four acres of land had been set aside and surrounded by a three-foot embankment of frozen dirt. Just the other side of the embankment was a chain of sentinels, their guns up and ready in case there was an escape attempt. A ridge of low hills surrounded and overlooked the camp. She could see the pieces of artillery planted there, pointed ominously toward the camp.

It was the men that horrified Carrie, however. Everywhere she looked were skeleton-like figures covered with flapping rags. Most were shoeless. Their eyes stared around numbly. Some looked up as the wagon rolled past. Most stared stoically at the ground.

"Do they not feed these men?" Carrie cried indignantly, her stomach revolting at what she was seeing.

"Not enough," Dr. Wild growled, his eyes burning. "I had heard the conditions were bad, but I wasn't expecting this."

"It looks like nothing more than a death camp," Carrie whispered, shuddering in the warmth of her thick coat. Some of the prisoners had tents—if such ragged caricatures could be given such a name—but many of them seemed to have no shelter at all. They stretched out on wooden boxes or simply lay on the frozen ground, trying to soak up all the warmth from the feeble sun they could. Some were walking around, flapping their bony arms in a futile attempt to get warm. Carrie turned away, tears glimmering in her eyes.

"I can't believe humans can treat each other like this," she whispered. A deep loathing filled her heart and spirit.

"It's horrible," Dr. Wild agreed somberly.

One of the men stopped flapping his arms and walked toward the carriage. Dr. Wild pulled back on the reins before they ran him over.

"Get away from there!" a guard called. The man looked his direction and then turned back to look appealingly at Carrie. "Move or I'll shoot!" the guard yelled menacingly.

Carrie stood up quickly and glared at him. "You'll do no such thing," she snapped. "This man is causing no harm." She drew herself up erectly. "We are here by order of the medical commission. I would appreciate it if you would let us do our job." The guard grumbled but turned away.

"Thank you," the prisoner said gratefully. "Might you have a blanket in your carriage? It is fearfully cold out here."

Carrie examined the obviously well-educated man. "How long have you been here?"

"Just since New Year's Eve," he said, shivering. "They marched several hundred of us across the bridge through a dreadful snowstorm. I'm afraid we were stripped of our uniforms and handed the rags I am wearing now. Very few of us were lucky enough to keep our shoes." He glanced at Dr. Wild. "Do you know anything of a prisoner exchange?"

"I know a loud cry is being made for one, but so far I've heard no solid news."

"I see," the man said. His shoulders slumped forward and the shivering intensified.

Carrie stood up and reached under the seat, pulling out the one blanket she knew was there. "I wish I had more," she said. "There is so much need."

"Yes, ma'am," the man responded. "I assure you I will share my blanket with several of my friends. We take turns sleeping in shifts around here." He smiled and turned away.

Carrie watched him go before she turned and stared at Dr. Wild. "How can we do any good here? How can we treat sick men who have no shelter, no way to keep warm, and no food?" She scowled, anger boiling up and threatening to choke her. "I wonder how many of these men die every night." Her own question was answered as she gazed past the embankment and saw hundreds of small mounds of frozen earth. Her lips tightened and she sat back down.

"We'll do what we can."

"Do they treat our men like this?" Carrie asked.

"Prisoner-of-war camps are never pleasant places," Dr. Wild said hesitantly.

"But to treat them like animals?" Carrie cried. "Some of these men probably have family in Richmond." She pursued her earlier question. "Do they treat our men like this?" she pressed.

"I don't know," Dr. Wild admitted. "I have heard unpleasant reports, but I daresay that at least the North is better able to feed their prisoners."

"Until they find out what is happening here," Carrie snorted. "I'm sure there will be retribution."

"I'm afraid you're right," Dr. Wild replied. "Carrie, everyone in the South is battling hunger. Our soldiers exist on little more than what these men get. General Lee is constantly sending out appeals for food to feed his men."

"I know it's bad everywhere," Carrie whispered in a broken voice, "but to see it with my own eyes..." She blinked against her tears. "It breaks my heart to think our soldiers are treated this badly. This is simply inhumane."

A heavy wagon rolling across the wooden bridge arrested her attention. She looked up and watched it slow and then stop. A well-dressed Confederate official stood and shouted for attention. Most of the men watching him remained where they were, looking up with disinterest. Some stood and moved over to where they could better hear him.

The official waved his arm and read loudly from a piece of paper in his hands.

"The government of the Confederate States of America announces a prison exchange of five hundred men."

Carrie looked out as the whole clearing fell silent. The reading continued.

"The exchange will take place day after tomorrow at ten o'clock in the morning." The official looked up and cleared his voice. "Everyone with last names that begin with the letters A through E will be included in the exchange."

Weak cheering met his announcement. Carrie gazed out over the crowded field, seeing expressions of joy mixed with those of black despair. "How wonderful," she exclaimed.

"Yes. It should help," Dr. Wild murmured.

The official waved his hand for further attention. "There is a report, not yet verified, that another five hundred will be released in a few days."

More cheering met this announcement. Carrie watched as the men slapped each other on their backs. Groups of men were soon huddled together. She was sure they must be talking about home and what they would do when they escaped the confines of the camp.

The next three hours passed rapidly, though Carrie battled anger and despair. The men brought to them were, for the most part, far beyond their ability to save. The cold and lack of food had ravaged their bodies beyond possibility of restoration. She helped Dr. Wild pass out what little bits of medicine they had, and tried to offer hope where there was none.

One of the men, emaciated and flushed with fever, gazed up at Carrie with tortured eyes. "Why do they treat us this way? Why can't we get simple food and medicine? I don't think that is asking so much." His words were slurred and broken.

Dr. Wild put a hand on his shoulder. "Many of our own men are suffering," he said kindly, in an attempt to explain what was in reality unexplainable. "I'm afraid the Union blockade of our coast is rather a stunning success. Far too little is able to get through, and

Richmond is harder hit than any of the other cities. The rather dubious honor of being the Confederate capital seems to make us a favorite target."

He took a deep breath. "I am so sorry you are being treated this way. If I had the power to change things, I certainly would," he said, shaking his head sadly. "I don't expect this to be of any comfort to you, but there are many of our own citizens starving to death this winter as well."

"Hurrah for war," the soldier said grimly, and closed his eyes as another spasm of pain gripped him. Minutes later, he was carried off by several of the guards.

"What will happen to him?" Carrie whispered.

"He'll be dead by tonight."

Carrie and Dr. Wild were loading supplies into the wagon when the commander of the prison stepped up onto a platform and called for attention. The prisoners crowded close this time, eager to receive any word of the prisoner exchange.

The commander looked out over the men, his hard face tinged with compassion. "I'm afraid the government official was mistaken," he began in a loud voice. "The first five hundred men to be exchanged will happen as planned, but they are merely to meet the quota for a special exchange arranged between our two governments. The prisoner exchange program has not been reinstated. No more men will be leaving." He stepped down and walked rapidly to his office on the far side of the encampment.

"Oh no," Carrie whispered, watching the prisoners. Hundreds of faces were suddenly gripped with a despair even deeper than what she had initially witnessed. To have been so close to freedom only to have it snatched away seemed more than some of them could bear. Dozens turned away weeping. Several, overcome with emotion, began to beat themselves in anguish.

Carrie wept along with the men. "How awful," she cried, longing to set all of them free. The wretched men she saw in front of her were no danger to anyone. They simply wanted to go home and be with their families, surely to forget there was such a thing as war going on. Most of the men had been so physically broken they would never fight again.

She looked at Dr. Wild. "Get me out of here," she ordered in a sick voice.

Zeke and Susie looked carefully at the map George had given them and stared at the crossroads stretched out in front of them. "I don't see it anywhere," Zeke said in a bewildered voice.

"Are we lost?" Susie's voice trembled.

Zeke looked over and wrapped his arm around her comfortingly. "Well, I wouldn't say we are exactly lost. I just don't know for sure where we be." He straightened. "We got to keep heading east. That be the way the fort is. Sooner or later we'll find something we recognize on this map. Then we'll know where we are," he said.

Susie managed to smile at his determinedly cheerful voice. She knew he was trying to lift her spirits. Tucking her head against the wind, she pulled her coat closer to protect against the driving rain and continued to walk.

"Look at it this way," Zeke called above the wind, his own face buried in his collar. "There won't most likely be soldiers roaming around in this here weather. I reckon they be burrowed up somewhere they can be warm."

Susie didn't bother to answer. Her commitment to reaching Fort Monroe hadn't diminished, but her enthusiasm for walking in the rain certainly had. She would welcome the opportunity to worry about Confederate soldiers if she could only have dry ground to walk on. Patting her pocket to make sure the letter was still wrapped securely against the rain, she stepped around yet another large mud puddle.

Her mind flitted back to the cozy, warm cabin she had shared with Zeke. She loved the plantation. She loved watching her brother and sisters recover from their mother's death and their father's imprisonment, and thrive under Opal's care. But finally she had reached the point where she could no longer ignore her restlessness. Moses dropping by brought Zeke's restlessness to a head, and made her recognize her own. She knew she was doing the right thing—she just wished she didn't have to be so miserable doing it.

The hours sloshed by as they plodded down the dirt road, struggling against the mud that reached out in a miry attempt to claim them. The wind rose and fell in intervals, but the rain continued to fall steadily. Susie was soaked through to the bone and shivering violently when she spied a structure through the undergrowth. "Zeke!" she cried, stumbling as a puddle reached out to grab her.

"You all right?" Zeke called. He stopped and tipped his hat so he could see her.

Susie pointed toward the woods. "There's a building in there."

Zeke made a beeline for the woods. Moments later, he popped back out and waved her over to join him. "It ain't nothing fancy," he said, grinning, "but I reckon it's a place we can call home for tonight."

Susie brushed away the cobwebs tucked in the corner of the door frame and eased into the little cottage, which had clearly been deserted for a long time. It was dark and musty, with little of the gray light outside filtering through the one small window on the back wall.

"There be dry wood in the fireplace," Zeke called. "Somebody must have left here real quick."

"Probably running from a battle," Susie said, sweeping the room with her eyes. "Why don't you get a fire started?" she suggested. "There's a broom in the corner. I reckon I can get some of the dust stirred around and out of our way."

Ten minutes later, a fire was crackling brightly in the fireplace. After the cabin started to warm up, Suzie took off her coat and draped it over a table, then did the same with Zeke's. A stack of wood in the corner ensured her they would be dry by morning. She looked around again. "I wonder why the Union soldiers didn't burn this place."

"Probably weren't worth much to them," Zeke shrugged. "From what I can tell, they went after the big places. I got reports that Moses and his men did bunches of damage. Other raidin' parties been out doin' their mischief as well."

"Well," Susie said, "I'm glad for a warm, dry place tonight. I know we need to get that letter to General Butler, but I don't think I could have gone much further in this weather."

"It was sappin' the life out of us, sho 'nuff," Zeke said, staring contentedly at the fire. "I reckon we should be there in a couple of days. In spite of the rain, I figure we made right good time."

Susie yawned.

Zeke looked up and smiled. "I saw some blankets over there in the corner. I'm sure they gots lots of holes in them, but they'll still keep us warm. You get some sleep," he commanded. "I'll keep an eye on the fire." He reached into his sack and pulled out some food. "Don't you want some food before you sleep? You ain't eaten nothin' since lunch."

Susie shook her head and reached eagerly for the blankets, which were indeed full of holes. "Tired," she mumbled. She was asleep as soon as her head hit the floor.

Several times during the night, she heard Zeke fussing with the fire, but the steady ping of rain on the tin roof always lulled her back to sleep.

When Susie woke the next morning, she stretched mightily. Her body was refreshed, though stiff, from her night on the floor. Zeke snored quietly beside her. She glanced over at the fire still burning in the fireplace. He must have gotten up not too long ago to stoke it. She looked at him lovingly, grateful to have someone to take care of her. Sitting up slowly, she glanced toward the window. With a wide smile on her face, she threw aside her blankets and got up, moving quietly so as not to wake Zeke.

She closed the door behind her and drew in deep breaths of the rain-freshened air, letting the first rays of the morning sun bathe her face with its golden light. "Thank you that the rain has stopped," she whispered to the sky. She could feel her spirits rising with the sun.

She didn't know how long she stood out there before she heard the front door open. She spun around with a wide grin. "The rain has stopped!" she cried joyfully.

Zeke stared at the golden globe on the horizon and nodded his head with satisfaction. "I reckon we'd better be moving on."

Two days later, the sun was just setting when Susie and Zeke approached the outskirts of what they knew must be Fort Monroe. They had not encountered anyone else on the entire trip. They had slept the last night out in the open, but since there was no rain, Susie couldn't complain.

"I told you we'd make it," Zeke said proudly.

"Who goes there?" a loud voice called.

Zeke stepped forward. "I be Zeke. This here be my wife, Susie."

"More contrabands?" the soldier sighed. "We don't have many runaways who show up in the dead of winter." He cast a practiced look at the sky. "Lucky you made it. From the looks of things, there's gonna be a big storm hitting tonight."

Susie glanced around. Rolling toward them across the ocean was a menacing bank of gray clouds. "We're not runaways," she said. "We have an important message for General Butler."

"That so?" the guard said skeptically.

Susie saw Zeke open his mouth to explain, but she interrupted him. It would do no good to explain their situation to this man. He had no authority to do anything. She could still remember Mrs. Hamilton talking about the way things were done in the army. "I think it might be best if you took us to your commanding officer," she said firmly.

Respect flickered in the soldier's eyes. "That so?" he growled again. He looked as if he were about to refuse, but nodded his head abruptly. "Come with me."

Not too much later, Susie and Zeke were standing in front of General Butler himself. He leaned back and stared at them. "You wanted to see me?"

"Yes, sir," Susie said. "We have a letter for you."

"A letter?" General Butler barked. "You could have given it to one of my aides."

"No, sir," Susie said. "Mrs. Hamilton said the letter was only to be given to you."

The effect of Mrs. Hamilton's name was immediate. General Butler pushed away some papers on his massive oak desk and leaned toward them. "Mrs. Hamilton, you say?"

"I used to work for her." Susie knew she had his attention now. "A few days ago, a young boy knocked at our door. He had been wounded by a hunter. He had this letter." She pulled it from her pocket. "We brought it on."

"How did you get here?" he asked, puzzled. "The rain has made the roads all but impassable to wagons."

"We walked," Zeke said.

"You walked?" Butler exclaimed. "Through all that rain?" He shook his head in admiration and reached for the letter.

Susie handed it over willingly, glad to know their mission had been accomplished. She watched as he read, wondering at the look of intense concentration that crossed his face.

General Butler looked up. "Thank you for bringing this." He pocketed it and looked at them more closely. "We need to find someplace for you for the night. Maybe for the next few days, if that storm hits. Then you can go home. I'll have one of my men take you."

"We're stayin'," Zeke announced. "I plan on being a soldier."

"Good," Butler announced with satisfaction. "We can use more of your kind." He turned to Susie. "What about you?"

"I'm staying, too. I am looking for someone in the camps. Maybe you can tell me where to find her."

General Butler barked a hoarse laugh. "Ma'am, there are thousands of contrabands in that camp. You're going to have your work cut out for you. I'm afraid I'll be of no help."

"Her name is Rose," Susie pressed. "She's a teacher."

"Rose Samuels?" Butler asked.

"You know her?" Susie gasped, unable to believe their good fortune.

Butler nodded. "I'll have one of my men show you where she lives." Then he stood and walked to the door, dismissing them. "Thank you again for your service. I can assure you it was of immense value."

Zeke beamed. "What do I do about bein' a soldier?"

"Report to Barrack Four in two days. A new regiment is being formed. You'll be a part of it."

Susie glanced over at Zeke's excited face as they followed Butler down the immense hall. She tried to be excited for him but found it impossible. She would support him in what he believed he had to do, but she was not going to pretend she wasn't terrified she would never see him again once he went to war. Taking a deep breath, she reached out and grabbed his hand.

He squeezed hers hard and leaned over to whisper, "Everythin' gonna be fine."

Susie nodded. She no longer believed things like that. Life wasn't so simple. If it was, her mama wouldn't have been blown up by an exploding shell, and her daddy wouldn't be languishing in some prison. Her whole family wouldn't be split up. She managed a small smile and then looked ahead.

Rose put an arm around Susie's waist and hugged her warmly as they watched Zeke's boat pull away from shore. Both of them waved until the ship was almost out of sight.

Susie sighed, fighting back the tears threatening to overflow. "Goodbye," she whispered one more time. Rose hugged her again and Susie managed a smile. "Thank you for coming with me."

"I know how hard it is," Rose said. "I saw Moses off again just a few weeks ago."

"Does it get any easier?"

"No," Rose said after a pause. "I suppose I should tell you it does, but I'd be lying. Every time Moses leaves, a part of my heart goes with him." Rose sighed. "I had two weeks with him, though. Two glorious weeks. John had a chance to get to know his daddy, and I soaked up enough love to last me until he gets back."

"What if he doesn't come back?" Susie whispered.

"There's no use starting with that kind of talk," Rose said. "You've got to believe the best and then deal with whatever comes your way when it comes."

Susie stared into her dark eyes and found the courage she needed.

Rose took her hand and squeezed it. "Everything will work out," she said. "I, for one, am very glad to see you. I always need help with the school."

"You sure I won't be in the way in the house?"

"I'm sure," Rose said, smiling. "We always need more help with the boys. You're welcome to stay there as long as you want to. With you being Opal's cousin, I feel like you're my own family."

Susie's mind turned to other things as they walked up the wharf. "George said he thought the letter I delivered had something to do with the prisoners in Richmond," she said hopefully. "Maybe my daddy will be getting out."

Rose frowned. "I've heard a lot of talk about the prisons in Richmond," she said. "They're awful places."

"You know anyone in the prisons?"

"No," Rose replied. "I had a friend who was in Libby Prison for a while, but he was released because he was a journalist. His name is Matthew. I remember the haunted look in his eyes when he got home." She shuddered. "I'm so glad he's not there anymore. I don't think he could stand it."

Chapter Twenty-Eight

Matthew was shaken awake by Captain Anderson. "Tell your men not to go to the tunnel tonight," he whispered. He moved quickly away, looking furtively over his shoulder to see if a guard had noticed.

Matthew stared after him, alarmed. What had gone wrong? Had someone discovered their tunnel? Stuffing down his questions, he rose soundlessly and moved from man to man, whispering Anderson's instruction, merely shaking his head and moving on when they tried to question him. All of them would have to get their questions answered later.

Matthew discovered the reason for Anderson's instruction the next morning.

"Line up!" a guard shouted, slamming open the door before most of the men were even up.

Grumbling, the men staggered up, their frozen muscles stiff, and formed an irregular line. Matthew glanced over at Anderson, wondering what had put the hard look on his face.

"Count down!" the guard barked.

Matthew held his breath as the men counted. His stomach was already grumbling with hunger even though he had done no work last night. If the count was off, they would be forced to count again. A room with over one hundred men took a while. Five roll calls later, the guard still hadn't come up with a consistent number. He cursed and slammed out of the room for more help.

Matthew hid a smile. The men learned a long time ago how to confound the guards. When they were counting one group, men would shift from a group already counted and move into another. Some ingenious fellows had rigged up hats stuck to poles. In the hurry of a count, they usually passed as prisoners. At other times, one prisoner would answer for another, careful to keep his head down to escape detection.

Matthew's smile disappeared when Anderson sidled up next to him. "Five men escaped yesterday afternoon," he mouthed.

"What?" Matthew was stunned. "How?"

Anderson looked around carefully before he answered. "I heard the guards talking. All of them managed to get Rebel uniforms. They walked right out the door."

"Brilliant!" Matthew whistled, thinking of the long hours of work they had put in on the tunnel.

Anderson grunted. "Only one of them is still out. The other four got hauled in this morning. The guards are trying to figure out how many actually escaped."

Matthew whitened. "The poor men." He was thinking of them down in Rat Dungeon.

"The poor *fools*!" Anderson snapped. "They were idiots to think they could walk out of here in broad daylight and not expect to be caught. They were asking for trouble."

"I guess you get so desperate you'll try anything."

"Well they've wrecked things for us for a while. Those guards are going to watch us like hawks."

"They'll find our tunnel," Matthew said suddenly. "The guards might miss it, but men stuck down in Rat Dungeon are going to find it for sure."

"They're not going down there," Anderson replied. "They are being transferred to another prison." He grinned when Matthew looked at him quizzically. "I do a lot of listening. I've learned it pays off. Anyway," he continued, "those men are being sent away. Richmond is catching a lot of flak from Lincoln about the prison camps. Seems enough stories have leaked out. Richmond is trying to cover their backsides, but the truth is getting out."

"Thank God," Matthew breathed.

"Don't get excited. Nothing is going to change. They're letting a few relief supplies filter through to Belle Island, but nothing is going to be any different. They haven't scheduled any prisoner exchanges. The guards have been told to look like they're easing up, but to watch us like hawks."

Matthew groaned. "We're so close."

"Yes," Anderson said grimly. He turned to walk away. "I'll let you know when it's safe again."

Matthew spent the rest of the day staring out the window at the empty lot they were digging toward. When Anderson strolled by in the afternoon, he called him over. "I've been thinking. We can't stop work on the tunnel now."

"The guards will be watching us too closely," Anderson protested. "It will be too risky."

"It will be more risky to *not* keep digging," Matthew insisted. "Those guards are going to be sticking their noses into everything. Sooner or later, they're going to find our tunnel. I, for one, am not willing for all of our work to be undone. Besides," he said, "if we lay back now, the men are going to get discouraged again. Too many of them are barely hanging on. I know they all came back after they saw how well the third tunnel is going, but it wouldn't take much to make them give up again."

"Let them give up," Anderson snorted. "We don't need them."

"No," Matthew agreed quietly, "but they need us. They're counting on us."

Anderson leaned back and studied him. "You have a plan don't you?" He smiled. "I should have known. What is it?"

"Keep the men working, but only at night when there is the least chance of detection." Matthew took a deep breath. "I'm going to go down there and work around the clock."

Anderson stared at him. "Come again?"

"It's the only way," Matthew insisted, swallowing the fear he felt at being alone in Rat Dungeon. He had thought it through. If they were going to make it out of here, they were going to have to take drastic action. He was the only one who had lived down in the dungeon. As much as he abhorred the idea, he knew he could stand it if freedom was waiting on the other side.

"You won't be able to do it," Anderson said flatly. "I know what it's like down there." He leaned forward. "We'll find another way."

Matthew shook his head stubbornly. "There's not another way. Look, Anderson, I'm going to be free. I'm getting out of this place. If no one else comes with me, that's fine, but I'm going to dig that tunnel and escape." He glared at his friend. "Are you with me or not?"

Anderson stared at him. Then suddenly he grinned. "You're the toughest newspaper reporter I've ever met." He reached out and grasped his hand. "We'll take four men down there tonight," he promised.

Matthew nodded. "Others of the men can answer for them at roll call. Someone different can answer for me every time. That way it will keep them guessing."

"What are you going to do if the guards go down into the hole?"

Matthew shrugged. "I guess I'll figure that out when the time comes."

One week later, Matthew leaned against the cellar wall and stared at the tunnel they were building. They had managed to conceal it fairly well behind a loose lattice of boards that they stuffed every morning with dirt, but close inspection could not help but reveal it. He shifted his weight as a rat scurried past his leg and nibbled at the food Anderson had brought down the night before.

Matthew knew he was close to the end of his endurance. His body ached from eighteen hours of digging a day. He allowed himself somewhere between four to five hours of sleep a day, grabbed in snatches when he thought he was safe from investigating guards. Anderson brought him food, but he was burning it off at a much faster rate than he was ingesting it. Hunger gnawed at his stomach. He was taking in his belt every few days. It was the loneliness, though, that was sapping his energy. Except for the five hours the men came down from upstairs, he spent every minute of the day completely alone. Buried in the tunnel, he sometimes had to fight to convince himself anyone was still alive in the world.

"It's worth it," he whispered fiercely, more to hear a human voice than to convince himself. His burning desire to escape had not diminished even a tiny bit. If anything, the passion burned brighter, fueled by every box of dirt he shoved out of the tunnel. He took another bite of biscuit and chewed it slowly to make it last as long as possible. As he ate, he allowed himself to imagine all the things that would be waiting once they reached freedom.

The clanking of the door leading down to the cellar jerked him back to the present. Matthew bolted upright, his pulse racing but his mind calm. Moving quickly but carefully, he dashed to the far corner, away from the tunnel, and pulled the straw aside. When the first guard descended the stairs, Matthew was crouched in the small hole he had dug. The straw was pulled back over it in what he hoped was a convincing fashion.

"I hate this place," one of the guards complained.

"Well, the commander said to check every single inch of this prison. Word has filtered through that a big escape is planned," another guard snapped. "The faster we do it, the faster we can get out of this hole." The revulsion was evident in his voice.

"I haven't heard anything about an escape," the first guard argued. "I heard some kind of rumor that the Federals were going to try some big breakout, though." He chuckled. "Let 'em come. We'll be ready for them."

Matthew sucked in his breath and froze, afraid even that small sound could be detected. His mind raced. Was Lincoln sending down men to set them free?

"Oh sure," the other guard scoffed. "Do you know what kind of chaos would be set loose in this town if all these prisoners were to get free? I'm plenty worried," he growled. "General Lee and his men are too far away to stop it if something big happens."

That seemed to shut the first guard up. Matthew strained to hear. Their footsteps rustled the straw, but it was impossible to tell where they were. He heard their footsteps stop. He held his breath and prayed they had not discovered the tunnel.

"What's this?" the first guard called sharply.

Matthew stopped breathing. After all their hard work, it looked like the game was up.

"Looks like old, moldy bread," the other guard snapped. "We're supposed to be looking for an escape route, not lunch."

"Where'd it come from?" the first guard growled defensively. "There haven't been prisoners down here for a month," he argued.

"One of the prisoners left it."

Matthew could almost see the guard shrugging his shoulders. He cursed himself as he realized he must have let some food drop from his bag at some point.

"The rats would have eaten it," the first guard insisted.

Matthew shifted his weight slightly, trying to ease the cramps ripping through his stiff muscles. He froze when the straw rustled above him.

"What was that?"

Matthew's blood ran cold when he heard footsteps approaching. If he hadn't been so frightened, he might have admired the man's intelligence and perseverance. He held his breath again when the footsteps halted inches from the edge of his crudely concealed hole.

A long silence followed.

"It was one of your rats," the other guard said in disgust. "Look, do you see any kind of an escape route out of here?" he snapped.

"No," the first guard said slowly.

"Neither do I. And I've had about all of Rat Dungeon I care to experience. We came. We looked. We didn't find anything." The angry tirade halted for a brief second and then continued in a patronizing voice. "Unless you'd like to go up and tell the commander you found a stale piece of bread. That will really impress him."

"It could mean something," the first guard insisted, but the enthusiasm was gone from his voice. "All right," he finally growled. "Let's get out of here." He paused. "I always felt sorry for the bums that had to stay down here."

"They got what they deserved," the other guard sneered.

Matthew longed to lunge out of the straw, take him captive, and leave him in the hellish dungeon for a few months. It wouldn't take him long to be singing a different tune.

"Maybe," the other guard said thoughtfully. "Still, I'm glad it wasn't me."

"If we don't get upstairs and give our report, it may be," the other man snapped. "Let's go."

Matthew waited several minutes after he heard the door slam shut before he staggered to his feet and threw himself on the ground. Sweat poured from his face and his breath came in shallow gasps. He knew exactly how close he had come to being discovered.

When Anderson and his men arrived that night, Matthew was waiting for them. "We've got to speed things up," he said urgently. "The guards suspect something. They're poking around everywhere." He quietly told them what happened, his voice barely above a whisper.

"They've been poking around upstairs, too," Anderson acknowledged. "But they won't ever think about pulling the stove out in the kitchen."

"Well, if those two guards who were down here today had better lights, they would have found our tunnel." Matthew knew his voice was desperate, but he couldn't help it. The strain was wearing on him.

Anderson reached out and put a steadying hand on his arm. "I've been doing some calculating. According to my figures, we should be there."

Matthew stared at him, his numbed mind not registering Anderson's words. "Be where?"

"Be in the lot behind the fence," Anderson grinned triumphantly. "I say we go up tonight."

Hope soared in Matthew like an eagle taking flight. He stared at Anderson and took a deep breath. "What are we waiting for?"

"You first, old man," Anderson replied.

Matthew crawled eagerly into the tunnel that was becoming like home to him. He knew every inch of the tunnel like the back of his hand. He could close his eyes and tell by the smell of the soil where he was. It took only a few minutes to scramble to the end of the tunnel. Once he was there, he began to dig upward, his heart pounding with excitement. The earth seemed to melt away before his eager digging.

Matthew gasped when his knife suddenly broke through the ground above. Fresh air came rushing at him. Matthew took deep breaths and continued to dig carefully. He reached back and touched Anderson's arm to signal that he had reached the top. Anderson's only response was to pat his leg excitedly.

It took only a few minutes to get the hole big enough to stick his head out. Breathing a prayer of thankfulness, Matthew eased his head up cautiously.

A sudden movement caught his eye, and Matthew immediately ducked back into the hole, his heart pulsating with fear. Frantically, he motioned for Anderson to back out.

"We hit the wrong place," he said quietly, his fear now replaced with savage disappointment. "The hole came out in an empty lot all right, but it's the one adjacent to the prison. I was almost seen by a guard standing not six feet from where I poked my head up." The sweat started to bead on his forehead as he considered how close he had been.

Anderson listened grimly. "I must have miscalculated."

"You might want to go back to the drawing board," Peter suggested, drawing a weak smile from all of them.

"I have an idea," Matthew said. All eyes turned toward him. "It's pretty hard to figure out where we are when we're tunneling underground. I've got to go back in and cover up that hole."

"How are you going to do that?" Peter asked.

"I'm going to take my shirt back, cover it with dirt and stick it up through the hole. It won't be perfect, but unless someone is really looking for it, they won't see it."

"Unless they walk on it," Anderson said.

Matthew didn't bother to respond to the obvious. His mind was racing too fast. "When I go back, I'll take one of my shoes off and shove it out of the hole." He glanced at Anderson. "You can look out the window, find the shoe, and refigure your calculations from there." He stopped and looked at Anderson expectantly.

Anderson grinned. "You really are smarter than you look." He nodded enthusiastically. "I think it will work."

"Except when you have to walk out of here to escape, you may wish you had that shoe," Peter observed.

"If I'm lucky, I'll pick it up on my way out." Matthew grinned, his hope once more restored now that another plan was in place. "Men, we'll be out of here in less than a week!"

Matthew's prophecy was correct. One week later, he backed out of the tunnel and motioned for Anderson to go in. He kept his eyes on the tunnel, not looking up at the men he knew were staring at him expectantly. He didn't want them to see the smile flickering on his lips. The original plan had been Anderson's. He should be the one who announced their success.

Five minutes later, Anderson backed out into the dim, yellow light from the three candles burning in the dank cellar. He looked up, a wide grin exploding on his face.

Silent joy erupted in Rat Dungeon. The four men watching shook hands and hugged each other exuberantly. Moments later, they were all clustered in the kitchen.

"What's it like out there?" Peter asked.

"Freedom never smelled so good," Anderson said joyfully. He took a deep breath. "This is just the first step," he reminded them. He went over, once again, the plan he and Matthew had devised for when they were out of the tunnel. The men listened closely, nodding that they understood.

"Each man here will tell those of the original group," Matthew said. "No one else is to know."

"Seems a shame for all that work to be used only by fifteen men," Peter said.

"It's not only for us," Matthew confessed. "We decided last week to bring Lieutenant Sadler in on the plans, on the condition he keep the hole a secret for exactly one hour after we make our escape. Then he can broadcast it. After that, it's up to each man."

Anderson stood, indicating a close to the meeting. "Everyone go to bed," he ordered. "We're going to need to be well-rested before we break out. We've done the hardest part, but what lies ahead of us isn't easy."

Matthew looked down at the hole leading to Rat Dungeon. "I think I'm going to stay up here tonight. I've become very appreciative of sleeping on hardwood floors while I'm shivering." All the men laughed as he led the way to their floor.

Matthew stared up into the darkness, unable to sleep now that freedom was so near. He prayed, knowing a hundred things could still go wrong. Someone could find either of the two holes they had broken through to the lots with. One of the men, in their excitement, could let something slip. A huge rainstorm could cause the ground to cave in around the holes they had dug. "God brought us this far," he finally muttered, rolling over and forcing his eyes closed.

Chapter Twenty-Nine

Carrie leaned back in the carriage seat, took a deep breath of the cold, crisp air, and smiled happily at Robert. "I can hardly believe we're going to a party."

"A starvation party. No food, but there will be plenty of music and dancing," Robert promised. "Thank you for coming with me."

Carrie smiled up at him again, snuggled close under the lap blanket, and watched Spencer's broad shoulders silhouetted against the starry sky. She knew Robert was saying that he understood how she felt about parties during such hard times as these. Carrie still wasn't sure how people could be in the mood for laughing and gaiety when the whole world was exploding around them, but the shivers of excitement running down her spine were beginning to give her a glimmer of understanding. In difficult times, perhaps especially in difficult times, one did whatever they could to infuse light into darkness, to bring laughter into despair. Scores of people during the brutal winter of 1864 were dancing and partying in gay defiance of the dark cloud covering, and threatening to suffocate, the capital city.

Carrie lay back and gazed up at the shimmering sky. After so many gray, cloudy days and nights, a brisk breeze had blown in from the north that morning, scattering the thick clouds as if they had been nothing more than dandelion fuzz. Now the sky was brilliant with a million stars, twinkling and winking as they blazed across the heavens. "It's beautiful," she said softly, staring up in awe.

"Yes, it is," Robert agreed.

Carrie turned to look at her husband and threw her head back, letting loose a loud whoop of happiness. Then she giggled. "Don't bother to tell me how unladylike that was. I simply won't care if you do. I'll merely think you're stuffy."

"I would never do such a thing." Robert's eyes danced with laughter. "I learned a long time ago exactly how impulsive my beautiful wife is."

Carrie turned serious. "I know how very fortunate I am. I've almost lost you in battle. You almost drowned in the ocean. And somehow you managed to escape Lee's order a few weeks ago for all able men to be taken to the front." She shuddered. "I can still see some of my weak soldiers climbing out of bed because they were deemed strong enough to fight," she said angrily.

"I'm glad President Davis still thinks I'm valuable enough to him to be able to stay in Richmond. I have no illusions that I won't be called back to the front eventually, but I'm determined to enjoy all the time we have together now."

"Exactly," Carrie replied. "I think of how many women have lost their husbands, their sons, their fathers. And I still have both of the men in my life," she said, tears shimmering in her eyes. She turned and took both of Robert's hands in hers. "Have I told you today how much I love you?"

"A few times." Robert gazed at her lovingly. "But I'll never get tired of hearing it."

The carriage rolled rapidly down the dark streets of the city. The cold weather seemed to have driven most of the residents inside to huddle around whatever inadequate source of heat they had. Most of the gaslights along the street remained dark because of scarcity of fuel, but Carrie saw nothing forbidding in the shadows tonight. Nothing could touch her as long as she was with Robert.

Piles of snow were still mounded on the sidewalks and along the edges of the street. Tree limbs, brittle in the cold weather, clapped and clacked against each other in a wild celebration of winter. An occasional dog, thin from lack of food, skulked across the roads, nosing into trashcans in the hope of finding a morsel of food human scavengers had overlooked. The few people they encountered had their heads tucked deep into their coats, not bothering to look up when the carriage rolled by.

As they drew nearer to the heart of town, activity picked up a little. More houses had dim lights glimmering from their windows. The sidewalks and streets were shoveled clear of snow. As they turned onto Franklin Street, Carrie drew in her breath with excitement. Bright lights shone onto the porch of the large three-story house they stopped in front of. She knew the light of day would reveal the drooping paint and fences, but for this one night, the old mansion—its yard covered with snow, its lines softened by the inky sky—reveled in all its former glory.

"I haven't been to a party since you proposed to me," she whispered.

"May this be a night you'll never forget," Robert said, holding out his hand with a smile. "I'm proud to be escorting the most beautiful woman here."

Carrie laughed. "At least I will be unique." Short of her wedding gown, which she would not consider wearing, Carrie had found nothing in her meager wardrobe that would be appropriate for any kind of party. Her faded blue dresses, worn and stained from her hours in the hospital, would never have done. She had long ago given away every other piece of clothing for bandages. The kind old lady next door had heard of her dilemma and come to her rescue, loaning her one of the few dresses she had saved back.

"I think you look like a doll," Robert insisted.

"An antique doll," Carrie commented. The dress was beautiful, but it was from another time. Its puckered sleeves and high, tight neckline were softened somewhat by the yards of creamy lace sewn onto a rose silk. It was a good thing she didn't care much for fashion, she had decided when she had held it up and smiled her gratitude to the old woman.

"Do you really care so much?" Robert asked in sudden concern. "I don't want you to be uncomfortable."

Carrie's laugh rang out through the cold, still air like a tinkling bell, causing several of the guests climbing the stairs to turn and look. "Care so much?" she scoffed. "Why, I don't care at all! There is a war going on, for heaven's sake. I hardly think anyone is going to be concerned with my apparel. If they are, I find I already feel rather sorry for them."

Robert drew her close in a warm hug and then set her back. "May I have the next dance, Mrs. Borden?" he asked solemnly.

Carrie shivered with delight, completely forgetting the cold as she envisioned the magic that always swept her away when she danced with Robert. She placed her hand in his eagerly. "Lead the way, Mr. Borden."

Once they greeted their hosts, Robert led Carrie into the large, brightly lit room. In the typical tradition of Richmond wartime parties, there was not a single drop of drink, nor a morsel of food anywhere in sight. No one seemed to mind. The room, warmed by a blazing fire and a throng of bodies, buzzed with conversation and music. Carrie relaxed as she looked around at the other women. She really hadn't cared much what she was wearing, but it helped to see other women in their everyday dresses, minus the jewelry that had once glittered brightly, but now had been donated to the Confederate cause.

Robert swept her onto the dance floor as soon as the next song started. Carrie started to protest that she had not greeted a single soul but clamped her lips shut. Those people would still be there when she was done dancing with her husband.

The old magic consumed her like it always had. The room, the people, the brutal winter, the raging war, all fell away, disappearing into a misty shadowland as Robert whirled her across the floor. For this moment, it was just them. Their love bound them close and spun them in a dance of joy.

***

Matthew had sat at the window all day, letting the brisk wind bathe his face as he watched the clouds chase across the sky and retreat before the bright blue that surrounded the setting sun. Now, the sky was brilliantly clear, alive with millions of stars. It was a perfect night. His body tingled with excitement. Three more hours, and they would all meet in the kitchen as planned. Matthew stared down at his shoeless feet, flexing his freezing toes, speculating on the fact that his anticipation was making him hardly feel them. His other shoe was stuffed inside his blanket. No shoes were easier to explain than one shoe. When a guard had questioned him, he merely shrugged and said, "Lost them in a bet." The guard had smirked knowingly and walked away.

Anderson eased over to join him. "There's not a single guard on our floor," he said quietly. "They cleared out early tonight."

"The scare of another escape is wearing off," Matthew replied. He grinned. "Boy, are they in for a surprise in the morning."

"You got that right," Anderson chuckled, slapping him on the shoulder. "See you in a little while."

Matthew watched him walk away, then turned back to his inspection of the outside. His shoe was still lying where he had left it. He could barely make it out, and only then because he knew where he was looking. No one had seemed to notice the worn out piece of leather.

In spite of his best efforts, his eyes lifted in the direction of Church Hill. He wondered if Carrie was still there, still safe in her warm house. His heart reached out to her, even as he forced his eyes to turn away. The few blocks separating them might as well have been a thousand miles. It was best that way.

Carrie pulled away from Robert, laughing breathlessly as they finished up a rousing Virginia reel. "They do have water, don't they? I'm about to perish from thirst."

"Only the finest water for my lovely wife," Robert said, bowing gallantly. "I'll be right back."

Carrie looked around the room while she waited. She was surprised to find she didn't know most of the other women in the room. She had been fairly familiar with

Richmond society before the war and even during the first year of it. The faces seemed to have all changed.

"Trying to find someone you know?" A teasing voice broke into her thoughts.

"Natalie!" Carrie gasped, spinning around and grabbing her old friend in a warm hug. "I had no idea you were still in the city."

"Kind of easy to lose people with the thousands pouring in," Natalie said. "For the life of me I can't figure out why people come here. Those of us who were born here can claim a reason to stay through starvation and suffering. It's the ones who come looking for it that leave me mystified."

Carrie laughed. "You haven't changed."

Natalie's eyes turned serious. "Oh, I've changed," she admitted. "I'm no longer the innocent little girl you traveled to Philadelphia with to visit my Aunt Abby."

Carrie's eyes misted over. "I miss her so much."

"You two formed a special bond," Natalie agreed.

"Have you..."

"Heard from her?" Natalie finished. "Getting mail from the North is about as difficult as getting a real cup of coffee in this city." She snorted. "Impossible."

Carrie laughed again. She had always enjoyed Natalie's easy humor. She assumed her friend had long ago left the city. Her family had a wonderful place in North Carolina. "Why are you still here?" she asked.

"I told you I'd changed," Natalie replied. "You thought I would be in North Carolina, didn't you?" She didn't wait for an answer. "I could be. My family left when McClellan threatened the city." She stopped, staring out over the dancers. "My place is here. My husband is fighting with General Lee."

"You're married?" Carrie cried. "I didn't know."

"Right after the war started." A tender smile played on Natalie's lips. "I met Theodore at one of the parties. It was love at first sight." She laughed. "And I don't even believe in love at first sight!"

"You've stayed in the city to be closer to him," Carrie guessed.

Natalie nodded. "I've only seen him twice in the last two years—once when they were marching through town. It was only for thirty minutes, but it was enough to keep my heart hoping." She looked sad for a moment but soon brightened. "In the meantime, I do everything I can. I've nursed sick soldiers in my home, made so many bandages I can do it in my dreams, and held benefits to raise money for our glorious cause."

Carrie decided not to comment on the *glorious cause.* "I hope you'll see him soon," she said.

Natalie smiled wistfully and shook her head. "Enough about me. What about you?"

Carrie started to fill her in. She was getting ready to tell her about Robert when he came striding toward them, two glasses of water in his hands. "And this is my husband," she finished with a smile.

"So you did marry this good-looking thing," Natalie cried with her usual abandon.

"Do I take that as approval?" Robert asked.

Natalie turned to Carrie. "I'm so happy for you." She gripped Carrie's hand. "How are you so lucky? How is it that such a dashing man in a captain's stripes is hanging out in Richmond?"

Carrie felt a twinge of guilt but shoved it aside. She had done her share of suffering. No one would commandeer the joy she had now. She was sure the future would steal it soon enough. "He seems to be indispensable to President Davis right now," she replied. "I am very fortunate."

The three chatted for a few more minutes until Natalie moved off with a promise to be in touch soon.

Robert handed over the glasses of water. "I'm glad she didn't look thirsty. I thought about being gallant and offering mine, but I have to confess I didn't want to." Quickly, he drained his glass.

Carrie followed suit. "Do you know many of the people here?" she asked.

"Richmond is full of new faces," Robert replied. "Most of the men here are connected with the government in some way. That's the only reason they're not with the army somewhere. Would you like to meet some of them? I'm afraid I'm not as familiar with the women."

"Yes, please." Carrie wasn't up to engaging in idle small talk tonight anyway. She much preferred what she knew would be the more serious conversation of the men. She had stayed close to her hospital work for months now, and was surprised to realize how much she missed the stimulation of conversation.

Robert led her up to a small knot of men. "Gentlemen," he said, nodding slightly.

"Welcome, Captain Borden, isn't it?" a short, round-faced man asked.

"Indeed it is, Mr. Whipple," Robert answered. He pulled Carrie forward. "I'd like you to meet my wife, Carrie Borden."

Mr. Whipple bowed slightly. "It's a pleasure, ma'am."

The other men in the group graciously acknowledged the introductions and then turned back to their talk. Carrie was content to listen. She was suddenly hungry to find out what was going on from a perspective other than her father's.

Mr. Whipple was the first to speak. "Our Congress has given Davis writ of habeas corpus again," he said sourly.

"I don't know that he had much choice," another man replied in a reasonable voice. "Our armies are being crippled by absenteeism. The number of deserters has increased, and many of the men who are drafted aren't showing up."

"I would venture it safe to say the enthusiasm for the war has rather declined," one added. "That's hardly a reason to give Davis such power."

"That's not the point," the man on Davis' side insisted. "We are losing battles because we don't have enough men. Lee is forced to stay on the defensive or plan rather moderate offenses because he quite simply doesn't have the men he needs to do something more effective." He took a deep breath, obviously gearing up for his final point. "There are so many absentees that if they were all to show up in camp at the same time, we would be able to face the North on equal terms."

Robert coughed and all eyes turned toward him. He was the only one present in uniform. "I'm afraid your sources might be somewhat incorrect. I agree there are a horrible number of absentees, but it is simply not possible for the South to match the North man for man. Their population is quite a bit more substantial than ours."

"Then you're saying there is no way for the South to win?"

Carrie watched Robert closely. How would he respond? He opened his mouth, but Whipple interrupted him.

"Don't y'all understand that the writ places in peril the sacred principle that led to secession in the first place?" Whipple protested. "I fear that with our whole country under martial law, and with our imminent president enforcing it..." He paused, his voice leaving no doubt of just how imminent he thought Davis was, and shook his head dolefully. "I fear our constitutional liberty has become a mockery. I think it would be much better for our country to be overrun by the Yankees, our cities sacked and burned, and our land laid desolate." He paused again. "I would much prefer that to our citizens' personal liberties being taken away by professed friends."

Carrie gazed with interest at his reddened face and bulging eyes. He obviously knew he was a minority, but he was quite determined to state his case. That he had done so with great passion could not be denied.

One man, a touch of irritation in his voice, swung to face Whipple. "Were you not in favor of secession?"

"Well, of course I was," Whipple snapped.

"Then surely you realize the price that must be paid. Oh, I know you're parroting the sentiments of our Vice President Stephens. You people are all the same," he snapped.

Whipple flushed even redder. "What do you mean?" he demanded.

"Everyone has to have someone to blame when things don't go right. This spring you were praising Davis," he reminded Whipple. "After the battle at Chancellorsville, you were touting that all of us had to make great sacrifices for the country—that no amount was too much." His voice grew scornful. "We run into a few setbacks, and now it's all Davis' fault. You criticize everything he does. How convenient to have a scapegoat!" Having spoken his mind, the man wheeled on his heel and spun away, his eyes flashing.

"He is a close aide to Davis," Robert whispered to Carrie.

Carrie nodded and continued to watch Whipple. The man's attack had subdued him, but he was certainly not cowed. His face was set stubbornly, his lips narrow with anger.

Another man spoke into the silence. Carrie remembered him as Mr. Count from North Carolina.

"I believe the president received a letter from Governor Vance of North Carolina recently."

"I heard something about that," Robert said eagerly. "What can you tell me?"

Carrie watched the tension dissipate as the attention swung away from Whipple. He took out a handkerchief and mopped his brow, listening eagerly. Carrie had to admire his courage. It was never easy to take a disparate stand when you were the only one of your belief present.

"Vance wrote to Davis to appeal for his help," Count began. "As most of you know, North Carolina's was not a loud voice for secession. We went along with the rest when Lincoln called for us to take up arms against the South, but I'm afraid we don't possess the passion some of the states do."

"Well, at least you're willing to look at it honestly," Robert said.

Count shrugged. "It's the truth."

Carrie looked at him more closely. She liked his kind face and intelligent eyes. Gray hair swept down over his creased forehead. She leaned forward closer to listen.

"Vance informed Davis there is much discontent in our state. He believes it can be removed by negotiation with the North."

"He is calling for submission?" one man asked in a shocked voice.

"Certainly not," Count said. "Vance is quite certain Washington will reject the fair terms we would submit to him, but he believes if our people see that, it will greatly strengthen and intensify the war feeling. He believes it will rally support for the government."

"Vance is saying that such a move would convince North Carolinians that the government cares about them and would never ask them to risk their lives any longer than necessary," Robert stated, his brow creased thoughtfully.

"Exactly," Count agreed.

"But negotiation has been tried," one man offered. "They wouldn't even receive Stephens six months ago. You can't negotiate if you have no one to talk to."

"And Davis has been announcing his desire for peace since the beginning of the war," another added bitterly. "We have made our desire to be left alone quite clear. I don't know what else can be done."

"Nothing can be done," another announced in a loud voice, stepping forward into the center of the circle.

Carrie tried to remember who he was. Finally it came to her. He was Mr. Mitchell from Georgia.

"President Lincoln has made his position quite clear. He has informed us in the last few months that we can only expect his gracious pardon by emancipating all our slaves and swearing allegiance and obedience to him and his proclamations." He took a breath. "In point of fact, Lincoln would desire that we become the slaves of our own Negroes." His burning gaze swept Count. "Can there really be in North Carolina one citizen who has so fallen beneath the dignity of his ancestors as to accept those terms?" His voice left no doubt where he stood.

Mr. Mitchell, realizing he had the attention of everyone, drew himself up and proceeded to fire another round. "It is with Lincoln alone that we could ever hope to confer, and he has made himself clear. He will never treat with us—on *any* terms. Our only possible recourse is to go on fighting until the enemy is willing to admit complete defeat. Not until then will it be possible to speak of peace."

A heavy silence fell over the group. As much as some might not want to admit it, the South had indeed set a course that was too late to change now. It was either fight on to complete victory, or admit to complete defeat. Gone were the days when Lincoln appealed for the South to return, saying he would not interfere with their right to own slaves. The viciousness of the war had changed all that. It had changed everything. The dark cloud that had descended on the land had blinded men to anything that might have ended the destruction. The only recourse was to fight on, hoping that the raging fire would leave something worth rebuilding when it burned itself out on the hearts and souls of men, women and children.

At eight o'clock sharp, Matthew and Captain Anderson moved the stove away from the kitchen fireplace and opened the hole. Solemnly, they shook hands with the other thirteen men who made the tunnel possible. No words were spoken. None were necessary. Everything had already been said.

Matthew took a deep breath and climbed down into Rat Dungeon for the last time. At least, he fervently hoped it was the last time. Peter, his partner in the allotted twosomes, was close behind him. Captain Anderson and Lieutenant Wilson were right behind them.

Matthew felt his feet hit the bottom and then lit one of the candles and attached it to the wall. Without waiting for the rest of the men, he dropped to his knees and began to crawl. He carried no light. He didn't need one. Every inch of the fifty foot tunnel was imbedded in his brain and heart. It had become his child. Now, it was offering him freedom. He could feel Peter breathing behind him. The two had come in together, and now they would go out together.

Matthew reached the end of the tunnel and raised himself to his knees. He carefully pushed aside the dirt-covered board that hid the exit. His heart pounding in his ears, he eased his head up slowly and looked around. The sky was crystal clear, the air so cold it made him gasp for breath. He grinned broadly, pushed himself up, and crawled out onto the ground. Reaching back a hand for Peter, he helped his friend up and then shook the dirt from his hair and beard.

Peter looked over at him and gave the thumbs up signal. Matthew reached over to shake hands with him and then they stood and walked out of the lot, heading down the dark street. Matthew held his breath, every second expecting a loud call to announce their presence. They strode briskly but steadily for two blocks and then turned right and ducked into the darkened shadow of a building.

Matthew brushed at the sweat on his face and tried to steady his breathing. They had done it! They were out!

Peter peered around the corner. "I don't see anyone else," he whispered.

"It's too soon," Matthew replied. "Anderson and Wilson were to wait three minutes before they came out. It hasn't been that long."

"It seems like hours."

Matthew nodded. Their stroll down the street had indeed seemed like a lifetime. He glanced ahead and waved his hand at Peter. "We have to keep moving," he said. "All of us are on our own from this point."

Peter peered around the corner again for a second before he followed. Matthew understood. He was fighting the temptation to rush back and make sure nothing had gone wrong. Four men would have offered more comfort than two, but they also would attract more attention. They had agreed everyone stood the best chance of escaping capture if they proceeded in groups of two. Matthew knew he might never see any of his friends again. They had indeed escaped the prison, but they were still deep in the heart of the Confederate capital. As soon as the alarm was raised, the search would be on. Matthew figured they had twenty-four hours at the very most to get out of Richmond.

Matthew glanced quickly at the street sign. He knew the city fairly well from his earlier visits, and he had prepared the other men the best he could. Turning right on Canal Street, he headed east for several blocks, then turned north on Twelfth Street. They passed the imposing Capitol Building, glowing softly from the brightness of the sky.

"It's beautiful," Peter commented.

Matthew was still too tense for casual talk. He knew they had a long way to go before they were safe. All his energy was directed toward one thing—getting out of there. He frowned as he realized the streets were practically deserted. He knew the cold weather was keeping people in their frigid homes. He also knew it would cause the two men to stand out even more. Their nondescript prison clothes would identify them as workers. The fact that neither of them had coats on a night that had already dipped well below freezing would make them look like lunatics. Matthew hugged the shadows as they strode along.

"Halt!"

Matthew hesitated as the commanding voice rang out in the still air but kept walking forward. Peter tensed and looked around but continued to follow him. Praying desperately, Matthew hoped that whoever had called out was not referring to them.

"Halt!" The voice was closer behind them this time

Matthew groaned and swung around. "Are you talking to us?" he asked with forced cheer.

A burly policeman strode up to them, scowling. "What are you fellows doing out this time of night?" he said suspiciously.

Matthew prayed Peter would let him do all the talking. His friend's strong New York accent would give him away in a heartbeat. "Just on our way home from work," Matthew continued.

"Where do you work?"

"Down at the iron works," Matthew said. He figured it employed enough men that it would make him the least suspect.

The policeman edged closer. "You ain't from around here, are you?"

Matthew's heart pounded faster. "My folks sent me up north to go to school." He managed to laugh. "I guess some of the accent rubbed off. I've been trying to get rid of it ever since I got home," he said with great indignation. "I don't want anyone to think I'm a Yankee!"

"That's a real good idea, son," the policeman said. His tone became friendlier. "How are things down at the iron works?"

"Can't complain," Matthew said, breathing a little easier.

"You're the first." The policeman leaned closer. "Ain't you got kids to feed? My friends with kids say they can't make enough to feed them with the prices the way they are." He paused. "Come to think of it, you don't look like you've eaten much yourself."

"No kids." Matthew decided to ignore the officer's observation. He knew exactly how thin he was. "Just a wife." An idea sprang into his mind. "But I reckon I'll be having one real soon. She's pregnant." He smiled. "And she's waiting for me. I promised her I wouldn't be late."

"Wouldn't want to keep the little lady waiting," the policeman agreed. He leaned forward and peered behind Matthew.

Matthew glanced over his shoulder. Peter had been standing back a little during the exchange. "Good to talk to you," he said cheerfully. "I guess we'll be going now."

The policeman held up his hand. "Wait a minute there."

Matthew's heart started pounding wildly again. He longed to run for it, but he had too much respect for the pistol strapped on the man's waist.

"What's with your friend here? Don't he talk?"

Matthew thought quickly. "He's been awful sick. Has laryngitis real bad. The cold air makes it worse on him."

"That right?" The policeman moved closer, staring under Peter's hat.

"That's right," Peter croaked in a hoarse voice, barely audible, before he doubled over in a spasm of coughing.

In spite of the seriousness of the situation, Matthew had to hide a grin. Peter's laryngitis was very convincing. He hadn't even been able to detect his New York accent himself.

The policeman still seemed unsure, but he nodded and waved his billy club. "The two of you get on home," he growled. "It's awful late to be out," he added. "Where are you going?"

Matthew cast in his mind for a plausible address. "Twenty-Sixth Street."

"Awful nice houses for an iron works man."

"A friend of the family," Matthew said, almost desperately. "They're letting me rent out a room. My friend here is next door."

"Be on your way then." The policeman turned and walked away, his heavy shoes thudding on the frozen dirt.

Matthew watched until he was out of sight and then sagged against the building, sweat pouring down his back.

"*Whew!*" Peter whispered. "That was close."

"Too close," Matthew said. "We're not going to get out of here tonight. We stand out like a sore thumb. There just aren't enough people on the roads. Anyone who sees us walking is going to remember us."

"What are we going to do?" Peter asked in alarm.

"Go somewhere and wait until it's light. We'll keep going as soon as the sun comes up. We'll be less noticeable then."

"We can't just stand around," Peter argued. "We'll freeze to death."

Matthew had to admit he was right. He stared up at the sky for a minute. "Follow me."

"Where are we going now?"

"You'll find out," Matthew snapped, angry that his carefully laid plans were going awry, yet filled with sudden anticipation.

Chapter Thirty

Mr. Whipple turned to Robert. "Captain, what is your perspective on the condition of our armies? General Lee's in particular."

Carrie hid a smile. All the armies were important, but it was impossible not to take a greater interest in Lee's. It was his, after all, that had rescued them from disaster time after time.

Robert frowned. "I'm afraid our armies are struggling right now. General Lee has the most experienced, efficient soldiers in our entire country, but I don't know how much more they can stand."

"What exactly are you referring to?" Count asked.

"They're starving," Robert said bluntly. "Lee's army is wretchedly fed and clothed. Last week their meat ration was cut again. The men are trying to keep their hopes up, but the brutal weather and their own hunger are sapping it from them."

"Meat is not available for anyone," Whipple protested. "They can't expect us to manufacture meat from nothing."

"There is plenty of meat," Robert snapped.

Carrie watched him compassionately. She had talked with him right after he returned from a two-day trip to visit General Lee's troops on the Rapidan River. He had been both angry and depressed.

"There is meat." Robert continued in a more reasonable voice. "Plenty of it in the border counties of our state, but the farmers refuse to take Confederate money for it."

"But there must be a way to obtain it," one man responded.

"There is," Robert agreed. "General Lee has suggested the government obtain it by barter. The farmers will accept cotton."

"But what if the cotton makes its way to the enemy?" Whipple asked.

"I'm afraid that won't matter if our army is incapable of fighting a battle," Robert snapped, his patience obviously stretched to the limit. "It is simply imperative we do whatever is necessary to make certain they are equipped for battle." His voice roughened. "In spite of some people's belief that our army can fight on passion alone, they also require blankets, food and clothing to keep them from freezing to death."

Carrie reached out and took his hand to let him know she supported him. He glanced down at her and squeezed it gently.

Whipple looked over at her. "Is your husband always so indelicate about how he states things?" he asked.

"My husband speaks the truth," Carrie said. "I believe that can be readily understood no matter how it is said." She cleared her voice, angry herself now. "How long did you serve in the army, Mr. Whipple?"

Mr. Whipple reddened, his eyes flashing with indignation. "I have been busy here in the capital serving my country," he snapped, his angry look clearly saying he didn't think she should be speaking.

"Well then," Carrie continued, "since you've obviously never been hungry"—she stared at his stomach—"and you've never been a soldier, you're hardly in a position to determine what the men in our armies need or don't need." She turned to Robert. "May I have the next dance, please?" Bowing her head slightly, she moved away.

"If you'll excuse me, gentlemen," Robert said, not bothering to hide the laughter in his voice. He was laughing outright when he caught up with her. "You should have seen his face! You definitely put the old windbag in his place."

"Oh, he's bent out of shape because a woman dared challenge him on something," Carrie scoffed. "He'd better get used to it. The women of the South are changing. When this war is over, they're going to know they can do things on their own, because they've had to. They aren't going to be content to play the helpless female any longer. They'll have to learn to stand up for their rights."

"And I have no doubts you'll be right in front volunteering to teach them," Robert said.

"Does that bother you?" Carrie asked, looking up for his reaction.

"Bother me?" Robert mused. "I'm proud of you. Not only are you smart and talented, you're also the best dancer in Richmond." He held out his arms. "May I?"

Carrie blinked away sudden tears and moved into his arms. "You're wonderful," she whispered, a catch in her voice.

"And don't you forget it," Robert grinned.

They danced for another hour before Robert begged for a reprieve. "This old man can't keep up with you," he pleaded.

"You're not old," Carrie said, looking at him appraisingly. "You just act old," she teased.

"Would you like to drink the next water I bring, or wear it, Mrs. Borden?"

"You don't have the nerve," Carrie said. The glint in Robert's eye told her she was wrong. "All right. All right. You do." She laughed. "I guess perhaps you don't act so old after all."

Robert leaned close to whisper in her ear. "Let's see how old you think I act when I get you home tonight."

Carrie blushed and pulled away. "Didn't you say something about a glass of water?"

"Coward," Robert teased. He moved away to blend in with the crowd.

Carrie moved to the back of the room and found a seat, content to sit in silence. The long day at the hospital combined with the hours of dancing had worn her out. Ten minutes later, Robert found her there. He approached with an apologetic look on his face. "Sorry I took so long. I ran into someone I've been trying to schedule a meeting with for a long time."

Carrie looked at him closely. "And did you schedule one?"

"He's leaving town tomorrow."

"But he can talk tonight." Carrie interpreted the look on her husband's face.

"Yes," Robert replied. "I told him I was occupied," he added quickly.

"No, you're not," Carrie said, rising to her feet. "You're the night person of this family. I'm almost dead on my feet, and you're still going strong. You stay here and talk to your person. I'll have Spencer take me home, and then he can come back for you."

"It really is very important. Are you sure you don't mind?"

"I'm positive. All I want is a soft bed right now."

"You'll keep it warm for me?" Robert said quietly.

Carrie met his gaze directly. "I'll be waiting," she promised. "Not that I won't probably be sound asleep," she added with a smirk.

Robert laughed. "Thank you. I have hopes this man can help with the army's food shortage. And don't worry about sending Spencer back," he added. "It's far too cold for him to be out so much. There are plenty of people going in our direction. I'm sure someone will have room in their carriage."

Carrie was shivering in spite of the warm blanket when Spencer finally pulled up in front of the house. "You're sure you won't come in and get warm before you go home?" she asked.

"No, Miss Carrie. I be just fine. My bed be callin' my name right loud."

"Goodnight then," she called as she walked up the sidewalk.

The house was completely dark except for one small lantern glowing in the foyer. Her father, expecting her to come home with Robert, had gone to bed.

Carrie had just reached the bottom step to the porch when she heard a rustling noise in the bushes. She tensed, straining to see if someone was there.

"Hello, Carrie."

Carrie gasped as a tall, emaciated figure, clad only in pants and a shirt, stepped out of the bushes toward her. She drew back instinctively. "Who is there?" she asked sharply. The voice had sounded familiar.

The figure moved closer. "I'm sorry I frightened you."

Carrie stared in disbelief. "Matthew?" she whispered.

"Yes," Matthew replied, not able to think of anything else to say.

Carrie shook her head, trying to think through the shock. "What in the world are you doing here?"

"I need your help," he said. "I'm afraid I may be putting you in some danger."

Carrie glanced around and pulled Matthew further into the shadows of the porch. Only then did she realize he was shivering violently. "You're freezing," she exclaimed. "I've got to get you out of the cold."

"I have someone with me." Matthew coughed violently, covering his mouth to stifle the sound.

Carrie knew now was not the time to ask questions. She stepped to the edge of the porch. "Come out," she commanded softly. "You're safe here."

Another man, not quite as thin as Matthew, stepped out of the bushes. "Thank you, ma'am."

Carrie stared at him. The New York accent was unmistakable. Grabbing Matthew's hand, she pulled him from the porch and started around the back of the house, making sure they stayed in the shadows. "We'll go in the back," she whispered almost inaudibly. She knew the thick door between the kitchen and the dining room would deaden any noise.

Robert stood at the window and watched Carrie go before he turned back to his companion. "I'm sorry you're leaving town tomorrow, Mr. Crutchfield."

Crutchfield shrugged his bony shoulders and ran a finely tapered hand through sandy hair flecked with gray. His dark eyes burned with intensity as he spoke. "Lee's men are starving. It sickens me that we are surrounded with farmers who are hoarding their feed in hopes they can get even more money for it. My heart goes out to the people in Richmond as well, but I can't help but hold more sympathy for the soldiers. They are starving while living in tents under rather brutal conditions."

"Do you really think you can talk some of the farmers into releasing their food?" Robert envisioned the haunted looks of hunger in the eyes of the soldiers he had visited two weeks earlier.

Crutchfield leaned closer and lowered his voice. "I have chosen not to make this public knowledge, but I have managed to obtain a rather large shipment of cotton." He paused and answered the question on Robert's face. "It is stored in a warehouse a few miles from here."

"How?" Robert sputtered, amazed.

Crutchfield merely smiled. "I find it more beneficial if I don't reveal my methods."

Robert grinned. "I understand. I simply hope it goes well."

"I can feed them," Crutchfield said, "but it is General Lee who will lead them." He paused and glanced at the room, then back at Robert. "You have talked to Lee recently. What hope does he feel for the spring?"

Robert frowned, choosing his words carefully. "Lee believes we are not in a condition to invade the North with any prospect of permanent benefit. We simply don't have the resources."

Crutchfield nodded. "Never have," he said brusquely.

Robert gazed at him and decided to speak his mind. Here, obviously, was a man not blinded by romantic fantasy of Southern splendor. "He hopes, by taking the initiative this spring, to fall on Meade unexpectedly and force him to retreat to Washington."

"Can it be done?"

"Lee has done miraculous things before," Robert said. "He hopes to use the element of surprise in his favor, even though he knows he is far outnumbered." He paused. "His goals are rather moderate by his own appraisal. He hopes that by throwing the Federals off balance, he can embarrass them and damage their plans enough to keep them flailing all summer. He hopes, in that way, to keep Meade from pursuing anything of great magnitude."

Crutchfield swung around to the window, staring out into the cold, his breath forming a layer of fog on the glass that eventually made seeing impossible. Still he stood there, his thin shoulders hunched in deep thought.

Robert waited. In the little time they had together, he had gained a deep respect for the other man's ability to see things clearly.

Crutchfield turned back around. "I'm afraid the Confederacy is up against it," he said. "In the military sense, it is quite impossible to win an unlimited victory. Yet in the political sense, it is impossible to consider anything else."

"It will be rather hard to fit the two impossibilities together." Robert was relieved to know other Southerners were beginning to understand the true picture. Not that understanding offered any answers. It merely painted the picture more clearly, but sometimes that was the first step to finding answers.

"Yes," Crutchfield murmured. "I'm afraid that, at the moment, neither our soldiers nor our statesmen fully grasp the implications of the terrible divergence in their appraisals of the situation. Each one seems to only grasp an understanding of their own viewpoint."

"Which is what landed us here in the first place," Robert said. "It is quite normal for two differing sides to only be able to see their own positions clearly." Crutchfield looked at him but didn't respond right away. Robert was glad. He was still trying to digest his conflicting emotions. He wasn't ready to discuss them yet.

"There may still be hope," Crutchfield said suddenly. "In November, the people of the North will have their next presidential election."

"So?" Robert was confused at the sudden switch in conversation.

"So, if the Northern people have been made to feel the war is simply too painful and discouraging to carry on any longer, they may simply vote Lincoln out of office."

Robert began to understand. "If Lincoln is out of office and the next president has gotten the message that war will no longer be tolerated, they may yet decide to leave us alone."

"Exactly," Crutchfield agreed. "It is obvious we don't have the capacity to achieve stunning victories, but we may indeed have the capacity to hang on. If we can hang on long enough, the North will get tired of it. Then the voters at the polls will determine what happens. They are tired of losing their men in this uncalled for act of Northern aggression. I believe many of them are willing to let us go if it means their men quit dying."

"Not to mention our own," Robert stated. "I hadn't thought of it that way, but it might just work. A military program based simply on the necessity of staying alive until the fall could gain what more ambitious programs have missed."

"I'm afraid it is our only chance."

Carrie opened the back door quietly, made sure the kitchen was empty, and beckoned Matthew and his friend inside. The kitchen wasn't exactly warm, but it was much better than outside.

Wrapping his arms around himself, Matthew tried to control his shivering body and chattering teeth. Peter was doing the same.

"Sit here," Carrie commanded. Within minutes, she had a fire blazing and a pot of hot water on the stove. She opened the closet and pulled out a loaf of bread, a bowl of beans, and several sweet potatoes left over from supper. She soon had hot food and hot coffee set in front of the two men. "Eat," she said. "We'll talk when you're warm again."

Matthew gladly complied. The hot food eased down his throat, bringing welcome warmth into his emaciated body. He glanced at the kitchen door and prayed that no one would come in to check on the noise they were making. He had taken a great risk to come here. He was confident he could count on Carrie to keep their secret, but he wasn't so sure about Thomas. He was a friend, but he was also a government official. If Thomas was discovered aiding and abetting escaped fugitives from Libby Prison, he would lose his job, and he could be branded a traitor.

Matthew shoved his empty plate back. At least his shivering had stopped. "Thank you," he said.

Carrie rushed over to hug him. Now that his immediate needs were taken care of, she looked full of questions. "It's wonderful to see you," she cried, "but what in the world has happened to you?"

Matthew took a deep breath and nodded toward his friend. "This is Peter Wilcher. He's also a journalist, from New York." He stopped and looked at Carrie squarely, wanting desperately for her to understand. "We have just escaped from Libby Prison."

Carrie sucked in her breath. "You've been there again? I didn't know."

"There was no way to notify you." Matthew leaned forward and took Carrie's hand. "We need your help."

"But how?" Carrie asked. "How did you end up back there? You're a civilian."

"Being a civilian and a journalist seemed to make us extremely valuable to them," Peter said. "We've been there almost seven months."

"Seven months!" Carrie gasped and shook her head. She took a deep breath. "I'll do whatever I can to help you."

Matthew gazed at her, his heart warmed by the compassion and friendship he saw there. A wild hope sprang into his soul. She seemed to genuinely care for him. Could it mean something more?

Carrie reached out to take his hand. "What can we do to help? Robert and I—"

"Robert?" Matthew gazed around, trying to ignore the burning sensation her hand produced. "He's here? You came home in the carriage alone."

"Robert was talking to someone at a party we attended."

"How is my old friend?"

"He's wonderful," Carrie told him. "The two of you would have much to talk about if there were time. I know there isn't." She paused. "Robert and I are married," she said happily.

Matthew blanched, thankful his already pale skin wouldn't betray him. "I see," he murmured. "Congratulations. You two were meant for each other." Over Carrie's shoulder, he could see the look of surprised knowing in Peter's eyes. Matthew didn't care. He cursed the wild hope that had once again betrayed him.

Carrie didn't seem to notice his lack of enthusiasm. "He should be home fairly soon. I can't imagine our hosts are going to want the house occupied all night."

Matthew stood. "I think it best we not be here when he comes."

"Why ever not?"

Matthew struggled to choose the right words. "I'm already putting you at great risk. It will not go easy for you if you are discovered helping us."

"I don't care about that," Carrie cried.

"No, but I do," Matthew said. "Robert is a whole different matter. I take it he is still serving in the military. What is his commission now?"

"Captain," Carrie admitted.

Matthew smiled grimly. "I won't risk having Robert branded a traitor. The army looks down on that." His voice made clear what he really meant. "If he would be willing to help me, it would simply be too much of a risk."

Carrie leapt to her feet. "*If* he would be willing to help you? How can you possibly say that? Robert is your friend."

"Who also happens to be the enemy." Matthew hated the hurt look in Carrie's eyes. He plowed ahead, knowing he had to speak the truth. "This war has torn apart many friendships. Robert and I haven't seen each other in a long time."

Carrie edged forward, her eyes blazing. "I will not hear one more word," she sputtered. "Robert and I talk of you often. I know exactly how he feels about you, and I know how much he misses you." She stopped, her eyes misting with tears. "We can help you, Matthew. Please let us. What are you going to do? Go back out in the cold and freeze to death until you and Peter are captured? You came here because you need help. Don't let your fears run you away now."

Matthew gazed into her eyes, his heart almost breaking at the love he saw there. Robert Borden was a lucky man, he thought bitterly. He glanced over at Peter.

"I say we take the chance," Peter said. "You said yourself we can't walk out of town tonight. Tomorrow morning we may be a little less noticeable, but there will also be guards and policemen looking all over for us."

Carrie gripped his arm. "Please listen to him. I have a plan, but I need Robert to make it work."

Matthew nodded. "I guess we have no choice." He put a hand on Carrie's arm. "I'm sorry I've put you in danger. I wouldn't have come here if I had any other choice."

"Oh, poo," Carrie said. "I wouldn't have had you do anything else."

Matthew grinned. "You haven't changed, have you? You always did know how to get your way."

"It's not so hard to get your way when you know you're right," Carrie quipped. She looked around. "There's a lot we need to do before Robert gets home. I'll need your help."

Carrie was waiting on the front porch when Robert arrived. "Hello, dear." She greeted him as he walked up the sidewalk, the carriage that had dropped him off rattling down the street.

Robert stopped and stared at her sitting on the porch swing. "What in the world are you doing out here in the freezing cold?" He stepped forward. "Is something wrong?"

"Not exactly." She didn't want to alarm him, but she put a finger to her lips. "I need to talk to you."

"We can't do that in our room where it's not five degrees?" Robert asked, obviously confused.

Carrie cast her casual attitude aside and leaned forward, all seriousness. "No one can hear us."

Robert sat down next to her, his face drawn with concern. "I'm listening."

Carrie took a deep breath. "Matthew Justin and a friend are in the barn."

Robert's eyebrows shot up. "What?" he breathed.

"They've escaped Libby Prison and need our help. I've told them we will."

Robert sank back against the swing, staring at her.

"You should see them," she hissed. "Especially Matthew. He looks like a ghost, and he has an awful cough. He tried to escape in September, and they put him in some awful dungeon for three months."

"Rat Dungeon," Robert said slowly. "They're in the barn?"

Something about Robert's grim tone made Carrie hesitate. "I told them you would be glad to help. Matthew didn't want you to know he was there. He said it would put you at too much risk if you helped an escaped prisoner."

"Well, I certainly am not going to advertise my activities tonight," Robert said with a narrow smile, "but he's my friend. If they're caught now, he'll get worse than Rat Dungeon. I'll see what we can do." His forehead screwed up in heavy thought.

Carrie grinned. "I have a plan."

"I should have known you would. Let's hear it."

Carrie leaned her head close to his, talking quietly.

When she was done, Robert sat back. "It just might work," he said.

Chapter Thirty-One

Matthew sat next to Robert on the carriage seat and tried to comprehend he was actually riding out of Richmond with a Confederate captain as an escort. He hugged his warm coat close and rearranged the blanket around his bony legs. A glance back revealed the tip of Peter's nose protruding from thick layers of lap rugs. Matthew rubbed his full stomach and thought about the basket of food stashed under the driver's seat. He looked forward and was unable to stifle a small laugh. "I never thought I would see Granite as a carriage horse."

Robert smiled, his eyes searching the darkness in front of them. "If it hadn't been for Carrie putting this harness on, I know he would never have gone for it. He'll do anything for her."

Matthew sensed Robert didn't want to talk until they were out of the town limits. He was content to wait. His fear of Robert's reaction had melted when his old friend barreled into the barn and swept him up in a warm embrace. While they lived in warring nations, their friendship had survived. It gave Matthew hope. Not only hope for himself, but for the nation as a whole. There were sparks of brotherhood and friendship everywhere that he hoped would fan into flame when the war ended.

Matthew leaned back against the seat and allowed his gaze to rove over the night sky, picking out favorite constellations. A glow in the east promised the rising of the sun. A heavy frost lay over everything. Tall clumps of frozen grass clattered noisily as the breeze tossed them about. Tears welled in his eyes. He had dreamed of freedom for so long. Even his fondest dreams hadn't felt this wonderful.

"Here we are," Robert said quietly. "If we make this, we should be okay."

Matthew looked up at the roadblocks looming before them. As they rolled nearer, two armed guards stepped out. He studied them closely. Their casual expressions indicated they knew nothing of the prison break. He relaxed slightly, but was still prepared to spring from the carriage if he needed to. Somewhere in the long night, he had determined he would not ever return to prison. He would rather die. He would risk a bullet in his back. He would not compliantly give himself up.

"Who goes there?" the guard called, his gun in a ready position.

"Captain Robert Borden." Robert drove close enough for the guard to see his stripes in the lantern light and pulled the carriage to a stop.

"Out awful early." The guard stepped forward. "Where are you going? Do you have a pass to leave the city?"

Robert handed it to him.

"How about the two fellows with you?"

"They have just been released from Chimborazo Hospital," Robert said. "They were both wounded during heroic action. The governor asked that I escort them home."

The guard leaned forward, staring into Matthew's face, and glanced back at Peter. "Where'd you get wounded?"

"Gettysburg," Matthew replied.

"What'd you do so heroic?" His voice was skeptical.

"They both saved the lives of their commanding officers," Robert snapped. "They almost died doing so." He paused. "Are all these questions really necessary, *Private*? These men have suffered a great deal. I hardly think sitting here in the cold is going to do any good."

The guard stepped back. "I haven't seen their papers yet."

Matthew held his breath as Robert handed over the forged papers, thankful the lantern light was dim and flickering. He wasn't sure the papers would pass intense scrutiny.

The guard, subdued by Robert's stern rebuke, merely glanced at them and waved the carriage on. "Have a good day," he muttered.

Robert waited until the wagon was out of sight around a sharp curve before he pulled Granite to a halt and leaned back against the seat with a deep sigh of relief. "I guess Carrie's plan worked."

"I can't believe the guard didn't say anything about Granite." Peter laughed. "Whoever heard of a Thoroughbred hauling a carriage for wounded soldiers?"

"He didn't look too intelligent," Robert said, grinning. "Which could be one reason y'all seem to be winning this war right now."

Matthew laughed. Robert hadn't lost his sense of humor. He grew serious and reached over to clasp his hand. "I don't know how to say thank you."

"Then don't," Robert replied. "Besides, we're not out of here yet. We still have a long way to go. If the guards found that tunnel, they could be right behind us. I'd rather not be sitting here waiting for them." He picked up the reins and talked quietly to Granite who sprang forward in a ground-eating trot.

Matthew gripped the sides of the carriage tightly as the frozen ruts and ridges sent pain shooting through his poorly padded body. Gritting his teeth, he stared ahead. He could endure anything that would put more miles between them and Libby Prison. His mind flew to his friends who had escaped with him. Where were they? Would they get out of the city? He longed to know, but realized there was no way to find out. From now on, he would have to put all of his energy into surviving.

"What was it like?" Robert asked, breaking the silence.

Matthew looked over. "Let's just say you never want to visit a prison." He shuddered, memories swarming his mind. "It's bad, Robert. It's really bad." He couldn't bring himself to describe it graphically. The experiences were still too fresh, too raw. He wanted to revel in his new freedom.

"How long have you and Carrie been married?" he asked to change the subject, as well as to convince himself it was true. He had buried any hope of having Carrie long ago. At least, he thought he had.

"Nine months," Robert said. "She's the most wonderful woman alive."

"Yes, I know," Matthew said. He felt Robert turn his head to peer at him. "You're both very lucky," he hastened to add. "I knew a long time ago you were meant for each other." He forced a cheerful tone into his voice.

Robert was quiet for several minutes and then glanced back at Peter, who was sound asleep. "I know how you feel about my wife, Matthew."

Matthew stared at him, meeting Robert's eyes. He wanted to deny it but knew it was futile. "I'm sorry," he said. "I've tried to change how I feel."

Robert nodded. "It's all right." He gave a small laugh. "How can someone who knows her not love her? It probably should bother me, but it doesn't. I know I can trust you."

Matthew breathed a deep sigh of relief. "I'm glad. I hope you know I would never have gone to Cromwell's house if I hadn't had to."

"I believe you," Robert replied. "It was hardly a foolproof plan of escape." He chuckled. "You were lucky Carrie came home late, or that she was even there. You're even luckier she's so smart."

Matthew heard the genuine note of friendliness in Robert's voice. He relaxed. "What has the war been like for you?" he asked, knowing it was safe to change the subject. The truth was out. He knew Robert would never bring it up again.

Robert shrugged. "It's changed me. I've seen things I hope to never see again. I've experienced things I hope to never experience again. I've changed how I feel about things, and what I believe."

"Such as?"

Robert pulled Granite down into an easier trot and seemed to consider the question. "I sent a letter to my mother a few weeks ago. I told her that if there were any slaves left on the plantation, she was to give them their freedom. They were welcome to stay if they wanted to start earning a wage when I returned. If they weren't interested, they could head north with papers saying they were free."

Matthew leaned forward in astonishment. "What happened to you?" He knew how adamant Robert had once been about his belief in slavery.

"A black family saved my life," Robert told him.

Matthew listened closely as Robert told his story, watching pain, sorrow, and then joy race across his face. When he had finished, Matthew sat, absorbing all he heard. "What about after the war?" he asked. "What are you going to do about your plantation?"

"I don't know," Robert admitted. "I'm trying not to look that far ahead. There are too many unknowns. Too many questions without answers." He shook his head. "All I've ever wanted to do is farm." He laughed. "If you can call what I did farming. Actually, I supervised slaves who did all the farming for me. I would like to go back to that, but I'm afraid it won't be there. If the South loses this war, I'm going to be broke. It takes money to run a plantation, and I won't have any." He scowled. "The future is nothing but a black hole."

Matthew ached for his friend and wondered what he could say. He was afraid Robert's appraisal of the situation was correct.

Robert shook his head. "Enough about me," he said, forcing a light tone into his voice. "I have all the things that are truly important. I'll face the future when it gets here. I learned a long time ago that the things we fear are not nearly so bad when we actually meet them face to face."

Matthew thought about the prison and found himself disagreeing. The prison had been every bit as bad as he had feared, yet it was behind him. He had to let go of his fears and face the future with courage.

"What next for you?" Robert asked.

"Back to the newspaper," Matthew said. "That is, once I get on the other side of Union lines." He stared out at the overhanging trees. "I promised the men still at Libby Prison that when I got out, I would tell their story. Sometimes the first step in stopping atrocities is bringing them to light. I intend to do that."

"And after that?"

"I'll always be a newspaperman. It's what I've always wanted to do. I guess it's in my blood."

"You're lucky," Robert said. "No matter what happens with this war, you'll always have a job. You'll always have something to do."

"And you'll always have Carrie," Matthew reminded him. "You're lucky, too."

Robert glanced over and smiled. "So get off my pity party. Is that what you're saying?"

"Take it any way you like, old friend." Matthew thought for a moment. "When I was stuck down in Rat Dungeon, I had a lot of time to think. I thought about what would happen if I finally got out of prison and none of the newspapers wanted me."

"Right," Robert scoffed.

"It could happen," Matthew insisted. "It would be plenty difficult, but I realized that if one door was to close for me, God would open another one. I finally decided it would be all right."

"I guess time will tell," Robert murmured.

"Will you have to fight again?" Matthew asked.

"Yes," Robert said. "This war is far from over. The South needs men too badly. I'm healthy, so I'll fight again."

"You know the South is going to lose, don't you?" Matthew asked carefully, hoping his friend wouldn't get angry. He saw a spark ignite and then die just as quickly.

"I know." Robert sighed. "I talked with a man last night who believed if we could hang on, the North would get tired of the war and vote Lincoln out of office. Then we could be an independent country."

"You didn't go for it?"

"Oh, it sounded good at the time, but I don't really believe it's true."

"It's not," Matthew agreed. "There is plenty of disagreement about how the war is being fought, and there are lots of people sick of it, but very few are thinking about throwing in the towel. At least, that was true last fall." He paused. "The North is not going to stop until there is complete victory."

Robert stared at him. "And what is that going to mean for us?" he demanded. I've heard different things about the plan for Lincoln's so-called *reconstruction*. The North may have conquered our country, but that doesn't mean they have captured our people's hearts."

"I know," Matthew said sadly. "Reconstruction is that black hole of the future you're talking about. There was a wild gulf between our countries before this war started. Now the gulf is even wider. Somehow, we must all find a way to bridge it."

Robert grunted. "Good luck. I fear the war may end, but the fighting will go on for a long time. You can beat people into submission, but you can't stop the flame in their hearts."

"Including yours?" Matthew asked. "Is the flame still burning?"

"It comes and goes," Robert admitted. "I'm trying to imagine rebuilding my life with the North as victors, but I can't say it's easy. Carrie keeps telling me to take it one day at a time, and I'm trying. That's all any of us can handle."

It was after noon when the carriage finally rattled down the drive to Cromwell Plantation. Matthew gazed at the grand house, his heart once more swept with memories.

"What a place!" Peter exclaimed.

The door opened and Sam stepped out on the porch, shading his eyes to see who was coming.

"Hello, Sam," Robert called, so as to not alarm him.

Sam stepped to the edge of the porch, and then his eyes opened wide. "Is that you, Mr. Borden? Robert Borden?"

"It is. I know it's been a while. I'm surprised you remembered me."

"Once I knew Miss Carrie loved you, I burned your face into my memory." Sam turned to Matthew. "Ain't I seen you somewhere before?"

"It's Matthew Justin, Sam. I spent Christmas here a few years back."

Sam peered at him. "What happened to you, boy? You don't look so good."

Matthew laughed. "Prison life doesn't seem to have done me much good."

Sam walked off the porch and approached the carriage. "That be Granite, sho 'nuff," he murmured. The old man stroked the horse's head. "I wasn't sure I would ever see this big horse ever again."

"We need a favor, Sam," Robert said.

Sam turned away from Granite. "I didn't figure you be droppin' in for a visit. What you be needin'? I'll do anything for Miss Carrie's husband."

❧

Matthew walked out onto the porch of the large mansion, breathing in the fresh air and enjoying the warm sunshine on his face. It had only been four days since Robert had left them and returned to Richmond, but he could already feel new life and energy flowing back into his body. His flesh was starting to fill out, and his hacking cough was better. The plan was to stay here for two weeks, build up their strength, and then try to get through to Fort Monroe.

The sudden sound of hoofbeats alerted him. He jumped up from the swing and ducked back into the front door. "Company," he called.

Sam was beside him in an instant. "You get a look?"

"No, I just heard them."

"You and Peter get on down to the basement. I'll take care of things up here." Sam paused. "You know how to disappear if you need to."

Matthew nodded as Peter appeared beside him. "Company," he said. "Let's go." They walked down the hall quickly, hearing the clomp of booted feet on the porch just as they ducked their heads underneath the cobwebs and descended into the dark basement. Matthew felt his way toward the lantern and lit it, keeping the flame low.

"Why are we down here?" Peter protested. "If those are Rebel soldiers and they start searching, we don't have anywhere to go. We'll be sitting ducks!"

Matthew held his finger to his lips. He hadn't told Peter the secret yet. The Cromwell family secret would stay just that unless there was a need. Carrie had given him a note to give Sam. When he had handed it to him to the day after Robert left, the old man merely raised his eyebrows. The next day, while Peter was sleeping, he had shown Matthew the tunnel.

Matthew could hear muted voices, but he couldn't make out any words. He ground his teeth in frustration. The clomping of boots drew closer, and one voice rang above the rest. "We have our orders. We're going to search."

"Oh no," Peter groaned, looking around frantically.

Matthew grabbed his arm and pulled him in the direction of the bookshelves. Seconds later, they were encased in the tunnel. Matthew grinned when he raised the lantern and illuminated Peter's face. "I told you everything would be all right," he whispered.

Peter shook his head, his eyes wide in amazement. "This is something." He opened his mouth to say more but snapped it shut again when they heard the basement door slam open.

Matthew turned off the lantern, not completely sure the faint light wouldn't glimmer through the crack. Total darkness embraced them as two men descended to the basement to talk.

"You really think some of them could be here?" one of them said.

"I think they could be anywhere," another deeper voice growled. "All I know is we have orders to search every building between here and Union lines."

"Must be a mite embarrassing to lose over a hundred men out of one of the most dreaded prisons in the South," the first man said. There was a brief silence. "I don't see anything, and there sure isn't anywhere to hide down here. Not unless they've buried themselves under cobwebs."

"I wouldn't put anything past those men who built that tunnel," the second man said, a tinge of admiration in his voice. "The commander of Libby Prison is fit to be tied. Took most of his guards and had them thrown into Castle Thunder. Said there was no way those men could have gotten out unless the guards had been bought off."

"Well, twenty-five of them have already been brought back." There was more heavy stomping. "Let's get out of here. We'll go see if any of the other men found someone."

Matthew waited until the door closed to relight his lantern. He and Peter stared at each other. "A hundred men?" Matthew finally said in amazement. "There must have been a mass exodus." His shoulders shook with laughter as he imagined men swarming through the tunnel they had worked so hard to build.

"I wonder who they've caught," Peter said. "I pity them, whoever they are."

Matthew sobered instantly. Visions of Anderson, Sprinkler, Wilson and the others rose in his mind.

"Sure does my heart good to think of those guards in Castle Thunder, though," Peter said in a more cheerful voice. "Won't hurt for them to feel what we did for a while. Maybe it will make them more human..." His voice trailed away as if he didn't believe it. He waved his arm in the air. "You want to tell me where this place came from? You seem to have a monopoly on tunnel escapes."

Matthew told him what he knew. "Carrie was determined to give us as much of a chance as possible," he finished, his voice thick with emotion.

"You say this tunnel goes out to the river?" Peter asked.

"Yes, why?"

"Let's not walk to Fort Monroe. Let's go down the river."

"Can't," Matthew said. "Moses took the only boat around here. I checked."

Peter was undaunted. "We'll make our own." He leaned closer, his eyes bright. "I lived on a river in New

York when I was a kid. I didn't move to the city until later. My brothers and I used to make rafts all the time. Sometimes, we would spend up to a whole week floating down the river."

"A raft..." Matthew mused. The James was a relatively calm river. They would encounter no rapids. If they hugged the shoreline, they would have plenty of time to disappear inland if someone in a Confederate boat spotted them. At this time of the year, very few boats would be on the river at all. He nodded slowly. "I think it will work."

"Of course it will work, Peter said with confidence. "I'd rather float down that river than walk another forty miles surrounded by Rebel soldiers as thick as flies."

Matthew felt his excitement growing. "We'll stay two weeks like we planned, and then we'll keep going."

Matthew felt and looked like a new man when he shook hands with Sam, and embraced Opal and the kids. "I hope to find a way to adequately thank you some day," he said.

"You just get yourself to Fort Monroe safe," Sam told him. "That be all the thanks we need."

"You sure you've got plenty of food?" Opal asked.

"Any more and the raft might sink." Peter laughed. He cleared his throat. "You people have changed my life."

Matthew looked at him curiously. He had felt a difference in Peter, but he hadn't known how to define it.

Peter looked uncomfortable for a moment and then cleared his throat again. "I didn't understand why Matthew was so concerned about the ex-slaves in the contraband camps," he stated with a shrug. "I guess the truth is, I didn't think about blacks at all. I had a full life that took all my energy. It was easy not to think about how slaves must suffer in the South. I didn't understand what the abolitionists were making such a big fuss about." He took a deep breath. "I guess I've discovered why. You people have been wonderful to me, and for no other reason than because I'm a human being."

"That's right, boy," Sam said.

"You knew nothing about me," Peter continued, "yet you treated me like family. I'll never forget it."

Sam reached out and put a gnarled hand on Peter's shoulder. "You remember one thing, Peter. Ain't many of us able to go out and change the whole world, but ever'one of us can help change the people God brings our way."

Peter nodded. "I'll remember," he promised.

Chunks of ice floating in the iron gray waters of the mighty James bounced off the raft as it floated easily down the river. The current was fairly strong, but the surface was marred by nothing but some tiny ripples.

Matthew leaned back and gnawed on a piece of bread. Soon the sun would set and the full moon would light their way.

"What are you thinking?" Peter asked.

Matthew smiled. "I'm thinking that this is one of my dreams come true. When I was a little boy, I used to dream of putting a boat on the river and just going. The rivers up around my home in western Virginia were either too shallow or full of rapids." He sighed. "Of course, my dream didn't include evading capture from Rebel soldiers."

"Back then, you would have thought that even more exciting."

"Yes, well, I find my perspective changing as I get older," Matthew said. "Want another piece of Opal's sweet potato pie?"

"Planning on gaining all your weight back in a month?" Peter teased.

"Maybe." Matthew cut a slice of pie and began to chew.

The moon rose a golden, glorious orb, just as the sun, shrouded in a veil of red, slipped below the horizon. It hung suspended on the skyline and then began to make its ascent, casting a luminous glow over the river spread out before them. The air was still and cold, causing Matthew to snuggle deeper into the blankets wrapped around him.

"It's hard to believe there's a war going on," Peter whispered, as if he didn't want to break the magical spell.

"I know," Matthew said. "It seems like if people could get outside and absorb enough of God's beauty in their hearts, maybe it would release some of the hatred and passion." He shook his head. "I wish it could be that easy."

The moon continued to rise until it seemed as if they were flowing right into it. Matthew held his breath, able to believe for the moment that the magical fairy-tale world spread out before him would embrace and hold him in its shimmering glow forever. There was no war. No prison. No Rebel soldiers. Reality was swallowed by magic and the whole world was full of peace.

A shot in the distance dispelled his fantasy world. He scrambled to his knees, threw aside the blanket, and peered into the dark shadows along the riverbank. "What was that?"

Peter knelt beside him, using the paddle to edge them closer to the bank, where the shadows could hide their presence. "We stand out like sore thumbs in that moonlight," he muttered.

They heard a loud crashing in the woods. Matthew stiffened, wishing fervently that he had a gun. Whatever was coming at them was clearly panicked.

Peter reached up, grabbed a low-hanging branch, and slung a length of rope over it to bring them to a standstill. If they stayed quiet, maybe no one would see them. The dark wood of the boat melted with the shadows, making them almost invisible.

The crashing grew louder and another gunshot roared in the distance, followed by muted shouting. "They went this way," floated to them on the breeze.

Matthew's heart pounded furiously, and his breath came in shallow gasps. Had someone seen them? Were soldiers pursuing them? "Cast us off," he ordered in a low voice. "We can't just sit here."

Peter nodded and quickly untied the rope. They had gone no more than ten feet before two dark shapes came hurling down the slope, splashing into the water. The two shapes began to swim furiously, their labored breathing loud in the still night. Suddenly Matthew's eyes opened wide with disbelief. "Catch them!" he whispered frantically. Already the frigid water seemed to be sapping the strength of the fleeing men. He grabbed his oar and began to paddle furiously. Another shot rang out behind them.

Peter sprang into action as well. The boat pulled alongside the two men, who were still oblivious to their presence. Matthew waited until the right moment to reach down and grab the lead man's arm, hauling him onto the raft. Peter followed suit with the other one.

"Don't talk," Matthew commanded, throwing all his weight back into his oar. The next gunshot sounded much further away. Soon, they could hear nothing except the slight breeze stirring the limbs, and the call of an occasional goose.

Matthew turned with a grin. "You can talk now, Captain Anderson."

Anderson, gasping for breath, stared at him but didn't move. "Wilson?" he finally whispered.

"We got him, too," Matthew said. Anderson nodded and then went limp. Both men were shivering violently, their hands and faces glowing a strange blue in the moonlight.

"Get their clothes off," Peter ordered.

Matthew knelt beside Anderson, grimacing at the thin, wasted condition of his body. He had obviously had a much harder time reaching this point. He shuddered as he imagined what the two men must have endured since their escape. He wrapped several blankets around the freezing man and glanced over to see that Wilson was now wrapped up just as securely. "They need a fire," Matthew said.

"We can't risk stopping," Peter protested. "Those woods are probably swarming with Rebel soldiers. It won't take them long to find us if we build a fire."

"You're right," Matthew growled. He moved over and began to rub Anderson's hands. When they began to warm, he performed the same service for Wilson.

Peter continued to paddle them down the river, holding them close to shore. Matthew didn't fear detection now, but he *was* afraid of what would happen to the two freezing men if they didn't get warm soon. They had gone at least ten miles when he told Peter to pull over to a clear area along the bank.

"It's not safe," Peter protested.

"We are not going to let these men die," Matthew said. "If it wasn't for Anderson, we would all still be in Libby Prison. His heartbeat is slowing down. If he doesn't get warm soon, he's going to die. The poor man is at the end of his rope."

Without another word, Peter eased the raft over to shore.

Matthew located a small, protected clearing in the woods and made a crackling fire. Then he returned to the boat and lifted Anderson, wincing again at how fragile his body was. Peter followed closely with Wilson. They laid both men next to the fire. Matthew added sticks until the heat radiated throughout the whole clearing.

"What do we do now?" Peter whispered.

"We wait," Matthew said, "That's all we can do. You keep guard for an hour while I watch them, and then we'll switch. If we hear anything, we put them on the raft and keep going."

The sun was casting a pink glow on the clouds when Anderson stirred, moaning softly.

Matthew jumped to his feet.

Anderson moaned again. His eyes flickered open and then closed again as if the effort was too much. "Where...?"

"You're with Peter and me," Matthew told him, nodding to Peter who had returned from watch to bring some tea they had kept warm on the fire.

"Matthew?" Anderson whispered, his face mirroring his confusion.

"You're safe." Matthew held Anderson's shoulders up while Peter held the cup to his lips.

Anderson gulped the warm liquid. "How...?"

"We'll explain everything later."

Anderson shook his head, obviously struggling to clear it. "S-soldiers," he stammered. "Everywhere."

"They're not here," Matthew reassured him, hoping his words would still be true in a little while.

Wilson stirred, and soon the two men were drinking and eating everything Matthew and Peter put in front of them. Matthew thanked Opal for piling so much food on them. There would be four of them from now on.

Anderson finally shoved his plate aside. "We have to get out of here," he insisted, his voice much clearer.

"You're too weak," Matthew protested.

A sudden muffled shout in the distance floated to them on the heavy morning air. Anderson staggered to his feet. "They've been after us for three days," he croaked. "They're not going to get me now."

Matthew leapt to his feet, catching the captain before he fell. He turned to Peter. "Leave the fire burning," he ordered. "They'll think we've taken off over land."

Matthew flung Anderson over his shoulder and raced for the raft, Peter and Wilson behind him. They were well downstream when they heard another shout. The campfire had been found.

Matthew gazed up at the sun. "We'll make it." He hoped he was telling the truth.

Chapter Thirty-Two

Moses had just strapped his pistol to his waist and stuffed his haversack with biscuits when Pompey sauntered over.

"You going somewhere?" Pompey eyed his preparations.

Moses nodded, his stomach churning. He reached for his coat and tried to shove down his nervousness.

"You don't act none too excited about it."

Moses knew Pompey was giving him the invitation to talk without attempting to pry. He turned and sank down on a log. Pompey followed suit. They had been back with Meade's army for about a month and a half now. "I've been called out to join a special mission." He still wondered what it was about it that bothered him so much. "I'm to ride with Colonel Dahlgren."

Pompey frowned in concentration. "That the fellow who lost his leg at Gettysburg?"

"That's him. He recovered, strapped on a new right leg, and is back in the saddle." In spite of his uneasiness, Moses respected Dahlgren's courage and determination, but something about the twenty-one year old colonel's brash attitude bothered him. When Captain Jones had called him into the tent to meet the colonel, Dahlgren had scanned him quickly and shrugged. "He'll do if I need a backup," he had said brusquely. Moses felt like a piece of meat being examined for sale.

Moses took a deep breath and crammed his hat on his head to shelter it from the rain that had been falling all day. A few degrees colder and the ground would be blanketed in snow. Moses would have preferred that to the bone-chilling wind enveloping him. "We're headed to Richmond," he said finally.

"Richmond?" Pompey echoed in surprise.

"General Kilpatrick and Colonel Dahlgren have cooked up a scheme to try to release the Union prisoners held there. Lincoln was in on it from the beginning. While we're down there, he wants us to distribute flyers talking about the amnesty he's offering to Confederate soldiers." He paused. "Seems they need some of Meade's infantry to stage a little skirmish and gain Lee's attention while several thousand of us cross over and head for the capital."

"Just several thousand?" Pompey asked skeptically. "To take the whole city?"

"Supposedly they have received reports about the meager defenses surrounding the city from one of the spies there. They believe them to be quite reliable." He managed a smile. "It will be a stunning coup if it works. Can you imagine five thousand prisoners free in Richmond? It could be the final stroke to make the city fall."

"Why you going'?" Pompey peered at him. "Especially without none of your men?"

Moses shrugged. "I'm going as a scout for Colonel Dahlgren. That is, if he needs me. He's already got a fellow, an ex-slave who says he knows the area well and can lead him to a shallow ford on the James River. Surprise and speed are essential to the success of the mission."

"You know that area well?"

Moses paused. "Not really. I grew up in Goochland County, but my owner didn't let us off the plantation very much. Captain Jones volunteered my services because he knew I came from there."

"But you ain't feelin' none too good about it."

Moses started to deny it but knew Pompey would know he was lying. "I'm not sure what's bothering me," he admitted. "There's something in my gut..."

"The gut don't usually lie, Moses," Pompey warned. "You pay real close attention to it while you be out there."

It was late on Sunday night when two lines of Union cavalrymen galloped by the Spotsylvania Courthouse in Fredericksburg. So far, everything had gone off without a hitch. General Custer had crossed the Rapidan River in a successful feint to draw Confederate cavalry after him. Yankee scouts had surprised and captured Southern pickets at Ely's Ford, east of General Lee, cutting telegraph lines to ruin communications with Richmond. Kilpatrick and Dahlgren had crossed the Rapidan River behind them and were now riding toward Richmond, unmolested because they were completely unknown.

Moses pulled his collar up against the raw cold. He was impressed with how things had gone so far. He still felt uneasy, but he was comforted by the smoothness of the operation.

When Dahlgren gave the order, a column of five hundred troopers split off from the original four thousand. The plan was for Kilpatrick to take his stronger force and attack Richmond from the north while Dahlgren crossed the James River and swung downstream on the south side to free the prisoners at Belle Island. Kilpatrick would dash straight in to free those at Libby and the other prisons. Dahlgren's men would cross over and join Kilpatrick, who would be stronger by several thousand more men. They would then torch the city and capture the Confederate leaders.

"We'll have some kind of party down there," one grizzled trooper called jubilantly.

"They ain't gonna know what hit them," another crowed.

The dark night swallowed them, concealing their presence as they galloped down the road toward Goochland and Louisa County.

Moses was quiet with his own thoughts. He was the only black face in a sea of white. He had grown accustomed to it over the last few years, but he didn't know any of these men—didn't know how they viewed his presence. The ex-slave Dahlgren had hired was riding at the front of the line where he could best direct them. Moses would feel safe only if he stayed on his guard.

They were approaching the river, north of Louisa County, when the sun lent a little color to the dark, rainy day. They stopped for a quick bite to eat and then jumped back into their saddles. "We're making good time, men!" Dahlgren called out. "No reason we can't do a little damage on the way down."

The men whooped and hollered. There had been absolutely no resistance. The Rebels had no idea they were about to be fallen upon. By mid-morning, the smoke from burning grist and sawmills dotted the sky behind them, melting invisibly into the thick cloud covering. Six canal boats loaded with grain had been torched and sunk.

Moses could feel the excitement rising to a fever-pitch as they neared where they would cross over, well into Goochland but still far enough west of Richmond to escape detection. The men were quiet now, the thud of horse hooves the only indicator of impending doom for the unsuspecting city.

Suddenly, the entire column ground to a halt. The rain had stopped falling, but the gray day still hung around them like a cloying cloak. The men shifted impatiently, eager to be on their way now that they were so close. Every second they were delayed could mean disaster.

"What are they doing up there?" one man muttered.

"It shouldn't be taking this long," another agreed.

A trooper dashed down the road beside the stalled column. "Where is Moses Samuels?" he hollered.

Several men twisted in their saddles to stare at him as Moses urged his horse forward out of line. "Right here, sir," he called.

"Colonel Dahlgren wants you up front," the trooper snapped. "Follow me."

Moses galloped after him. What had happened that would demand his services? It took several minutes to pass the long, stalled column. When he reached the banks of the river, he sucked in his breath. The usually calm James River bulged at its banks, straining to find a way to release the water rushing in a foaming cascade. He glanced away and was suddenly riveted by another drama.

Colonel Dahlgren stood beside his horse, staring down at the water with undisguised fury. Standing a few yards away from him, trembling with obvious terror, was the ex-slave Moses had seen from a distance earlier that morning. His breath was coming in quick gasps and his eyes were bulging.

The colonel swung around. "Trooper Samuels?" he snapped.

"Yes, sir." Moses urged his horse forward and swung easily to the ground when he reached the colonel.

"You're from around here, aren't you?" Dahlgren barked. "What do you think of this river crossing?"

Moses hesitated and then spoke honestly. "I wouldn't recommend using it, sir."

"Why not? I was informed this crossing would be shallow enough for my men."

"I'm sure it usually is, but the rain the last few days has made it impassable, I'm afraid." Moses tried to control the pounding of his heart. Why had Dahlgren really called him up here? It was obvious to anyone with any intelligence that the river was impassable. Dahlgren didn't need him to point out the obvious.

Dahlgren, his eyes blazing with anger, spun on his good leg toward the cowering guide. "You tricked me!" he yelled. "You set me up!"

"No, sir!" The terrified man fluttered his hands wildly. "I ain't done no tricking." He sucked in his breath. "How I supposed to be knowin' the river be up like this?"

Dahlgren spun toward Moses, his eyes flashing. "Where can I cross the river?" he demanded.

Moses knew he was risking the colonel's fury as well, but he met his eyes squarely. "I'm not aware of another place, sir."

Dahlgren's anger spewed over. His face turned red and the veins bulged in his neck as he swung toward the wild-eyed guide. "You may think I'm beat, but I'm not," he screamed. "I'll find another way into Richmond." He scowled, reached out to strike the guide and then seemed to change his mind.

Moses watched in fascinated horror. The colonel was obviously out of control.

Dahlgren wheeled away, stared at the river for another long moment, and spun toward several of his men. "Hang him," he ordered.

Moses gasped. He noticed dozens of black men gathered on the side of the clearing. He had heard that slaves, learning of their mission, had left their plantations to join in on the excitement. They stared at the drama now, disbelief on their frightened faces.

"Please!" the guide pleaded in a strained voice. "I ain't done nothin'. I ain't done nothin' wrong!"

Moses felt sick at the fear he heard oozing from his voice.

Dahlgren waved impatiently at the group of men he had spoken to. "I said hang him!" he ordered again. "And be quick about it. We've got to get out of here."

His men stared at him for a moment until one moved forward with a rope.

Moses stared in disbelief at the scene unfolding in front of him. He opened his mouth to say something, but there was nothing he could do. He had witnessed a scene like this before. He recognized the look of demented fury that wouldn't listen to reason. He had seen it on the face of the man who had hanged his father. At nine years old, he had watched his father be lynched by a man he dared to cross. Moses battled the sickness rolling in his stomach.

A sudden cry at the edge of the clearing grabbed his attention. Out of the corner of his eye, he saw several of the watching slaves edge toward the tree where the rope was being hung. He glanced toward the troopers arranged in the open clearing, staring at the drama taking place before them. Moses made up his mind.

He moved toward the slaves. "Get out of here," he said quietly. The cavalrymen behind him began to cheer and taunt the guide as he was led over to the rope. Moses breathed a sigh of relief. The noise would cover his words. "You can't stop it," he told them in an agonized voice. He held up a hand when one of the slaves started to speak. "Things could get out of control. He might not be the only one." He knew they would understand his meaning.

The one who had started to speak stopped dead in his tracks and stared at him. The rest locked eyes on him as well.

"I'm sorry," Moses choked. "They're not all like this," he added, knowing his words would mean nothing. These men would never forget what they were seeing happen at the hand of Union soldiers—the men who were supposed to be their liberators. The men they had followed eagerly all day. He glanced over his shoulder and saw the guide being lifted to a horse, his mouth gagged, his arms and legs flailing in futile resistance.

"Leave now," Moses said urgently. "Save yourselves."

The group hesitated, then turned as one and melted into the trees. Most of them had already learned the lesson that resistance against the white man was futile. Their faces were both angry and forlorn as they turned for one last look and disappeared. Moses gazed after them wishing fiercely that he could join them, yet knowing that if he disappeared, he would be immediately suspect. Dahlgren would assume he had been in cahoots with the guide and would have him hunted down.

Moses swung into his saddle just as the horse was pulled out from under the guide. Bile rose in his stomach as the man jolted to a stop at the end of the rope. The crack of his neck as it broke rang out over the sound of the gushing river. Moses turned away, tears of helpless rage filling his eyes. Somehow, he had to maintain control.

A cheer rose from some of the soldiers. Others watched grimly, their faces set in anger and pain. One exchanged a long, sorrowful look with Moses, his pinched expression revealing his feelings. Moses straightened, taking heart from the one who shared his pain.

Dahlgren scowled up at the dead man and swung away. "Let's keep moving," he ordered. "Crossing the river is out of the question. We'll go straight downriver. We still have the advantage of surprise."

Robert had just walked up to the house after a long meeting with a government official when the tower bells in Capitol Square began to peal wildly. He stopped on the porch, turning to look down on the city, which was shrouded by the dark, rainy afternoon.

Thomas appeared beside him, a worried look on his face. "What do you think it is?"

Robert shrugged. "Only one way to find out." He turned toward the house. "I'll get our gear."

He reappeared, his arms full of rain gear and haversacks that May had hastily stuffed with food. Micah rounded the corner with Granite at the same time Spencer drove up in the carriage. Thomas climbed in quickly, and they were off.

When he and Thomas reached Capitol Square, a large force of the Local Defense had already assembled. Robert gazed out over artisans from the armory and a battalion of government clerks, many of whom were mere boys. Their faces were determined, their eyes blazed fiercely.

Governor Letcher appeared on the porch of the Capitol, his mouth set in a grim line. "A Federal cavalry force is advancing on the city from the west," he announced in a booming voice. "We shall not give up our city!"

A rousing cheer greeted his words.

Colonel Custis Lee stepped to his side. "I've commandeered all the horses and wagons available. We are heading out to Westham Plank Road a few miles west of the city. We'll set up our block there."

Custis Lee looked up and saw Robert standing in the crowd. A relieved smile broke over his face. He shouted directions to the men and then wove his way down to join him. "I'm glad to see you, old man. I'd heard you were still around here. Up for a little action?"

"Lead on." Robert smiled and gripped his gun tighter. His heart pounded as he realized how close the Federal cavalry had gotten. Thoughts of Carrie working in the hospital, oblivious to the close proximity of danger, steeled his determination to force the invaders back.

They heard an explosion of artillery north of the city. Lee glanced up. "I had heard reports of two cavalry units," he said. "The other one must have hit our outer defenses on Brook Road." He shook his head. "They'll have to hold their position. My orders are clear to head west." He turned and leapt on his horse.

Robert mounted Granite, while Thomas climbed into a wagon. Within moments, the three hundred-member force was moving rapidly out of the city.

Carrie glanced up at Dr. Wild. "I'm through with this man."

Dr. Wild nodded. "I'm almost done as well." His words were interrupted by the wild clanging of the tower bells. He lifted his head, listened for a moment, and bent back to his work.

Carrie looked up at the line of men still waiting to be treated. This was her third visit to Libby Prison. Ever since Matthew's harrowing description of his stay, she was determined to do what she could. She had precious little time between her duties at Chimborazo and the black hospital, but still, she felt she was making a slight difference. There was medical service offered to the prisoners, but it was never enough. Not that much could be done. Most of the prisoners suffered from hunger and exposure. No medicine would cure that. Once again, Carrie prayed that the prison exchange program would start back up. Some of these men would not last much longer.

A guard appeared at the door. "You need to go now," he ordered.

"But our time isn't up," Carrie protested. "We have another hour left."

"Not today you don't." The guard motioned for them to leave.

Carrie wanted to argue, but she didn't want to jeopardize their visiting privileges. That they were here at all was a miracle. Ever since Matthew and the others had escaped, security had been tightened. The men were subjected to dozens of roll calls a day, sometimes four or five in the middle of the night. If any man was seen too close to a window, a guard would shoot first and ask questions later.

As Carrie packed her bags, she noticed looks of excitement on some of the men's faces. She wondered about it, but kept packing. The prison commander met them at the front door.

"What seems to be the trouble?" Dr. Wild asked. "Have we inadvertently caused a problem?"

"It's the Yankees causing problems." The commander scowled. "We've had reports that the Yanks are going to try to stage a prison break. Word came in of Union cavalry to the west and north of the city."

Carrie snapped her head around toward Capitol Square. Robert and her father must even now be reporting for duty. Her heart pounded as she wondered what the night would bring.

"They won't get these prisoners," the commander growled. The doors pushed open, and men carrying heavy barrels wrestled through the doors. He turned back to Carrie and Dr. Wild. "Those barrels are full of gunpowder. I'll stay at my post until I see a Yankee head for this prison." His lips thinned. "Then I'll blow this place sky high."

Carrie gasped. "You're going to kill everyone?"

He gazed at her as if she were a rather unintelligent child. "Ma'am, you tell me what I should do. Those Yanks get here and set these prisoners free, and we'll have five thousand men marauding this town eager for revenge. We don't have enough guards to stop them if they come. All the local troops have been called out to guard the roads. I'll do whatever it takes." He spun on his heel and disappeared into his office.

Carrie stared after him.

Dr. Wild took her arm gently. "I'll take you home."

Carrie nodded, her heart screaming in protest, even though she knew there was nothing she could do. She glanced back at the prison several times, wondering if she would ever see it again. The thoughts of the men inside and the fate they faced made her shiver. While her rational mind told her they could indeed be dangerous to the city, her heart told her they were men who just wanted to return home to their families where they could be warm and well-fed. She shuddered as she thought of Matthew, glad he had escaped before now.

She would go home to sit by the window and wait for Robert and her father to return.

Dahlgren led his men east, straight toward Richmond. The rain continued to fall, making the roads slick and thick with mud. The sudden boom of cannon made him pull his horse up sharply.

Moses was now close enough to hear every word.

"Kilpatrick is storming the outer defenses," Dahlgren said with grim satisfaction. "We are less than five miles from the city. We will wait for darkness and then advance. Richmond's limited forces will have their hands full with Kilpatrick. We'll give him time to break through, and then smash through ourselves." His voice was once more full of brash confidence.

Moses tried to control the loathing in his heart, but he could not block out the image of the guide swaying from the tree, his eyes bulging lifelessly, his tongue already swollen when Moses had dared to look back. He had lost all taste for any kind of fight, but he knew he had no choice but to press on.

"Dismount, men," Dahlgren called. "We'll take a short break before we press forward to victory."

His men cheered and moved eagerly to find some kind of shelter from the rain. Horses dropped their heads and turned their backs to the rain.

Moses leaned against a tree and munched on a biscuit, even though he had lost his appetite. The episode today pointed out to him once more, in graphic detail, just how far his people still had to go. They may have been mustered into the army out of dire need, but too many people still saw them only as animals, expendable when they were in the way or no longer useful. He fought to control the bitterness swelling in his heart, knowing it would serve no purpose. Giving in to bitterness would only mean another victory for Dahlgren. His determination to help change things for his people forged into solid steel. One day, this war would be over, and then the real battle would start. Not the battle for a country, but the battle for equal rights for the blacks of America.

"Mount up!"

Moses scrambled to his feet as the order rang through the night. It was time. The five miles passed quickly as the road fell away before their horses' galloping hooves. Moses knew they must be approaching the outskirts of the city.

A sudden burst of gunfire split the night.

"Forward, men!" Dahlgren shouted.

Moses leaned low over his mount's neck and surged forward, his gun drawn and ready. There was sporadic firing, and then silence.

"Drove right through them," one man crowed. "Richmond is ours!"

Robert saw the line of men running toward them in the night. He stepped out in front of them and held up his hand. "Who goes there?" he called.

A young boy, barely fifteen by the looks of him, stopped and stared up at him wildly. "They're coming. They pushed right through our lines."

Custis Lee strode up. "How far back are they?" he snapped.

"Not far," the boy gasped.

"You're doing a fine job, son. We're going to stop them here. Line up with our men, and make sure your gun is loaded."

Robert watched as the fear faded from the boy's eyes and his shoulders straightened with renewed confidence.

"Yes, sir!"

Lee turned to the men awaiting his orders. "This is it, men! We stop them here."

A brief cheer rose in response to his words and then a grim silence descended. Robert exchanged a somber glance with Thomas and took up his position beside him. He knew exactly how outnumbered they were. All he could hope was that the officer leading the Union cavalry didn't have that information. Tonight, the darkness was their friend.

The sound of thudding hoofbeats broke the silence. Robert stiffened, his gun in a ready position. He felt the proximity of the troopers before he actually saw them in the misty night.

"Fire!" Lee roared.

The explosion of gunfire rang out in unison. The charge stopped abruptly. Sharp gunfire erupted from the Federal lines, but Lee had chosen fine defensive positions for his men. The Local Defense unit continued to pepper the cavalrymen with deadly gunfire. Robert could see men falling, their guns clattering to the ground.

"Retreat!"

"We stopped them!" Thomas called triumphantly as the troopers turned and dashed back into the darkness, followed by the rousing cheers of the Local Defense.

"They were counting on surprise." Robert watched the last dim shapes disappear. "We spoiled it for them."

"Will he try again?" asked a young boy close by.

"I don't think so," Robert said. "He was counting on the element of surprise. Now that it has been spoiled for him, I think he will concentrate on getting his men out. From the sound of things, the attack against the northern line was repulsed as well." He nodded with satisfaction. "We stopped them."

Moses watched several men fall around him. He ducked as he felt a bullet whiz by inches from his head. He was firing, but in the darkness he really had no idea what he was firing *at*.

"Retreat!"

Moses clutched his rifle, spun his horse quickly, and urged him into a gallop, glad to leave the blistering gunfire. Their attack had hardly been a secret. It was obvious the city had been forewarned and was waiting for them. He heard Dahlgren cursing, but he felt no sympathy for him. The man deserved whatever he got. It was the men following him that deserved the sympathy.

As they rode, the rain turned into a stinging snowstorm. Moses pulled his coat closer and yanked his hat further down over his eyes. His mind turned to the dead guide. Had anyone found him? Had some of the slaves returned to cut his body down? Somehow he didn't think so. Their terror had been complete. They would have started running as soon as they were out of sight. They wouldn't stop until they had reached the plantations they started from.

"We'll be lucky if we get out of here alive," the trooper trudging beside him grumbled. "General Lee himself is probably headed this direction."

"Why weren't we told the city was so well defended?" the one behind him added. "That had to have been a regular line of infantry we ran into back there. I wonder how many of our men we lost."

"All I want to know," another chimed in, "is how we're going to get out of this mess. We can't just waltz back through Lee's lines."

"We're headed east," Moses said. "I think the colonel is taking us to Fort Monroe."

"Think we have any chance of getting there," another trooper asked, "*before* we freeze to death?"

Moses would have chuckled if he wasn't still gripped by the horror of the hanging. He merely shrugged. "Good a chance as any, I guess. It will take us about two hard days of riding to get there."

"Great," a soldier groaned. "I wonder if I'll still be able to feel my body by then."

Moses grimly hoped that he couldn't. He clearly remembered the pimpled, blond-haired kid's cheers when the guide was lynched. He clenched his teeth and stared straight ahead. He had to keep his thoughts to himself.

The long night passed slowly. The snow continued to drive at them mercilessly, icy pellets hitting their bodies and driving into their faces. Moses kept his hat pulled as low as possible, but it was impossible to completely protect his head. To make the time pass, he thought of Rose and John. He could envision them in their little cabin huddled beside the fireplace on a night like tonight. He longed to be there to hold John, to put him to bed, to watch his little body snuggle down into the blanket.

He shook his head. He had to think of something else before the longing for what he couldn't have consumed him. He was holding on to the hope that they were indeed headed to Fort Monroe, and that he would have a chance to see his family before he returned to his men. In spite of the late snowstorm, spring wasn't far away. The year's new campaign would start soon. Just a glimpse of his wife and new son would make it a little easier to bear another long separation.

A sudden shout in the distance caused him to jerk his head up. Pushing his hat back, he tried to see into the blinding snow. The sharp report of guns floated back to him on the breeze. He frowned, unsure of what to do.

"What's going on up there?" a soldier shouted.

They all plowed to a halt as the sound of gunfire continued. Minutes later, a trooper, his head bare and his coat stained with blood, raced by them. "It's an ambush!" he yelled. "They've killed Dahlgren. Most of the men are surrounded." Whipping his horse, he disappeared into the night.

"Let's get out of here!" two of the men surrounding Moses yelled. They turned abruptly and disappeared into the driving snow.

Chapter Thirty-Three

Moses watched the two terrified men disappear. He pitied them. They had no idea where they were, and no idea where they were going. They would be hopelessly lost in the snowstorm in minutes. He took several deep breaths and tried to think clearly. The gunfire had stopped, so there was no pitched battle taking place. He had been riding near the end of the column, and now he found himself completely alone. The snow was falling heavier, deep drifts lining the road.

He considered his options. He could charge ahead to see what had actually happened, or he could do what many others had done and simply disappear into the snow, hoping for the best. Moses had an advantage over most of them. He wouldn't have to head much further east before he would be in familiar territory. He scowled, wishing he could see through the thick whiteness surrounding him. Had Dahlgren really been killed? Why was there no shooting?

Moses sat quietly for several minutes, and then, with a wistful glance east, he swung off his horse and looped the reins over a nearby branch. He couldn't ride off without knowing what happened. There was little chance his presence would make any difference, but he had to know. Slipping quietly through the woods, eyeing landmarks keenly so he wouldn't get lost himself, he edged forward, every sense alert.

He felt their presence before he actually spotted the three Confederate soldiers mounted on their horses just below a slight rise. Moses froze and sank down until he was level with the ground. Heart pounding, he tried to discern his next move.

"You reckon there's any more of them out there?" one soldier asked, his voice floating dimly through the snow.

"If there are, they're lucky," another scoffed. "We've got over a hundred men surrounded up there. That fellow leading them is deader than a skinned possum. We'll be escorting them boys to prison in the morning."

Moses bit his lip when he heard of Dahlgren's death. He tried to feel sorry, but he could still see the guide swaying from the end of the rope. He couldn't help but feel justice had been done. Dahlgren had schemed up an impressive plan—a brilliant one if it had worked. But it had failed miserably. The dashing colonel was dead.

"They were plumb crazy thinking they could waltz right in and take our city. I heard they were hoping to free the prisoners. Looks like them boys just added to the number."

Moses had heard enough. Dahlgren's men were surrounded. There was nothing he could do.

Suddenly, a tree limb, concealed by the snow, snapped under his heavy weight. Moses cringed and froze.

"What's that!" one of the soldiers yelled.

"Probably nothing," another guard replied, "but just in case..."

A shot rang out.

Moses sucked in his breath as a bullet landed feet from where he stood. He knew the snow was too thick for the men to see him. He remained still, knowing any movement might give his position away. Ten minutes passed—long minutes when his feet started to turn numb and his hands hurt from the cold.

"Told you it wasn't anything," the soldier called again. The three resumed talking.

Moses waited another few minutes, then melted into the darkness. When he reached his horse, he swung into the saddle and headed east. He was going to Fort Monroe.

Anger had replaced the panic that gripped Richmond during the Union threat.

Thomas strode into the house and threw down the newest edition of the newspaper. For once, Carrie understood his anger and quite agreed with it. She had been shocked when the news came forth about the letter found on Colonel Dahlgren's body after his death.

"The paper has finally published a complete copy of the letter Dahlgren was carrying," Thomas said. "Let me read it to you." He coughed, almost doubling over.

Carrie reached over and picked up the paper. "I'll read it. You're still trying to recover from that nasty cold you picked up out there on the road."

"Just read the underlined parts," Thomas replied. "I wanted you and Robert to hear them."

Carrie nodded, put down her coffee, and began to read.

"*You have been selected from brigades and regiments as a picked command to attempt a desperate undertaking—an undertaking which, if successful, will write your names on the hearts of your countrymen that can never be released...*

Many of you may fall, but if there is any man here not willing to sacrifice his life in such a grand and glorious undertaking...'"

Thomas grunted in disdain, and Robert shook his head.

"*...or who does not feel capable of meeting the enemy in such a desperate fight as will follow, let him step out, and he may go hence to the arms of his sweetheart, and read of the brave who swept through the city of Richmond.*

We hope to release the prisoners from Belle Island first, and, having seen them fairly started, we will cross the James River into Richmond, destroying the bridges after us, and exhorting the released prisoners to destroy and burn the hateful city, and to not allow the Rebel leader, Davis, and his traitorous crew to escape.'"

Carrie slammed the paper down. "I think they were going too far."

"Finish reading what I underlined," her father urged. "There is more."

Carrie searched until she found it. "*Once the prisoners are loose and over the river, the bridges will be secured and the city destroyed. The men must keep together and well in hand, and once in the city it must be destroyed, and Jeff. Davis and his cabinet killed.' "*

"What is going to happen?" Carrie asked when she finished reading. She knew the whole city was in an uproar.

Robert wiped his mouth and put down his napkin. "The city is demanding reprisal of course. They want some of Dahlgren's men put to death as a warning to the Federal government that we won't sit back and let things like this happen."

"Didn't General Lee send a letter in response to all this? Thomas asked.

"Yes. He agreed the papers should be published so the whole world could know the kind of war being waged against us. He wanted attention brought to the atrocious acts they are plotting and trying to perpetrate." He paused. "He also said he would not recommend the execution of the prisoners that have been taken because these papers can only be considered evidence of Dahlgren's intentions. There is no clear indication as to how much his men knew of the full scope of the plan. They were merely following orders."

"Are they going to execute these men?" Carrie asked. As angry as she was, there had already been too much killing. Adding to it would accomplish nothing.

Thomas shook his head. "Most of Davis' advisers recommended that at least some of the raiders be put to death, but Davis resisted. He was backed up by Lee who still has a son in Yankee hands. I think they both fear even more brutal reprisal."

"So we do nothing." Robert sighed. "Except be glad they were unable to carry out their plan."

"It's not that simple," Thomas said. "In a war that has already changed a great deal, I foresee an even darker future."

Carrie grimaced. Her father wasn't being bitter. He was stating facts the way he saw them. "What do you mean?" she asked.

"From the beginning of the war, many in the South have believed Lincoln personally provoked the war. He has been an easy target of blame for each new escalation of casualties and cruelty. It doesn't really matter who wrote those papers. The effect is the same. When you take into consideration the threats that have already been made against Davis…"

"Like the fire in his cellar," Carrie interrupted. "Or the attempt to shoot him just before Christmas."

"There have been rumors of other plots as well," Thomas said. "Davis is convinced Lincoln has approved a new level of warfare."

"One that includes arson, pillage, and assassination," Robert finished.

"The war is simply becoming more vicious and inhumane as it drags on," Carrie murmured in dismay. "Is there any way for it to end?"

Thomas shrugged. "I've heard of new steps being taken. Davis and his cabinet have already approved covert operations to encourage the anti-war underground in the North. They have authorized five million dollars for that purpose."

"But why?" Carrie asked, confused.

"If they can cause enough terror in the North, it may strengthen the peace movement there," Robert answered.

"Davis hopes it can swing several northwestern states away from reelecting Lincoln in the fall."

"How then can we condemn what Dahlgren has done, when our government is making plans to do the same kinds of things?" Carrie didn't expect an answer.

Matthew and Peter oared the raft ashore and held it steady while Anderson and Wilson clambered off. The James River had become extremely wide, with the trees scattered too randomly to offer any real protection. They had decided during the night to go the rest of the way on foot.

"Maybe we're close enough to Union lines that the Rebs will stay away," Peter said hopefully.

Matthew glanced over at Anderson and Wilson. In spite of two days of rest and plenty of food, they were still too weak to put up much of an escape attempt if they were pursued now. Their strength had been exhausted in the mad rush that had deposited them in the frigid waters of the James River. "Let's hope so," he said.

Anderson seemed to read his thoughts. "I think you two should go on without us. We'll just slow you down."

Matthew snorted. "We left Libby Prison together. We will reach Fort Monroe together," Matthew said. "We've gotten this far. We'll make it the rest of the way just fine."

"How far do we have left?" Wilson asked in a weak voice.

"I don't know for sure," Matthew admitted.

"Well," Anderson said, drawing a deep breath. "I suppose there is only one way to find out." He strode forward and glanced over his shoulder. "Are the rest of you coming?"

They had walked for only two hours when it became obvious Wilson needed a rest. He had been sick in the prison shortly before the escape. The harrowing experiences he had suffered since then had rendered him a shell of the man he had been when Matthew first met him.

"Let's stop to eat," Matthew suggested, nodding toward Wilson when Peter and Anderson looked at him in surprise.

They were huddled next to a log just yards from the road when they heard hoofbeats. Thick underbrush concealed their position, but all four men froze. Matthew motioned for the others to stay and crept forward until he could see the road. His blood chilled when he saw a unit of ten Rebel soldiers round the curve. They were talking and laughing, obviously not concerned with stealth.

"Picked up two more today," one of them laughed. "You should have seen that man's face."

Another soldier laughed harshly. "You should have heard him. When we ran him down, he drew himself up real proud." He deepened his voice to imitate his captive. "My name is Captain William Springer of the United States Army. I have tunneled my way out of Libby Prison and escaped. I will not return alive. Go ahead and shoot me."

Matthew felt sick. Springer had stuck with them when all the other men had given up in despair. He had talked about what he was going to do when he got home to his wife and three girls. He had come so close.

"Did he shoot him?" another soldier asked.

"No," he responded. "We roughed him up with a rifle butt real good, then threw him in a wagon. I guess he's on his way back to Libby Hotel. He was still begging someone to shoot him when I rode off."

"I kinda feel sorry for him," one of the soldiers admitted. "I spent a little time in a Union prison. I felt the same way."

"Yeah?" another quipped snidely. "I wouldn't be broadcasting your feelings. Folks in Richmond are still plenty upset about that prison break. It's been almost three weeks now. At last count, only forty-five of them prisoners have been brought back. That leaves a lot who are gonna be up North snubbing their noses at us."

"Well I don't reckon we need to be hanging around here anymore," one called. "Some of those fellows obviously made it through, because we just barely missed a clash with some Union cavalry today. I been seeing signs of them all over. As best I can figure we're only a few miles from their lines. I'm done hunting for prisoners. I'm glad to be going home."

Right then, Matthew was wishing for a rifle. Anger pounded in his ears, blurring his vision and making breathing difficult. For one wild moment, he considered dashing out of the woods and attacking the man who mimicked Springer. He restrained himself. He still had to get Anderson, Peter and Wilson the rest of the way. He couldn't get himself captured now. Besides, what good what it do?

Tell the story, the voice in his heart reminded him. *Tell the story.*

Matthew waited until the men disappeared, their talking and laughter gone, before he turned around to the other men. They stared at each other with sick, angry eyes for a long moment.

"We're almost there," Matthew said. "Let's get going." They had to continue, for their sake, and for the sake of those who had tried and failed.

The sun was still high in the sky when Matthew peered through a clump of trees and saw a splash of Union blue. He leaned forward, looking more closely to make sure he wasn't mistaken and about to walk into a nest of Rebel soldiers. He could clearly see several Union soldiers strolling back and forth, their guns on their shoulders.

"We made it," Matthew choked, his voice thick with emotion now that the end was in sight. He put an arm around Anderson to support his faltering steps, and they edged out of the forest. Peter, with Wilson slung across his shoulder, walked out behind them. Wilson had collapsed a half mile back. Peter had been carrying him ever since.

As they moved closer, a Union soldier glanced up and moved to intercept them. "Who goes there?"

"My name is Matthew Justin," he called, gladness ringing in his voice. "I am a journalist with the *Philadelphia Tribune.* I have another journalist and two Union officers with me. We have escaped Libby Prison and are requesting sanctuary."

The soldier lowered his rifle and rushed forward. "Hey fellows," he called back over his shoulder. "Four more of those jail-breakers made it!"

Two days later, once more rested and well-fed, Matthew approached the cabin General Butler had directed him to. He smiled in anticipation and knocked softly on the door. He heard footsteps and the door was flung open. His smile disappeared as he looked into the unfamiliar face of a young woman. "I'm sorry," he said graciously. "I'm afraid I must have the wrong house."

"Not necessarily," the girl said. "My name is Susie. Who are you looking for? Even if she doesn't live here, I reckon I might know her."

"I'm trying to locate Rose Samuels."

"Well then, I reckon you be at the right place. Only she ain't here right now."

Matthew tried to swallow his disappointment.

"Don't look so sad, mister." Susie smiled. "She's down at the school." She paused, her eyes suddenly cautious. "Who are you?"

"Matthew Justin. I'm an—"

"Old friend of hers," Susie finished, her smile broader now. "I'm Susie. I'm living here while my husband serves in the army. Rose will be sure enough happy to see you. She's told me all about you and how you saved her from Ike Adams. You go right down to that school. Moses left a few days ago. Seeing you will make her real happy."

"Moses was here?" Matthew asked. "I thought he would be somewhere with the army."

"He is now," Susie said. "He took part in the attempt to set those prisoners free in Richmond, but it didn't turn out so well. He made his way back here along with about fifteen soldiers he picked up along the way. He had two days with his family and then left again. He should be with General Meade's army now, along with my Zeke," she added proudly.

Matthew listened in amazement. There had been a prison break attempt? What had happened? He was suddenly very eager to talk with Rose and get the answers. He turned to go and then hesitated. "Shouldn't I wait here? I'd hate to interrupt."

Susie shook her head. "It won't be an interruption. Besides, I think her afternoon session is about over."

Matthew nodded. "Thank you."

Minutes later he stood inside the door of Rose's school. He watched for several minutes as she moved from student to student, checking their work. She stooped down to smile at a little girl, talking to her quietly for a few moments, and patting her on the head. The little girl looked up with a grateful grin and then turned back to her work.

Rose, seeming to realize she was being watched, glanced toward the back of the room. Her face creased in a puzzled frown for a moment and then a huge smile exploded on her face. "Matthew Justin!" she cried, running down the narrow aisle.

Matthew stepped out into the aisle and caught her in a warm embrace. Both of them were laughing when he set her back down.

Without warning, Rose pulled him toward the front of the classroom and turned him to face the mass of inquisitive faces staring at him. "This is my friend, Matthew Justin," she began. "He is a journalist from Philadelphia. He writes stories about what is happening in the war. Maybe he'll tell you a story."

Matthew looked at her in surprise. She knew nothing about how he had spent the last eight months.

Tell the story.

He looked into the children's young faces. He realized they were not too young to hear about men's cruelty to each other. Their wise eyes said they had already experienced more than he probably ever would. They were not too young to accept the challenge to make a difference. And they were not too young to know they could take action to change their circumstances. Maybe starting with the young children meant their hearts could be protected before it was too late.

He took a deep breath. He and Rose would have plenty of time to talk later. "I'd like to tell you a story," he began.

An Invitation

Before you read the last chapter of Dark Chaos, I would like to invite you to join my mailing list so that you are never left wondering what is going to happen next. ☺

Join my Email list so you can:

- Receive notice of all new books & audio releases.
- Be a part of my Launch celebrations. I give away lots of Free gifts! ☺
- Read my weekly blog while you're waiting for a new book.
- Be part of The Bregdan Chronicles Family!
- Learn about all the other books I write.

Just go to www.BregdanChronicles.net and fill out the form.

I look forward to having you become part of The Bregdan Chronicles Family!

Blessings,
Ginny Dye

Chapter Thirty-Four

Spring had once again descended upon Richmond, its soft breezes chasing away the chill of winter and coaxing flowers from the barren ground. Ice had disappeared from the river, replaced by prisoner exchange boats. After failing to liberate prisoners with the raid on the capital city, Lincoln decided to reinstate the flag-of-truce boats plying the waterways of the two countries. The prisons were still full, but the horrible overcrowding had eased.

Carrie was waiting on the porch when Robert rode down the street on Granite. She looked at the two of them proudly and then glanced away when her vision became blurred with tears. "Get a hold of yourself," she whispered fiercely. "You knew this time was coming."

Robert trotted up to the gate and swung off Granite. He stood and looked at Carrie on the porch, but he made no move to join her.

Carrie waited. She knew he was once again imprinting her face on his mind. She gazed at him, willing all the love swelling in her heart to show on her face. Finally, Robert moved up the sidewalk and drew her into his arms.

"What is the report from Lee?" Carrie asked, more to delay the inevitable than because she cared.

"General Lee is taking a realistic view of what we are facing this summer," Robert told her. "A detailed report has been sent to Davis. He is urging the Secretary of War to build up reserve supplies in Richmond. He has also suggested that all residents whose presence is not required be forced to go elsewhere." He paused. "He told Davis that if anything happens to interrupt the flow of rations to the army, he might have to retreat all the way to North Carolina."

"I see," Carrie said, studying Robert's face. She sighed. "You know I won't leave the city. My work is here."

"I know," Robert said in an anguished voice.

"The city has been threatened before," Carrie said, trying to alleviate some of the fear on Robert's face. "Why is Lee so pessimistic now?"

"Meade's army has been taken over by the Union's General Grant. Lee knows he can't count on cautiousness and inactivity to give him the advantage. He has an army of dedicated fighting men, but once again, they are seriously outnumbered. And he doesn't have Stonewall Jackson to pull off any stunning surprises." Robert paused. "General Grant is an imposing commander." He glanced toward the city, his frown deepening. "Lee knows an attack could come at any day. He cannot even call all of his artillery in because of lack of forage. He doesn't have the means to keep everything alive."

"Supplies are still so critical?"

Robert nodded. "Lee is recommending the end of all railroad travel until the army's mobility has been restored."

"Has he lost all hope?"

"General Lee?" Robert scoffed. "The odds might be against him, but he is already devising ways to confound the Federals."

"And if he can't?"

He met her gaze. "Then it will all be over."

Carrie didn't want to talk anymore. She moved forward and pressed her body against Robert's. He gathered her close and pulled her over to the swing where they sat in silence for a long time, simply absorbing each other's presence. Everything had already been said that could be said. Just as they had expected, Robert had been called back into active duty. With the renewed threat against Richmond, every man possible had been called to arms.

Robert finally stood, pulling her close into another long hug, before he stepped back. "I have to go."

Carrie managed to smile. "I have something for you." She moved across the porch to the magnolia tree and picked off both of the blooms that had flowered that morning. She carried them over, presenting one fragrant blossom to Robert. "The day we got married, my father brought me the first bloom of the season. I made a wish on it." She gazed at the man she loved more than anyone in the world. "I wished that you and I would have a long life of happiness together." She paused. "I'm wishing the same thing today."

Robert fingered the bloom tenderly and stuck it in his pocket. "I'll be back," he promised. "We still have a lot of living to do."

Carrie watched until he and Granite were out of sight, her magnolia bloom crushed to her breast, tears streaming down her face. When she could no longer see them through her blur of tears, she raised the milky blossom to her lips and kissed it gently. She would keep it on her mantel until Robert returned. It would remind her every day of the dream burning in her heart.

The dream that one day the dark chaos would end, and nothing would ever separate them again.

To Be Continued...

Available Now!
www.DiscoverTheBregdanChronicles.com

Would you be so kind as to leave a Review on Amazon?
I love hearing from my readers! Just go to
Amazon.com, put Dark Chaos into the Search box, click
to read the Reviews, and you'll be able to leave one of
your own!

Thank you!

The Bregdan Principle

Every life that has been lived until today is a part of the woven braid of life.

It takes every person's story to create history.

Your life will help determine the course of history.

You may think you don't have much of an impact.

You do.

Every action you take will reflect in someone else's life.

Someone else's decisions.

Someone else's future.

Both good and bad.

The Bregdan Chronicles

Storm Clouds Rolling In
1860 – 1861

On To Richmond
1861 – 1862

Spring Will Come
1862 – 1863

Dark Chaos
1863 – 1864

The Long Last Night
1864 – 1865

Carried Forward By Hope
April – December 1865

Glimmers of Change
December – August 1866

Shifted By The Winds
August – December 1866

**Many more coming... Go to
DiscoverTheBregdanChronicles.com to see how
many are available now!**

Other Books by Ginny Dye

<u>Pepper Crest High Series - Teen Fiction</u>

Time For A Second Change
It's Really A Matter of Trust
A Lost & Found Friend
Time For A Change of Heart

<u>When I Dream Series</u> – Children's Bedtime Stories

When I Dream, I Dream of Horses
When I Dream, I Dream of Puppies
When I Dream, I Dream of Snow
When I Dream, I Dream of Kittens
When I Dream, I Dream of Elephants
When I Dream, I Dream of the Ocean

<u>Fly To Your Dreams Series</u> – Allegorical Fantasy

Dream Dragon
Born To Fly
Little Heart

101+ Ways to Promote Your Business Opportunity

All titles by Ginny Dye
www.AVoiceInTheWorld.com

Author Biography

Who am I? Just a normal person who happens to love to write. If I could do it all anonymously, I would. In fact, I did the first go round. I wrote under a pen name. On the off chance I would ever become famous - I didn't want to be! I don't like the limelight. I don't like living in a fishbowl. I especially don't like thinking I have to look good everywhere I go, just in case someone recognizes me! I finally decided none of that matters. If you don't like me in overalls and a baseball cap, too bad. If you don't like my haircut or think I should do something different than what I'm doing, too bad. I'll write books that you will hopefully like, and we'll both let that be enough! :) Fair?

But let's see what you might want to know. I spent many years as a Wanderer. My dream when I graduated from college was to experience the United States. I grew up in the South. There are many things I love about it but I wanted to live in other places. So I did. I moved 42 times, traveled extensively in 49 of the 50 states, and had more experiences than I will ever be able to recount. The only state I haven't been in is Alaska, simply because I refuse to visit such a vast, fabulous place until I have at least a month. Along the way I had glorious adventures. I've canoed through the Everglade Swamps, snorkeled in the Florida Keys and windsurfed in the Gulf of Mexico. I've white-water rafted down the New River and Bungee jumped in the Wisconsin Dells. I've visited every National Park (in the off-season when there is more freedom!) and many of the State Parks. I've hiked thousands of miles of mountain trails and biked through Arizona deserts. I've canoed and biked through Upstate New York and Vermont, and polished off as much lobster as possible on the Maine Coast.

I had a glorious time and never thought I would find a place that would hold me until I came to the Pacific Northwest. I'd been here less than 2 weeks, and I knew I would never leave. My heart is so at home here with the towering firs, sparkling waters, soaring mountains and rocky beaches. I love the eagles & whales. In 5 minutes I can be hiking on 150 miles of trails in the mountains around my home, or gliding across the lake in my rowing shell. I love it!

Have you figured out I'm kind of an outdoors gal? If it can be done outdoors, I love it! Hiking, biking, windsurfing, rock-climbing, roller-blading, snow-shoeing, skiing, rowing, canoeing, softball, tennis... the list could go on and on. I love to have fun and I love to stretch my body. This should give you a pretty good idea of what I do in my free time.

When I'm not writing or playing, I'm building I Am A Voice In The World - a fabulous organization I founded in 2001 - along with 60 amazing people who poured their lives into creating resources to empower people to make a difference with their lives.

What else? I love to read, cook, sit for hours in solitude on my mountain, and also hang out with friends. I love barbeques and block parties. Basically - I just love LIFE!

I'm so glad you're part of my world!

Ginny

Join my Email List so you can:

- Receive notice of all new books
- Be a part of my Launch Celebrations. I give away lots of Free gifts!
- Read my weekly BLOG while you're waiting for a new book.
- Be part of The Bregdan Chronicles Family!
- Learn about all the other books I write.

Just go to www.BregdanChronicles.net and fill out the form.

Made in the USA
Lexington, KY
18 March 2016